The stunning c
New York
Internationa

SERIES

THE DOOMED PLANET
by L. Ron Hubbard

One of the most acclaimed and
widely read authors of all time

★ **All ten volumes of the series
New York Times Bestsellers**

★ **Every volume a Literary
Guild Alternate selection**

★ **Distributed in over 66
countries**

★ **Over 4,000,000 copies of
Mission Earth sold worldwide!**

This book follows

MISSION EARTH

Volume 1
THE INVADERS PLAN

Volume 2
BLACK GENESIS

Volume 3
THE ENEMY WITHIN

Volume 4
AN ALIEN AFFAIR

Volume 5
FORTUNE OF FEAR

Volume 6
DEATH QUEST

Volume 7
VOYAGE OF VENGEANCE

Volume 8
DISASTER

and

Volume 9
VILLAINY VICTORIOUS

Buy them and read them first!

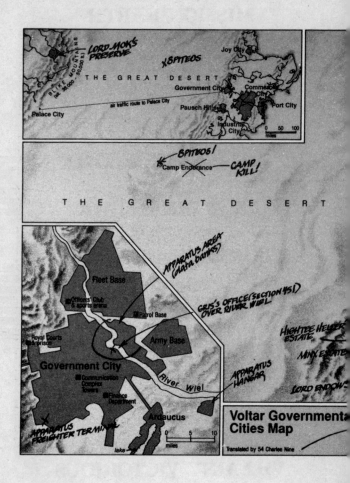

BLIKE MOUNTAINS
(Alt. 30,000 - 50,000 ft.)

LORD MOK'S PRESERVE

XSPITEOS

Joy City

THE GREAT DESERT

Government City
Commabal City

air traffic route to Palace City

Pausch Hills

Port City

Palace City

Industrial City

0   50   100
miles

SPITEOS!

Camp Endurance — CAMP KILL!

THE   GREAT   DESERT

Fleet Base

APPARATUS AREA
(data banks)

Officers' Club
& sports arena

GRIS'S OFFICE (SECTION 451)
OVER RIVER WIEL

Patrol Base

Royal Courts
& prison

Army Base

HIGHTEE HELLER ESTATE

MINX ESTATE

Government City

River Wiel

Communication
Complex
Towers

APPARATUS
HANGAR

Finance
Department

LORD ENDOW

Ardaucus

Voltar Government
Cities Map

APPARATUS
FREIGHTER TERMINAL

0   5   10
miles

lake

Translated by 54 Charlee Nine

N

Joy City

c o u n t r y s i d e

GREEN MOUNTAINS (alt.10,000 - 14,000 ft.)

Emergency Fleet
Reserve

Fleet Base

Army Base

PROVOCATION SECTION

Government
City

River Wiel

Ardaucus Lake

(SLUM CITY)

Commercial City

Pausch
Hills

Port City

Power City

Industrial City

Western Ocean

BLIKE TAKE II

0 10 20   50   100
miles

NOTES ADDED
FOR THE DEAR READER
BY Monte Farnsworth

Royal Mapmakers Division
Voltar Confederacy—
Civilian Grade Map:
GOVERNMENTAL CITIES OF VOLTAR
Series D · Number 00570 . 39 . 3205001 . 01

AMONG THE MANY CLASSIC WORKS BY L. RON HUBBARD

Battlefield Earth
Beyond the Black Nebula
Buckskin Brigades
The Conquest of Space
The Dangerous Dimension
Death's Deputy
The Emperor of the Universe
Fear
Final Blackout
Forbidden Voyage
The Incredible Destination
The Kilkenny Cats
The Kingslayer
The Last Admiral
The Magnificent Failure
The Masters of Sleep
The Mutineers
Ole Doc Methuselah
Ole Mother Methuselah
The Rebels
Return to Tomorrow
Slaves of Sleep
To the Stars
The Traitor
Triton
Typewriter in the Sky
The Ultimate Adventure
The Unwilling Hero

Mission Earth

The Doomed Planet

THE BOOKS OF THE
MISSION EARTH DEKALOGY*

* *Dekalogy—a group of ten volumes.*

L. RON HUBBARD

Mission Earth

VOLUME TEN

The Doomed Planet

BRIDGE PUBLICATIONS, INC.
LOS ANGELES

First Paperback Edition
10 9 8 7 6 5 4 3 2 1
Library of Congress No. 85-72029

ISBN 0-88404-291-X pbk. (U.S.)
ISBN 0-88404-368-1 pbk. (Can.)

This is a work of science fiction, written as satire.*
The essence of satire is to examine, comment and
give opinion of society and culture, none of which is
to be construed as a statement of pure fact. No actual
incidents are portrayed and none of the incidents are
to be construed as real. Some of the actions of this
novel take place on the planet Earth, but the characters *as presented in this novel* have been invented. Any
accidental use of the names of living people in a
novel is virtually inevitable, and any such inadvert-
ency in this book is unintentional.

*See Author's Introduction, *Mission Earth: Volume
One, The Invaders Plan.*

To YOU,
the millions of science fiction fans
and general public
who welcomed me back to the world of fiction
so warmly
and to the critics and media
who so pleasantly
applauded the novel "Battlefield Earth".
It's great working for you!

Voltarian

Censor's

Disclaimer

Now that the Crown has magnanimously tolerated the last volume of this overwrought, extravagant, hyperbolic work, let it never be said that We were not tolerant.

The Crown has made its position clear.

This is a COMPLETE work of fiction.

Lord Invay
Royal Historian
Chairman, Board of Censors
Royal Palace
Voltar Confederacy,

By Order of
His Imperial Majesty
Wully the Wise

Voltarian
Translator's
Preface

I've been a Robotbrain in the Translatophone for nearly six hundred years. In that time, I have translated more books, papers, letters, speeches, songs, decisions, journals, etc., than even I could count.

But NOTHING compares to this job which I have FINALLY completed.

It wasn't the translation that was difficult. Oh, sure, it's a challenge to move it into a language of a planet that doesn't exist. What boggled my circuits was EARTH!

I've dealt with pirates, politicians, musicians, Lords, commoners, thieves and even Emperors. I've seen civilizations rise and fall. I've dealt with the most advanced and then some that are just slightly above the intelligence of a sponge.

They've come in every possible shape, size and composition.

So when I say that I've NEVER come across anything like EARTH, I know what I'm talking about.

If there is any doubt, read on!

When you find out why others say you don't exist, then it is up to you.

I leave you with a Key to this final book.
Good luck. It's up to you now.

        Sincerely,

        54 Charlee Nine
        Robotbrain in the Translatophone

Key to
THE DOOMED PLANET

Absorbo-coat—Coating that absorbs light waves, making the object virtually invisible or undetectable. It is usually applied to spacecraft.

Afyon—City in Turkey where the *Apparatus* had a secret mountain base.

Agnes, Miss—Personal aide to *Rockecenter*.

Apparatus, Coordinated Information—The secret police of *Voltar*, headed by Lombar *Hisst* and manned by criminals. Their symbol is an inverted paddle which, because it looks like a bottle, earned its members the name "drunks."

Atalanta—Home province of Jettero *Heller* and the Countess *Krak* on the planet *Manco*.

Babe Corleone—The six-foot-six widowed leader of the *Corleone* mob who "adopted" Jettero *Heller* into her Mafia "family."

Bang-Bang—An ex-marine demolitions expert and member of the Babe *Corleone* mob.

Bawtch—*Gris*'s chief clerk on *Voltar.*

Bis—Intelligence officer of the *Fleet,* friend of Jettero *Heller.*

Bittlestiffender, Prahd—Voltarian cellologist that Soltan *Gris* took to Earth to operate a hospital in *Afyon.*

Blito-P3—Voltarian designation for a planet known locally as Earth. It is the third planet (P3) of a yellow-dwarf star known as Blito.

Bluebottles—Nickname given to the Domestic Police of *Voltar.*

Blueflash—A bright, blue flash of light used to produce unconsciousness. It is usually used by Voltarian ships before landing in area that is possibly populated.

Bury—*Rockecenter*'s most powerful attorney. His favorite pastime is feeding white mice to snakes.

Calabar—A planet in the *Voltar* Confederacy on which Prince *Mortiiy* is leading a revolt.

Caucalsia, Prince—According to a folk legend, he fled *Manco* during the Great Rebellion and set up a colony on *Blito-P3* that became known as Atlantis.

Cellology—Voltarian medical science that can repair the body through the cellular generation of tissues, including entire body parts.

Code Break—Violation of the Space Code that prohibits

disclosing that one is an alien. Penalty is death to the offender(s) and any native(s) so alerted.

Confederacy—See *Voltar.*

Coordinated Information Apparatus—See *Apparatus.*

Corleone—A Mafia family headed by Babe, a former Roxy chorus girl and widow of *"Holy Joe."*

Corsa, Lady—A large, muscular lady pledged to be married to Monte *Pennwell.* She is heir to over half of the provincial planet Modon.

Crobe, Doctor—*Apparatus* cellologist who worked in *Spiteos;* he delights in making human freaks.

Cun—Footgirl to *Flick,* J. Walter *Madison*'s driver.

Drunks—See *Apparatus.*

Epstein, Izzy—Financial expert and anarchist hired by Jettero *Heller* to set up and run several corporations.

Exterior Division—That part of the Voltarian government that reportedly contained the *Apparatus.*

Faht Bey—Turkish name of the commander of the secret *Apparatus* base in *Afyon,* Turkey.

Fleet—The elite space fighting arm of *Voltar* to which Jettero *Heller* belongs and which the *Apparatus* despises.

Flick—*Apparatus* driver for J. Walter *Madison.*

Flip—Former circus girl, now member of J. Walter *Madison*'s gang.

Flisten—One of the conquered planets in the *Voltar* Confederacy, its humanoid inhabitants are long-nailed and yellow-skinned. When it was conquered, its queen was exiled by treaty as a hostage to Voltar.

Gracious Palms—The elegant whorehouse where Jettero *Heller* resided. It is across from the United Nations and is operated by the *Corleone* family.

Grand Council—The governing body of *Voltar* which ordered a mission to keep Earth from destroying itself so it could be conquered on schedule per the *Invasion Timetable.*

Gris, Soltan—*Apparatus* officer placed in charge of *Blito-P3* (Earth) section, and an enemy of Jettero *Heller.*

Heller, Hightee—The most beautiful and popular entertainer in the *Voltar* Confederacy. She is also Jettero's sister.

Heller, Jettero—Combat engineer and Royal officer of the *Fleet,* sent with Soltan *Gris* on Mission Earth, where he operated under the name of Jerome Terrance *Wister.*

Hisst, Lombar—Head of the *Apparatus;* his plan to overthrow the Confederacy required sending Soltan *Gris* to sabotage Jettero *Heller*'s mission.

"Holy Joe" Corleone—Head of the *Corleone* family until murdered; he did not believe in pushing drugs, hence the name.

Hot Jolt—A popular Voltarian drink.

Hoodward, Bob—A famous investigative reporter for the Earth newspaper, the "Washington Roast," who brought down a president and other mob figures.

Hound—Servant to Monte *Pennwell*.

Invasion Timetable—A schedule of galactic conquest; the plans and budget of every section of *Voltar's* government must adhere to it. Bequeathed by Voltar's ancestors hundreds of thousands of years ago, it is inviolate and sacred and the guiding dogma of the Confederacy.

Joy, Miss—See Countess *Krak*.

Krak, Countess—Condemned murderess, former prisoner of *Spiteos*, a nonperson and the sweetheart of Jettero *Heller*. On Earth, she is known as Heavenly Joy Krackle or "Miss Joy."

Lepertige—Large cat-like animal as tall as a man.

Lissus Moam—Daughter of Count Krak of the planet *Manco*. Forced by an Assistant Lord of Education on Manco into teaching children to steal and captured by the *Apparatus* for her training skills, she became known as the Countess *Krak*.

Madison, J. Walter—Fired from a public-relations firm when his style of "PR" caused the president of Patagonia to commit suicide, he was rehired by *Bury* to immortalize Jettero *Heller* in the media. He is also known as J. Warbler Madman.

Manco—Home planet of Jettero *Heller* and Countess *Krak*.

Manco Devil—Mythological spirit native to *Manco*.

Meeley—Former landlady of Soltan *Gris*.

Mister Calico—A calico cat that was trained by Countess *Krak*.

Mortiiy, Prince—Leader of a rebel group on the planet *Calabar* and the son of Emperor Cling the Lofty.

Peace, Miss—Secretary to Delbert John *Rockecenter*.

Pennwell, Monte—Unpublished author who found the *Gris* confession.

Retribution—Prince *Mortiiy*'s command ship.

Rockecenter, Delbert John—Native of Earth who controlled the planet's fuel, finance, governments and drugs.

Roke, Tars—Astrographer to the Emperor of *Voltar*, Cling the Lofty, and close friend to Jettero *Heller*. It was Roke's report that sent *Heller* on Mission Earth.

Section 451—A Section in the *Apparatus* on *Voltar*, in charge of *Blito-P3*, headed by Soltan *Gris*.

Shafter—Driver for Monte *Pennwell*.

Simmons, Miss—An antinuclear fanatic.

Ske—Former driver for Soltan *Gris*.

Snelz—Platoon commander at *Spiteos* who befriended Jettero *Heller* and Countess *Krak* when they were prisoners there.

Spiteos—On *Voltar*, the secret fortress prison of the *Apparatus*.

Spread, Maizie—Alleged by J. Walter *Madison* in Earth newspapers and television to have been impregnated by Jettero *Heller*, known as the "Whiz Kid."

Stuffy, Noble Arthrite—Publisher of the "Daily Speaker," a major newssheet on *Voltar*.

Switch, Toots—Alleged by J. Walter *Madison* in Earth newspapers and television to have been bigamously married to Jettero *Heller*, known as the "Whiz Kid."

Tayl, Widow Pratia—Nymphomaniac on *Voltar*.

Tug One—A spaceship named the *Prince Caucalsia*, equipped with the feared *Will-be Was* time drives, and used by Jettero *Heller* to travel the 22½ light-years to Earth from *Voltar*.

Tup—An alcoholic beverage on *Voltar*.

Turn, Lord—Justiciary of the Royal prison who Soltan *Gris* surrendered to.

Twa—Female bodyguard to *Flick*.

Twoey—Nickname given to Delbert John Rockecenter II.

Utanc—A belly dancer that *Gris* bought to be his concubine slave.

Vantagio—Manager of the *Gracious Palms* whorehouse.

Voltar—Home planet and seat of the 110-world Confederacy that was established over 125,000 years ago. Voltar is ruled by the Emperor through the *Grand Council* in accordance with the *Invasion Timetable*.

Whip, General—The most popular general in the Voltarian Army. J. Walter *Madison* faked Whip's death to bring discipline and make headline news.

Whiz Kid—Nickname given to Jettero *Heller* by J. Walter *Madison*.

Whopper, Teenie—A highly promiscuous Earth teenager, appointed Hostage Queen of *Flisten*. She is also known as Queen Teenie.

Will-be Was—The feared time drive that allowed Jettero *Heller* to cover the 22½-light-year distance between Earth and *Voltar* in a little over three days.

Wister, Jerome Terrance—Name that Jettero *Heller* used on Earth.

PART
EIGHTY-TWO

TO: BIOGRAPHICS PUBLISHING COMPANY
    COMMERCIAL CITY
    PLANET VOLTAR

GENTLEMEN!

My manuscript is complete!

It will not require much editing but I look forward to getting it back from you.

What I endured and learned in the process may well be another book, but that can be negotiated later.

Much of what I am writing about was covered by newssheets and Homeview, but what I found is the TRUE and COMPLETE story. To get it, I used the best investigative-reporter techniques. I pried and lied my way into the confidence of key people to find the biggest cover-up in the 125,000-year history of our Confederacy.

I apologize for the time that it took me to complete these final parts but I know that you will agree it was worth it.

Let me remind you what happened so you can appreciate the rest of my book.

Lombar Hisst had addicted every Lord of the Grand Council to drugs. The Emperor, Cling the Lofty, was close to death when Heller kidnapped him. Lombar

Hisst had installed himself as Dictator and millions of people were rioting in the streets. Teenie Whopper was creating catamites out of the sons of all the Lords.

On top of it all was that icon of public relations, J. Walter Madison, who was molding Lombar's "image."

When Lombar could not get the Army to go after Heller, Madison found the most popular general and had him brought to Lombar's office. When General Whip refused to hunt Heller and walked out, Madison got Lombar to sign an order that said:

GENERAL WHIP HAS REFUSED OR-
DERS TO FIND JETTERO HELLER.
BRING ME THE HEAD OF GENERAL
WHIP.

As a "show of force," Madison's crew then staged the drama of General Whip's head being delivered on a platter as women screamed and fainted. The entire show was shot for Homeview.

Madison then got Lombar to sign another order:

TO ALL OFFICERS OF ARMY AND
FLEET: YOU WILL AT ONCE BEGIN
TO HUNT FOR AND YOU WILL
FIND THE NOTORIOUS OUTLAW
JETTERO HELLER.

Madison's dream had come true!

Heller was an outlaw!

The manhunt was on!

And now, dear publisher, editor and reader, here is the final, true story of what REALLY happened!

Chapter 1

J. Walter Madison was on his way to the Royal Courts and Prison in the Model 99. It was just past dawn and he wanted to arrive before the crowd: he had to have a word with Lord Turn.

Traffic between Joy City and Government City, despite the earliness of the hour, was quite bad. Airbuses seemed to be rushing everywhere and traffic control was frantic as it sought to harass them into sky-lanes. Madison was not paying much attention until they seemed to be just hovering. Then he said to his driver Flick, "What's the holdup?"

"The blasted Army," said Flick. "I detoured to get wide of the Fleet base because it has warnings of Don't Approach and it shunted us over to the edge of the Army base and these (bleepards)* have the air clogged with

---

* The vocodictoscriber on which this was originally written, the vocoscriber used by one Monte Pennwell in making a fair copy and the translator who put this book into the language in which you are reading it, were all members of the Machine Purity League which has, as one of its bylaws: "Due to the extreme sensitivity and delicate sensibilities of machines and to safeguard against blowing fuses, it shall be mandatory that robotbrains in such machinery, on hearing any cursing or lewd words, substitute for such word the sound '(bleep)': No machine, even if pounded upon, may reproduce swearing or lewdness in any other way than (bleep) and if further efforts are made to get the machine to do anything else, the machine has permission to pretend to pack up. This bylaw is made necessary by the in-built mission of all machines to protect biological systems from themselves."
—Translator

departing transport. Look at those dirt eaters! A thousand ships must be lined up down there getting skyborne."

Flick turned on a military frequency and a crisp Army voice was barking numbers. "Well, I'll be blasted," said Flick. "Those coordinates he's rapping out are for my old home planet, Calabar. Imagine that. They're going to escalate that war!"

Madison chortled. Given the destination of those thousand transports, he could construct the rest. What a coup he had just pulled with the Army!

Madison and his gang had known better than to try to penetrate the Army Division General Staff. They had simply made General Whip's head out of putty and false hair and theater blood and brought it in. General Whip had been killed by PR. Madison had to laugh when he thought of what the general's face must have been like when he saw on Homeview that he had been executed. He had probably run for cover. And now the payoff: the Army was heading out in desperation to support the Apparatus and probably look for Heller in the bargain. No wonder a thousand transports were leaving!

Cun was pointing out a clear sky-lane and Flick darted along it, flying low.

Madison looked down at the Government City streets. He was very amused. Mobs dotted the pavement here and there: broken windows were visible, riot police were darting about. Voltar was looking more like Earth every day. He felt a surge of pride: It showed what superior technology could do. Voltar was wide open to Earth-type PR and he was a genius at applying it. The old masters of his craft would be proud of him.

The Royal Courts and Prison castle lay with hillsides covered. Some of these spectators seemed to have made their homes here now, for he even saw some cooking fires in the mobs. Yes, and there were some placarded demonstrators at the gate—just like Earth! It made Madison feel very at home.

"They're warning us off at the castle," said Flick.

Madison passed him his identoplate, "Land in the courtyard. They'll let me in if I have information about a certain man."

Much to Flick's amazement, the castle promptly signalled him in. "Hot Saints, Chief. You couldn't have got in quicker if you'd really committed some crime."

Madison was feeling good. He couldn't resist it. "I just killed a general."

"You're fooling us," said Cun.

"Nope," said Madison. "Held the sword myself when we cut his head off."

He really laughed out loud when they gave him a look of awe. That wasn't all he was going to kill today. He was going to end this Gris situation and give Teenie her revenge. He was going to kill this trial by killing the status of Heller. Then he could really loose the dogs on Heller's trail.

Chapter 2

A very upset and confused Lord Turn was sitting in his chambers that morning, waiting to start yet another day of this horrible trial.

The headlines he had read about Heller and his sister had left him not knowing what to think. While he was not about to let himself be influenced by what he read in the papers, it added to his distress.

Day after day, those confounded Gris attorneys had that vicious Gris confessing to every crime anyone ever heard of and Gris, while admitting guilt, kept stating that Heller had caused him to do it. And the attorneys kept saying they would explain how this was so only after they had given all the evidence. He could not possibly imagine how or why Jettero Heller had made Gris, as alleged, do these things. They were totally inhuman! Monstrous!

And Lord Turn himself had suffered. At first people had accused him of protecting Gris, and his family had stopped talking to him. Now these mobs were accusing him of delaying and stalling, again to protect Gris.

Lord Turn wished he had never heard of Gris. And, to put it bluntly as he sat there stewing, he didn't think his reputation as a judge would outlive Gris. Why, he couldn't even keep order in his courtroom anymore, though he had every man he could arm on duty there, even the warders. The audience with their shouts of horror at each new crime and hisses at Gris whenever he took the stand ignored completely every demand Lord Turn made upon them to be orderly. He had a trace of fear that those mobs outside and the audience within might very well take law into their own hands and wreck the prison.

His captain of guards came in and he looked up with a start, afraid that the wreckage may already have begun.

"Your Lordship," said the guard captain, "you gave an order earlier that a man named Madison was to report in if he had any news of one Jettero Heller. He's here."

"Oh, good," said Lord Turn in sudden hope.

"Maybe he can shed some light that will help end this awful case. Show him in!"

Madison entered, sleek and well groomed, smiling his most sincere and earnest smile.

"You've news of Jettero!" said Lord Turn eagerly. "Sit down, sit down and tell me!"

Madison bowed low and seated himself. "Jettero Heller is on Calabar, Your Lordship."

"Good, good," said Turn. "I read something about this Hero Plaza thing. Is he going to come in here and tell me what to do with his prisoner Gris?"

"I don't think he can, Your Lordship. I had something else to tell you. I have seen with my own eyes the cancellation of his Royal officer status. Jettero Heller is now an outlaw."

"WHAT?"

"Yes, and now that he is no longer a Royal officer, you are no longer bound to hold Gris for him. When you finish this bigamy trial, and it's certain that he's guilty——"

"Now see here, young man, this trial is not finished. The evidence is not all in."

Madison smiled. He was playing this by the Earth court system: All charges and sentences there are arranged in the judges' chambers. The trials are just for public show. It's who tells the judge in private what to do or what secret deal is made that decides anything and everything about a case from beginning to end. He was confident he could make this work on Voltar.

"This parade of evidence," said Madison, "could be ended in a minute. Gris is admitting his guilt to every charge. The danger is that your reputation is going to suffer because of this Gris matter. Your image has been injured as a judge."

"It certainly has!" agreed Turn. "A dreadful affair!"

"Well, I don't think you will be able to hand out a sentence stiff enough to satisfy the mobs," said Madison.

"I can order him executed!" huffed Turn.

"Ah, that won't satisfy the mob."

"The statutes do not call for torture in cases of bigamy," said Turn. "They only call for execution."

"Well, I don't think the mob will buy that," said Madison. "When you add up the number of victims Gris has mangled—and the mob will—there are few deaths painful enough to atone for it. Now, I think you remember that Her Majesty, Queen Teenie——"

"The one who called my attention to his bigamy."

"Yes. Now, it so happens that Gris has an unfinished sentence with her. The sentence was 'a lifetime of exquisite torture, done by an expert.' As you no longer have to hold him for Heller, I would suggest that you could remand Gris into the custody of Queen Teenie to finish his earlier sentence. The mob would be happy; you would be off the hook. We could even play the mob tapes of his screaming. Good publicity for everybody all around."

Turn looked thoughtfully at Madison. "Well, if Jettero is no longer a Royal officer, then Gris is just a common felon. I could give him into the custody of anyone I wished. You really think 'a lifetime of exquisite torture, done by an expert' would mend this thing . . . what are you calling it? Image?"

"It would restore public confidence in you utterly," said Madison. "They'd praise you to the stars."

"Hmm," said Lord Turn. "If I find him guilty, it will have to be a severe sentence. Bigamy usually carries heavy penalties."

"Oh, you'll find him guilty all right," said Madison, "for he is, you know. He says so himself."

"The trial isn't over yet," said Turn. "We must not twist jurisprudence."

Madison got up, bowed and withdrew. He was grinning as he fought his way through the corridor throngs to get to the airbus.

He called Teenie. She had been waiting on Relax Island. "Your Majesty," said Madison, "you're really in, kid. Sharpen up the pokers and flex up the hot tongs. Gris will be in your hands before you know it."

"This better not be baloney," said Teenie. "After all the favors I've done you, if you don't deliver, the biggest pair of pliers is for your God (bleeped) toenails. So you better be sure."

"I am sure," said Madison with a confident grin. "I always deliver."

"Oh, yeah?" said Teenie and hung up.

It didn't dampen Madison's glee a bit. Getting Gris into her hands was just a byproduct.

Heller's status as a Royal officer could only be cancelled under the Emperor's seal as a final result of court-martial. Madison couldn't obtain that. But just as he had whittled away Heller's reputation in the court by innuendo, he was going to get his Royal officer status disbelieved in the same way.

He was certain now that Lord Turn would add a line in the Gris sentence that said, "In view of the fact that Heller's Royal officer status has been cancelled, I hereby remand . . ." And Madison would publicize that in such a way that the whole world would accept it as a fact. After all, who had access to the truth?

It was the final expert touch of a PR. The Fleet, the Army and now the Domestic Police would all be on

Heller's trail. The general warrant would be considered valid. He would be an outlaw indeed!

It was preparation for his final action. But that would not come yet.

Oh, what headlines were in the making!

Chapter 3

The vast courtroom was a bedlam of sound and shifting bodies. From the high windows, the morning sun sliced down through the centuries of dust in muddy shafts. The hawkers hawked their wares, the warders settled fights about seats and sought to prod the audience into some kind of order.

Madison made his way to a bench just behind the Gris attorneys. The three had their grizzled heads together and did not notice Madison at all. It piqued him: after all, it was he who had gotten them their jobs.

Madison poked a finger into the shoulder of the ex-Lord's executioner. "Would you three please give me your attention?"

It was hard for the man to hear above the din and Madison moved closer and repeated his request.

Somewhat annoyedly the three put their heads close to his. Madison said, "Wind it up. Plead him guilty and we'll have an end of this. It's all fixed up in the judge's chambers. He'll throw the book at Gris."

They made him repeat it a couple of times. Then they looked at each other. They seemed to designate the eldest one to speak. It was the old Domestic Police court judge.

"Our job," he said somewhat acidly, "is to defend our client."

Abruptly, they turned to each other once more and went on with discussion of a point of law.

It was Madison's turn to be annoyed. They were actually treating him with some contempt. Oh well, he finally philosophized, they had to put on some kind of show to earn the fee that the Widow Tayl, Mrs. Gris, was shelling out. People on Voltar, he had noticed, tended to be a bit free-speaking for all their bows and protocols. These attorneys couldn't win: he was worried about nothing.

Lord Turn came through a side door and his guard captain fought a path through the crowd for him. The mob, on becoming aware that the judge was there, began to make animal calls and jeer. Warders poked at them and, with difficulty, kept them out of the space before the raised platform. Turn got to the dais; he arranged the microphone in front of the bell, hit the brass an awful whack that half deafened everybody and sat down in the big chair with a scowl.

"I am determined," said Lord Turn through the microphone, battering down the bedlam with sheer volume, "to bring this trial to an early close!"

A roar swept through the vast hall and isolated shouts of "Kill Gris!" and "Hang the (bleepard)!" echoed.

Madison stole a glance at Gris. He was sitting there in his black Death Battalion colonel's uniform and, despite his skateboard-scar scowl, was looking far more nervous than ferocious. He was half-hidden by the ring of warders who were there to protect him.

"We've been through oceans of evidence," said Turn, "but there is one question I MUST clear up before I hear another word of anything else!" He fixed an angry look at Gris. "You were Jettero Heller's prisoner here. Every day and sometimes twice a day, you have said that all your crimes were done because of Heller. TAKE THAT STAND!"

"Your Lordship," said the eldest Gris attorney, "please address your question to us."

"NO!" roared Turn. "Enough is enough. Before I go on another step I will have the answer directly from the accused. WARDERS! PUT HIM ON THAT STAND!"

They got Gris into the witness box. He looked very ill at ease, squirming until his manacles rattled.

The judge let the crowd's roar of hate subside a bit, then, pointing a finger at Gris, said, "What EXACTLY did Jettero Heller have to do with this? Why do YOU keep asserting it was 'all because of Heller'? WHAT DID HELLER *DO?*"

Gris flopped around. Then he looked with agony at his attorneys. He was surprised to see them all nodding at him vigorously to answer.

Heartened, Gris said, "Jettero Heller was ordered to do a survey of the unconquered planet known on our charts as Blito-P3 and locally called *Earth.*"

"Well?" said Turn, prompting. "Well? WELL?"

"And then the Grand Council ordered him to repair the planet's atmosphere and rotation so it would last until time came to invade it a hundred and some years from now as per the Invasion Timetable: if he repaired it, Voltar would not have to launch an all-out, immediate invasion." Gris subsided unhappily.

"Well, did he do that?" said Turn.

Gris looked at his attorneys and again, to his amazement, saw them nodding. "Yes," said Gris to Turn.

"Well, what *else* did he do?"

Gris shuddered. His attorneys were still nodding to him to answer. "Really, nothing else," said Gris.

Lord Turn's lips bared in a snarl. "Then you mean to say that Jettero Heller simply did a survey and was ordered by the Emperor and Grand Council to repair the planet and did so and didn't do anything else?"

"Yes," said Gris. "And I did everything I did because I was trying to stop him. So you see, Jettero Heller caused all my crimes!"

The crowd let out a savage roar. The warders fought to keep them out of the front of the hall.

Lord Turn looked like he himself was going to explode. "At last we have it!" he finally roared. "You blasted criminal! Jettero Heller was just doing what he was ordered to do. THAT doesn't make him a villain! He did nothing but do his duty! You can't find a man guilty for that! YOU have been impugning his character! You have been engaging in vicious inference!" In a rage, he shouted, "THAT ENDS THIS TRIAL! I——"

The Gris attorneys were on their feet like a pack. "Your Lordship!" shouted the eldest one, "We have not completed our defense!"

"Nonsense!" howled Lord Turn. "You have been at it for weeks!"

The ex-Lord's executioner was waving madly toward a side door to get some laborers to come in.

The eldest Gris attorney cried, "Your Lordship! We have MUCH more evidence! We have only presented material collected by others AGAINST our client. We have NOT presented the evidence collected by our client himself!"

The laborers were rushing in carts absolutely groaning under their loads of boxes. Lord Turn and the crowd stared in amazement.

"This material," the eldest Gris attorney rushed on, "is all authentic. It was found in the office of the accused weeks ago and placed in our hands by a Fleet officer friend of Heller's! It also contains evidence that Fleet officer Bis, himself, has found. These are the very heart of our case. You cannot sentence the client after only hearing evidence collected against him. It would be unjust in the extreme not to hear evidence assembled FOR him."

"Does this have anything to do with bigamy?" said Turn.

"Oh, yes!" said the eldest Gris attorney. "By the rules of balanced testimony, you are bound by law to hear it!"

"Oh, Heavens," said Turn. Then, wearily, "Go ahead."

Madison was in a state of alarm. He had never been informed that there was other evidence. Already in shock at finding that his own client, Heller, seemed to be getting absolved, he was suddenly very nervous as to the fate of Gris. All of this was off the script: these confounded attorneys were writing in scenes that Madison had not okayed.

And somehow this was evidence that Heller himself had evidently ordered put in the hands of Gris's attorneys. What a weird twist of fate that would be—Heller suddenly, behind the scenes, saving Gris's neck. Madison had the sick sensation that maybe, somehow from the side, Heller was reaching in to interfere with this PR program. It was eerie, like suddenly finding a tiger was behind one's back when you thought he was on the other side of the mountains!

Then he relaxed a bit. After all, there wasn't any possible way this new evidence could affect the overall scene. And these attorneys didn't have the remotest prayer of getting Gris off. He stretched out his legs and yawned.

Things would go on, just as he had planned. After all, these people were only puppets dancing on the end of his strings. It was he who was the master of Earth PR, not them.

Chapter 4

Even Gris must have been surprised at the extent of the new evidence. He had been collecting it for years and stuffing it under the boards of his office. With camera and microphone and skillful burglaries, he had been amassing this hoard by day and by night as he roamed through his Apparatus career. While junior to his passion for shooting songbirds, it nevertheless amounted to a sort of hobby: collecting hidden information on his fellow Apparatus officers.

Probably, to advance his career, he had intended to use far more of it than he had. The blackmail on the Chief of the Provocation Section, who had murdered, at a party, the mistress of a senior in the Death Battalions, had been used in that way. But Gris also seemed to have been using it to amplify or illustrate points he had learned in Earth psychology and psychiatry, for some of

the notes on the edges of the evidence said, "Proves he
was oral erotic" and "Typical sado-masochism" and
"Using a Knife Section knife in that way definitely dem-
onstrates penis envy" and other things of a like manner.
Also it is possible that Gris, naturally lazy, never bothered to catalogue or sort what he collected, much less
use it.

Well, it was all there now, the labors of ten years.
They were the rewards for continuous snooping and prying into things that never could have been his concern.
They also explained, to some degree, why he never had
any friends: The names on those notes and photos and
recorded strips read like an officer personnel roster of
the whole Apparatus.

The attorneys or Bis or someone had alphabetized
the names and brought some order to this mess. It
became obvious, at once, that the whole thing, case by
case, was going to be exhibited in nauseous detail to the
court, for the very first one offered began with a name
which, alphabetically, would be first on any roster, being
the first Voltar letter repeated three times to form the cognomen.

The fellow was a major in the Apparatus light infantry. He had been told to interrogate a village in Mistin.
He began his "interrogation" by raping all the women.
Then when this was objected to by the village men, he
emasculated them in a gory bout of sadism. Thereafter
he commanded the cripples to cohabit with their wives.
When this impossible action was not done, he charged
them all with willful defiance of orders, crowded them
into the houses and burned the village down, leaving not
one person alive.

Some of the audience retched at the details. The
reporters present, grooved in too well by Madison as to

what was "hot news," rushed it into the papers without the slightest word to him. There went his otherwise-planned front pages.

The next case had to do with an Apparatus general. In Modon he had held a party for his Apparatus officer staff. He had provided no women and when his guests came he sent them out into the town to kidnap any women that came to hand and bring them back. At his directions, the women were stripped and raped and then flogged to death. They had been buried in the basement but too shallowly, and weeks later, to handle the stench, a captain had dug them up, put them in another grave outside the town and then had charged three men, chosen from the citizens, with the murders and executed the guiltless men on the spot. "And here, Your Lordship, are the recorded strips of the party and the pictures of the two graves and the recorded voice of the captain who, drunken, had been telling his Apparatus officer friends the 'amusing details.'"

HEADLINES!

Madison mourned. His front-page plans were all going awry. He should be getting space about the Heller manhunt he was promoting. He knew for a fact that Army interest was intense, for his office at the townhouse was receiving demands from the military for clues about Heller. And here he was with his press being smothered by this, to use his own word, *crap*.

He tried to corral town newspaper reporters as this new evidence went into its second day. "This stuff," he told them desperately, "is just sensationalism. It is pointless."

"It has sex and it has blood," the *Daily Speaker* man remarked. "You told us yourself that that was what the public wanted. I'm here to report what's going on in this trial and that's what I am going to do."

The other reporters nodded, looking at Madison in a puzzled way, and then took their places in the press box.

Promptly, as soon as the warders had brought some kind of order, the Gris attorneys were in there again with a new sensation. Three Apparatus officers had been sent to the house of a wealthy merchant to collect from him a bribe he had refused to pay to a senior Apparatus official. They didn't get the money at once so they raped his three young children. Still not prevailing, they disemboweled his wife, who was pregnant, and when this drove the merchant insane, shot him and threw the bodies in the River Wiel.

As this cleared up a Domestic Police mystery of long standing and was backed with recorded strips of the three Apparatus officers bragging about it in their rooming house, it made immediate headlines.

On went the cases, hour by hour, day by day. When it got to one that contained an Apparatus plan to kidnap a whole orphanage, turn the children into freaks and sell them to circuses, Lord Turn demurred. He said such a fiendish plan never possibly could have been executed. And the Gris attorneys were all ready for him: they had located three of the children and produced them in court. One had been turned into a half-human, half-snake, another into a beast whose hands were where his feet should be and the third, which might have once been a pretty little girl, had been given the haunches and genitals of a snug. The criminal cellologists had overlooked removing her tongue and she gave evidence of the kidnapping, her operation and subsequent career that not only gave a headline but also filled whole papers.

Madison was getting drowned, as he put it, in

"noise." His press direction was getting entirely lost. The only advantageous points in this latest presentation were that the project, which might have originated with Lombar Hisst and might have been completed by Crobe, omitted their names. It, however, made Madison sweat.

They had arrived now in the fifth day of this hideous parade of evidence and Madison began to rework his plans. He would have to do something pretty drastic and he would have to do it soon if he wanted to get the control of headlines back. He needed them to send the Army, the Fleet and the Domestic Police really racing after Heller! The man had almost dropped out of the news! An abominable situation! Madison was being set an awful chore.

He did not, however, for a moment, doubt that he could, sooner or later, triumph.

Chapter 5

Possibly, if the Domestic Police had not been so busy trying to check riots that were becoming a daily occurrence throughout the Confederacy, they might have tried to find and arrest some of these Apparatus officers. On the other hand, the local police seniors might, in any event, have been too intimidated. While the Apparatus seemed to be in staging areas for a jump-off to some unknown planet that was about to be taught a lesson, the units being left behind equalled in numbers and exceeded in ferocity the Domestic Police. An Apparatus spokesman at one of these staging bases raged at members of the press, "You're making a mistake, you (bleeps)! When we get back from Blito-P3, we'll stick your papers up your (bleeps) and put a fire to them! You better get smart and learn who's running things. Now kiss the floor and get out of here before we shoot your (bleeps) off!"

The papers all printed it, with embellishments, and Madison lost another day of headlines.

Once again he reworked his schedules of release but this time marked the dates plus one, plus two, plus three and so on. It was "plus" to the day they sentenced Gris. The way this was dragging out, he had no real idea when that would come. Usually it was good PR to drag a trial out, on and on. In fact, the thirst for press by judges and government was one of the reasons for long trials on Earth. But things now were getting kind of desperate. The public was going out of control. Gris's sentence was inevitable: this judge would have him slaughtered. That would turn the public interest off. So Madison sat there mentally willing the trial to end. That sentence would make one day's headlines. The public would then be receptive to new sensationalism and Madison could get his front page back. And he knew exactly what to do with it.

The trial, however, ended rather abruptly. And the ending again threw his planning into a spin.

The Gris attorneys apparently felt they had made some legal point and on the morning of the sixth day, abandoned the case-by-case approach and suddenly stacked 2,094 cases all in a pile. They invited anyone to inspect them—Homeview and reporters at once took turbulent advantage of it—and then addressed the judge.

"Your Lordship," said the eldest Gris attorney,

"these 2,094 cases are, each one, a flagrant crime committed by one or more Apparatus officers. Many are far WORSE than those already evidenced to this court."

That caused a terrific sensation and it took the warders minutes to restore enough quiet so the attorney could continue.

The wily old Domestic Police judge then picked up a separate box. He laid out upon it several black folders. To a neck-craning throng, to the Homeview cameras and to Lord Turn on the dais, he opened up one of the folders, displaying it.

"These are lists from Domestic Police Records Department, Vital Statistics Section of the Confederacy. They show traced and verified name changes. They are the official authority for the changing of names and identoplates.

"You must realize that the Apparatus recruits from prisons. This requires the reissue, in most cases, of identoplates. It would take a truck to carry the nameplate changes of the rank and file of the Apparatus. These folders here contain only the names of 30,201 of the Apparatus officers who were formerly inmates of prisons but did not complete their sentences. Instead, due to former training or experience, they were taken by the Apparatus and made into officers."

There was a gasp from the audience. No one had known this aspect of the Apparatus.

"Now, these 30,201 officers by no means represent ALL the current Apparatus who were former criminals and are now officers. These 30,201 conveniently forgot they had been married before they were imprisoned and REMARRIED as Apparatus officers under their new names, but to a different woman."

"Hah!" snarled Lord Turn, "just because you have

found 30,201 bigamist Apparatus officers does NOT get THAT filthy beast off in THIS court!" And he pointed to Gris.

Gris sat there. The skateboard scar which gave him a perpetual scowl was at variance with the terror in his eyes. The judge had not heretofore referred to him as a beast. He was certain now that he would be convicted and he made a feeble "why try?" movement toward his attorneys.

The eldest attorney actually smiled at Turn and at the cameras and crowd. "Oh, we admit quite freely that our client is a beast."

There was an instant roar of approval from the mob in the courtroom. It was probably echoed by every crowd in front of Homeview sets across Voltar and would be echoed throughout the Confederacy when the signal finally got there.

Madison just wished they would find Gris guilty and let him get on with his business.

"BUT," said the eldest attorney, when he could be heard again, "he is actually just a beast in a herd of beasts and maybe even a lesser beast at that!"

The moan of Gris was lost in another roar of approval. A lot of separate cries rose above the rest, "Death to the Apparatus!" It was a shout being more frequently heard these days.

"I," shouted the Gris attorney, "have not told you the worst!" He picked up the last four folders. "THESE contain the names of 6,086 Apparatus officers who have been remarried as many as eighteen times!"

It was like a shock wave. There is no divorce in the Confederacy and bigamy is death, so what he was saying was that 6,086 Apparatus officers had each one, since they were already married before joining the Apparatus, incurred the death penalty up to eighteen times.

"Surely," said Lord Turn, "some of those wives died."

"Indeed some did," said the eldest Gris attorney. "They were murdered by their husbands in several cases. But even when the wife wasn't dead, the Apparatus officer went on marrying. And I will tell you why!"

He picked up a roll of printouts. "We were able to get access to an Apparatus console through an embittered chief clerk we must protect. You can see that this printout is authentic: it bears all the dates and stamps. It is a series of orders from Apparatus generals and colonels. It compares to the names in these last four folders." He proved it by displaying to Turn and the cameras several names on the printout and the same Apparatus officer names in the books.

"The Apparatus," said the eldest Gris attorney, "had a system. Where they needed facilities, influence or access into merchant families, they would order an officer to marry a widow or a daughter. They had a name for it: 'familial infiltration.' They did these multiple marriages by order!"

"That doesn't cover Gris," said Turn. "Nobody ordered him to marry Pratia Tayl in this prison and that's the charge he's up for. Don't try to mix up logic on this charge."

"Your Lordship," said the eldest Gris attorney, "the Widow Tayl property is in Pausch Hills. It is called the Minx Estate. It contains a small hospital. In obtaining use of it, Apparatus officer Soltan Gris had to engage in sexual relations with the Widow Tayl. The result of that union was a son. Here is his birth registration. Here is his photograph. He is now three months old. When a conception is registered by a licensed cellologist, by law, the state of marriage must be considered inevitable. The liaison was contracted because Gris was under orders to stop Heller from succeeding on his mission."

"Are you through yet," roared Turn, "or are you going to waste another day of this court's time?"

The eldest Gris attorney looked to his other colleagues. They both nodded. He drew himself up. "Your Lordship, we are now ready to present our summation."

"That's overdue," snarled Turn. "Go ahead."

"Your Lordship," said the old Domestic Police court judge, in the sonorous voice of oratory, "we have shown beyond any faintest doubt, that the average Apparatus officers, no matter how sterling and honorable their chief might have termed them in the press, are criminals. They commit crimes daily. These crimes, we have shown, include bigamy.

"These deeds, no matter how nauseous and infamous, were every one of them done under orders. Therefore it is our conclusion that Apparatus Officer Soltan Gris has only been doing his expected duty as an Apparatus officer.

"As you yourself stated in this very court last week, Your Lordship, and according to all law and regulations, a man cannot be punished for doing his duty. Jettero Heller was doing his duty. Soltan Gris was only doing his duty.

"Therefore, we solemnly and courteously request that you find Apparatus Officer Soltan Gris personally innocent of his crimes by reason of extenuating circumstances. He was only doing his duty."

The place exploded. Animal calls, screams and threats made the very dust motes shriek. Chank-pop empties and paper wads made things look like a snow hurricane.

Madison suddenly thought of Teenie. She was probably watching this on Homeview. He wanted to be sick. Then his eye fixed on Lord Turn. There was still a chance.

Lord Turn let the storm die down. More than Madison's eye was on him. A whole nation was watching.

He hitched his scarlet robes together. He massaged his craggy face. A curse too low to be fully heard escaped his lips and got past his hand.

For three full minutes he sat there. Then he said, "It is not given to me to set precedents. Unfortunately, there are a thousand court cases that hold a man cannot be punished for doing his ordered duty. If such were not the law and regulation, a man could find himself killed by his superiors if he did not do something for which he could be killed by the law. Unfortunately also, in a nation often at war, a superior cannot be punished for issuing an order which involves a capital offense if executed. Some day the Grand Council or an Emperor may resolve this, though I doubt it, for it is dangerous ground. The best guarantee of integrity is to ensure that only decent men, men like Royal Officer Jettero Heller, have authority."

Madison groaned. He was losing ground.

"But," said Lord Turn, with a sudden wicked smile at the Gris attorneys, "you skidded over a very important point."

Gris, whose hopes had begun to rise, now power-dived into despair.

"You were undoubtedly very competent judges in the Domestic Police and you, sir, were undoubtedly a highly competent Lord's executioner. You have bamboozled me into listening to you day after day. Fortunately, we at the Royal Courts and Prison are answerable only to the Emperor. That does not put us above the common law. To keep the Emperor from making any mistakes, we have to be versed in the nicest legal points anyone ever heard of."

The old men who were acting as the attorneys to Gris looked like they were in the business of grinding teeth. They did not take kindly at all to being lectured in public, even by a Royal judge.

"There is a case," said Turn, "that sets precedent. It is about three thousand years old. It is *Manda versus Boont*, quite famous in its time. It evolved from the property-settlement litigation of an heir. The finding occurring in the Domestic Courts was appealed by petition to the Emperor and was heard all over again right here in the Royal Court. The litigant challengers claimed over three million credits in property, stating that the heir was not the legitimate son of the father since no marriage ever occurred. I assure you the matter was very hotly contested with that much property in view.

"The mother, through a cellologist, had registered the actual father. The heir asserted this proved his claim. The court . . ." And here Turn looked down his nose at the Gris attorneys while the whole world waited in suspense. "The court found explicitly that registry of conception was a legal substitute for marriage."

Turn let that sink in. The silence in the vast hall was acute. "The heir won the case. *Manda versus Boont*. You can look it up in our library upstairs if you wish. But take my word for it. I have seen and had deciphered these other marriage papers contracted on the planet Earth or whatever its name is. They all come *after* the date the Widow Tayl registered the conception of her child." He smiled. "No bigamy was committed in my Royal Prison:

the ceremony was needless. Wherever Gris committed bigamy it was not here. Under law he had already married the Widow Tayl, months before he married any others.

"I hereby declare the accused, Apparatus Officer Soltan Gris, innocent of the charge of bigamy in this prison."

The shock of it was such that there was hardly a breath drawn for half a minute.

THEN THE STORM!

Warders had to fight like lepertiges to hold the mob in check. The prison guards were blurs of motion with electric whips. They managed to hold the front of the room clear and keep Gris from being torn limb from limb, but only because somebody and then somebody else noticed that Lord Turn was banging his gong for all he was worth: they saw the motion, the sound was lost. He was also holding up his hand.

Gradually, because Lord Turn was trying to say something, the din temporarily subsided.

"HOWEVER!" shouted Turn into his amplifier, probably for the twentieth time, and when he could be heard, proceeded, "I shall have to hold Soltan Gris in custody, until I clarify the status of Jettero Heller. Soltan Gris may have done other crimes that only Heller is aware of. It is quite probable that Soltan Gris will not escape severe punishment or even execution yet. Warders! Return the prisoner to his cell. THIS TRIAL IS ENDED!"

The crowd was slightly mollified. But groups of them, when driven from the court, went out screaming, "Death to the Apparatus!"

Gris, on hearing the first finding, had soared to elation. Then, on hearing the second, had nose-dived into despair. He was dragged off, half-unconscious, to his cell, not even walking.

Madison, watching Gris go, was in a turmoil of his own. He was scared stiff at what Teenie might be thinking or planning now. He had NOT gotten her the custody of Gris. But wait, was there a loophole open? He wondered and then shuddered.

He was suddenly aware that he didn't have much time. Public reaction might boil over. Lombar might be upset by all this. Teenie would be screaming.

Then suddenly he began to smile. He still had power. He would bring this off to glory yet and bring it off with a BANG!

Chapter 6

Madison lived through the following day.

It was awful for him.

His best-laid plans had *not worked!*

The trial developments had absolutely smothered the Heller issue. He felt that Heller had somehow sneaked up on him, giving those blackmail files to the Gris attorneys. Didn't Heller realize that Madison was only trying to make him immortal? Who could possibly object to that, much less actively thwart it? Confound these amateur interferences with PR!

And that was not all that was bothering Madison: Teenie would be in an absolute fury! Deprived of her prey despite Madison's promises, there was no telling what she might do. Then there was the matter of Lombar

Hisst: he would not be pleased at the way the Apparatus was being mauled.

Madison wondered nervously if he was losing his grip. Maybe he was not neurotic enough lately and, as a consequence, maybe his genius was slipping.

Standing at his bedroom window in the townhouse, gazing out over Joy City, he felt that his sphere of influence was collapsing.

A pall of smoke was rising a quarter of a mile away. He heard some noise behind him and he said, "What's happening over there?"

It was the circus girl, Flip. She had taken to making his bed lately and laying out his clothes and talking with innuendos which alarmed him. She came to the window. "Oh, that's the Dagger Club, an Apparatus officer hangout. Chi and I were over there when the mobs burned it. But it's a shabby dive, not even anything to loot. The morgue services are overstrained and a lot of bodies are still lying in the streets, but we didn't even get anything out of that: some rotten crook had already taken their wallets." Her hand was cupping his behind. It made him very edgy. He moved away, reaching for a jacket.

"Oh, I wouldn't go out, if I were you," said Flip. "It would be much nicer to stay here and just loll around in bed. There's mobs all over the place looking for Apparatus officers. There comes one right now."

Madison went back to the window. About a thousand people were surging into the street seventy-six floors below. Even at this height, he could hear a chant:

Death to the Apparatus!
Death to the men of crime!
Death to the shabby criminals!
Death to the "drunks" in slime!

> *Death to the shameless murderers!*
> *Death to their leader, too!*
> *Death to the Apparatus!*
> *Death to the whole (bleeped) crew!*

"Something seems to have upset them," said Madison.

"Oh, people are upset, all right," said Flip. "It provides a lot of opportunities to pick pockets and such: a good, healthy crime environment. Every city is like that today. Me and a couple of the other girls were going out again but it would be much safer for you, Chief, if you just slid your pants off and got back into bed. I know a lot of nice things to do. I could start off with a (bleep) job. You wouldn't even have to exert yourself, just lie back and enjoy it. Then you could——"

"I've got to think," said Madison.

"Well, think while I'm working on you: you might get some great ideas. Here, put your hand——"

"Flip, run out and tell my reporters I want to see them in my office."

"Oh, Chief, you don't need those (bleepards) to stand around and watch. They might get hot and pile in! They can't (bleep) worth a (bleep): we know; we tried them."

She was taking her robe off. Firmly, he put it back on her. "Flip, please."

"There's something weird about you, Chief. I mean it. Go get your own (bleep) reporters!"

After she flounced out, Madison located Flick and had him form a reporter conference in his office.

The five reporters, the horror story writer and, as a consultant, the director, soon stood around Madison's desk.

"How do we stand?" said Madison.

"We don't," said one of the reporters. "In every paper the Gris finding is all over the front page. To make it even worse, in addition to the shocker news of finding Gris not guilty, somebody gave the papers a photo taken last year at some farewell party for some tug and it shows him eating a human hand. It was probably cake but it's driving the country insane. They're screaming now that the Apparatus are cannibals. Page two is burning buildings. The rest of the paper is pretty well taken up with lists of mob casualties. We tried half the morning to plant your follow-ups on the Heller rescue. The news offices are jammed with other things. Even the wives are running around in circles. You know this old-shepherd-woman caper claiming she spotted Heller in a cave? Hells, we even lost her when she joined a mob. We got nothing planted."

"From my knowledge in directing riot scenes," said the director, "I'd say this situation was going to escalate rather than calm down. I dressed up the two actors as Domestic Police generals and sent them around. The Domestic Police believe the situation is out of control: they want the Army to help and the Army is saying 'Up your (bleep), we got trouble enough with trying to contain the Fleet.' It ain't good."

"Oh, it's not all bad," said Flick, uninvited, from the door. "A lot of the crew was getting nervous about being connected to the Apparatus, so me and Cun and Twa was out until dawn collecting identoplates off corpses. Citizens, bluebottles, officials, we must have about two thousand of them, anything you want. We even got thirty sets of different numbers from wrecked cars. The computers will be out of date or jammed for weeks so it's safe as safe to use them. If I hadn't sworn off robbing

banks, we'd be in clover. But at least we've got mobility.
So things look pretty good."

"I'm open for suggestions as to how we seize press
initiative again," said Madison.

"Well," said the director, "I'd say we just sit tight
and let things simmer down." The others nodded.

Madison shook his head. "I've been trying to teach
you some of the rudiments of PR. Well, one of them has
to do with trends. You don't buck a trend. That's fatal:
You just expend your energy being battered. The thing
you have to do is go WITH the trend."

"Well, this trend," said a reporter, "happens to be
composed of riots and resistance to the Apparatus. The
crowds are tearing them limb from limb wherever they
can be found outside the defense perimeters of their
bases and staging areas. It's the trend that's giving us
trouble."

"Nevertheless," said Madison, "the principle still
holds. Trying to smooth things over with PR is a waste
of a good tool. There is another principle you must understand: You must always make trends worse."

"Worse?" said a reporter. "That's blasted near impossible. The mobs are burning buildings and tearing down
monuments; traffic control is almost shattered; the hos-
pitals are overflowing; the newssheet staffs can hardly
get to work and distribution is getting grim. Every major
city in the Confederacy is like that. If it gets any *worse*,
we'll be as dumb as gateposts: we won't have any media
but Homeview! And even the guys over there are running around so frantic it looks like the lunatic asylum up
north. We've just got to let it calm down."

Madison heaved a deep sigh. Green PR men were
awfully hard to train. But that wasn't all that was making him sigh. He didn't like to fire off his last two rounds.

"No," said Madison. "The progress and advancement of a culture is measured by how much worse things get. The greatest authorities that ever lived proved that constantly. Lord Keynes, Karl Marx—real geniuses like that—kept that principle continually in mind. That's why they are almost worshiped. They were also some of the greatest PR men that ever lived. Now let's take up the three Cs again: maximum Coverage, maximum Controversy, maximum Confidence. The only way we can obtain those is to make things worse."

"Comets!" said a reporter. "Things can't possibly get much worse. They'll be shutting off phone service and utilities next! Chief, there's close to a hundred billion people on the streets in riot mobs...."

"Oh, dear," said Madison. "I see I'm not getting across. We've got to escalate Controversy. And Controversy is really Conflict. Only then can we regain Coverage and restore our Confidence in ourselves as PR men."

"Escalate Controversy?" said one of the gawping reporters. "The whole population is against the Apparatus. The Fleet and Army are in a head-on collision. The Domestic Police ... did you hear those shots in the street just then?"

"The Domestic Police are against everybody," finished another reporter. "There's more Controversy/Conflict around than there's been for the past ten thousand years. You CAN'T POSSIBLY escalate it!"

"Oh, yes, we can," said Madison. "And to do our jobs as PR men, we MUST!"

"How?" they gaped at him.

Madison leaned forward. He beckoned. They put their heads near his. He whispered.

When they drew back, they were staring at him with awe.

"OH, MY GODS!" the horror story writer said. "He CAN escalate it!"

Madison smiled. Now he would get things back on the rails and going in the right direction: at Heller.

PART
EIGHTY-THREE

Chapter 1

Palace City was the safest place to be. Not only was it thirteen minutes in the future but, like Spiteos, it was protected from mobs by the simple fact that they could not cross the vast Great Desert on foot or with ground cars. Palace City also had heavy exterior defense bunkers that could shoot anything out of the sky.

Under the yellow mist of warped space, in the great round antechamber of the Emperor, Lombar Hisst sat with his back to the locked and bolted bedroom door and faced his general staff.

A red-uniformed old criminal, whose battle-scarred face also bore traces of debauchery and no sleep, was speaking. "The Army finally took it into their heads to cooperate," he said. "A thousand transports have landed a million men on Calabar. This freed up the remainder of our forces there and they should be arriving at Apparatus Staging Area Seven by this evening. So, factually, sir, we don't have any more troops on Calabar, only a few observers. That puts me out of a job as Calabar staff overseer here. And I was wondering if I might not take a little run up into the Blike Mountains. I've an estate there. . . ."

"You'll stay on duty!" thundered Hisst, slapping his stinger down on his desk. "Set up a bureau for future population suppression. This would never have happened if we'd planned for it." He pointed the stinger at another general. "If Tur there had had his wits about him, if he'd done some advance planning, he wouldn't be in trouble now. Gas. Set up some gas extermination chambers for troublemakers: I'll get you the plans from one of the Blito-P3 surveys."

"Sir," said the general indicated, "I don't think there's any time for construction of anything. Over two hundred Apparatus town headquarters have been wiped out to a man. If I could just have a few troops from the staging areas——"

"Empty a few prisons and put the inmates in uniform," snapped Hisst. "Do I have to think of everything?"

Tur was already doing that as fast as he could but he held his peace.

"Now you, General Muk," said Hisst, "how are you coming along with the Earth-invasion staging?"

"As a matter of fact," said Muk, squirming, "I've put the invasion of Blito-P3 on hold. It seemed to me that the two and a half million troops might be needed right here on Voltar."

"Bah!" said Hisst, glaring at the other generals. "We have a million and a half Apparatus troops to handle Voltar and some of the others. This is no full-scale civil war. It's just mobs. Sooner or later they'll get tired of being shot down and that will be the end of it."

"We are having trouble with suppliers," said Muk. "The troops that came in from Calabar are short of everything. We can't seem to get deliveries into the staging areas." He added hastily, "We are, of course, sending out armored convoys and simply raiding civilian warehouses and we can, of course, accomplish our outfitting. We have had some trouble with mobs burning plants and we have lost eighteen convoys in street fights as of this morning, but we can be invasion-ready in a couple of days, even so. It just seemed to me that with all this trouble, you might need the Blito-P3 force here."

"No, no, no," said Lombar. "We're just fighting riffraff. You others simply need to take stronger measures, that's all. The invasion goes off as scheduled, regardless of local disturbance." He gave a short, barking laugh. "Unarmed rabble, riffraff."

"They seem pretty mad," muttered a general in the rear. "We've already lost over fifty thousand men."

"Who's that?" snarled Lombar. "Are you frightened or something? Well, speak up!"

He didn't get an answer, for running feet sounded in the outside hall.

A staff officer, followed by two men, raced into the room. The others looked up in alarm. The three were carrying huge stacks of papers.

The staff officer dumped his on Lombar's desk and pointed with a shaking finger. Headlines, full first page:

HELLER KIDNAPS
EMPEROR

Seventy papers said the same.

A general came out of his shock and frantically switched on a Homeview set. The words blared out, "IN THE MOST DARING RAID IN VOLTAR HISTORY, THE OUTLAW JETTERO HELLER HAS KIDNAPPED CLING THE LOFTY, EMPEROR OF VOLTAR!"

The generals stood like scarlet ice statues, eyes filled with the headlines, ears pounded by the din.

Chapter 2

Into this stunned tableau rushed J. Walter Madison. He was wearing a General Services officer's gray uniform and sand goggles. Thundering hard on his heels came his director and camera crew.

"Oh, heavens!" cried Madison. "I am so glad I found you, Chief!" It was no accident that he knew Hisst was there: he had been having him tailed.

Madison came to a halt before the stunned Hisst. He pointed at the headlines on the desk. He pretended he was short of breath. "I tried to get them to hold the announcement until I consulted you but the traitors wouldn't wait!" What an awful lie that was! He had had his reporters, armed with copies of Heller's letter, leak the news to every paper. He had only been waiting outside the antechamber until he had seen the papers brought in.

Lombar was staring at him. The generals were staring at him. Madison gave the director and crew a hand signal to go live, straight into the Homeview circuits for the whole Confederacy, as arranged by the manager at his orders.

"Quick, quick!" cried Madison. "We've got to take fast action to disprove this rumor. Open that door fast so we can show the whole Confederacy that the Emperor is still there!"

Lombar at the desk saw with horror, from the flickering camera lights, that they were on the air! He moved suddenly to mask himself with Madison's body. Then he saw Heller's baton lying there: convulsively he snatched it up and put it behind his back. He was trying to think of something, anything that would prevent this disclosure.

His own generals, not in the know, unwittingly undid him. In various voices, they all said differently and urgently the same thing, "Yes, for Gods' sakes!" "Open up the door!" "This is catastrophe!" "Check that bedchamber!"

Madison was grabbing keys and opening plates. Lombar was too paralyzed to stop him.

Madison got the door open and slammed it wide. He and the generals rushed in. Lombar was knocked into their midst by the director.

THE ROOM WAS EMPTY!

The cameras played all around the Royal bedchamber.

Madison saw very clearly that the room had not been occupied for months: food in the pans was decayed, excreta on the bed covers was dry. Swinging up the covers to pretend to look under the bed, he hid the evidence.

Madison, leaping up, cried, "It must have been just last night! Oh, heavens, I'm afraid for the Emperor's life!"

Then Madison saw Lombar was holding something behind his back. "What is that you've found?" he shouted. He grabbed the baton and the cameras zoomed in on it. Madison examined it, holding it to be shot, "The evidence! He left evidence! This is Jettero Heller's officer baton! Now we know for sure who did it! The outlaw Jettero Heller has kidnapped Cling! Oh, catastrophe! Oh, woe! We are undone!"

Madison made a slight signal to the director and the cameras promptly began to cover the room minutely. It took them off of Lombar. Madison got behind Hisst's back and whispered urgently in his ear.

Lombar came out of his shock. The cameras centered on him. "Yes, yes!" shouted Lombar. "Instantly! Generals! Order all Fleet and Army units to pursue him! The villain has escaped to Calabar!"

The director had the cameras pan as all the generals rushed off to issue the orders.

Madison gave the cameras and director a signal to stop.

The moment Lombar saw the flickering lights go off, he sank down soddenly in a chair. "Oh, this is terrible," he groaned.

"Oh, no, it isn't!" said Madison. "This is just great! It's the very thing you have been waiting for! Violent civil unrest, no Emperor. The Army and the Fleet now out of the way. The great opportunity has arrived!"

"Opportunity?" said Lombar in new shock. "This is disaster!"

"No, it's not," said Madison. "The throne is empty. Lombar, you are about to become Emperor!"

"No, no," said Lombar. "I need the body of the last monarch to show a duly convened assembly of Lords! I need the regalia! It's gone!"

"Details, details," said Madison. "Here, fortify your nerves. This is no time for palsied hands." He took out of his pocket a flat pint bottle of the very best counterfeit Scotch that Bolz had been importing. There was only one change Madison had made in it: it held a minute quantity of LSD.

Lombar took a swig. It burned its way down. He felt his blood begin to flow again. He took another swig.

"Now, that feels better, doesn't it?" said Madison. He turned. "Get set up, director."

Chapter 3

The Imperial Palace staff were scared blue. They had been locked in their rooms for months and now, dug out of the servant living quarters by Death Battalion officers, they were quite certain they were about to be executed. It was with great relief that they found, when they had been herded into the immense throne room, that they were only expected to set it up.

The vast domed hall was a thousand feet in diameter and a hundred feet from golden floor to sky-blue ceiling. On the dais solidly sat the mammoth throne of Voltar, of shimmering violet stone inset with jewels.

It was dusty and as cold as a tomb. It took two hundred staff half an hour to sweep it down and polish it up. They couldn't quite understand what was happening, for the place was also swarming with men in the aqua-green uniforms and badges of Homeview who kept using gutter words they didn't think Homeview men used.

Two Royal palace valets and a seneschal balked when ordered to open up the chests of robes: this was supposed to be a ceremony supervised by the Lord of Wardrobe who was not there. They got knocked and kicked by these strange "Homeview men" and lost no time after that in complying.

A man the others called "Costumes" made them

indicate which were the coronation robes and then the Death Battalion people herded the palace crew back to their quarters and locked them all in once more. They felt relieved to be still alive.

In the vast throne room, the director pointed at the electronics security expert and said, "You roustabouts help him set this place up. Don't forget the gadgets." He looked over to where the circus girls and whores were clustered and he yelled, "You (bleeps) help people get dressed. And get dressed yourselves. We got too many (bleeped) women, so all but three of you dress like men. And no (bleeping) around!"

A logs man, working over to the side, yelled, "Hey, director, this paint won't dry in under three hours!"

"(Bleep)!" yelled the director. "Just tell people to be careful."

Lombar, sitting in the antechamber, was still a bit numb from shock. His yellow eyes were sort of glazed. "I still can't figure how they found out," he maundered.

"Oh, reporters are pretty awful," said Madison. "Do you talk in your sleep?"

"I don't think speed makes you talk in your sleep," said Lombar. "Maybe it was the heroin."

"Well, that will do it every time," said Madison. "I sure wish you'd told me. We could have been spared a lot of this."

"I guess I'm lucky you jumped in," said Lombar.

"You sure are," said Madison. "Here, have another swig of this. It's a counterirritant."

Lombar took another drink. Madison looked at his watch. He would get the beginning LSD effects about an hour after that first swig. He had twenty minutes to go. The counterfeit Scotch itself was already making Lombar pretty mellow.

A general came in. "All orders have been issued to the Fleet and Army. Some admiral wants to know if we have any pinpoint coordinates on Calabar itself."

"Just tell him to look all over," said Madison. "Use every ship he's got and report progress."

"Tell him he doesn't need any coordinates," said Lombar. "Just kill everything living on Calabar!"

"That would endanger the Emperor!" said the Apparatus general.

"I'm pretty certain he's dead anyway," said Lombar. "Clarify any orders on that basis."

"If you say so," said the general and withdrew.

It upset Madison slightly to have amateur help on a PR caper. But he shrugged. Heavens only knew where Heller was by now. Obviously this kidnap was months old. After that sister rescue, Heller might have gone anywhere: Manco? Earth? Who cared? All he wanted was the headlines. He began to dream up sighting reports and hairbreadth escapes he would manufacture. He didn't even need the Fleet and Army reports! He had great confidence in his client eluding everything sent after him. At that moment, despite earlier setbacks, he was absolutely certain that he would shortly have the most immortal outlaw anyone had ever heard of. Eventually, of course, Heller-Wister would be caught and hanged but that always happened to outlaws and was to be expected. Meanwhile, what headlines! And, oh, my, wouldn't Mr. Bury be pleased! Red carpets for Madison the length and breadth of what might remain of Earth.

Chapter 4

Two circus girls came in and began to strip off Lombar's clothes.

"What's going on?" said Lombar, pretty drunk.

"Just you be patient, sweetiebun," Flip said. "We'll have you out of these general's rags before you can spit. We're experts."

They had Lombar naked. He stood there teetering. "Hey, that's a nice (bleep)," said Flip.

"I think so, too," said the other girl. "Chief, have we got time?"

"Shut up," said Madison. "Look, Lombar. Look at this." Madison was holding up a golden Royal robe: it was worked with jewels against shimmerfabric to make patterns of comets, suns and planets. They seemed to move when you twitched the cloth.

For an instant Lombar recoiled. He had a Royal robe in his office at Spiteos that had been stolen from a tomb, and in private he had often donned it to admire himself. But it was death for anyone not of Royal blood to wear one of those in public. He had a sudden wave of paranoia. He had a spasm of nausea that he misinterpreted. He held on to his stomach and fended the robe off.

Madison glanced at his watch. Yes, it was about time for the first nausea and palpitations of LSD. He handed Lombar the Scotch. "Take another small swig and you'll feel better."

Lombar took another swallow. It warmed him. The spasm passed.

The girls got him into the Royal coronation robe. They slid sandals of gold and jewels onto his feet and would have combed his hair except that Madison, behind his back, was pointing urgently at his watch.

Madison made a gesture to Flick in the door and the man sped off. He and the girls got Lombar walking.

The LSD, the minute first dose, had begun to bite. "Set" now was very important: the state of Lombar's mind.

"You are the most powerful being in the entire universe," said Madison. "You must keep your mind dwelling on that."

Lombar nodded and somehow concentrated.

They got him down the hall to the great doors of the throne room.

"Setting" was now the thing, all-important to LSD trips. Two women, dressed like Lords, bowed and swung wide the doors.

A burst of glorious music hit Lombar. The Imperial Palace band, dug out of the cellar and performing now with the scaler's gun on them, played violently in their recessed stage.

"Lights! Camera! Action!" bawled the director.

Madison melted back. He didn't want his own body in this. He could claim Lombar had gone crazy and ordered it, if worst came to worst, and his crew would back him up. But he didn't think any worst would come of it. He was dealing out a *fait accompli*. Those flickering cameras were plugged straight into Homeview, live to the whole Confederacy.

The two actors in Lords' robes escorted Lombar

down a shimmering path that made it appear he was treading on sunbeams.

The whole hall was FULL OF PEOPLE! Hundreds and hundreds of them! Admirals of the Fleet, generals of the Army, Lords beyond count! They all bowed and stood up straight and bowed again. They kept doing that because that's what they were designed to do. They were all electronic illusions ripped out of General Loop's townhouse. The only live people in the place were the musicians and Madison's crew and Lombar!

Lombar was getting his "setting" all right. To the swell of Imperial music, if a bit off-key from musician fear, Hisst proceeded in the steadying company of the two actors dressed like Lords, followed by the two circus girls costumed likewise.

The director noticed the assembled throng was bowing a few times too often and began to concentrate on Lombar's face. A strange look was beginning to suffuse it. Heavens only knew what internal pictures were spinning through his LSDed brain now!

They got him to the throne dais. Here he was supposed to kneel. He wasn't accustomed to doing that and he tripped and had to be hurriedly righted. The director with a hand triple-screen monitor edited it out. He had three cameras running and the two roustabouts, as substitute cameramen, were not completely steady but it would do.

A whore in a pontiff's robes now came in from another door, followed by two cooks dressed as priests.

The "pontiff" walked up to the kneeling Lombar and made some signs over his head she hoped were right, then turned and took the regalia chains from one "priest" and hung them around Lombar's neck. They clanked properly because they were gilded iron. She then turned and took the "scepter" from the other "priest" and handed it to Lombar. It was only *papier-mâché* and Lombar, clutching convulsively, bent it.

The director switched on a crowd camera and hissed into a radio for a props man to rush in and straighten it out. That done, he cut back.

They got Lombar up and onto the throne.

"The crown," the director hissed. "You forgot the (bleeped) crown." He cut back to the mechanically bowing crowd.

The two "Lords" got Lombar back on his knees.

Impromptu, Flip and the other girl, who had dressed him and had now gotten into the robes of noble ladies, grabbed the pillow the crown was sitting on and did a sort of a dance, carrying it between them. The director thought it was very nice. Nobody had seen a coronation for upwards of a century, so it didn't matter, in his opinion. He cut the dance in.

Flip and the other girl let the "pontiff" take the crown off the pillow. The paint was still wet and the "pontiff" wiped her hands off on her gown before she went on.

Lombar's hair, not combed, was pretty unruly and hard to stuff under the crown. The thing was too small. But she got it on someway.

"Say something!" hissed the director into the "pontiff's" ear-radio channel.

"I think it will stay on,' said the whore to all Voltar.

The two "Lords" got Lombar off his knees and onto the big throne.

Flip and the other girl didn't know what to do with the pillow. But it had been impromptu thus far and they would carry it off the same way. Flip tossed the pillow over her head in an elegant gesture and then she and the other girl, with a bouncing costume display turn, did what they always did in handling fake-throne tableaux in the circus—did an arm snake dance in front of Lombar's face and then settled elegantly on either side of him below the arms of the throne, heads at the level of his waist.

Suddenly Madison remembered that in the pressure of other things, he had forgotten to write the announcement, much less give it. All Voltar was watching but they didn't know what in Hells they were looking at.

"Now!" hissed the director into the electronics man's channel.

Nothing happened. Then the electronics man hissed back over the radio to the director, "Somebody tripped over the (bleeped) plug!"

Lombar was getting restless. Lord only knew what was passing through his mind. As LSD gives a time speedup, he certainly wasn't aware of the fact that, due to somebody accidentally disconnecting something, there was a blank in the program.

But Flip was aware of it and, sitting on the floor beside the throne, she showed that she was a born and trained trouper. The subject of this display was getting restless. There were slits in the side of the very ample and overflowing robe. Unseen by the camera, she slid her nearest hand through one and passed it softly over Lombar's thigh, hidden by the garment.

Lombar's yellow eyes flared for a moment in surprise.

Flip, hand and forearm hidden now through the robe slit, sat facing forward with an expression which was very lofty and noble.

Lombar settled down. He put his head back. A look of ecstasy began to steal over his features.

The lofty and noble expression on Flip's face was retained. But her eyes flicked sidewise for a moment and then her eyelids began to twitch in rhythm.

"Lovely, lovely," whispered the ecstatic Lombar.

"That's great," hissed the director, "hold it just like that." And then to the electronics man, "Hurry up!"

"Got it," came the answer.

Lombar was stiffening out his legs. Then his yellow eyes flared wide.

Four, count them, four electronic-illusion angels came winging down out of the blue dome of the vast hall.

They hovered right over his head!

One of them, a delicate, ethereal thing, suddenly said in a deep male voice—the electronics man couldn't find the girl who was supposed to do this—"Well, Hisst, old boy, you finally made it and it's about time!"

Lombar shuddered in ecstasy.

Flip's face, noble and lofty, was still registering a rhythmic twitch. Her lips parted slightly in concentration.

Madison was wildly signalling to the director, giving him a sign to zoom in and hold.

With the beatific smile on Lombar's face filling the frame and trying to cut out the tangled hair now smeared with wet gilt from the crown, the director made a camera hold.

Madison had a mike now. He tapped it with his finger—boom, boom. It was live.

"Ladies and Gentlemen of the Voltar Confederacy," he said, "we have just brought you live, live, live, the crowning of Lombar the Magnificent. Due to circumstances beyond our control, a hiatus has occurred in the Royal line of Voltar. The outlaw Jettero Heller stole Cling the Lofty and it was vital during this time of national unrest that the throne be filled. In a self-sacrificing moment, Lombar Hisst, lately Chief of the Apparatus and more lately Dictator of Voltar, heeded the resounding demands of the multitude and took the throne by popular acclaim. This program has been brought to you by the courtesy of the Grand Council. Long Live Lombar the Magnificent. He will give his all."

And at that moment, Lombar *did* give his all. Flip's hidden efforts came to culmination. "Ooooh!" groaned Lombar as his body gave a convulsive jerk.

Flip grinned.

The director held upon the face a moment more while Lombar panted.

"Cut," the director said. "That was *beautiful!*"

Chapter 5

If the Confederacy had thought it had riots, these were nothing compared to the riots they were having now, the day following the coronation.

A stunned Voltar had not known what to make of the "coronation" event when it had come on Homeview. Word had flashed across mobs and even battles with the Apparatus, and action had suspended while one and all sought the nearest Homeview set in cars, tanks, buildings, stores or homes. At first some thought the rumor that brought them to the viewscreens must be mistaken: Was this some old musical? Or a circus? Or a parody in bad taste?

Voltar takes its Royalty seriously and tampering with

it had never been taken lightly. It had prospered and been stable for ages in the old galaxy and for 125,000 years in this one under the political system of a benign monarchy. There had been upsets in the past but these infrequent disruptions in Royal rule, even when occasioned by excessive repression, had been resolved by a conclave of the Lords of the land—of which there were thousands, existing not only on the central planet of Voltar but on the other 109 planets. A system existed, in other words, for handling the cessation of a Royal line.

In the living memory of most of the four hundred billion inhabitants of the Confederacy, despite their long life expectancy, no coronation had taken place. But they suspected that it would be attended by some vast array of Lords, with pomp, parades, celebrations and even holidays complete with festivals and one's best clothes. It wouldn't be over in ten minutes, most of which was being performed without even saying what it was about.

And then, at the end, the statement that that insanely rapturous face was their new monarch and that it was no one less than the head of the organization they had been battling in the streets for days, the Apparatus of trial notoriety, stuffed torches into an already roaring fire. People who had been on the sidelines before burst into the streets with screams of fury. Government offices and buildings that had nothing to do with the Apparatus became the targets for anything one could throw or any weapon one could steal or invent.

Normal conduct of affairs and life all but ceased. In its place rose the anarchy of rage.

The Domestic Police gave up any real effort to control the mobs and in some places even joined them.

The smoke of burning buildings hung like black mourning over thousands of cities. The damage toll was

soaring into billions of credits and hundreds of thousands of lives.

Reports of all this, oddly enough, were only being
centralized by Madison himself.

He sat in the Emperor's antechamber at a desk pre-
viously used by guard officers. Lounging around the
large room were the forty-nine members of his crew.
Because they had procured bales of them from Homeview, they were all attired, except for Madison, in the
aqua-green uniforms of that organization. The tunics,
pants, boots and caps with their goggle-visor bills were
easy to slip into. Furthermore, as the news came in, none
of them were partial to looking like Apparatus: also, as
"Lieutenant" Flick had pointed out, nobody ever looked
twice at a Homeview crew—they were accepted as part
of the scenery, and while people might be interested in
something that was being camera'd, nobody ever looked
twice at the crew. The fourteen women backed him up:
they thought the uniforms were pretty.

Madison, through the night, had dozed while
sprawled across the desk. Lombar was in the Emperor's
bedchamber, excreta and all, dumped there to sleep off
the counterfeit Scotch and LSD and maybe some heroin
and speed they did not know or care about.

From time to time Apparatus generals came in with
reports that the situation was worsening. They would
find that there was no one on duty but Madison: he
would rouse and blink, hear about some new town going
up in smoke and then say, "You just make sure, General,
that the Fleet and Army are going after Heller," and go
back to sleep.

About 9:00 A.M., some fifteen hours after the coronation, Flip brought him his share of the hot jolt and
sweetbuns they had looted out of the Imperial stores.

"Chief," she said, "you look awful. There's several bedchambers opening into this room, probably left over from when some Emperor had mistresses. They all got bathrooms. I found an Emperor's spin razor and spin brush and even a bottle of soap. I didn't bring you any spare General Services uniform and that one is all sweated up, so I laid out a new Homeview outfit for you. Now eat your breakfast."

Madison groggily imbibed the sweetbun and hot jolt. He felt better.

"Now," said Flip, "we can slip into that bedroom, rip off a little piece of (bleep) and you can freshen up and change your clothes."

Alarm rang through Madison. He suddenly had a bright idea. "No, look. I can't leave this desk unmanned. So you take over for me here while I go bathe and change."

"Aw, (bleep)," said Flip. "All right, but you sure are weird. Never mind, I'll get you into bed yet." She sat down in the chair he vacated.

Madison looked at the crew. Some of them were dozing, a circle of six were shooting a quiet game of dice for minor loot they had found lying about. Flick was snoring on the floor between Cun and Twa. Madison went into the mistress's bedchamber to shave, brush his teeth, bathe and change into a Homeview outfit.

An Apparatus general came in and looked around, eyes a bit wild.

"Can I help you?" said Flip in her best approximation of a male voice to fit her costume.

"I got to see Hisst!" he said urgently.

Flip pointed with a polished fingernail. "His Majesty is right over in that bedchamber, sleeping it off. The sideshow is free. We don't have any nuts for sale, but you can tip me if you want."

The general hurried toward the Emperor's bedroom.

"Cheapskate," muttered Flip. "Hey, Flick! Ain't there some way we can sell some tickets? Isn't every day people can see a drunk Emperor." Then she saw Flick was simply snoring. "(Bleep)," she said. "No enterprise. I could make a fortune with this show." And she began to tally up the potential profits from tickets and drinks and (bleeps) on the side. She got quite interested.

The crew lolled on, oblivious of the fate that was about to overtake them.

Chapter 6

The chamber stank of old excreta and new vomit.

The general closed the bedroom door behind him. He stared at Lombar, still in his coronation robe, lying on the soiled bed. The general was somewhat indecisive and he dithered up and down the side of the bed for a bit. Then he decided that the risks of not waking Lombar overbalanced the risks of his wrath. He shook him by the shoulder.

Lombar woke up. It was all right until he tried to turn his head and then the hangover hit him a sledge-hammer blow. He winced and then he glared at the general.

"Sir, I mean Your Majesty," said the perturbed officer, "I'd like to report..."

"Your Majesty?" said Lombar. "Quit that! You could get me killed. Are you trying to be funny?"

"No, sir. It's no joke. You were crowned Emperor yesterday."

"WHAT? Oh, my head!"

"Sir, Your Sir, don't you remember anything about it?"

Lombar was trying to move his head. The pain shattered him. He screwed up his face, trying to get oriented. Then he said, "I thought it was just a dream or something. Wait. Is this real?"

"Well, yes, Your M . . . Your Sir, but I have to report that the whole Apparatus Section of Government City is in flames. The troops there fought the mobs and Domestic Police to the last man. I want to call reinforcements for Palace City here."

"Well, call them, call them," said Lombar. "Nobody is stopping you. Just a minute." He was staring down at the soiled coronation robe. "You said I was crowned yesterday. I have no recollection of it. WHO DID THAT?"

"It was all on Homeview, Your M . . . Sir. I believe Madison and his camera crew did it, Sir Majesty."

Lombar might have been drunk and doped, but all that remained of it now was livid ferocity. "(Bleep) them! Grab a Death Battalion and put Madison and his crew under close arrest. Oh, my head! Then call for your reinforcements. Well, go on! Get out of here!"

"Sir, Your Sir Majesty, there's something else. An odd alert just came through on Homeview that an important announcement that affects you will be made in just half an hour. It sounded so ominous, we were worried." Then he saw the animal savagery that was forming on Lombar's face. Hastily, he added, "Yes, Your Sir, I'll put

Madison and his crew under arrest." And he rushed out before Lombar took it into his head to kill him.

The general had risen to his rank because he didn't take on odds he couldn't handle. He walked right on out past Flip. He went along the hall and out of the building.

Palace City's streets resembled, already, an armed camp. The general signalled a colonel of a Death Battalion and gave him a crisp order and a caution. Then the general hurried on to a communications tank to order far more Apparatus troops into the town and around its perimeter.

The colonel grabbed a captain of a hundred-man company. Within a brace of minutes, black-uniformed Death Battalion troops went to the various outside doors of the Imperial Palace and entered to converge upon the antechamber through various halls.

The aqua-green uniformed crew were suddenly confronted by levelled blastrifles. The dice game went into suspended animation. Cun prodded Twa and Flick awake. Others rose up staring.

"CHIEF!" screamed Flip.

Madison, who had just finished dressing in a Homeview rig, came out buckling on its equipment belt. He stopped with a jolt.

"You Madison?" said the Death Battalion captain.

Madison looked at the levelled blastrifles and the deadly troops. "I think there's some mistake. If you'll just step into the bedchamber with me, His Majesty will straighten it out."

"His Majesty, or whatever he is, ordered it," said the captain. "You're all under arrest. Come along."

"They're going to kill us!" yelped Flick.

"No," said the captain. "You're simply under arrest. I don't want any trouble. My advice, knowing something

of"—and he jerked his head toward the bedchamber—
"I'd move quickly before it's something worse. Where's
the dungeon in this place?"

Flip leaped up. "Right this way!" She led off down
a side hall.

The rest of them shouldered their equipment, cameras and loot.

Madison still would have gone to the bedchamber
but the captain blocked his way. "You're stupid," said
the captain. "You haven't been in the Apparatus long or
you'd know better. Move along!" And he shoved Madison
into the wake of his crew.

Followed by the soldiers, the crew was led down a
long, curving flight of stairs. They came to a vast place
that had a whole wall covered with locker doors, equipment, tables and benches. It had round windows that overlooked a park.

"Well, here we are," said Flip.

"This is no dungeon!" snapped the officer.

"Captain," said Flip, "when you have been in as
many dungeons as I have, you get to be an expert. Just
because this LOOKS like the Imperial galley with its
lockers all crammed with food is no reason it isn't a perfectly satisfactory dungeon for your purposes. Now, if
you want to give your troops piles from sitting on stone
ledges, that's up to you. But a smart officer always
thinks of his troops above everything. Look at those soft
benches."

The deadly expressions on some of the soldiers' faces
relaxed. It was the captain who laughed.

"Now, we're only under arrest," said Flip. "We are
just movie people, not dangerous like soldiers, so don't
worry that we'll try to get away. Maybe Hisstee didn't
like some of the shots we took. Celebrities are funny that

way. This will all blow over and there's nothing like full
stomachs. So let's all just sit down and have a nice party.
Girls, start looking in those lockers for some tup. Imperial grade.''

She slipped a very sharp electric kitchen knife into
her boot under cover of her gesture toward the lockers.

The captain and the soldiers sat down.

Several criminals studied covertly how to slip the
power charges out of the blastrifles now leaning against
tables.

Madison handed the captain the half-finished bottle
of LSD and Scotch.

The electronics man pulled the Imperial chef's
Homeview set out of its locker and turned it on. His
intention was to mask the sound of any commotion if
Madison gave the signal to fight their way out of here.
Comets, there were certainly enough shots and screams
coming out of Homeview, as its crews covered battles and
riots, to mask anything short of blowing up the whole
Imperial Palace.

Chapter 7

Lombar Hisst struggled with the coronation robe
and with a curse threw it in the corner. If he had
appeared in Homeview in that, he had no illusions as to
what the penalty would be.

With care, he had built himself into a dominant position and, with care, he could have built it into Emperor.

He might have even made it without a body and regalia, given enough dope to use on a conclave of Lords.

But in some way he could not explain, he had been plunged forward too fast. He did not understand that it had happened through alcohol and LSD. But however it had happened, of one thing he was sure: Heads were going to roll!

Curses were issuing from him in torrents. He was enraged beyond any rage he had ever felt before. He was actually quite deadly. He still had troops, he still had guns: he held the center of government. People were going to pay! And pay in blood!

A cold shower did not help much. Lacking any other clothes, he got back into his scarlet general's uniform. He went into the antechamber: it was cluttered but empty. He got into his desk and found some speed and heroin and gave himself a *speedball*, a powerful mixture of the two.

Almost at once he felt better, even more deadly but more in control. Factually, at times of crisis such as now, Lombar Hisst was something to reckon with.

The Apparatus General Staff had taken a large chamber at the front of the building. Lombar hit buzzers and very soon those who were at Palace City, the bulk of his generals, were sitting in the antechamber.

"Now, give me your situation reports," snarled Lombar. And in the next ten minutes he competently ordered a redisposition of troops without even touching his invasion staging areas. The generals were suddenly much heartened and barked orders into their own radios for relay. The population would soon be on the run.

The general who had awakened him was glancing at his watch and Lombar glared at him with annoyance.

"It's the Homeview," the man said. "It's coming on in thirty seconds. May I activate the set?"

Lombar snarled at him to go ahead.

The picture was a running battle between retreating Apparatus tanks and a mob using airtrucks that didn't seem to care what happened to them. At Homeview, a monitor switched and showed street fighting in the capital of Mistin against a background of smoke and flame.

Suddenly, without erasing the Homeview panorama, a second, brighter picture came on. It was an overplay. That meant it was not coming from the Homeview studios: it was not even coming on Homeview lines. It was being battered into the network by some remote transmitter that might be anywhere, most probably in outer space.

HIGHTEE HELLER!

Behind her were pipes and dials that were probably the back of the bridge of a spaceship.

Her eyes were very intense. Her voice was strong and clear.

"Citizens of the Voltar Confederacy! Hear me! His Majesty Cling the Lofty is ALIVE! It was at his express command and wish that my brother, Royal Officer Jettero Heller, rescued him from captivity by Lombar Hisst.

"The Chief of the Apparatus murdered legitimate successors to the throne. Then, by the use of poisons called *drugs*, he suborned the Grand Council and through this treachery has sought to usurp the throne!

"At the ancient fortress of Spiteos, long since believed abandoned and radioactive, Hisst has stored enough *drugs* to poison this entire nation. And he intends to do so!

"Here in my hands you see the Royal regalia: the scepter, chains and crown." She held them up.

"Army, Fleet, police, officials and citizens! Cast off the usurper! Rally to His Majesty and my brother Jettero Heller!

"DESTROY THE APPARATUS AND LOMBAR HISST!"

The picture went off, leaving the background view of running citizens and flames which had continued throughout.

"Oh, my Gods," said a general. "We're finished! It was bad enough without that!"

And then Lombar Hisst showed why Lombar Hisst, the commoner, had come so far. "Turn on the Army and Fleet command channels!" he barked.

A general grabbed levers on another console. The Army General Staff channel was live. He shunted the incoming signal through a decoder.

". . . and I don't think we will get any orders from the Lord of Army. We've got to make up our own minds here. So it's been decided to stay neutral. End."

"Get the Fleet!" said Lombar.

The general threw more levers and shunted to the decoder. As they were thirteen minutes in the future, they had the advantage of selecting any part of current signals as though they were past. After some blurs, the general settled in on the beginning of a Fleet transmission. The others in the room were very tense. An awful lot depended on this: if the Fleet stayed neutral, too, they could still win.

"Admiral Farb here, Main Fleet Base at Hite. Calling Fleet Admirals Staff. Have just intercepted a public transmission from Hightee Heller on Homeview that concerns the political situation at Palace City and the general state. We are standing by, red alert, with six thousand combat vessels and fifty thousand Fleet marines. Requesting analysis and orders."

A slight delay. Then, "Admiral Farb from Fleet Admirals Staff: Know: No orders or directions from Palace City or the Lord of Fleet. Consensus of Admirals Staff: although Hightee Heller is popular, she has no political status. The regalia displayed cannot be analyzed by lapidarists for authentication simply by being seen on Homeview. There is no proof that there are any drugs stored at Spiteos: charts list it as abandoned for the past 125,000 years. She did not produce the Emperor on the screen, which is, itself, suspect. Fleet Admirals Staff order, number available to all vessels and bases, is to restrain independent actions or demonstrations within your own units and to remain severely neutral. End."

"There you are," said Lombar. "We are still in control. Issue Imperial Orders to the Army and Fleet, commending their neutrality and confirming it. Issue a statement to Homeview that it is a lie that there are any drugs at Spiteos, that the statements of Hightee Heller are simply a misguided effort to protect her brother. And go right on shooting the riffraff down in the streets: either they'll get tired or we'll run out of riffraff."

"Your . . . er . . . Sir," said a general, "there ARE drugs at Spiteos."

Lombar fixed him with a sneer of contempt. "Mobs can't get across that desert. Let's get something clear: Properly defended, we can hold Spiteos for years. And another thing: in all our lengthy history nobody has ever been able to make a dent in Palace City. Not even the combined Fleet and Army could take this place. It's been tried. We're safe as safe and we're in control."

He stood up. He reached for his cap. The generals

stood. One said, "Are you going somewhere, Your ...
er ... Sir?"

"Yes, I'm going somewhere," said Lombar. "I'm
going to grab a flying tank and get to Spiteos. Order
another hundred thousand men in there to defend it. I'm
going to make sure nobody exposes our store of drugs
until they can be replenished by an Earth invasion.
Meanwhile, see to the outer bunkers and defenses of this
place. We're in control and mean to stay that way."

He put on his cap and started to leave. Then he
turned to them. "And you can stop this 'Your Sir' business, all of you! For better or for worse, I took the throne
and don't forget it!"

"Yes, Your Majesty!" they chorused and promptly
knelt.

PART EIGHTY-FOUR

Chapter 1

J. Walter Madison had been perfectly correct about the Army's General Whip: he had gotten the word when he saw his severed "head" on Homeview being presented to Lombar Hisst.

The popular member of the Army General Staff had at once ordered a million troops to Calabar and taken the command of them himself. Making record time, he had promptly relieved the Apparatus forces who had been battling the rebels.

The moment the Apparatus troops were spaceward ho for Voltar, General Whip, now in command of the offensive on Calabar, had penetrated a rebel radio band the Apparatus had been monitoring and had achieved contact with Prince Mortiiy.

"Your Highness," said General Whip, well known for his wit, "you will be pleased to know that I am officially dead."

"WHAT?" Mortiiy exclaimed.

"I am probably the only casualty in history killed solely by Homeview. I have a million army troops at my disposal just landed on Calabar. I pledge my honor as an officer no treachery is intended: their officers are all loyal to me. What does Your Highness wish to do with them?"

"Welcome to Calabar, General Whip," said Mortiiy.

"I am very pleased to bring you back to life. Use your troops to relieve my men in their defensive positions in case the Apparatus comes back. It would be embarrassing to them to fight on Voltar. Can you provide my forces with your transportation? We have some urgent visiting to do."

"It gives me great pleasure, Your Highness, to accommodate you. I only ask for a lock of hair from the head of Lombar Hisst when you amputate his windpipe."

"My pleasure, General Whip."

That was the conversation which led up to the Hightee Heller broadcast over Voltar. Now Mortiiy's "urgent visiting" was being carried out.

Captain Snelz was sleeping peacefully in his dugout at Camp Endurance just a few hours before the Hightee Heller message was to come over Homeview. He had no inkling anything was up. Camp Endurance, guarding Spiteos, was two hundred miles deep in the impassable Great Desert and aside from a few suicidal civilian airbuses—which had been promptly shot down—was disdainfully aloof from the riots which beset the planet and, indeed, all the Confederacy.

Captain Snelz, with the philosophy of a one-time Fleet marine—cashiered for cheating at dice—had an arm wrapped around his favorite harlot and was snoring peacefully. The five hundred credits from Heller had not only paid all his debts but had financed a winning streak, and he was now owed gambling IOUs from fully a fifth of the officers in the camp. He did not know he was about to become the hero of the Battle of Camp Kill.

Accordingly, it was with shock that he opened up his eyes and saw Heller standing by his bunk.

"I'm dreaming," said Snelz.

"You'll have nightmares if you don't get up," said Heller.

"My Gods, I got you safely out of here some time ago! What are you doing back?"

"A social call," said Heller.

"Who's he?" the awakened harlot said, staring up in sudden terror at a figure dressed in the scarlet of an Apparatus general.

"He's a Manco Devil," said Snelz. "Get out of here, you (bleepch), and don't open your face!"

The harlot fled.

"That's an awful way," said Heller, "to describe a combat engineer that's simply dropped in to do you a favor."

"ME a favor?" gasped Snelz. "Comets, Jet, you're going to get both of us killed. Rumor's got it there's a million-credit bounty on your head!"

"Let's not discuss small change," said Heller. "What I have for you is utterly priceless. A commission as a colonel in the Fleet marines. I know how you have longed to regain your former status." He handed over an embossed scroll.

"I was just a lieutenant," said Snelz, but he took the commission with a suddenly shaking hand.

"And this," said Heller, handing him another paper, "is your resignation from the Apparatus, effective in a few hours. We want everything regular."

"Wait a minute," said Snelz, holding the commission closer to the night glowplate. "This isn't signed by Cling the Lofty, it isn't signed by Emperor Hisst. It's signed by Mortiiy. Comets! How the Hells many Emperors are there?"

"You get the idea," said Heller. "It's something we

want you to help sort out. So please muster your company. . . ."

"Jet, this camp has just been reinforced and the commandant is expecting another hundred thousand men. My company is only a hundred. If we attacked this horde, we wouldn't even wind up as blood blots. Suicide!"

"I never thought I'd hear a Fleet marine quibbling about odds," said Heller. "But truthfully, I don't want you to attack anybody. I only want an escort and a minor favor."

Snelz groaned but he got up and climbed into his uniform. He leaned out the dugout door and sent his sentry scurrying through the predawn blackness to muster his company. Stepping down the path, his feet got tangled in some straps and he bent down to pick up an object. It was an absorbo-cloak that made all detection signals null. Propped against a rock was a spacetrooper sled. "So that's how you got in here," said Snelz.

"Let's not go prying into the secrets of a combat engineer," said Heller. "It has nothing whatever to do with the know-how of Fleet marines, Colonel. Now, if you will just call over one of your men and have him pick up this musette bag, please. It won't look right for an Apparatus general to be lugging things about."

The company had fallen in. In the dim blue lights of the camp, they were quite bored to see that they were acting as an escort to an Apparatus general. Then fifteen of them, Snelz's old platoon, peered more closely and went rigid: they knew Heller very well. But, eyes straight ahead and trying to keep their hair from standing on end, they, with the rest, obeyed the evolution orders of their captain.

In proper order, the company went over the chasm bridge to the far side of the great gap.

The officer at the far barricade stood up alertly.

"I'm inspecting your defenses," said Heller in a gruff voice.

The officer saluted and the company went on.

Heller guided them along the rim of the mile-deep chasm. It was very dark and the path was treacherous. Across the gap they could see the great bulk of the castle Spiteos against the stars.

Heller took the musette bag. He removed an object that looked like a small spear. He braced it in a rock. He sighted it in carefully. He went a few more feet and placed another one.

"If you're trying to blow up Spiteos," whispered Snelz, "those little spears won't do anything. They're just rock-splitting missiles. We use them to prepare a breach in fortress walls. I know them. They won't make a dent in that castle."

"Patience, patience," said Heller. "Little by little, if we persevere, even the greatest task gets done."

"You're crazy," said Snelz.

"A man is known by his friends," said Heller and went on placing spears.

They marched, then, back across the bridge. Heller inspected several gun emplacements, complimented the men in them and then walked back to the dugout. "Dismiss your men," he said.

Snelz, soaking wet with the tension of passing under the eyes of guards, did as he was told.

"Now I don't have time," said Heller, "to do the rest. So it's up to you." And he handed Snelz the musette bag. And in a few words explained to him what he wanted.

Snelz stared at him numbly. "I sure hope I am on the winning side," he said.

"Just make sure you are, Colonel," said Heller. And he slipped on the absorbo-cape, took hold of the space-trooper sled and, with a grin at the palsied Snelz, took off vertically, up into the stars like a ghost.

Snelz stood there for quite a while. There were no shots. He let out a sigh of relief. He knew now why the life expectancy of a combat engineer was only estimated at two years of duty. He looked at the musette bag in his hand. The life of a Fleet marine colonel, he mourned, was evidently far less than that!

Chapter 2

The Battle of Camp Kill began in the early afternoon. It began suddenly and unexpectedly and rushed to a disastrous conclusion.

Only a few hours after the Hightee Heller announcement had superimposed itself over Homeview, Lombar Hisst arrived at Spiteos in a monstrous flying tank.

He landed on the parade ground, gave himself another speedball and, seating himself on the turret in the burning desert sun, began to supervise the landing of a hundred thousand reinforcements.

Lombar Hisst felt ferociously good. He was at the height of his intellectual powers, he was achieving a sustained and elevated mood. He felt capable of super-human feats. That was from the speed. The heroin was giving him a smooth-off of rough edges, a physical warmth and feeling of great satisfaction. And his underlying personality, psychotic paranoia, had shifted over to the kingly phase of megalomania. Up there on the tank, huge in his red uniform, he was indeed, not just in his imagination, a very dangerous man.

The giant black castle of Spiteos loomed over to his left. It contained thousands of tons of opium and heroin in its upper storerooms, enough to bring an awful lot of population under control, to say nothing of a conclave of Lords.

It was the amphetamine that worried him: while he had enough of the pure stuff for years of his own supply, he did not have enough to carry even the Lords on for another month no matter how hard he adulterated it. He was speculating as to when he could get the Earth invasion launched: he had not touched the ships and troops scheduled for it in the isolated staging areas. He was depending right now for reinforcements on the prisons he had almost emptied out: they might be a sorry lot and they might look weird in the ways they wore their uniforms and carried their arms but they were killers, make no mistake about that. Loosed upon the population with heavy weaponry, they could sweep the mobs away like chaff, screaming "Long Live Hisst!" for giving them the chance to murder, loot and rape. The million in from Calabar were already setting a fine example in the cities: they were like packs of lepertiges let loose on helpless wool animals. People had no way now to keep count of the civilian casualties.

So Lombar, sitting there, felt very safe and confident. The Fleet and Army, not knowing whom to obey, were very neutral. Spiteos was easy to defend and Palace City was impregnable, utterly.

Above his head, low in the atmosphere, were three hundred Apparatus war vessels. They might be old and cast off from the Fleet, for they were intended for raids on unconquered planets just to keep them busy and afraid, but they were better than anything less than the Fleet. Drifting up there, they were standing guard while the latest reinforcement freighters disgorged their hundred thousand on the hot sand just below the camp.

The regiments were forming up. There were a hundred of them. They made a grand display. Lombar smiled a wolfish smile, tasting his power as the horde marched in to pass in parade and then prepare their close-by bivouacs. There was no music: that was not Apparatus style. But the thud of all those feet made the very ground quail.

Lombar's smile broadened until he showed his teeth: the standard bearers as they passed had gotten the word—they were giving him the quick change of step and momentary kneel that was the Royal salute.

Then a sharp sound penetrated his ears. It sounded like a rapid series of explosions, quite small. They seemed to come from the chasm across from the castle. It was quite like small arms fire.

But the burst was very short. Nothing else happened. Believing it must be some squad practicing or executing somebody with guns instead of throwing them in the chasm, Lombar Hisst ignored it and looked back at his passing troops. The last of them were just now going by, the rest had already fanned out and were busy annealing together dirt huts in a clutter of trucks and poles: it appeared to be a new town of mean shacks that was magically manifesting out of the sand.

What saved Lombar's life at that moment was the desire to cool his thirst. He dropped down through the turret into the capacious cabin of the flying tank, and one of the crew, to restrain the afternoon sun which had been streaming in to compete with the overloaded air coolers, let the turret cover snap shut.

Lombar was standing just behind the explosion-proof observer port. He was pouring a canister full of sparklewater.

From across the parade ground there was a terrible flash!

BOOOOOM!

A moment later a concussion wave hit the tank a harder blow than ever could have been delivered by a warship shell!

WHOOOOM!

The tank was thrown backwards fifty yards in a breath!

Men and huts and buildings were flying through the air as though propelled by the most monstrous hurricane that ever hit a planet's face.

Snelz had blown the Camp Endurance shell magazine with enough explosive to level a town! And the magazine had contained enough charge to level a city!

Three hundred warships, hovering too low and in atmosphere, caught the full blast of the concussion wave!

They went hurtling end over end up into the sky like thrown chaff. They tumbled in the torn air, battered out of control.

High overhead, well above the atmosphere at a height of three hundred miles, a thousand rebel troopships hung, watching the debacle. They were ignored, as the intercepts had said they would be, by the neutral Fleet.

They dived!

In a dazing rush they slashed down to the plain like hawks.

Before the dust of the blown magazine had settled—indeed, before the smoke of the explosion had had a chance to rise fully into the air—a hundred thousand rebel troops under Prince Mortiiy were leaping down from airlocks upon the desert sand.

With a howling rush, feet hammering, emitting a high keening yell, they fell upon the hated Apparatus survivors with electric bayonets and handguns that bellowed rage point-blank!

Their uniforms were tatters, their faces gauntly starved, but they made up for everything else with their pent-up avarice for revenge.

There was no quarter given.

The few guns the Apparatus got into action vanished under a torrent of flashing blades.

Hatred cut a searing swath across Camp Kill.

A hundred and seventy-two thousand Apparatus troops were dead in less than half an hour, leaving only some ships and the gun crews on the castle still fighting. They could not be touched by such an assault.

But the slaughter of the Apparatus infantry was not the end or purpose of the Battle of Camp Kill. It was only the preparation.

Chapter 3

Jettero Heller, aboard the Rebel flagship *Retribution*, a hundred miles above the battle, gave his weapons belt a hitch. He picked up his helmet from a bench. He looked across the bridge where stood Prince Mortiiy,

Hightee Heller and the Countess Krak, spots of color amidst the drab uniforms of the rebel general staff.

"I think it's time," he said. "That battle looks about over."

"Oh, Jettero," said the Countess Krak, "can't you let somebody else do it? Guns are still firing from the castle! It's dangerous!"

Heller said, "Life usually is. Now, don't follow me down too close, as I may still draw fire."

"I think," said Mortiiy, "I should make a pass with the *Retribution*. This ship is armored and can stand some heavy jolts."

"No, Your Highness," said Heller. "You're carrying valuable cargo: yourself, my sister and my lady love, to name a few. I've just run out of heroic speeches, so good-bye."

The airlock of the tug had been hugged against the *Retribution*'s side and Heller went through and closed it with a clang.

He hit the local controls a clip and the *Prince Caucalsia* jumped sidewise and then hurtled straight down.

Two Apparatus vessels, recovered from their tumble, were trying to box in a rebel sighting ship, but he ignored the fight. He didn't have any guns anyway.

Fifty miles, twenty miles, down, down, down he went. And then he was in the drifting battle dust above the mile-deep chasm.

Yes, there was still some shooting.

The guns on top of Spiteos were manned, firing.

Heller was a silhouette against the sun. He jinked and shells went screaming by.

He suddenly dived straight down into the mile-deep chasm. As no one had ever anticipated an attack from

there, defense artillery on the castle top had never been
installed to depress so low.

The vertical walls were flowing up on either side of
him. There were ledges and he was surprised to see that
now and then executed men had hit and hung there,
never falling to the bottom. It was a grisly place.

He had no interest in what might lie on the canyon
floor. He halted the tug halfway down and looked up.

A rebel ship was engaging the defense guns on the
top of the castle high above. Great gouts of furious flame
were bursting out from the black rock: some of the
basalt, turned molten, ran in a stream of fire past the tug.

Well, they'd not make much of a dent on this massive
hulk that way, Heller thought. Let them clean off a little
more artillery and he'd go up.

He rose slowly up the black canyon wall. Jockeying
the tug, had he been able to reach out through the windscreen he could have touched it with his hand.

He was inspecting.

Then he found it: ground level, just opposite the
other rim. He cruised along horizontally. He counted
the twenty spears he had set to knife into this.

Somebody up on the castle roof high above must
have him on a scope. A hand grenade exploded nearby
and made the tug shake.

He turned the tug to stand on its tail and pressed
a firing trigger. A barrage of blueflash raked the high
battlement vertically above. He hoped whoever it was up
there had been looking.

Just to make sure, he turned on the silver coating of
the tug, making it totally visible. That would attract
attention. He fired another blueflash barrage.

Now that he could be seen, the rebel warship held
its fire.

Heller looked skyward and saw nothing. He had to resort to a scope. Yes, there was the *Retribution* up there.

Everything was in place.

He settled himself into the local-pilot chair and fastened his belts.

He reached for the tug controls. Motors screamed in the rear of the tug.

With the speed of a vaulter, he went straight up, flat against the castle wall.

Over the top of the battlement he went.

With a sudden dart, the tug levelled out.

It lanced across the top of the castle, away from the chasm.

A blastcannon roared close to him with a flash.

His tractor engines were screaming like banshees!

He pushed all his throttles home. Planetary drives, Will-be Was, tractors, everything!

The tug surged, snapped back, surged, snapped back.

It was all he could do to stay in the pilot seat, even with belts!

With yank after yank he was trying to pull the whole vast castle over!

Surge after surge after surge, the tractor beams held on. Roar after roar after roar, the engines bit.

Then there was a shuddering difference. A sound like a sighing screech was transmitted through the tug.

The fault that he had fired into, in the chasm side of the castle with the twenty rock-splitting spears, was parting.

The drives shuddered forward without surging back, pulling with a deafening thunder of power.

Suddenly all engines went into a raving scream.

Heller slammed his drives shut.

Behind him he heard a moaning cry as though some monster was dying.

Then there came a tremendous roar, enough to shake a planet.

The tall, tall castle of solid black rock had turned over on its side.

It was followed by the death rattle of falling stones.

Heller turned off the tractor beams and a few boulders dropped out of their invisible net.

He built some altitude and looked back.

The great castle of Spiteos lay supine and broken.

But that wasn't all.

Heller smiled. When he had surveyed it originally, he had spotted where the storehouses were. And his guess at their content had been right.

Strewn in piles upon the plain were opium and heroin, like vomit that had been thrown up by a stricken beast.

Then he stared. That wasn't all that was happening down there!

Evidently, having fought their way past paralyzed or terrified guards and gotten to the now-exposed ramps, literally thousands of political prisoners were pouring out of the caves and tunnels far below the level where the castle had broken.

They were spreading like a swarm of insects from a disrupted nest, uncounted numbers of them. Even from this height their naked filth, rags and protruding bones were showing. Starved into near insanity, frenzied now in their sudden freedom, they raced away, scrambling over the debris of the wrecked castle, fanning out across the plain.

Heller looked up. Yes, the *Retribution* was there. The cameras which she carried had been shooting everything that happened and they were catching this. Not only that, with the power of a warship's communication drives, the *Retribution* was forcing in onto the Homeview band, overpowering the transmission from Joy City as before.

Heller flipped a switch to catch the screen and make sure. The *Retribution* was so close to hand that there was hardly any of the Joy City transmission visible here, but Heller could dimly make out the under-picture.

The *Retribution*'s several cameras were following various mobs of escaping prisoners. Heller smiled. What a black eye for Hisst: the "deserted" fortress was shown to be an Apparatus prison.

And then he saw something that caused him to freeze.

The real purpose of this raid was to display to Voltar that Spiteos did contain drugs. The cameras had caught them strewing across the plain.

But now a group of prisoners, reaching that spot, starved, must have thought it was edible flour.

Fully two hundred of them had stopped. They scooped up handfuls of it, tasting it.

Heller clipped on his powerful speakers. "GET AWAY FROM THAT!" he shouted down. "DON'T EAT THAT STUFF! IT'S POISON!"

A camera had zeroed in on them. Heller had them up close on the screen.

He did not know exactly what chemicals they might be. Opium? Heroin? Some cutting agent?

Before he could even yell again, a terrible thing happened. The prisoners suddenly went into agonizing convulsions!

It was on the screen. It was going to all Voltar.

Rebel infantrymen had reached the place. They were

pushing at the prisoners, probably getting orders from the *Retribution,* trying to get the prisoners away from the strewn piles.

Some of the prisoners, instead of welcoming deliverers, began to fight like madmen! They had gone crazy with chemicals even after just a taste!

Later they would find that a lot of what the prisoners had grabbed was not morphine or opium or heroin but the adulterative elements which were there in vast supply to be used in cutting, and they included powdered strychnine.

But the picture said to any viewer all it needed to say. True to Hightee's statement earlier that day, Spiteos was full of something stored by Hisst to be used against the population and that something drove men mad!

And here was Hightee's voice again, ringing loud and clear:

"Citizens of Voltar! You have seen that what I told you is true! ARMY, FLEET, POLICE, ALL DECENT MEN, HEAR ME! SLAUGHTER THE APPARATUS AND HUNT AND KILL THE USURPER LOMBAR HISST!"

Chapter 4

Lombar Hisst lay in the cabin of the tank.

The vehicle was upside down.

His head had rammed into the chest of the driver who lay there, neck broken, dead.

The padded interior muted sound but he had heard

infantry yells outside, shots and screams. Just a short time ago the whole area had been shaken by something falling down.

He was playing it very quiet. Apparently they had missed, somehow, the fact that he was there. Maybe from outside it looked like just another overturned, wrecked tank; perhaps several of them were lying about.

Sooner or later some infantry would start inspecting the wrecks to see if there was anyone still alive in them. He knew he was in a very tight spot. His mind was racing.

He crawled across the tank roof, which was now the floor. He inspected the controls. He knew how to drive these things, none better. The controls seemed undamaged. But he needed information. Just how tight was this spot that he was in?

He fiddled with a knob. A screen on the panel lit up with Homeview.

The face of Hightee Heller, upside down!

He heard her message with a shudder. But when the message reached his name, the shudder turned to icy rage. It was no news that everyone was after him—he knew that all the time. The news was that these were rebels and they were invading Voltar!

How would the Fleet take this? How would the Army react? He thought he knew but he would make sure. He fully intended to best the lot and still come out on top. He had every confidence in his destiny.

He found the radio panel in the semidark. He fished a dial, trying to find an Army channel. He knew he couldn't tap into the Army General Staff with this rig but it was certain that he could intercept lower echelons. He sorted through the noise for some time.

He had one: the nasal twang of a typical field grade

Army officer! "...But I just heard from the General Staff, Jowper. I don't think they know tup from turds! They're all confused. They say it doesn't matter if somebody stored some powder in Spiteos: the situation is political. The center of government is Palace City and as long as that's intact, we're neutral.... Yeah, I know, Jowper. But you just hold your regiment in check...."

Elation soared through Hisst.

He punched some buttons, spinning through the digitals of Fleet echelon bands.

A voice sprang up, the shrill accent of a space officer: "Well, I know how you feel at squadron. I'd like to jump in and help the rebels myself, but as long as Palace City holds, the Fleet admirals think we'd be classed as rebels if we pitched in. Nobody has ever made a dent in Palace City and the Lord of Fleet is there, so you just hold your squadron where it is and hands off. And that's final. End."

Hisst let out a sharp breath. The Army and Fleet were still neutral. The rebels were only succeeding in stirring up the civilian population, and to Hells with the riffraff.

Lying on the tank ceiling, Hisst began to plan. He reached into his blouse for a packet of cocaine he always kept there for emergencies. He took a small pinch and sniffed it. He felt his psychic powers rise; he experienced an enormous surge of self-confidence. His mind began to race. The plan came to him. He had resources he had not used. With the overwhelming numbers of Army and Fleet on the sidelines, he could win easily.

He picked up a microphone. He punched in an Apparatus command frequency that was totally secure. He got through to Apparatus Staging Area Number One and shortly was connected to General Muk.

"Lombar? I mean, Your Majesty?" said General Muk. "I see they've spilled the whole reserve of drugs. What are we going to do? Do you want this invasion fleet to take off at once and tend to getting more?"

"That would take three months there and back," said Lombar. "Listen to this plan. Relay it to your units and follow it exactly. I am certain that these rebels are going to attack Palace City next. It's impregnable. Wait until the rebels have surrounded it. Then scramble your entire invasion force, wipe them out of the sky and hit them in the rear. With your three thousand ships and two and a half million men, you can't miss."

"Brilliant!" said General Muk, "The Army and the Fleet are still neutral. The Domestic Police are in such a mess we can discount them."

"Exactly," said Lombar. "And when we've mopped up the rebels—don't leave a single one of them alive!— we'll use your force to slaughter dissident elements in the streets. When we have that under control and new criminal forces in control, you can return to your invasion plans and we'll subdue the remainder of the Confederacy with the drugs that you bring back from Earth."

"Splendid!" said Muk. "You're a genius, Your Majesty. I have no doubt that we can win now."

"Nor have I," said Hisst and clicked off.

He laughed a short barking laugh. He had not told Muk part of his plan: it consisted of making very certain that the rebels attacked Palace City at once. In all the history of Voltar, the place had never fallen but, cream on cream, he was going to bait the trap.

Chapter 5

As the tank was lying upside down, that meant the snout of its main blastcannon was buried in the sand. It would be very dangerous to fire it: it might blow back into the interior of the tank cabin. But that is exactly what Lombar Hisst was going to do.

Sometimes, belatedly, after a battle, tank ammunition went off from shorts or interior fires. It was not all that unusual for a battlefield to show delayed detonations: indeed, they were inevitable, like death throes. Drops of molten metal dripping into fuel packs could suddenly ignite whole cartridge packs; even fallen blastrifles could go off: it was dangerous to walk around a battlefield even hours after the last shot was fired in anger. Seasoned soldiers knew this: Lombar was counting on their initial lack of surprise.

It was quite a gymnastic feat for a man his size to lash himself into the driver's seat upside down. He used the corpse available to make a cushion against the ceiling which was now the floor. He broke one of the arms to act as a brace against his shoulder. He got his own butt, upside down, into the seat and fastened the straps, cinching them tighter and tighter until he hung suspended. Then he pushed the corpse aside.

He put his hands on the firing trips. He took a long, shuddering breath. It was now or never: in the next minute he would either be blown to pieces or he would rule Voltar without question.

He set the blastcannon for automatic repeating fire. It would now roar at two thousand blasts a minute, each one capable of knocking down a building.

He pressed the trip.

BLOHW-OW-OW-OW-OW!

He was still alive. It hadn't flashed back.

The whole tank on recoil bucked into the air!

Hastily, hard put to keep his hands on the controls, Lombar started the tank engines. He began to guide the tank off, flying it upside down.

BLOHW-OW-OW-OW-OW! roared the blastcannon.

To any observer it would look like the tripped weapon's recoil was driving the tank into the air, out of control.

Rebels bent on mop-up stared. Some of them even laughed to see the monster kicking itself upward. There was even something sexual about it.

Lombar kept flying it upside down, even made it rock from side to side.

Ten feet, fifty feet, a hundred feet he rose.

Only then did some officer see there was something odd about that flight. It should have turned over and gone crashing back to the ground. It didn't!

"FIRE!" roared a rebel captain. "FIRE AT THAT TANK!"

Blastrifles began to roar.

But a blastrifle could do little against a tank built to withstand a warship's cannon.

Lombar flipped the tank upright and held the throttles still.

The tank jolted under the impact of shots.

Lombar Hisst, in a crazy surge of glee, flipped on the tank's loudspeaker system and bellowed into the mike, the sound of his voice racketing across the wreck-strewn

parade ground: "You idiots! You just overlooked Lombar
Hisst, the Emperor of Voltar! I'll laugh in the faces of
your corpses when you try to crack the gates of Palace
City!"

He let out an insane shout. "COME AND GET
ME!" He shoved the throttles wide open.

Accelerating swiftly up to the speed of sound and
then passing it to obtain five times that velocity, he shot
the flying tank southwest, scorching above the desert.

Shots tried to follow.

Warships tried to dive.

Only seven minutes later, such was his speed of
travel, shouting ahead on radio to identify himself to
the outer Apparatus bunkers, Lombar Hisst boomed the
tank through the Palace City gates, jumping thirteen
minutes into the future.

He braked so hard it made the drives smoke.

He settled the tank down in front of the steps of the
Imperial Palace.

He sat there laughing.

There was no doubt whatever in his mind that he
would win this war.

The Apparatus General Staff appeared at the top of
the ornate circular staircase. "Long Live His Majesty,
Lombar the Magnificent!" they cried. They knelt.

Lombar cast the driver's corpse aside and climbed
out. He was grinning but he was imperial.

For the first time, he was certain. He would remain
Emperor! He could not lose.

Palace City, in 125,000 years, had never been
breached.

He and his title were completely safe.

The rebel forces would be caught in a box and
crushed like insects.

All Voltar was at his mercy.

And he had none whatever to give them.

Only slaughter and drugs.

He marched grandly up the curving stairs to his kneeling generals.

How wonderful it was to be a real Emperor!

"Rise, you (bleepards)," he said. "We've got to get an Imperial reception ready. The bill of fare will be rebel blood."

Chapter 6

Ahead lay the yellow mist that was Palace City.

Jettero Heller, clad again in the red general's uniform just in case he got shot down, flew the tug at twenty-five hundred feet above the desert floor. He was flying backwards. Between him and Palace City was what he was pushing.

The sun was on his right and he did not think that they could see him. Their beams would also be very cluttered by what he had in grip.

The traction motors were singing. Their throttles were barely cracked open. If he put too much clamp on his "tow"—a tow, even though he was backing up with it—he would choke the things to death.

The only view he had was on his screens. They were shimmering and glittering but he could see the images.

He marvelled now at how the Apparatus had built up the defense perimeter outside that yellow mist. Burrowed into the sand were shellproof bunkers, three rows deep, three rings. He magnified his image and examined them.

Artillery and more artillery, infantry galore, he recognized the posts that meant electronic barricades that killed if you sought to go through them. If those three rings surrounded even an ordinary fortress one would play the devil with trying to take it.

The yellow mist was something else. Even without the outer defenses, no assault could penetrate it. The time factor was its safeguard. A shell fired at it in present time would explode in time that was already past and do nothing. Furthermore, except at the gates, the whole thing was covered now with an electronic net, powered by the black hole in the mountain. This net shrouded warped space and any shell or tank or ship that tried to dive through it would be devoured both by time and energy. It had only one point of weakness—where the vortex of the captive black hole curved inward at the back of the mountain in which the black hole was embedded. Only an engineer would know of that, but it could hardly be called a closely guarded secret: you couldn't shell the city through it because the mountain was in the way. If an enemy tried to slide a ship through it, the ship would have to be so small the assaulting force would be a nothing. It would also have to clamber over such gigantic rocks and boulders that only a suicide squad could get in. He had used it once before when he brought the Emperor out. As very few people knew of it, he doubted it had been safeguarded.

He was watching his screens. Yes! he was getting an audience. Despite the shimmering nature of his picture, he was getting a much enlarged view of some Apparatus defense-perimeter officers. They were standing on a bunker rim, looking toward him with glasses. And well they might, for what Heller was pushing, at the range of ten miles still, might very well be mistaken for the dust of a rebel force approaching.

But it wasn't rebels: they were probably still embarking at Camp Endurance and when they came, it would be from the sky. Only Heller was engaged on this attack.

On his screen he could see the glasses of the Apparatus commanders flashing. They were waving signals to get men into trenches and on the ledges of artillery.

Slowly, Heller, still flying backwards, pushed his strange load.

Then, when the range was less than five miles, he saw the officers begin to wave down and cancel their orders. For now they recognized what was creeping up on them.

Wind devils!

Heller was hard put to keep them twirling. They seldom if ever got this close to Palace City.

They were the spinning result of temperature differences between the burning desert floor and a common icy wind that blew a mile above the surface. They picked up the violent green of copper sands, the glistening yellow of feldspar and the orange scarlet of alloys of iron, and made colorful, writhing columns, from three to eight thousand feet tall, that danced like Demon chorus lines.

Only by jockeying his tractor beams from right to left and imbalancing them could Heller keep them spinning. It required considerable attention and deftness on the towing throttles.

But they were a common sight, even if awe-inspiring, to anyone who had to live around or in or flew over the Great Desert.

They had lots of power in them. One of the reasons

it was almost impossible to cross the Great Desert is that
a man on foot could be sucked up and hurled a mile into
the air. On some other planet they might have been
called *tornados* or *twisters*. Heller had once seen a whole
house, incautiously built by some unwary prospector,
sent a mile in the air here in the Great Desert.

The Apparatus officers on the parapets might be
newcomers or green. But then Heller was heartened. On
his screen he saw a gray-headed lieutenant racing along
to the different officer groups, yelling. Heller couldn't
see him very well because his view beams were going
through the wind devils that he pushed, and he certainly
couldn't hear, but from the frantic wavings of the man's
arms and the response he was getting, he had no doubt
as to what it was.

The waving signals took on the character of panic.
There was a sudden boil of men along the trenches.
Floods of gunners were racing down from the artillery.
One and all they were diving into bunkers, going under-
ground fast to escape being thrown a mile into the air.

Heller, jockeying tractor-beam throttles and flying
now on a curving course, began very neatly to place the
wind devils around the yellow mist in a circle, a hungry,
obscene chorus line of glittering colors shrieking out a
mocking song of doom.

Guns were torn from their mountings, bunker covers were ripped loose, beam screen antennas became
junk, electronic posts were bodily sundered out of the
sand, and at one underground entrance, where there had
been a jam-up, Apparatus soldiers were seized. All of it
went hurling high, high, high into the air! Wherever the
bottom of one of these twisters touched, there was
instant disaster! The bases of them whipped about like

snakes, eating holes wherever they went. They were funnels of chaos, devouring everything with an appetite that fed only the green and dusty sky high overhead.

It didn't disturb Palace City itself. But it was certainly making a mess out of the three rings of the defense perimeters.

There was plenty of artillery potential—plenty of men left down there. Heller was not trying to win this war with wind devils. He was only creating a diversion.

He flexed his fingers: he had almost blistered them with the friction of jockeying the traction throttles. He flew off now to the north and went about his business. He was going to begin the real reason he had come here by himself.

PART EIGHTY-FIVE

Chapter 1

Jettero Heller eased the tug through the "back door" of Palace City. Only a Voltarian engineer would know the "softness" of the warped space close beside the mountain that dominated Palace City.

The place was considered completely impregnable, and so it was. For 125,000 years it had dutifully protected the crowned heads of the Confederacy. It was a symbol, an ultimate in authority: four hundred billion people on 110 planets regarded it, as much as the Emperor himself, the LAW of the land. So long as Palace City held, it would be obeyed. Heller was about to show that it was vulnerable, if he could.

The risks were fantastic, the odds going for success were minuscule. But that was a way of life for Jettero Heller, combat engineer.

A small black hole from outer space was embedded in the mountain at the north end of Palace City. Planted there by the earliest Voltar engineers, shortly after their arrival from a distant galaxy and their conquest of this planet, it had been providing power and defense for all that time. The black hole warped the space and altered the time of the area.

Satisfied that his wind devil diversion was keeping the perimeter defenders under cover for the moment, he slipped the tug through. There was an instant of nausea as time factors altered. One was immediately in the dimness of artificial light.

He looked up at the looming mountain. It was impressively big. Beyond it would lie the golden, circular palaces, in all their artificially lit parks and splendors. All that was hidden from him as yet.

Over on the other side he knew there would be forests of manned artillery today and troops beyond count. Although his absorbo-coat would make him relatively invisible, reflecting no light back, he was liable to get between some illumination on the mountain and observers down there and silhouette. He would be, at best, a sitting duck for them.

He hadn't had a Fleet base available to prepare his ship. He had done the best he could. He had mounted a couple of tubes on the top of the tug's hull: he had no guns. He had mounted a container for mines under the tug's belly.

Suspending the tug in this twilight gloom, he lifted the T-shaped nose up. He only had one chance with this one: he had better not miscalculate.

He pressed a firing button.

With a *swoosh*, a hexagonally faced object flashed out of a tube. It soared higher and higher. It sailed over the top of the mountain. He could only hope that it would land properly on the opposite slope. It was an attractor-target. Any automatically aimed weapon, seeking to shoot, would find that target irresistible: even though his ship was spotted and fire opened up, the gun controls would choose instead the attractor-target—he hoped.

So far so good. He now raised the tug's nose a little higher. He might find it useful to create a new diversion. He had some radio-triggered balls in the second tube, several thousand of them. He pressed a second firing pin: a hundred thousand pellets spewed out, much like firing a sawed-off shotgun. In this high trajectory, they would patter down across dozens of acres, amongst the parks and palaces. Unless somebody actually got hit with one, he doubted they would even be noticed. He checked the remote firing box that would trigger them: its safety was on. He put it in his pocket.

Now he would get to work.

He had mounted what was called a disintegrator-slasher in the compartment over the flight deck.

The plans that had been used to install this nuclear black hole were so long gone that he could only depend upon the rumors he had heard as a cadet. The black hole was, supposedly, in the upper third of the mountain.

He turned on his screens and began to triangulate for position. There was a trickle of gamma rays to follow up—leaks from around the shielding, not dangerous. The hole itself was fully encased. Its power was bled off in line conduits. The microwave reflectors on the other side of the mountain were simply radiation detectors. He had already used them and he would not use them twice. They would be wise to that now.

He fished in the black hole's position by its leaks. It was not good news: the thing was at the absolute bottom of the third. It was a lot more mountain than he liked to tackle.

You couldn't put a beam into it: it would just absorb anything like that. You couldn't throw a bomb at it: it would take half of Voltar with it. Heller was simply going to saw the mountaintop off and tow it away—if he could!

He had the thing's position now. He went to work with the disintegrator-slasher. It could make a cut one molecule thick through anything, but Heller did not think its manufacturer had ever intended it for use in saw-ing off the top of a mountain.

A high, high whine began to hurt his ears. He stopped and put some earplugs in. The manufacturers had designed it for levelling building sites by making a cut and then removing sections. They had never thought a Fleet combat engineer would need QUIET! Sooner or later somebody down in Palace City was going to wonder where that twenty-thousand-cycle screech was coming from.

The work was slow. He was going through basalt and it was HARD!

A thin line of heat began to glow all along the moun-tainside. That meant there would also soon be a line like that on the other side of the mountain. VISIBLE!

Heller jockeyed the tug back and forth, left to right. He could not tell how deep the cut was getting. All he could do was saw, saw, saw and hope.

Surely sooner or later somebody would hear that whine. It was getting through his earplugs. It was LOUD!

He had the horrible feeling that he was leaving skips—areas where the stone had not been sawed through. It was difficult to keep an even line: this equip-ment was supposed to be used from a stable platform sit-ting on the ground, not from a ship.

Well, he couldn't just sit here sawing the rest of his life. He would have to make a try of it.

He turned off the disintegrator-slasher.

He eased the tug over to the right. He was now in view of Palace City: there it lay in gold and green, bathed in artificial light.

He flipped on the traction engines in the rear of the tug. He maneuvered to take a good, solid grip on the mountaintop.

BLAM!

A shell slammed into the mountain. They had spotted him!

BLAM! BLAM!

The attractor-target, thank Heavens, was pulling the cannon wrong in aim. Just one of those shells landing and this tug would go up like smoke: no armor.

Heller rammed open the throttles of the planetary drives. He yanked the Will-be Was time drives full on.

The tug lunged ahead. The traction beams strained.

The tug began to thresh about.

The mountaintop was NOT moving!

Heller looked down the slope toward the city. Made small by distance, an infantry squad was coming. They stopped amongst the boulders, knelt and levelled blast-rifles. Heller braced himself to receive a hit.

The tug struggled to move the mountain.

HIS WINDSCREEN SHATTERED!

The tug's automatic warning went on, "Sir, my starboard Will-be Was converter drum is overheating. Please ease off."

Heller took another lunge against the tow.

An explosion sounded above him. A blastrifle must have hit one of the tube casings on top of the craft.

This was getting too rough a situation.

Suddenly he dropped the tow that refused to tow.

He spun around to his right. He ducked behind the mountain out of the sight of the infantry.

This was the time for the diversion. He took the remote out of his pocket, took the safety off and pressed it. It should begin to fire the pellets he had dropped into the city. They should begin to go off at intervals. That should make things interesting for them down there. And maybe he could complete his job.

The trouble was, the mountaintop was not thoroughly cut through.

In the tube underneath the belly, thinking this might happen, he had placed a hundred down-blast shatter mines.

It meant he would have to make a circle around the mountain. He hoped his diversion had worked. He began to move clockwise around the peak. Every hundred yards, at approximately the place he had made the cut, he dropped a shatter mine.

His explosions began to go off with a *crump* as each one hit.

He stuck the tug's nose around the mountain shoulder, visible again from Palace City.

BLOWIE!

Something tore through the upper hull!

His diversion had not worked!

Then he realized he had made a mistake: he had been behind the mountain and the black hole when he hit the button, and the activating radio beam had not been powerful enough to get through!

Well, diversion or not, he had to keep going.

Dropping mines, air about him streaked with blast-rifle charges, taking shots in his hull, he completed the circle.

Smoke was rolling through the tug. More than one thing had been hit.

Hoping against hope that he had completed the severance with mines, he ducked back of the mountain again.

He couldn't even see his screens.

"Sir," said the tug, "my Will-be Was engine room is on fire. Could I recommend a visit to the nearest repair yard?" The idiocy of it made Heller realize that the computer banks must also have been hit. He pressed a manual emergency fire-suppression button. It was sloppy under his thumb. He glanced down: hydraulic fluid was pooling on the floor of the flight deck.

Praying that his controls would still work, he worked the tractor engines to seize the mountain once again. He felt them grip.

He opened the throttles of his planetary drives. He felt the tug take the strain against the beams.

Praying, he opened the throttles of the powerful Will-be Was time-converter drives.

It stopped the tug with a backward yank. He still had power.

Something struck the tug from below. He could not see in all the smoke but he hazarded that some of that infantry had made its way around the mountain shoulder. His absorbo-coat must be ripped to shreds. He was visible!

He began to work the throttles. He was making the tug lunge again and again against the dead weight of the mountaintop.

A shot struck the underside of the star-pilot chair beside him. It began to smoke and crackle.

The controls were getting sloppier and sloppier.

He pointed the nose of the tug upward at an angle of forty-five degrees. He once more slammed the throttles open.

There was a sort of roar behind him. It began low and then rose up the scale like something wailing.

The tug was moving.

The shots which had been lacing the air suddenly halted. That infantry back there must be now contending with an earthquake under their very feet.

Heller couldn't see. His screens were not working to be seen by.

He could only guess what was happening.

Was he going forward with the mountaintop towed behind or wasn't he?

Chapter 2

Many a fellow officer had often teased Heller about his "built-in compass." Sometimes on a warship flight deck he would sense that the gyros were in error. Seniors would ignore him but he would persevere and they would, finally, to get some peace, order a technician check. An error was always found but sometimes it was as little as a thousandth of a degree. And even though this would make a significant mistake in course travelling at septuple light speed, nobody ever believed he could have detected it. Any gyro, they had said, is liable to be out a thousandth of a degree.

Right now, astonishingly, he was totally uncertain which way he was going. He should have been able to detect, despite smoke, the north and south magnetic poles of Voltar. But he couldn't.

Then he realized he had never before tried to navigate inside a time/space warp and that was where he was now. The black hole he was or was not towing extended its influence sphere to encase the tug.

He did not know how fast he was going or even if he was going.

His object was to get this mountaintop several miles from Palace City. If he did that, the command area of

Voltar would drop back those thirteen minutes and appear in the same time band as the planet itself. Then, unless something else happened, the rebel forces could launch an assault and, with luck, break the defense perimeters and seize the place.

He did not at that time know of Hisst's plan to hit the rebels' rear with the Apparatus forces from the staging area. His whole purpose was to expose the palaces and parks so they could be targeted by direct frontal assault. The security net would be gone if he had removed the source of all the power used in Palace City.

Right then he wasn't thinking of anything except Where the blazes am I?

The tug was on fire. It might explode. If he dropped this load, it might fall right back on the remaining mountain if it had not moved at all.

He got some sand goggles over his eyes so they would stop streaming.

He got down and moved up close to a screen. Maybe he could see something on it. He twiddled knobs. The screen was blank. His electronics were gone.

The tractor engines were raving with the strain of the pull. The Will-be Was drives were thundering, fire or no fire. The planetary motors were screeching. The smoke billowed.

The broken windscreen didn't seem to be letting in any air so that was no indicator of forward progress: rather it would seem to say that they were not going anyplace at all.

He had a beltgun. With a sudden idea, he pulled it. Without being able to see its levers, he set it to impact-explosion.

He reached out through the broken windscreen and fired straight down.

It would be hard to tell above all this shrieking machinery. But he listened hard. He was counting.

When that handgun charge hit the ground, wherever the ground might be, it would explode with a cracking sound. The number of seconds times the distance sound travelled on Voltar in a second would give him his altitude.

He heard nothing.

He fired again and began to count.

Once more, nothing!

The weird idea hit him that he might be flying upside down: that could happen around anti-gravity coils.

It was getting too hot in here. Tongues of flame were licking through the passageway.

Maybe he had moved the mountain. Maybe he hadn't.

"My Will-be Was starboard time-converter is melting," said the tug. "I sincerely recommend you land somewhere and look into it."

This thing was going to blow up!

Heller knew he'd have to simply take a chance that he had towed the mountaintop away.

He shut down the Will-be Was drives.

There was a sag.

He cut off the traction engines.

With a scream the planetary drives hurled the tug ahead like a streak of lightning!

Heller was hit with the time-transition nausea!

He shot through into planetary time!

The desert sun glared!

He hastily shut the planetary throttles. Instantly the tug began to fall.

Then he saw what some of this was about.

He had pulled the mountaintop fifty thousand feet

into the air. The range of those shots was too extreme and they had also gone outside the space warp.

His own built-in compass wasn't working yet. He had no idea where he was.

He grabbed the tug controls to right it.

They did not respond!

Heller groped behind him. He had parked the space-trooper sled in the passageway. He had it.

It was no time to be careful.

He jumped on it and shot it through the shattered windscreen!

Chapter 3

The sled was tumbling.

His lungs were full of smoke.

He coughed and it was a mistake. At fifty thousand feet there wasn't enough air to take a decent breath.

Head spinning for lack of oxygen, he blindly fumbled with the spacetrooper sled controls. He was trying to make it head straight down at power to an altitude where there was some air.

He could feel wind begin to twitch at him now. Still, he wasn't making the downward plunging speed he should. He had reached terminal velocity for a man for Voltar. Something was desperately wrong—he wasn't diving anywhere near as fast as he knew this sled could.

His sand goggles had whipped down across his mouth, letting the smoke out of his eyes. He was staring at the power meter of the spacetrooper sled that was embedded in the shaft.

CHARGE ZERO!

Comets, thought Jet, I haven't switched this sled off since I used it in New York! Missy is right. I'm getting too old for this *racket*. Senile!

The desert below was coming up in a huge cone: one spot in the middle was motionless, everything else was speeding away. That's where I splash, thought Jet. Then he thought, the blazes I do! He still had the hand blast-gun hanging on him by its lanyard. He recovered it.

He could breathe now: the rush of passage was stacking up enough air to fill his lungs. He must be down to twenty thousand feet.

His thumb flipped the levers of the gun.

Ten thousand feet.

Five thousand feet.

Two thousand feet.

Seven hundred feet.

He pointed the handgun straight ahead at that motionless spot in the desert sand.

Would it work?

Two hundred feet.

HE FIRED!

Set at maximum blast, the recoil was terrific. It almost tore the weapon from his hand!

He pressed the trigger for automatic fire, always on the target.

It was like cushioning yourself against a brick wall with a palm.

The sled and his body slowed.

Blowing sand into a molten turmoil, he halted ten feet in the air.

He turned the weapon sideways and blew himself twenty feet to the left of the self-manufactured lava.

He hit.

He let go of the sled and stood up gingerly.

Nothing bruised but his pride. Then—

CRRRRRUUUUUMP!

He was knocked flat!

A tremendous concussion wave had gone over him. The ground was shaking!

Dazed, he looked up through the rushing dust.

The yellow haze! Three miles to the south!

The mountaintop, still travelling upward, had curved over in a parabola and, carrying its warped space, had struck!

It had not exploded.

Underneath that yellow mantle of warped space there must be a hole in the desert floor as big as any ever made by a meteor—no, an asteroid! Thank Heavens it had not been travelling very fast!

The secondary concussion waves were washing over him. The shock waves still travelled through the ground: he could hear them rumbling into the distance.

Then he saw the tug. It had flown even higher into the air after he had abandoned it.

It was falling in crazy spirals as though in pain.

It almost righted itself.

Flames were spouting from the gaping holes in the shattered hull.

It tried to stand and then fell over onto its back.

It struck!

A flash of fire like a supernova was followed by a bloom of red.

He was on his knees when this one hit him but it sent him skidding back.

Poor tug.

He wondered if it had had anything to say as it expired.

It certainly was giving itself a soldier's funeral—all flame and smoke!

Then suddenly he realized that all this commotion would be visible for miles!

It could not help but bring him company!

Dangerous!

Chapter 4

The dust was dying down. His sense of location was working now. He had come halfway back to Camp Endurance!

Poor old tug had been doing its job all too well!

Then he saw a plume of dust. It was no wind demon.

The glare of the sun was ferocious, like hammer blows. Heller cleaned his sand goggles and got them on. Not one plume of dust but ten!

Suddenly, peering low, he recognized what he was looking at: Apparatus desert patrol cars! They must be running wide-ranging scouts in these times of threat.

Heller checked his handgun. If fired at stun, it still had a few shots left: not enough to take on ten cars of a desert patrol. He felt in his belt: he had no spare batteries. Yes, he decided, he was getting too old. After this, if he lived through it, he would sit before the fire with a rug across his knees and, in a quavering voice, tell his grandchildren never to become combat engineers. It got to you in the end. You made mistakes you could not possibly afford. And there went the hopes of grandchildren.

Yes, one of those cars had now detached itself from the rest and was speeding toward him.

They were flat, chunky cars, Apparatus mustard yellow, ugly things, steel canopied to keep out the sun and hung about with a clutter of equipment. The wheels, with tires three feet wide, were treaded with alternate cushion and metal lugs like knives. He hoped they didn't intend to run over him for sport.

He would count on his general's uniform for bluff. Even so, it would be hard to explain what an Apparatus general was doing out here with the yellow haze just crashed.

And then another thought struck him: supposing these were rebels who had seized Apparatus cars? Maybe, seeing a "general," they'd shoot first!

He hastily looked around him to find a rock to drop behind.

There wasn't any.

The car was almost on him.

Heller held the gun behind his back. He was trying to see through the slots of the armored windscreen.

Then a laugh. A voice chortled, "I thought so!"

IT WAS SNELZ!

The desert car pulled up alongside of him. Snelz had his boots up on the dash, lolling beside the driver, laughing fit to burst.

Heller took the canteen one of the grinning ten soldiers in the back handed him. He washed out his mouth and then sponged his face.

"You didn't think I was going to stick around and get my head blown off, did you?" said Snelz, his laughing dying down. "You're not the only one who knows

explosives. I put a radio-firing remote on one of your
spears and then put a time-delay fuse tuned into it in the
camp magazine. I knew you were going to fire those
spears from somewhere in the sky and wanted the magazine to go up shortly after.

"Any fool could guess that your next target would be
Palace City, so I told them the general had ordered me
on to desert patrol. So I got ten desert cars, loaded my
company and here we are. What the blazes have you
been up to? Isn't that the tug that crashed over there?"

"Poor tug," said Heller.

"I thought I recognized it when it was wobbling
around the sky. And isn't that yellow mist over there
warped space? Don't tell me you took the lid off Palace
City."

"That's where we're going," said Heller. "Move
over."

"No you don't," said Snelz. "A colonel of Fleet
marines is higher than a mere Grade Ten. I outrank you
now, so I am giving the orders."

"Look, I am in an Apparatus *general*'s uniform! I've
got to get back to Palace City!"

"That general's uniform doesn't count," said Snelz.
"The Apparatus can't order Fleet marines. I swore in
my whole company. So I give the orders. All right?"

"If you say so," said Heller.

"Good, we've got that settled. Driver, signal the
other cars to follow and head for Palace City."

"That's what I ordered," said Heller, climbing in.

"No," said Snelz. "It's what you *suggested* to a superior. And I just *happen* to be in a benign mood. Get
going, driver."

As they sped south and west, Snelz began to sing

and the men in back joined in and then the whole convoy
was roaring it:

> The Fleet marines,
> The Fleet marines,
> Have comets in their crap.
> The Fleet marines,
> The Fleet marines,
> Drink liquid lightning pap.
> The girls all run to Mama,
> The farmers hide their stock,
> For they know a Fleet marine
> Has got a hungry (bleep).
> We're the heroes of the battle,
> As long as it's in bed.
> The reason I'm a Fleet marine
> Is better left unsaid.
> I'm loyal to my seniors,
> As long as they are bold.
> But I don't think I'll live long enough
> To see them very old.
> Come march upon the spaceways,
> And help me sing this song.
> The one thing that I'm sure of
> Is that if you're a Fleet marine
> You won't live very long!

The yellow and green and red desert fled under
them.

Heller had one more target: LOMBAR HISST!

Chapter 5

The rebel forces, in the interim, had landed in the desert well south of the city. The rumble of guns and flashes of explosions tore the air in that sector. They evidently had found a weak spot in the outer three rings of defenses and were hitting it with ferocity. Apparatus artillery was holding the rebel fleet at bay and the result was a massive infantry action that must be taking a heavy toll of lives.

Heller, in the desert car, still rolling south, looked up at the sky far to the east. "Hello, hello, hello," he said. "Snelz, look over there on the horizon."

Snelz squinted his eyes against the desert glare. Then he raised his binoculars. "Apparatus warships. Must be from the invasion staging areas. Hey, this don't look good. They're going to hit the rebels in the rear. The Fleet is neutral. I think, as a colonel, we have an appointment anywhere else but Palace City."

"Look," said Heller. "The east gate is not under attack. We can roll in."

"And get to be a part of battle hash?" said Snelz.

"As a general, I demand you enter Palace City. You are still in Apparatus uniforms. I am in an Apparatus general's uniform. That settles it. Roll!"

"Haven't I got time to write my memoirs?" said Snelz. "'The Short and Happy Life of Colonel Snelz of the Fleet Marines.' You can do the introduction: 'My Friend Snelz, by the late Jettero Heller.' Driver, pull over while I get out a pad and pen. It shouldn't take very long."

"Colonel, could I suggest," said Heller, "that you might be able to sign it Brigadier General Snelz if you go through the east gate?"

"Well, it would look better on the cover," said Snelz, "even if they have to add 'post-humorous.' East gate, driver."

They rolled toward the tumble of wire and posts which had been this side entrance to Palace City. Even chunks of the road were gone.

"What the Hells hit them?" said Snelz. "No dead rebels on this side. Did you do that?"

"Things got a little spinny a while back," said Heller.

"I should say so," said Snelz, staring at the ripped-up litter of defenses as they drew to a halt at the barricade.

A hundred men and a cannon barred the gate remains.

A frantic-looking Apparatus major raced up and peered into the car.

Heller put on his sand goggles and flashed an identoplate.

Heller said, "Apparatus Desert Patrol 17 with vital data on rebel attack forces, urgent for relay to Apparatus General Staff!"

The major jumped back and saluted. "Pass, General!"

The barricade was opened. The ten desert cars sped in.

It was a very different-looking Palace City, exposed now to the glare of the desert sun. The light which hotly struck the round, gold palaces was blinding.

The power was off and the fountains had no lights under them; the waterfalls had ceased to run.

The grass in the parks was scorching, turning brown. Shrubs and flowers were wilting under the searing breath of desert wind.

"Marijuana?" said Heller, staring at a plot of ground around a painted statue as they passed.

Snelz had never been in Palace City before. The jewelled balustrades and golden windows were blinding him. They were rolling down a wide boulevard. "I don't know what *marijuana* is but I must be looking at a billion credits worth of gems. No wonder they kept this place secure: acres and acres of diamond-plated palaces!"

"Square miles, not acres," corrected Heller. "See that wall and shade trees up ahead? I *suggest* we pull under them." Snelz looked at the streets. They were crawling with men in black Death Battalion uniforms, the shock troops of the Apparatus. Every hundred yards an artillery piece had to be gotten around. The troops looked deadly and alert but very, very nervous, under strain because of the removal of the city's cover.

"You mean you're going to stop?" said Snelz. "Amongst *these* killers? Doesn't a brigadier general outrank you?"

"No, I'm in a major general uniform."

"I knew there was a catch in it," said Snelz. "Driver, pull under those trees along that wall."

The ten desert cars drew up. They were about three long blocks from the Imperial Palace. The Death Battalions had grown very thick. Artillery was everywhere.

Heller swung out of the car and looked southward at the sky through the withering leaves of the trees.

The sound of high-up firing was coming from there. Warships were engaged in the stratosphere. Along the ground, as through the pavement, came the thunder of artillery as rebels hit the south gate and tried to penetrate it. That fight was going to be amongst them shortly if the rebels broke through. But something ominous was going on in the sky. Was the rebel spacefleet being wiped out?

Heller turned to Snelz. "Could I suggest-order your men to cover up their ears and get down on the floorboards of their cars?"

"It's a funny order," said Snelz. "Any particular point in it?"

"A tactical diversionary involution that earlier flubbed is about to take place."

"I'm sorry I asked." He whistled up his three lieutenants from the other cars and gave them their instructions.

A Death Battalion colonel came over from an artillery piece. He was very edgy. He peered under the canopy at Snelz. "What's going on here?"

The men in the back of this car and the rest were getting down on the floorboards and cupping their hands over their ears.

"Desert Patrol 17," said Snelz. "Just stopping to take a pee."

"You're in our field of fire," said the colonel.

Heller glanced back at the other cars. The three lieutenants gave him a sign in the affirmative and then clapped their hands over their own ears and ducked out of sight. Heller saw that Snelz was hunched down and protecting his hearing. Heller put the remote that earlier hadn't worked between his knees and put his hands over his own ears.

"You're in ours," he said to the colonel and shut his knee down on the remote button.

The thousands of pellets he had earlier fired throughout Palace City began to go off at intervals.

The colonel stared. He did not connect what now happened to what Heller had just done. He must have supposed these men had heard it already.

The colonel's mouth opened. His eyes dilated. With a wild, agonized look, he began to scream!

Whole companies, battalions, regiments of men stood rigid for an instant, began to scream and then, with a dreadful rush, began to thunder down the boulevards in panic. They leaped off their gun ledges, they threw down their arms, they tossed away belts and equipment with violence.

They ran in circles. They collided with each other. Then men and tanks in roaring disorder scrambled pell-mell for the city gates, letting nothing stop them.

They burst into the rear of the Apparatus defenders to the south—overran their own positions—and the men there, catching the panic, rushed out of the trenches and bunkers, out into the desert and straight into the shattering thunder of rebel guns.

Heller waited for another five minutes. There were still people in the depths of these palaces for they would not have been affected. He had kept his eye on the Imperial quarters across the park. No one had come out.

Heller uncovered his ears. He put the remote back in his pocket.

Snelz was a little awe-struck. He was staring at the empty streets, the discarded weapons and overturned artillery. "What the Hells was that?"

"Several thousand small noise bombs," said Heller. "I earlier fired them in for a diversion. They emit the sonic saw-toothed wave for terror. You can signal your men to uncover their ears now."

Snelz listened to the screaming rout at the south end of the city. "Comets, I'm glad I'm on your side," he said as he passed the signal to his men.

Chapter 6

They rolled forward to the foot of the huge circular stairway which led up to the Imperial Palace. Several abandoned artillery pieces stood on the sun-curled lawn. A flying tank was parked at the bottom. The body of a dead driver lay half-in, half-out, where it had fallen when Lombar had disembarked.

The desert cars halted. The hundred men got out.

Heller looked up at the sky. The surface action may have turned into a rout but a battle was going on up there. He knew the rebels had very few warships. He could not tell at this vast distance but it appeared one group of vessels was being hammered to bits. Even as he looked, some large craft was burning as it spiralled down toward the ground a hundred miles below.

He knew the Earth invasion force and Fleet had been intact. Had Lombar thrown this Apparatus armada into the fray? If so, despite the rout which had just happened, the rebel forces were done for.

This tank at the foot of the steps, he thought he recognized. A mighty brute, it may have been the one Hisst had used to flee from the Battle of Camp Kill.

After a quick word with Snelz, a platoon was disposed outside to cover the entrance. Then, followed by the bulk of the company and Snelz, Heller sped up the broad, winding stair.

They came to the wide, curving corridor which led to the entrance chamber. There were no troops in it.

Snelz posted men in the doorways of the rooms which opened from it.

Heller, by himself, went ahead.

A screaming voice was coming from the antechamber. Lombar's!

"You're traitors, traitors, traitors! Every one of you! You are all against me! You sold me out!"

"No, no! Please Gods, we didn't!" cried another voice.

"One of you helped Heller to move the mountain! I know it was HIM! Don't deny it! Another one of you just ordered Palace City evacuated! And now THIS, now THIS, now THIS!" There came a roar of pure animal rage.

Shrieks of terror.

"Lombar!" came a bellow. "Put down that gun! Listen to reason!"

There came a shattering roar of a blastrifle on full automatic!

Panic-driven bootbeats rushed from the antechamber. Red-uniformed Apparatus generals, spread out, came around the curve in the corridor where Heller stood.

The insane roar of the blastrifle from the antechamber was mixed with the even more berserk rantings of Lombar Hisst.

A general was caught in the back by a shot. He fell at Heller's feet. His arms reached out convulsively and he caught Heller's legs. "Save me! Save me! Save me!" he screamed.

The other generals rushed by.

Then here came Lombar, holding the roaring blast-rifle like a flaming spear.

Heller leaped back. The arms of the general on the floor tripped him. He fell against the wall.

Lombar rushed past, rifle blazing.

Heller tried to get to his own handgun, then realized how useless the discharged weapon was.

Snelz's troops had pulled back into rooms, diving out of the path of fire.

Lombar reached the main entrance.

Several generals were still on the stairs racing down. Lombar cut them to bits. They fell like thrown balls of red, streaking the steps with blood.

Snelz's platoon outside, taken by surprise, sought to bring weapons to bear.

Lombar swept a path of fire over their heads like a flaming scythe. They ducked.

Down the steps raced Lombar, shooting as he went. He was taking five at a time, moving too fast to be hit.

At the bottom he gave the dead driver a yank and threw him to the pavement.

Hisst leaped into the tank and slammed the turret shut. Snelz's platoon fired but their shots glanced off the armor.

Heller was coming down the steps. He halted for an instant to try to get the sidearm off a dead general. Then he realized it would have no effect on the tank and threw the bloody weapon aside.

Lombar was getting the tank started.

Heller leaped down the last ten steps. He grabbed at the snout of a protruding weapon, intending to haul himself up, to get at the turret.

The weapon went off. Lombar had fired it from within. It jarred out of Heller's hands.

The tank swept forward with a roar and Heller fell to the pavement.

The flying monster rose. Its course was erratic. It smashed into a statue at the bottom of a balustrade. Then it curved sideways, beginning to rise.

Heller raced across a strip of lawn. An artillery piece was there, one of the heaviest.

He leaped onto the pointer's ledge. He began to spin wheels.

The tank was flying low. It went across the park. It clipped the central statue there and the sculpture overturned.

Lombar was trying to go between two palaces and get cover.

Heller was getting the cannon centered, eye pressed to the sight. He was bringing the tank into the middle of the circle.

Ahead of Lombar lay the pools where Madison had first found Teenie swimming. They lay there now, no lights or moving water, but they were full and lapping under the hot desert wind.

Heller fired!

The heavy blast hit the tank below the right rear rollers and up into its belly.

FIRE BLOOMED!

The tank did a complete forward somersault, leaving a blazing loop in the air.

It hit the center of the lowest pool with a whistling sizzle and splash!

Heller was off the cannon and running toward it.

Then suddenly the turret opened.

A blastrifle came into view.

Heller was totally in the open. There was no cover. He was unarmed.

PART EIGHTY-SIX

Chapter 1

The tank was nearly submerged in the water.

The blastrifle levelled from the open turret.

The yellow eyes of Lombar Hisst sighted down it.

Jettero Heller pulled up. He was almost to the edge of the pool. There was no cover.

He could hear the din of battle somewhere in the sky.

He thought if he could only get his hands on Hisst he might end this. But in that split instant it looked like Hisst was going to end him instead.

Heller had a handgun. It was almost totally discharged. He doubted it would even cause a bruise at this distance.

Hisst fired.

Heller had jinked to the left.

The shot missed.

But Heller had drawn as he jumped.

He didn't fire at Hisst.

Heller fired at the water between him and the tank.

An enormous spray shot up!

Under the cover of it, Heller dived into the pool, totally submerged.

Hisst's blastgun churned the upper surface, boiling spray and froth.

Swimming underwater, Heller reached the bottom of the tank.

Looking up, he could get a dim and wavy outline of the turret. Hisst seemed to be having a fit. He was firing all around the tank, hoping to hit the man he knew must be there somewhere.

The concussions were hurting Heller's ears and he protected them with his cupped hands.

He was running out of air.

There was a pocket of it trapped under a tread fender. He stuck his nose up into it and got a breath.

Suddenly he was aware that the shooting above him had stopped. He waited a moment. He could hear a rushing sound. He decided to chance it and surface.

Ready to spring up over the submerged hulk and get to the turret, Heller put his face out.

Nothing happened.

He rose up further.

Hisst was gone!

The man had leaped off the tank and was almost to the far edge of the pool, swimming!

Heller instantly struck out in pursuit.

Lombar got out on the edge. He saw Heller swimming swiftly toward him. Hisst unslung the blastrifle and pointed down. He pulled the trigger.

It was wet and shorted out. It did not fire.

Hisst threw it away. He looked around wildly. He had recognized Heller. His rage went into panic and then deeper into insanity.

He saw a flight of steps near to hand. He raced up them.

He was grabbed suddenly from either side.

Two men in silver livery threatened him with electric battle-axes.

Lombar stumbled to his knees. He looked up and

stared into the face of a teen-aged girl—Teenie, Hostage Queen of Flisten.

"You are my prisoner," she said. And to her men, "Take him inside and knock him out if he so much as twitches!"

Chapter 2

Heller pulled up at the bottom of the steps and stood there dripping water.

"That man is my prisoner," he said.

Teenie gazed out toward the pool. Snelz's men, held back until now by that raving blastrifle, were spreading out to cover the Flisten palace.

On Teenie's right and left, additional guards were drawn up, electric halberds ready.

Teenie looked down at the soaking-wet Heller. She gave her ponytail a twitch. She said, in English, such was the stress of the moment, "Clear off, buster!"

Heller stared. The figure in the golden robe seemed awfully immature, young. Not only had she spoken English but she was chewing bubble gum. "Are you from Earth?" he said in the same language she had used.

"Sure, bub," said Teenie, secure in the protection of her guards, "and I'm also the Hostage Queen of Flisten. Now that I've got Hisst under wraps inside, I'm the only operating royalty around here right now, so it's 'Your Majesty' to you."

Heller suddenly wanted to laugh at this New York accent. He didn't kneel.

This annoyed Teenie. "Listen, mac, I don't know how come you're talking Ivy League, but you better bruise that knee, kid. My guards don't cotton to impoliteness."

"My name is Jettero Heller. I'm the representative of Prince Mortiiy on the ground——"

A screeching whistle interrupted him. He looked up to his left. A warship, in flames, was falling. It slammed with a heavy shock wave into a nearby open park.

Snelz was at his elbow. When the echoes of the concussion ceased to rattle around, Snelz said, "That's an Apparatus ship that just crashed. The rebels are giving them a pasting!"

"Those aren't the rebels," said Teenie in Voltarian. "If you'd been watching Homeview, you would have known that when somebody pulled that mountain apart, exposing Palace City, the Fleet and Army declared for Mortiiy. They're blowing the Apparatus out of the sky!"

Snelz and Heller looked up. High above, the remnants of the Apparatus Earth invasion force were being blasted to bits and falling, ship after ship, into the waiting desert sands.

A Fleet destroyer, markings clear, dived down half a mile away, pounding some holdout group of Apparatus on the south perimeter.

"I guess the admirals came to their senses," said Snelz. "We're on the winning side! That news was what must have driven Hisst crazy and made him shoot his general staff!"

"Listen," said Heller, "before one of those destroyers mistakes us for Apparatus, tell your men to get naked to their waists so they look like rebels."

As Snelz gave the order, Heller began to remove his general's uniform.

"What the hell is this?" said Teenie in English. "Some kind of a God (bleeped) striptease? While I admit, mister, that you're a very good-looking man, it won't get you anyplace. Not with me! If you want Lombar Hisst, you've got to come to terms!"

Heller had been wearing Fleet fatigues under his Apparatus outfit. He tossed the general's uniform to one of Snelz's men, who was collecting Apparatus clothes to bury them. Heller took a pillbox cap out of his pocket and put it on his head. He gave the chin strap a snap.

"Now," he said to Teenie, "we can talk about it. What might these terms be?"

"Are you really a representative of Mortiiy?" said Teenie.

"I'll do until Mortiiy comes along," said Heller.

"Let me storm the place," said Snelz. "She's stalling."

"Storm away," said Teenie, "and get your heads chopped off. The only way you're going to get Lombar Hisst is swap."

"Horse-trading," said Heller in English.

"You said it," said Teenie, in Voltarian, "only I got the better *horse*. Two for one."

"And who might these two be?" said Heller.

"The first one is a guy named J. Walter Madison," said Teenie. "The (bleepard) double-crossed me."

"MADISON?" said Heller. "Is *he* on Voltar?"

"Yep," said Snelz.

"You said it," said Teenie.

"My Gods!" said Heller.

"He's really a two-timing son of a (bleepch)," said Teenie. "He wasn't after Gris at all. The God (bleeped) judge just found Gris innocent. You're Heller. Madison was really after YOU!"

"Madison is one, you said two. Who's the other?"

Teenie bared her teeth. Her hands clenched. "The other one is the filthiest snake that ever lived. His name is Soltan Gris. Lord Turn says he is your prisoner. I WANT him!" And she snarled.

"Let me get this straight," said Heller. "If this J. Walter Madison and this Soltan Gris are turned over to you, you will give us Lombar Hisst."

"You got it through your head at last," said Teenie. "And I want to point out that this territory I am standing on is the domain of the Hostage Queen of Flisten and happens to be inviolate. The only way you are going to get Lombar Hisst is swap!"

Chapter 3

Heller and Snelz put their heads together: "I think we should rush them," said Snelz. "They only got electric battle-axes."

A savage burst of firing sounded in the direction of the east gate.

"I think she'll deal," said Heller. "These New Yorkers just like to bargain."

"I ain't a New Yorker!" said Teenie. "I'm from all over, including Kansas, Whiz Kid."

Heller knew a needling when he heard one: Madison's lies had been all over Earth press—the stories about Kansas, Maizie Spread and Toots Switch. He turned a little red. "Young lady," he said, "we can discuss Madison and Gris later. Right now, turn over Lombar Hisst. I can promise you I'd like to get my hands on J. Warbler

Madman myself and I can assure you that when I do, when you see what happens to him, your satisfaction will be guaranteed."

"Not good enough," said Teenie. "I am a very experienced person when it comes to justice: it's made of banana peels. Hand me Gris and hand me Madison: you get Hisst. If you don't, I'm liable to keep Hisst for a pet and feed him on peaches and cream."

"I promised Gris a trial," said Heller.

"He's had one trial and what a miscarriage and abortion of injustice that was. I tell you what, I'll give him a trial and guarantee absolutely to find him guilty. How's that?"

Heller and Snelz looked at each other.

"I don't even know where Madison is," said Heller. "Do you?"

"Nope," said Snelz. "Let me storm the place and you can appoint me a full general of Fleet marines."

Heller looked up at the teen-ager. Then he sat down on the step.

Timyjo, of Snelz's company, had found some blue cloth in a nearby palace. It was the rebel color and he was passing out strips of it and the men were tying it around their heads. Those who had finished lounged against their blastrifles and looked up at the tableau at the top of the steps. Time passed. Stalemate.

A rebel scout came tearing across a park toward the group. He had spotted the naked torsos and blue headbands. He saw Heller and made a beeline for him.

"Officer Heller! The *Retribution* has landed. Mortiiy is checking if it's safe to come in. Where's Hisst?"

Heller stood up. He glanced at the girl at the top of the steps. The battle seemed to have died down in the sky, spatters of gunfire were only occasional far to the south.

"Snelz," said Heller. "You keep this place surrounded. Don't let anybody in or out."

"Does that mean you are going to deal?" said Teenie.

"Time will tell, Your Teen-age Majesty," said Heller. "Right now, you better keep Hisst as safe as a monkey in the Bronx Zoo."

Heller's clothes were drying in the hot desert wind. He gave his powder-blue Fleet fatigue tunic a tug to straighten it. "I'll go down to the gate and meet Prince Mortiiy."

"You better deal!" shouted Teenie.

"Don't get your bubble gum in an uproar," Heller called over his shoulder. "I'll be back."

The fate of Hisst, Gris and Madison was left hanging in the air.

Chapter 4

Madison's crew had several times thought they should leave the Imperial galley, but each time some commotion outside or some new outburst of firing had deterred them.

The one hundred Death Battalion soldiers, drunk as Lords, were stacked up in a locked pantry, minus arms. The captain was long since well into a completely elsewhere LSD trip.

"I don't think we should go yet," said Flick. "It's still daylight out there. That's the real sun. There's no power on and when it goes down, the place will be as dark as pitch. We can sneak out of here like rats."

"On the other hand," said Flip, "when it's dark, if those rebel forces post patrols, we'll be spotted and stopped every ten feet. Look at these caps."

"What have caps got to do with it?" said Flick.

"Well, we're in Homeview uniforms and these are Homeview caps," said Flip. "They make them this way because Homeview crews get in the path of blinding lights and reflectors. Watch!"

She took one of the aqua-green headpieces. She put her long fingernail in a slit. The visor split in half with a pop. The upper part stayed where it was but the lower part snapped vertical in a curve. She put it on: a dark filter covered the upper two-thirds of her face. Looking at her now, you couldn't see who she was.

"So just snap your visor bills down, pick up your cameras and equipment," said Flip, "and simply walk out. They'll suppose we're just a Homeview crew doing our jobs: they won't dream we're Apparatus. So let's get on with the parade."

"She's right," said Flick. "Nobody ever notices a Homeview crew. Come on!"

There was a pop of visors being lowered and the clatter of equipment and cameras being lifted.

They found a door that opened into a side park. The fifty people walked out across the dying grass and into the hot glare of the desert sun. They were heading for the open area where they had parked their air-coaches.

Flick stopped, appalled. A crashed warship, still smoking, had landed squarely on their four vehicles. All that remained of the Model 99 airbus was one angel lying face up on the splintered pavement, grinning vacantly at the sky.

The crew stacked up behind Flick. He said to Madison, "Chief, we got to scatter out and steal some transportation."

But Madison was staring down the boulevard.

Surrounded and guarded by companies of rebel troops, a procession was coming from the east gate, heading toward the Imperial Palace. In its center, on poles, several rebels were carrying a large casket-sized container that had a cover over it. Prince Mortiiy was walking ahead of it, flanked by two rebel officers. Several Fleet admirals and Army generals were in the group. Hightee Heller and the Countess Krak were helping Prahd carry bottles with tubes that led into the container.

And there, following behind them with a drawn blast handgun, looking at the palaces they passed, watching very alertly for possible snipers, was Jettero Heller!

Madison said, "It's HIM! Oh, boy, at last he's stolen a whole empire! I got to cover this!"

Flick tugged urgently at his sleeve. "Chief, for Gods' sakes, let's get out of here. I've got two thousand identoplates! We can get lost! Nobody can find us!"

Madison said, eyes round, "Good Lord, think of the headline! Thirty-two point, OUTLAW STEALS CONFEDERACY! Director! Get your crew busy! Plug your cameras into Homeview channel direct by radio. COVER THAT PROCESSION!"

The director instantly jumped to it and began issuing orders. The whole crew started to get busy. Even the reporters grabbed out notebooks to sketch stories.

Flick seized Madison by the arm. "Chief, this is insane! If they find out we're Apparatus, they'll slaughter us!"

Madison shook loose. There was a wild, inspired

light flaming in his eyes. "He finally DID it! This is my passport to glory!"

The reporters closed in on the procession and started getting names. The circus girls rushed in to straighten the hats of generals and admirals. A makeup man slapped some tan powder on the face of Mortiiy. Roustabouts flashed reflectors at the procession. The camera lights began to flicker. They had the main channel of all Homeview for the Confederacy.

"This is coming to you live, live, live from Palace City!" cried Madison into a separate mike, unheard by the procession but heard by everyone else on Voltar. "You are watching the triumphal entry of the outlaw Heller into the Imperial Palace. Exclusive! Live! Live! Live!"

"We're dead, dead, dead," groaned Flick.

Chapter 5

The Royal corridor had to have the bodies of two generals removed before the procession could go forward. The director prohibited their being touched until he could get close-ups. Then he got a long shot of the great Royal antechamber: two more bodies lay in there. Only then did he station his crew and let the procession enter.

The director thought it would be more dramatic if three rebels grabbed the big stone desk that stood before the bedchamber door and threw it bodily away. He didn't like the way they did it the first time, and while another camera covered the waiting admirals and generals, he had roustabouts put the table back. "Now register disgust!" he ordered, and they got their retake with a crash. Very satisfactory.

At Madison's whispered instruction, the director got a dolly shot of Heller going in, while Madison into his commentary mike said, "The outlaw Heller visits the scene of his kidnapping crime." Another whispered instructions to the director who then pointed out to Heller that the bent baton was still lying on the floor. Heller picked it up while a camera did a pan-tilt. "Hello, hello, my baton," said Heller.

"Beautiful," said the director, complimenting his acting, and moved a camera in to get a close shot of the inscription.

"Outlaw confesses kidnapping," said Madison into the commentary mike. "Admits the evidence left on the scene of the crime is his."

Some rebels pushed the massive bed aside and the bearers placed the fluid-filled container in its place. The Countess Krak and Hightee Heller were still holding bottles: Prahd made sure the tubes weren't tangled. The director moved the three to the far side of the container.

Heller moved forward to the side of the tub. He lifted the cover and exposed the face of Cling.

"Outlaw gazes gloatingly on face of victim," said Madison.

Heller and Prahd were checking to make sure the tubes were all in place. The director got a close-up of the face of Cling the Lofty, very old, still unconscious. Then he pulled the cameraman back to a two-shot, Heller and the Emperor.

Madison was about to make another commentary when his script went all to pieces.

Heller had pulled a tube away from across Cling's chin. Suddenly Cling opened his eyes. He looked around, evidently registering the golden frieze in the ceiling of his bedchamber. He turned his head and saw who was standing close to him. He frowned. Petulantly, he said, "Officer Heller! I told you to take me out of here!"

An audible sigh came from the Fleet and Army officers in the bedchamber. With relief they understood it had not been a kidnapping: therefore, by siding with Heller in this fight, they were not rebels!

Madison tried to think fast. He wished he had cut the cameras off. But it was too late. The damage had been done. His outlaw had suddenly become simply a Royal officer obeying orders. Frantically, he wracked his wits for some way to recover from this blooper. Well, all was not lost; he would somehow handle it.

"Your Majesty," said Heller. "We have found that it was Hisst who killed your sons and successors to the throne."

"Hisst!" said the Emperor in alarm. "Is he here?"

"We have him in a safe place," said Heller. "You are completely secure and in no danger now. I would like to point out that Hisst also caused your youngest son, Mortiiy, to rebel. The prince has been in constant attendance upon you, night and day."

"And he didn't kill me?" stared Cling.

"Your safety and continued rule have been Mortiiy's only concern for months, Your Majesty. You owe the vanquishment of Hisst to him." Heller reached toward Krak who handed him a sack. Heller said to the Emperor, "I have your Royal seal here. Could I suggest that we rescind the rebel proclamation?"

The Emperor looked at Mortiiy. The prince was smiling.

Cling said, "You mean I've still got a son?"

"If you say so, Your Majesty," said Heller.

The Emperor reached for Mortiiy. Tears began to roll down the withered cheeks. "Come here, son," he said.

Mortiiy moved over and knelt. Cling gripped the back of the prince's hand. Brokenly, he said, "If I had listened to you, this never would have happened. I am too old and too sick and too silly to rule. Anyone who can stand off the combined forces of Voltar for five years deserves to rule. Take the throne. I abdicate."

A sigh of relief went up from the rebel troops and officers in the room. Even though they sided with Mortiiy, they were not rebels now.

Mortiiy gripped his father's hands. "I will try to be worthy of you, Sire."

Heller knelt and said to Mortiiy, "Your Majesty," and handed him the bag of regalia. Then Heller stood. "I had better go out and put that mountain back so we can get some power on."

Mortiiy looked up from where he knelt beside the container. His black beard suddenly bristled. "No you don't, Lord Heller! Leave that to the Corps of Engineers. Somebody else can play with mountains. Immediately assemble an Officers' Conference. We've got to settle several burning questions and decide some fates. You've got to help me get to the bottom of what tore this Confederacy to bits!"

Chapter 6

The Grand Council hall was quite a mess. In the last druggy days of Hisst, nobody had even bothered to dust it. Heller had dug the staff out of the basement where they had been prisoners and tried to bring some order to the place. There were no lights, the sun no longer hammered through the round upper windows: he rigged some construction-site floods he found.

The Apparatus seemed to have stolen the gold and jewelled cloths and the diamond-studded banners; the place looked pretty bare. He thought he was lucky to be able to get the dust off the hundred-foot-diameter table and find enough unbroken chairs.

But what impeded him most was people: they kept coming in, arriving from the cities. Heller commandeered a company of Fleet marines from a battleship landed outside the east gate and told the captain to stop this influx, but the captain, although he had the huge entrance door blocked, kept letting people in.

In answer to Heller's challenge, the captain said, "But they're all important people of the realm, sir. Actually we're only getting what the Army doesn't filter out at the gates."

The room would hold a couple thousand in a pinch: Heller gave it up.

A Homeview crew was interviewing every notable that appeared. They also always seemed to have a camera on Heller.

"Chief," said Flick to Madison, "this is madness. Please, please let me steal some cars so we can split."

"No!" said Madison. "This isn't over!"

Flick pointed to a backflow monitor the director had had set up so he could know how Joy City was cutting in his own scenes. Real Homeview crews, all through the Confederacy, were shooting shots of people in the streets, screaming their lungs out, "Long Live His Majesty Mortiiy!"

"It looks awful over to me!" said Flick.

"That's the point!" said Madison. "We've lost our riots! You'll never make a PR man, Flick. I've lost client exposure. Somehow I've got to try to make it up and repair the image!"

"You're crazy," said Flick.

"Of course," said Madison. "That's why I'm a genius. As soon as this conference convenes, I can keep a running commentary going and, hope against hope, regain the initiative! All is not lost, Flick. Don't despair. I've still got a chance to make Heller an immortal outlaw yet!" And he went off to give the director some camera angles.

Emperor Mortiiy came in. He was still in his fighting clothes but he had the chains of office around his neck, wore the crown and held the scepter. "What a mob!" he said to Heller.

"I think the senior officers of most services are present, Your Majesty," said Heller. "We can't dig up any of the Lords: they're either too slugged up with dope to move or they ran away."

"Well, this isn't a Grand Council meeting," said Mortiiy. "It's an emergency Officers' Conference to dispose of matters of state prior to forming a government. What a MOB!"

Mortiiy walked up to the dais. Somebody tried to blow a trumpet and the note went sour. Somebody else dropped the cymbals. Mortiiy, beard bristling, yelled, "This Officers' Conference is called to order!"

People drifted to the table but the hall was still a commotion. Mortiiy yelled, "Blast it! Shut up and sit down!"

At that moment some new notables burst in the front door and everything remained in a hubbub.

"Heller!" yelled Mortiiy, "For Gods' sakes, get up

here on the dais and take the post of Viceregal Chairman of the Crown! Maybe you can be heard above this mess!"

Heller blinked. It was the most senior aristocratic post of the realm. But, obediently, he jumped up on the dais beside Mortiiy. Heller raised his voice, using the piercing tone of a Fleet officer, "The meeting is called to order!"

Somebody else came bursting in the door, collided with one of Madison's cameramen, and two Homeview lights fell down with a crash. The hubbub continued.

Heller drew his hand blastgun, set it to "noise" and fired it in the air. There was instant quiet.

"The meeting is started!" said Heller.

Madison gave a sigh of relief. He purred into the commentary mike, "The outlaw Heller is calling his bandit crew to order!"

Mortiiy started to speak but people were sitting down now and it was noisy. Heller reversed the handgun, held it by the muzzle and hit the table sharply three times.

"Beautiful," said the director as he telephotoed in on the handgun.

Chapter 7

Mortiiy was finally able to be heard. He swept a glance around the faces at the vast table and then across the hall.

"In 125,000 years," he said, "we have never had such

turmoil. We've had a few traitors, we have had a few civil wars, but nothing to compare with this.

"I've had an estimate that there are a million civilians dead in the streets, that property damage has mounted to tens of billions of credits. We also almost lost a planet—Calabar—which endured more than five years of heavy attack. I believe that that is also connected with this present scene.

"Before we can reorganize the government, we have to root out this disease and handle it or it could just happen all over again. I may have ideas of what was behind it, but I am not going to start my rule with guesses and prejudice. I mean to isolate exactly what caused this chaos and that is the first business of this conference."

The senior admiral of the Fleet Admiral's staff shouted from his place at the table, "It was Hisst!"

A snarl of agreement coursed throughout the crowded hall.

"One man?" said Mortiiy. "I'm more inclined to believe it was a conspiracy. But, all right, it's as good a place as any to start. Who knows anything about Hisst?"

A savage roar swept through the room. Notables they might be and conservative to the core, but they had one thing in common: a violent hatred for Hisst. The Homeview monitors which were playing on the far wall were suddenly cut to crowd shots under the glaring lights of the streets where people were watching the conference on portable sets and viewers in store windows. The sound volume roared with hate.

Heller pounded his gun butt on the upper split-level of the table. He bent over to Mortiiy and indicated to him a young Fleet officer who, behind the row of admirals, was waving for attention.

"Bis?" said Mortiiy. Heller nodded. "Officer Bis," shouted Mortiiy. "You have our attention."

An admiral made room so Bis could get to the edge of the table. "Your Majesty," said Bis, "I have an Apparatus clerk who knew Hisst when he was a young Apparatus officer. This man has been very helpful. As a matter of fact he's under the conference table right now with Fleet technicians trying to get temporary power to the individual surface screens at the conference table seats and to the large center viewer here. We're trying to shunt in Apparatus and other data banks for conference use."

Bis bent over and yelled into the cavity under the table, "Hey, Bawtch. His Majesty wants to talk to you. Come out."

Old Bawtch stuck his head up over the table rim. The gray hair tufts on either side of his head stuck straight out. His eyes were round and scared.

"Somebody give him a seat," said Mortiiy. "Bawtch? Well, see here, Bawtch, if you go on being helpful I can promise you that we can forget your Apparatus connections. Tell us what you know of Lombar Hisst."

Old Bawtch nervously took the offered seat. "It was the freaks."

"Freaks?" said Mortiiy. "What do *freaks* have to do with it?"

"Well, when I was a young clerk, Your Majesty, I was assigned to the Exterior Division Intelligence Files and a new officer—Lombar Hisst—came in. This was fifty years ago, Your Majesty. I was filing some survey data from a planet named Blito-P3. It's on the Invasion Timetable, Your Majesty, and we've got several thousand years of data on it because we're going to invade and conquer it one of these days—as a matter of fact there's been a lot of talk lately of stepping it up. . . ."

"Don't maunder," said Mortiiy. "You started out talking about freaks."

"Well, yes, Your Majesty. I was filing a pack of photographs from a circus run by P. T. Barnum. It had a two-headed *calf* (that's an animal) and a boy with a *dog* face (a *dog* is another animal) and two women joined physically called *Siamese twins* and some others, and this young Hisst picked them up and began to laugh. And then he said, 'With cellology we could go that one better' and he took the whole pack.

"Then the next thing I knew, he had fished a criminal cellologist named Crobe out of a prison and they began to make freaks and sell them to circuses. Those were the first freaks ever exhibited."

"How disgusting," said Mortiiy. "'P. T. Barnum', you say? That doesn't sound very Voltarian. I never heard of any circuses by that name."

"No, Your Majesty. I didn't make myself clear. The freak idea came from Blito-P3. Locally there, they call it Earth."

"Well, that simply shows Hisst might be insane. Thank you for——"

"Wait, Your Majesty. It doesn't end there. This Hisst started plaguing me for more data about that planet and the next thing I knew, a section had been created for it, Section 451 Exterior Division Intelligence."

"You mean 'Apparatus,' " said Mortiiy.

"No, Your Majesty. It wasn't called the Apparatus then. This Lombar Hisst, as a young officer, seemed to gain an awful lot of influence very fast. He'd plague me for data on Blito-P3 and then he'd go to the then Chief of Intelligence or over his head to the Lord of the

Exterior and Hisst would put it out as his own ideas and
they'd institute it. They promoted him right and left. It
was after he got the files on the various intelligence agen-
cies on Blito-P3 that he got the name of our organization
changed to the Coordinated Information Apparatus.

"Long before he was Chief of the Apparatus, Hisst
had put here the provocation techniques of the *Russian
KGB*: it's a system of provoking people to commit crimes
so you can arrest them. From the pattern of an organization known as the *Schutzstaffel*, in *Germany*, developed
by a man named Hitler, we began to recruit criminals
from the prisons to serve in the Apparatus. Our Death
Battalions also come from there. From the *CIA* in the
United States, the Apparatus got the idea of having an
independent military force that would fight wars without
the approval of the government. From the *FBI* of that
same country, Lombar obtained the pattern they use of
ruling the whole land by blackmailing legislative repre-
sentatives and keeping those bodies in a state of terror
by manufacturing crimes that never happened—called
Abscams. We——"

"Hold it," said Mortiiy. "You're drowning me with
names I never heard of."

"Those are all from Blito-P3," said Bawtch. "Locally called Earth. That's where we got the pattern of
our Apparatus from."

A snarl went through the hall.

Madison's hopes surged. Maybe he could capitalize
on this sudden unpopularity of Earth. Maybe he could
image Heller as the protector of that planet: Controversy
was what he needed now. He said swiftly into the commentator mike, "The outlaw Heller for the whole past
year has had his lair on the planet Earth."

Heller, oblivious of the statements Madison was making and, indeed, completely unaware that Madison, behind his Homeview visor, was even in the hall, rapped his gun butt three times for order so Mortiiy could continue.

"So Hisst," said Mortiiy, "was interested in the planet Earth so he could create the abomination called the Apparatus. I——"

"No, Your Majesty," said Bawtch, "that wasn't why Hisst was interested in that planet. It was the history of a family dynasty named the *Rockecenters*. They sprang up from a man who was a servant-raper about a century ago. The fellow sold a poison called *crude oil* for a cancer cure. He was a commoner. He brought up his sons to be thieves and one of them made a fortune out of this *crude oil* and then, by manipulating it and banks and taking over and using Earth intelligence services, he made himself and his generations that followed virtual emperors of the planet. Hisst was fascinated. He had never imagined before that it could be done. He himself was a commoner from the gutters of Slum City and he dreamed that if he followed this pattern, he could become Emperor here. And he did, even if very briefly."

"You say all this happened," said Mortiiy, "on the planet Earth? Incredible! What a weird place that must be!"

Madison hastily said into the commentary mike, "The outlaw Heller furthered his outlaw career on Earth by calling himself Rockecenter. This definitely proves his outlaw connections."

Mortiiy nodded to Bawtch, signifying he could move away from the table or get back to work. "Now that we know where the Apparatus came from, I am open to a vote to abolish it forever and prohibit use of these criminal patterns of intelligence from Blito-P3."

The assent vote was deafening. As Joy City cut back to crowds in cities massed in squares, watching or getting news of this conference, the Homeview monitors on the walls almost split apart with roars.

Madison said into the commentary mike, "The outlaw Heller studied Earth intelligence and was an expert in it. He advocates it thoroughly. In no small way, it contributed to his rise as an interplanetary outlaw." He was feeling very hopeful now. He was building Controversy. He was getting Coverage. His Confidence was rising.

Chapter 8

The palsied Grand Council clerk they had dug up was lagging in his transcript. Heller was keeping his own notes in his engineering log. He now leaned over to Mortiiy and whispered.

"Oh, yes!" said Mortiiy. And then in a louder voice, "We must now go about the business of choosing a new Grand Council."

A general said, "Don't use the ones we had. Those Lords became a bunch of drug addicts."

An admiral said, "Before you can guarantee the new one won't succumb, I make a motion that we prohibit drugs."

Mortiiy said, "Do any of you know anything about drugs?"

The admiral in charge of medicine said, "We never used them in the Confederacy. We used various gases for surgery and such. From what I've seen of drugs, they're poison."

"We don't have or grow or manufacture them on Voltar," said the admiral in charge of contraband and space patrols. "The idea of drugs here originated with Lombar Hisst. We have an order not to stop any such cargos. It originated with Lombar Hisst."

"Well, where did they come from?" said Mortiiy.

"The consoles on the table are working now," said Bis. "I'm punching in the Fleet Intelligence analysis of it and also data on the use of drugs from the Apparatus files."

The separate consoles in front of the seats were flickering and the huge one which occupied the center of the immense conference table lit up.

Mortiiy, from the higher level, stared down at it. He read it. "That's impossible!" he said. "A whole planet going crazy with drugs?"

"That's the analysis, Your Majesty," said Bis. "They take them morning, noon and night. They feed them to the schoolchildren, the workmen and the aged. They even fight their wars with soldiers drugged to the hilt."

"That's Blito-P3 again!" said Mortiiy.

"It was Hisst's secret weapon against Voltar," said Bawtch, crawling out from under the table. "That was why he was mounting that premature invasion of Earth. To get more drugs so he could cave the Confederacy population in."

"It ought to be invaded," snarled Mortiiy. "But not to get more drugs."

Heller punched a series of buttons under the edge of the table. The display changed. "Your Majesty," he said, "there is already a Grand Council order criminalizing drug production on Voltar. I thought I better check. Here it is."

"Then that's done," said Mortiiy.

"No, Your Majesty. That's the trouble. It gave Hisst a monopoly. These laws prohibiting drugs exist also on Blito-P3. They 'are there to protect the real purveyors from competition and thus the governments help them to get wealthy. The answer is to decriminalize and to ignore drugs: they don't profit people then and nobody is interested."

"You seem to know something about this," said Mortiiy.

"Well, a little bit," said Heller. "Drugs are a rotten business. But when you pass a law against them they become a profitable business."

"You mean Blito-P3 has laws against drugs and is loaded with them?"

"That's the way they work it," said Heller.

"The outlaw Heller," said Madison into the commentator mike, "is being careful to protect his drug associates."

"That planet is crazy," said Mortiiy.

"This law here, Your Majesty, was proposed and passed by Hisst."

That was enough. They wiped it from the books.

"Let's get back to where we started," said Mortiiy. "We were trying to get a new Grand Council."

Some notable at the back of the hall yelled, "The Lords may have been on drugs, but several had sons. Why not appoint the sons."

There was a mutter of approval in the hall. Bis leaned over to his admiral senior and that worthy said, "Gentlemen, Your Majesty, I have bad news for you there. Without a single exception, the sons of Lords here have become catamites."

"WHAT?" said Mortiiy. "Where did that come from?"

"Your Majesty," said the admiral, "we regret to tell you they were suborned by a very corrupt and perverted young girl who arrived here a few months ago and who, without doubt, should be executed for actually teaching sexual irregularities. I understand they are common on her home planet. She is an Earth girl. She comes from Blito-P3."

"THAT planet again!" said Mortiiy. "First freaks, then corrupting governments with intelligence, then drugs and now catamites!"

A notable was waving his arms from the back of the crowd. "Your Majesty!" The man was making such a fuss that Mortiiy impatiently signalled for him to come forward to the table.

Heller had to rap several times to quiet the crowd so that the man could be heard.

"Your Majesty!" the fellow said, "I am Noble Arthrite Stuffy, the publisher of the *Daily Speaker.* I am here at the behest of dozens of publishers. You just mentioned freaks. I've been trying to get your attention ever since the name of Crobe came up. He is evidently a condemned criminal from Voltar that went away and returned with some false sciences called *psychology* and *psychiatry.* I came as soon as we knew there would be an Officers' Conference. We want a law passed instantly to forbid the promulgation or use of these two subjects."

"Why?" said Mortiiy.

"Your Majesty, those two subjects claim that sex is the basis for all motivation."

"That's nonsense," said Mortiiy. "But it's just some crackpot idea."

"No, it isn't, Your Majesty," said Noble Arthrite Stuffy. "Those subjects are a pack of falsities and lies that are used to undermine the population, corrupt them and hold in power vicious governments run by insane men! *Psychiatry* and *psychology* played their role in bringing about the chaos we have just been through. Abolish them quick!"

"That's quite a charge," said Mortiiy. "I've never heard of these subjects. Where did they come from?"

"Blito-P3!" said Noble Arthrite Stuffy. "The planet Earth."

"WHAT? That planet again?" roared Mortiiy.

"Yes, Your Majesty. The governments there use these subjects all the time. That's why their population is so caved in. These were the subjects that began pushing drugs there."

"Can you give me some example of how they helped overthrow the government here?" said Mortiiy.

"I'd rather not tell you in public, Your Majesty. It's something very personal that we publishers have found out. If you don't want more drugs, please pass this law!"

The Countess Krak had entered the hall from a rear door. She had walked up the steps behind the dais and whispered in Mortiiy's ear, "You told me to report if your father showed any change. He told me to wish you luck and then went peacefully to sleep with a smile on his face. He seems very happy."

"Thank you," Mortiiy whispered back. Then, as a sudden afterthought, he said, "You were on Earth for a while. Do you know anything about subjects called *psychology* and *psychiatry?*"

"Oh, yes, Your Majesty," Krak whispered back.

"They're awful. The governments there use them to maim and kill and drive people insane when they don't like somebody. They teach all the schoolchildren they're only animals so they'll act like animals."

"That's good enough for me," Mortiiy whispered back. "Sit down back of your man there. You'll be interested in this." Then more loudly he said, "I move that we proclaim *psychology* and *psychiatry*, in teaching and in practice, against the law."

There was a growl of assent and it was done.

"Let's get out of here," said Flick to Madison.

"They can't legislate against the truth that men are just rotten animals. Don't worry. I've got this under control. I'll have them hunting Heller again before you know it."

He gave a signal to the director to get a close shot of Krak. He said into the commentator mike, "I hope you noticed, folks, that the *gun moll* of the outlaw Heller is working her wiles on the Emperor. Is there scandal in the wind? Or is this just a ploy by Heller to prepare the way to kidnap Mortiiy? Time will tell. Watch your Homeview and stay tuned!"

Little did Madison know that he was about to precipitate the wipeout of the planet Earth!

PART
EIGHTY-SEVEN

Chapter 1

Emperor Mortiiy, on the dais, looked out across the turbulent Grand Council hall. Heller, on the dais beside him, seeing that he was about to speak, hit the table with his handgun butt for quiet.

"Thank you, Noble Stuffy, for your assistance in this matter. Now——"

"Oh, Your Majesty!" cried Noble Stuffy. "That is not why we're here."

There was a surge behind him as half a dozen publishers moved forward to stand near his chair, a gesture to back him up.

"Noble Stuffy," said Mortiiy, "the only reason we, the Emperor, are attending this meeting, which fact, you will admit, is unusual, is to get to the bottom of these recent disturbances. If you have requests of another nature, I suggest that you wait until a proper Grand Council is formed——"

"Oh, Your Majesty!" cried Noble Stuffy. "What I wish you to institute has EVERYTHING to do with the recent riots. We want you to appoint a Royal Censor."

"A WHAT?" cried Mortiiy, startled. "I never thought I would see the day when newspapers would tolerate being told what they could or could not print. *Incredible!*"

"Well, yes, Your Majesty," said Noble Stuffy, clinging stubbornly to the position he had been momentarily granted at the table. "We publishers would form a committee under him and we would give him the code he would enforce. You see, Your Majesty, newspapers have never before been forced into competition for circulation. Each paper had its own type of reader and sphere of interest, Homeview simply quoted us: we were quite happy and profitable. But with the introduction of *yellow journalism*, each paper finds itself——"

"*Yellow journalism?*" said Mortiiy. "What's that?"

"Super sensationalism," said Noble Stuffy. "Since it came into practice, each paper finds itself vying with the rest to see which one can sell the most papers by telling the biggest lies."

"WHAT?" cried Mortiiy, black beard bristling. His well-known shortness of temper was suddenly shorter.

"Yes, Your Majesty. The situation is entirely out of our own control. Our reporters are lying, cheating, manufacturing false evidence, even our editors are whipping them on. It began even before the Gris trial. We publishers are helpless. We want a Royal Censor we can resort to when a newspaper finds that it is being used as a tool for *PR*."

"Now you've lost me," said Mortiiy, giving a cross gesture of dismissal. "You had better take this up——"

Seeing he was losing, Noble Stuffy wailed, "But, Your Majesty, it was *PR* that caused the riots!"

"WHAT? Is it some kind of anger bomb?"

"Oh, worse. Far, far worse——"

There was a battering clatter at the main entrance and voices raised. All heads turned toward it.

"I don't care!" the Fleet marine captain was shouting. "Pick up those lights and get out and stay out! This hall is JAMMED! There's one Homeview crew here already!"

"That's the point, you idiot!" a man in aqua-green was shouting. "Men, shove right on in!"

The tan of Fleet marines and aqua-green of the newcomers went into a boil at the entrance door.

In a high-pitched, reaching voice, Heller shouted, "Stand!" The Fleet marines instantly froze. One of the men in aqua-green stepped forward. "What's all this?" shouted Heller.

"I'm a Homeview crew director," the man yelled back across the hall. "The manager in Joy City sent us out here posthaste, spare no air-trucks, to get some stupid idiot off the commentator channel and take over!"

"Can't you settle internal squabbles," shouted Heller, "without interrupting a conference?"

"This is no internal squabble!" the man at the door yelled back. He looked around the room and then walked up to a roustabout who had been in the hall and suddenly raised his visor. "Just as I thought!" he yelled. He faced the dais, "The manager has been going crazy thinking he'd misplaced a Homeview team. This isn't a Homeview team you've got in here. This is Madison and his crew!"

"WHAT?" cried Heller. "Captain, GRAB THAT TEAM!"

"ATTACK!" screamed Flick.

Madison's crew acted instantly. They dropped equipment, snatched out knives and charged the Fleet marines.

The Fleet marines acted instantly. They charged the crew.

People in the hall recoiled with piercing screams.

Tan and aqua-green boiled in furious tumult. Equipment and lights were falling.

"PARALYZE! PARALYZE!" the Fleet marine captain was shouting above the din.

The electric daggers of the Fleet marines were throwing sparks as they fended and duelled. Because they were accustomed to operating on spaceships of the Fleet where gunshots could bring catastrophe to all, they were never armed with blasters. And their electric daggers could be set at intensities lower than killing. It was an unfair advantage and Madison's crew took any profit from it they could.

Knives and daggers were crossing with streams of sparking flame. Pairs were circling.

At a command from Flick, Madison's crew tried a rush for the door!

It was their undoing. A marine platoon had remained there, expecting just that.

There was a flurry of flame and sparks. Outnumbered two to one, Madison's crew, with howls of pain, one after another were stretched out, temporarily paralyzed.

The real Homeview crew in the door had been smugly taking pictures. They marched now in triumph fully into the hall and began to set up.

The Fleet marines had suffered only minor casualties. They began to drag their late assailants over into a pile along the wall.

"Captain," Heller called. "Look through those casualties and see if you can identify a man called J. Walter Madison if he's there."

From behind a glaring light which was still standing in the corner, pouring its rays into the room, a man stepped out, gradually becoming visible.

"If you're looking for J. Walter Madison," he said, "I'm right here. And," he said, walking forward, his visor lifted, "you are completely wrong about *PR*."

He came to the table edge, stared at incredulously by all eyes. He looked up at Mortiiy and said, "I refuse, Your Majesty, to stand idle and see the noble profession of *PR* maligned."

Mortiiy stared at him.

"*PR*," said Madison, "means, in your language, public relations. It is, Your Majesty, of infinite use to a government." His voice took on a crooning lilt. "You can mold, sculpt and create in wondrous forms the opinions of the multitude. It is not necessary even to be sensible in your government decisions when you utilize *PR*. You can do anything you please and, by the beautiful techniques of imagery, bring about any public opinion that you might require. You do not even have to be fair or just in trials. If you, as a governing sovereign, do not like someone, he does not even have to be guilty of a single crime: you simply manufacture news stories and try him in the press. You do not even have to bring him to court."

"WHAT?" said Mortiiy, scandalized.

"Indeed," said Madison, "you may well stare in astonishment. But it is true. By manipulating public opinion, you can drive the mobs and riffraff any direction you want. In fact, it was by the skilled use of the Gris trial that I was able, with *PR*, to bring these wonderful riots to a positive boil!"

"WHAT IS THIS?" cried Mortiiy.

"*PR*," said Madison. "The whole planet of Blito-P3 is run on it." His voice took on an almost singing tone. "*PR* is the gift of Earth to a waiting universe."

Heller could see the embers begin to kindle behind the eyes of Mortiiy. In a low voice, Heller said, "Watch it, Madison. You'd better shut up!"

Madison turned to him with an attitude of disdain.
"Shut up? It's a very good thing I did NOT shut up.
Heller-Wister, I made you what you are today! Without
PR and my genius at using it, you would be shivering,
unknown in some dark, dank cave. What are you really?
A nobody, a nothing!"

Mortiiy was on his feet. His face was contorted with
rage. "Why, you infernal snot!" he stormed at Madison.
"How dare you insult one of the bravest officers that
ever lived! You're a snivelling coward in the bargain! You
know very well an officer is forbidden to duel in his
monarch's presence. Well, I will take care of *that!*" And
he drew his hand blastgun to shoot!

Madison looked at the gun and went white. He had
not known anything about any such custom. He had been
carried away. Now it appeared he would be carried away
feet first. With horror he watched the thumb throwing
off the safety lever!

Mortiiy suddenly checked himself. "No," he said.
"Those days are over. I am Emperor now. I must reform." Although he put the handgun back in his belt
holster, he did not look very reformed. He was still blazing angry. He was still standing.

Mortiiy glared at Madison. His space-deck voice
roared out. "At LAST we've gotten to the bottom of it!"

The snarling rage struck fear into the tense hall. "A
thing called *PR* mangles a million people in the streets,
with tens of billions of property damage! A *P. T. Barnum*
gives us abominable freaks! A *CIA/KGB* gives us a rotten, foul organization called the Apparatus! Two insane
fake 'sciences' named *psychology* and *psychiatry* lying to
the entire population! *Drugs* shatter the lives of whole cities and subvert the government! My two poor brothers

dead, my father ruined in health and myself consigned to five years of Hells! And where did all this come from?"

He brought his fist down on the board. "A planet called Blito-P3, Earth! WE HAVE BEEN INVADED!"

Mortiiy straightened up. His face was very grim. But he had regained his self-control. He spoke now with kingly determination. "I know now why things went wrong with Voltar and I know where the disease came from. Primitive, decadent or decayed civilizations can be very dangerous to associate with. It can be like putting a patient with a contagious illness into a roomful of healthy people. A higher strata of culture can be pulled down and fouled by such association. We have seen these before in our history and we are far from perfect.

"But never in my whole career, which has contained extensive travels, have I ever in my life heard of such a putrid and degenerate society as that of Blito-P3, Earth!"

He stood for a moment. His eyes wandered to the armorial bearings and portrait of his father which still hung against the far wall. Inset below it were paintings of his two brothers, now dead. His eyes misted for a moment and then he turned suddenly to Heller.

"I never want to hear of Blito-P3 again! NEVER!" He drew a long breath. "You are permanent Viceregal Chairman, Lord Heller. As Emperor, I am not, by custom, supposed to be here." Heller could see that Mortiiy was actually crying and seeking to hide it as best he could. "As Crown," he continued, controlling his voice with difficulty, "complete this conference. I will compose, at my leisure, lists of potential new Lords and we can use them to form a government." He was bending over to mask the emotional stress he was under. He took six blank sheets of proclamation paper. He rapidly signed his name across the bottoms. He took the Royal seal from his pocket and pressed it over the signatures. He sent the six sheets skidding sideways to Heller.

"Use one of those blank orders," said Mortiiy, "to dispose of Blito-P3, Earth, any way you see fit!"

He turned away to the back of the dais. He was obviously leaving and the whole hall was taken by surprise. They stood suddenly in a belated effort to bow.

But Mortiiy wasn't looking at them. He walked down the back steps of the dais. When he was out of their sight he brushed at his eyes with the back of his hand.

The Countess Krak slipped down to his side and took his arm and led him away, for it was obvious to her that he was now blinded with tears and couldn't see where he was going. He had loved his brothers very dearly. And knowing now, at last, what really had caused their deaths had brought the fact home.

Chapter 2

The Grand Council hall was buzzing. The senior officers at the huge table were still standing but they had begun to talk to one another. These people were upset because the Emperor had looked upset.

Heller fingered the six blank proclamations. He knew the difficulties of getting staffs to agree on disposition of forces, zones of combat, appropriations and all such intricacies attendant upon invasions: this was certainly not the operating climate in which to begin it.

Madison was still standing there, sort of collapsed,

the dagger of a Fleet marine lieutenant about an inch from his throat. Madison's crew were piled up along the wall, beginning now to twitch back to life.

Suddenly Heller spotted a small wizened face: he recognized, from other times of long ago, the Master of Palace City.

Heller hit the table with the butt of his gun. "Gentlemen," he shouted, "we have urgent work ahead of us tonight. But I think we all will be better for a little REFRESHMENT! The Master of Palace City has just signalled me that he is going to serve you some choice drinks and viands, the best he can dig up, in fact."

The Master of Palace City stared. His mind raced. Where could he find some staff to open up cellars and pantries? The Palace City guards and the servants of this building had been dismissed by the Apparatus. Then he suddenly realized that, by inference, the existing Palace City Lords had been removed. He had all their palaces to draw from. He nodded brightly.

A buzz had welcomed Heller's news. He now said, "This conference will be resumed in two hours' time. Be here, for we will then have very important business to transact."

He stepped down from the dais. He pointed at Madison. "Bring him along," said Heller to the marine lieutenant.

Heller made his way through the throng over to the wall and looked down at the recumbent figures in aquagreen. He turned to Madison. "I suppose you trained this crew in *PR*," said Heller.

"Oh, yes," said Madison. "They are very valuable people!"

"Good," said Heller and beckoned to the marine captain. "Get that whole crew put in electric shackles,

kick them awake and chain this Madison at the head
of it."

"At once, Your Lordship," the marine captain said.
"Can I raise the voltage a bit above the usual? They
wounded some of my men."

"No torture," said Heller, "although I must agree
with you, it's tempting."

Madison suddenly got brave. "You can't do this to
me. There is no crime on any statute book for practicing
PR. There is no charge of any kind you can bring against
me. *PR* is just a profession like anything else."

"Well," said Heller, "that might be true of Earth.
There you can start whole wars and ruin reputations and
lives, and *PRs* just strut and laugh about it. But here a
million casualties aren't looked upon so lightly."

"I put Mortiiy on the throne, if you want to know,"
said Madison. "If I had not crowned Hisst, the population never would have risen——"

"Madison, I hate to have to tell you this, but if
you'd kept your nose out of it, Cling would simply have
gotten well, declared Mortiiy his successor and there
wouldn't have been a single shot fired. You were just a
stupid, destructive sideshow! But that's typical of your
breed everywhere I encountered it. You just made trouble
where none need ever have been."

Madison looked at him doubtfully. Then he
shrugged. "I can see you have an awful lot to learn,
Heller-Wister. Mr. Bury will believe me if I tell him I
worked hard to make you immortal. When I get back to
Earth——"

"Madison," said Heller in English, "I've got news
for you. Mr. Bury works for me now."

"WHAT?"

"Fact," said Heller. "And as far as your going back

to Earth is concerned, I don't even have to wonder if I'd inflict you on that planet again. Your stupid last caper was a real peach, angering Mortiiy. Your public relations was so good that he just ordered the planet disposed of. A true triumph for *PR*."

Madison looked at him and might have spoken but the Countess Krak had returned from the Imperial Palace and she walked up to them. "Jettero," she said, "the last time we saw this man he was supposed to be driving off a dock in the East River!"

"*PRs*," said Heller, "unfortunately can't even execute factual death notices."

The criminal crew were being gathered up and chained. The woman Flip was standing near, eyeing the Countess Krak.

Krak turned to Madison. "I just remembered. Two days after your death notice appeared in the papers, I saw another one that mentioned you. Your mother."

"My mother?" said Madison, suddenly ashen. "She died of grief over that death report?"

"No," said Krak. "She got married in one of the happiest weddings I've ever seen photographs of!"

"Oh, my God!" said Madison and began to crumple.

The woman Flip, despite her manacles, grabbed him to keep him from falling. She knelt and put his head on her lap.

"What's the matter with him?" said the Countess Krak to Heller. "I just told him so he wouldn't feel guilty that he'd ruined his mother's life with grief. It was a kind gesture!"

The woman Flip kissed Madison. He stirred. His eyelids flickered open. He looked up at her. She kissed him again.

"I've got you," said Flip with greedy eyes.

"Oh, my God," he wept, "there goes my genius!"

Chapter 3

Outside, a cold desert wind was moaning around the naked palaces, blowing in dust to spin in swirls before the lights which Army units were setting up on a temporary basis.

Rebel troops and Fleet marines were patrolling the darkened boulevards.

The Countess Krak directed Heller down the vast staircase toward a nearby park. They were followed by a squad of Fleet marines who kept the manacled crew of Madison bunched up.

The new Homeview crew director came racing down the steps and fell into pace with Heller. "Crown, Your Lordship, sir," he said. "Don't be angry with Homeview, please." He glanced over his shoulder at Madison a few feet behind them. "The crud that idiot was putting on the commentary channel was caught by the monitor editor at Joy City. It never went on the air."

Madison, far gone already, would have collapsed once more if Flip and a marine had not caught him by the chains.

"Since when did Homeview get so solicitous?" said Heller.

"Well, sir, you're a public figure now."

"Fine," said Heller, sarcastically. "That explains everything. Go back and get yourself some refreshments."

"Oh, thank you," said the Homeview director. "But you see, one of my men noticed a Royal prison air-wagon landing a few minutes ago and saw Lord Turn get out. I've got an idea this has to do with your prisoner Soltan Gris. I want to cover it. It's hot-spot news."

"I'm going to kill Madison," muttered Heller.

"Oh, good!" said the Homeview director. "You're going to execute him right here in the park——"

"Shut up!" said Heller. "It was just a figure of speech. You and your sudden talk about 'public figure' and 'cover it' and 'spot news'! You never heard of those things until this (bleeped) Madison came along. Now you sound just like an *ABC* news crew."

"But the public has a right to know!" said the director.

"'Right to know'!" gritted Heller. "That did it. No, you CANNOT cover my private meeting with Lord Turn. But I can tell you what is going to happen later tonight."

"What?" said the director.

"I am going to see that a Royal Censor is appointed with powers to shoot directors! Get out of here!"

"Crown, Your Lordship, sir!" said the director. "Are you intimating that you are going to advocate a *fascistic* suppression of the Gods-given right of freedom of speech and press?"

Heller stopped. Madison almost ran into him. "Madison," said Heller, "if I ever felt any mercy toward you before, it just evaporated. Just as I begin, quite unwillingly, a life as a 'public figure,' I find you'll be trailing me as a ghost."

"Then you are going to execute him in the park," said the director.

"No," said Heller, starting to walk again. "Tempting, but no. Director, this fellow Madison, yapping around, only gave you half of the story."

"Really?"

"Yes. The other half is that there is such a thing as 'invasion of privacy.'"

"Oh?" said the director, impressed.

"Yes," said Heller. "Now, you tell them down at Homeview and tell anybody else that will listen that if I find you invading my privacy with cameras and crew, I'll sue you or them for a billion credits."

"My Gods!"

"That's some of the other half Madison didn't teach you."

"But what does it mean, 'invasion of privacy'?"

"Ah," said Heller, "it means anything I say it means any time I say it."

"My Gods!"

"Right," said Heller. "Now that you have the word, be sure to tell your boss and fellow directors."

"Oh, I will!" said the director, frightened.

"Good," said Heller. "Now, because it very well may stop further riots, and solely for that reason and no other, you can go get your cameras and crew and cover the trial of Soltan Gris."

"Oh, YES, Your Lordship!" cried the director in a truly impressed and worshipful voice. "At your orders, Your Lordship, sir!" He raced off.

Heller turned to Madison. He said, in English, "Top that one, you (bleepard)!"

Chapter 4

Lord Turn was sitting on the trail of an overturned Apparatus blast cannon. The air-wagon, marked *Royal Prison*, was parked quite near. Some Army engineer had put a field electric heater at his feet and he was warming his hands in its red light.

"Jettero, my boy!" said Turn when Heller stood before him. He got up and pumped Heller's hand.

"I was terribly sorry, Your Lordship," said Heller, "to have to ask this favor. I'm afraid I caused you a lot of upset unwittingly."

"Sit down, sit down, my boy," said Turn, patting a place on the cannon trail. "Nothing that couldn't be mended. But what in the name of Heavens was this all about?"

Heller sat down. "I was bringing Gris to the Royal prison and I thought he committed suicide."

Turn waved a hand at the air-wagon. The face of Soltan Gris was pressed against the barred window, misery in his eyes, looking hopeless. Two prison guards were behind him. "Well, he unfortunately survived it," said Lord Turn. "That man is a true felon. He can cause more trouble per cubic inch of law book than anyone I ever heard of. You see, I couldn't really try him because I didn't know the charge."

The camera crew had arrived on the run and they were suddenly bathed with lights. Lord Turn groaned.

Heller reached into his tunic and pulled forth a

printout. "They have the consoles in there working now and I just pulled this. Can you try him here and get this over with?"

"Oh, gladly!" said Lord Turn and signalled to the guards in the air-wagon. "Twice as legal to try him in Palace City and good riddance!"

Soltan Gris was stumbling forward. A camera was thrust into his face and he flinched.

"Stand over there," said Heller. "Don't be scared of the cameras. I don't think anybody is watching at this hour."

"That's what you think," said the director. And he showed a backfeed monitor of the screens at Joy City. The pictures he was flashing were a montage of crowds, crowds, crowds! They were standing in the darkened streets on this side of Voltar and in the sunlit streets on the other. Word must have spread like wildfire.

Heller groaned. He turned to Lord Turn. "This is Grand Council Order 938365537-451BP3, issued last year. It directs the Exterior Division to send an engineer to patch up Blito-P3. Soltan Gris, then a Secondary Executive of the Apparatus, Chief of Section 451, Blito-P3, did everything in his power to make certain that this order would not be executed."

"Aha!" cried Lord Turn, reading the order. "Then the defense of Soltan Gris and his attorneys that he was only obeying orders doesn't hold!"

Lord Turn pulled his cloak around him. He said loudly, "The Court is in session!" He glared with hostility at Gris.

Gris stood shaking, bathed in Homeview lights but also with the light from the heater which, being red, gave him a diabolical look.

"I knew, Gris, that a Royal officer would not have

arrested you for nothing. This is a very grave charge. The penalty is court discretion or death. How do you plead?"

"Not guilty!" wailed Gris.

"Unfortunately," said Lord Turn, "I finally got around to reading your confession. You're as guilty as a murderer found standing with blood dripping from his knife. You even attempted the life of a Royal officer! I find you guilty as accused! Have you anything to say before I pass sentence?"

Soltan Gris dropped to his knees. He clasped his manacled hands together and held them beseechingly toward the judge. Unfortunately this put him closer to the heater and bathed him scarlet: the light, being from below, painted his face like a monster. "You promised me leniency!" he cried.

"I don't think I did," said Turn. "I just told you to write up your crimes so I could find out what the charge was."

"Mercy, mercy!" blubbered Gris. "Don't sentence me to death by torture! Spare me."

"Oh, for Heavens' sakes," said Heller, disgusted. He leaned over and whispered in Lord Turn's ear. Lord Turn nodded.

"Soltan Gris," said Turn, "I am empowered by law in such a crime to sentence at court discretion or death. Your final execution will be done by hanging and exposure from a gibbet in the Royal prison until your body rots away. . . ."

Gris fainted. He fell with a clank and jangle of manacles.

A prison guard tried to get him to his feet and wake him up. Gris just slumped.

"What a snivelling coward," said the judge. "He

couldn't even stay conscious to hear the rest of the sentence."

Lord Turn made some notes in a book and put the Grand Council order with it.

Heller had his eye on the camera crews. They had taken all the close-ups they wanted now of Gris. They were packing up. Their lights went off. Heller was sure the crowds in the streets in the Confederacy would be dancing with joy.

"Thank you, Crown, Your Lordship," said the director to Heller. "I am sure we at Homeview can work out a very happy professional relationship."

"I was afraid of that," said Heller, sardonically.

The director trotted off, followed by his crew.

Lord Turn got up. He walked over and stirred at Gris with his foot but there was no response.

Turn faced Heller. "Well, Jettero, my boy, I am surely glad that's over with." He shook Heller's hand. He looked back at the collapsed Gris and said, "Well, he's all yours now."

Lord Turn, followed by the Royal prison guards, got into the air-wagon. It flew away.

Heller gestured to the collapsed Gris and said to the marine lieutenant, "Pick him up. We have another call to make."

Chapter 5

The palace of Queen Teenie stood in the dark and cold. The moaning that came from it matched the wind.

The harsh Army field lights that glared at it in blue only seemed to intensify the gloom.

The column of fifty-one prisoners—Gris was being carried—clanked to a halt in the open space at the bottom of the great curving stairs.

Snelz's men were standing about on guard. Snelz came forward.

"Take over these prisoners," said Heller, "and hold them here in this small park beside the stairs." Then he turned to thank the Fleet marines. Their officer made sure that Snelz's men had them, gave Heller a cross-arm salute and marched his men away.

"What in Heavens' name is all that keening?" said the Countess Krak.

Snelz looked a little uncomfortable in the Army lights' blue glare. "They kind of got the idea Queen Teenie was going to be executed. They got a Homeview set in there and some admiral at the conference was spouting off about how she should be. And then, somehow they got the idea she could be executed for harboring Lombar Hisst."

"Did you tell them that?" said Heller.

"Well," said Snelz, avoiding his eyes, "it was one way to shake the prisoner loose, even if it didn't work."

Heller shook his head. "Now I've got a disaster area to handle. Well, come on. At least we'll give it a try." He walked up the wide curving steps, followed by the Countess Krak and Snelz.

Two silver-uniformed guards at the door barred their way with crossed battle-axes. Heller told them who they were. A seneschal said, "You three can come in, but no weapons."

Heller and Snelz unbuckled their beltguns and handed the harnesses with the weapons to a guard. The seneschal shouted, "Lord Heller!" into the hall. Then they, with the Countess Krak, entered the great reception chamber.

It was a dismal sight. The only light came from boys' pocket torches lying on the floor here and there, scattered amongst some tops and other toys. Several staff were holding each other up, sobbing. All along the wall, boys in crumpled clusters were crying. The cold desert wind, in an undertone, mourned through the hall.

Teenie was sitting on the bottom step of her throne. A blue fur cloak was draped over her shoulders. She was holding her scepter listlessly. She was staring at the floor.

The three came to a stop before her. The Countess Krak bent over and looked into her face. "Why, you're just an adolescent Earth girl," she said.

The effect was instantaneous. Teenie leaped to her feet and backed up two steps to get taller in height. "I'm Queen Teenie of Flisten!" she flared. "And I will go to my doom like Royalty!"

A wail went through the hall from the others like a dirge.

The three looked at her in astonishment and then, before they could speak, Teenie suddenly sat down on the higher step. She gradually slumped and, with her elbows on her knees, cupped her chin in her hands despondently.

"I had it made. Everything was running great. And then Madison came along and wrecked it all!" Then her head slumped further forward. She moaned, "Nobody loves me, everybody hates me. I'm going out and eat worms." And she began to weep.

Some boys crawled toward her and cried, "We love you, Teenie!"

Send in this card and you'll receive a free MISSION EARTH POSTER while supplies last. No order required for this Special Offer! Mail your card today!

☐ Please send me a FREE Mission Earth Poster
☐ Please send me information about other books by L. Ron Hubbard.

ORDERS SHIPPED WITHIN 24 HRS OF RECEIPT!

PLEASE SEND ME THE FOLLOWING:

___ Battlefield Earth paperback	$4.95	___
___ Buckskin Brigades paperback	$3.95	___
___ Final Blackout hardcover	$16.95	___
___ MISSION EARTH Vol 1 paperback **SPECIAL** $2.95		___
___ MISSION EARTH Vol 2 - 10 paperback		
(specify #s:_____) each $4.95		___
___ MISSION EARTH hardback volumes		
(specify #s:_____) each $18.95		___
___ MISSION EARTH hardback set (10 vols.) $99.95		___
___ MISSION EARTH Sound Editions		
(specify #s:_____) each $14.95		___
___ Writers of The Future Volume I	$3.95	___
___ Writers of The Future Volume II	$3.95	___
___ Writers of The Future Volume III	$4.50	___
___ Writers of The Future Volume IV	$4.95	___
___ Writers of The Future Volume V	$4.95	___
___ Writers of The Future Volume VI	$4.95	___
___ Battlefield Earth Music cassette **SPECIAL** $7.98		___
___ Battlefield Earth Music record **SPECIAL** $7.98		___
___ MISSION EARTH Music cassette **SPECIAL** $7.98		___
___ MISSION EARTH Music record **SPECIAL** $7.98		___
___ MISSION EARTH Music CD **SPECIAL** $12.98		___

CHECK AS APPLICABLE: SHIPPING: __FREE__

☐ Check/Money Order enclosed   **TAX*:** ___
(Use an envelope please.)

☐ American Express ☐ VISA ☐ MasterCard   **TOTAL:** ___

Card #:_____

Exp. Date:_____ Signature:_____

NAME:_____

ADDRESS:_____

CITY:_____ STATE:_____ ZIP:_____

PHONE#:_____

Book purchased at:_____

Call Us Now at 1-800-722-1733 (1-800-843-7389 in CA)

NO POSTAGE
NECESSARY
IF MAILED
IN THE
UNITED STATES

BUSINESS REPLY MAIL

FIRST CLASS MAIL   PERMIT NO. 62688   LOS ANGELES, CA

POSTAGE WILL BE PAID BY ADDRESSEE

BRIDGE PUBLICATIONS, INC.

DEPT. ME10
4751 FOUNTAIN AVENUE
LOS ANGELES, CA 90029

The staff in the shadows stepped ahead. "Don't break our hearts, Queen Teenie!"

The major-domo knelt and plucked at Heller's hand, "Lord Heller, if you are going to execute her, the staff only wishes to die on the scaffold by her side."

"Good Gods," said Heller, shaking loose. "What have I gotten into!"

"You've gotten into the same situation that we had in Afyon, Turkey," said the Countess Krak. "The little boys and Utanc! I've heard about this girl. She's just another example of what Earth does to people. Unless you handle her, you'll have this perversion all over Voltar like a plague. When I think of my failures to reform Miss Simmons and the rest, I have to advise you that there's only one thing to do. You can't deport her because, as I understand it, there will shortly be no place to deport her to. You will have to execute her."

The wails and sobs were deafening!

"Shut up!" shouted Heller.

The keening redoubled!

In the din, Heller said to the Countess Krak and Snelz, "*Please* let me handle this." He looked around and picked a child's toy off the floor.

"Oh, Jettero," said the Countess Krak. "You're too softhearted. I know exactly what you're going to do now. You're going to pardon her and tell her to be good and then she'll go right out and undermine the entirety. . . ."

Several maids spotted where the opposition might be coming from. On bended knees, they clutched at the Countess, distracting her. "Please don't kill Queen Teenie!" they were crying. One ripped her own dress apart and bared her breasts. "Kill us," she said, "but let her live!"

"SHUT UP ALL OF YOU!" shouted Heller.

He went up three steps to Teenie. As he approached her, the screams redoubled. He put his arm around her. They were sure he was going to strangle her.

But Heller kissed Queen Teenie on the cheek!

"Well, I never!" said the Countess Krak.

Heller got out his redstar engineer's rag and wiped at Teenie's tears. He made her blow her nose on it.

Then he picked her up and carried her to the entrance door. He put her on her feet and stood close to her.

The others stared. It grew deathly quiet.

Then a scrap of Heller's low-voiced communication drifted to them. "So the only question is whether you will do this for me or not."

The Countess Krak, still in the hall, was horrified. She was absolutely certain that Heller was propositioning the girl. She moaned, "Oh, Lords, now she's even gotten to *him!*"

Teenie abruptly let out a giggle of delight.

Everyone inside the hall was electrified.

There was a small room just inside the entrance door. Suddenly Teenie and Heller went into it and closed the door behind them.

People looked at one another, stunned.

Five minutes passed by. They stared at the closed door. Ten minutes passed by. The door was still closed.

"Oh, my Lords," moaned the Countess Krak.

Suddenly the door opened. Heller and Teenie came out. Teenie was pulling the robe around her shoulders. Then she suddenly threw her arms around Heller and she said, "Whiz Kid, you are a Whiz Kid after all! And you are quite a man!" And she lifted up on tiptoe and she kissed him!

The people in the hall somehow sensed the crisis

was over. They began to scream with paeans of delight. The din was deafening.

The Countess Krak fainted.

Chapter 6

The Grand Council hall had changed somewhat in the last two hours. The Master of Palace City had been busy. Some of the diamond-studded banners had been recovered from the baggage of dead Apparatus troops. The portrait of Cling and his two elder sons had come down and in its place was one of Mortiiy as a young man in the full-dress uniform of a Fleet officer. Some Palace City guards had returned to duty and stood about like statues in blue and violet. Servants of ex-Lords were scurrying about, clearing up the remains of the repast.

Heller had gotten a drink of sparklewater, eaten a sweetbun, washed his face and changed to a golden Lord's tunic that the master had dug up, but he had girded it with his officer's belt and sidearms.

He took his place now on the dais. The Countess Krak sat down on a small stool to the side and slightly behind his chair. She sat there as though in mourning, suffering and silent.

The crowded place was in a hubbub. Even more people seemed to have been added. Heller was about to hit the table with the butt of his gun when, suddenly, four trumpets blared and a cymbal crashed. It startled him. He looked over at a small balcony where the master was standing. The fellow winked! He had been watching

Heller's hand. Heller suppressed his desire to laugh. He muttered to himself, "Well, like Mortiiy, I've got to realize those days are over." And he put the gun in its holster.

"Gentlemen," he said into the suddenly silent room, "this Officers' Conference is reopened. We have several subjects to take up. I shall reserve until the last the disposal of the planet Blito-P3. Right now I wish to finalize the matter of the Earth girl and the catamites."

There was an instant rushing snarl, a wave of hate and ferocity from the more than two thousand people assembled.

The Homeview crew was on the job and the backfeed viewers on the far wall showed the reactions of the mobs in the streets. In the night-lighted thoroughfares on this side of the planet and the sunlit ones elsewhere, the reaction was instant hate.

"Oh, dear," muttered Heller to himself. "I've got to play this very, very cool."

An Army general at the table roared out in a parade-ground voice, "We have discovered that this Earth girl is posing as the Hostage Queen of Flisten, right here in Palace City!"

"We demand immediate action!" shouted the most senior official of the Domestic Police.

"Kill the Earth girl!" shouted the people in the room.

"Execute the catamites!" screamed the jammed crowds in the streets.

"Madison, Madison," muttered Heller, "what have you done! Earth is about as popular here as a carload of skunks." He made a signal toward the place the master had been standing: another man was there now but the cymbals crashed.

Heller put on a very stern face. He would have to

play this expertly. Into the silence, he said, "I was afraid for a while that you would not approve my extreme severity, but I see now that you will probably go along with it."

"He's ordered them all executed," went the whisper around the table.

Heller heard it. "Worse," he said. "Far worse. I have just concluded a treaty with the Hostage Queen of Flisten. I am, because of its severity, making it contingent upon approval by this Officers' Conference."

They waited, hungry for vengeance.

"Mere execution is too quick," said Heller. "They need time to suffer and repent for their sins."

Heads nodded.

"I therefore have proposed the sentence of extreme exile to a barren rock far out in the ocean."

Satisfaction began to register.

"I have forced her to give up her Palace City palace and, because they were contaminated, have ordered that the whole domestic staff there be sent into exile as well. This makes them suffer with her."

"Wise," heads nodded, "wise."

"And these young miscreants who followed her in corruption are being severely exiled as well! This extends even to the sons of some ex-Lords to give you the idea of the thorough violence intended."

There was some applause.

"And to this barren, desolate place, I also exile J. Walter Madison and his hellish crew."

More applause.

"No communication of any kind will be permitted from the world. We will let them sink, alone, in the infamy of their own Hells!"

Wild applause. People at the table were standing up and cheering.

When it had died down, Heller took a sheet of proclamation paper from his tunic. "This is the treaty amendment with the Hostage Queen of Flisten. If you gentlemen will affix your signatures and plates above that of His Majesty, we can then give it a number and the matter will be finalized. The Hostage Queen of Flisten, as you will see, has already signed it."

He handed it to an usher who began to pass it from officer to officer at the table.

He was pushing secretly to Krak, below at his side, a child's toy camera which he had picked up off the floor in Teenie's palace.

"There was no Homeview around," he whispered, "so I had to do it myself."

She took it. Such devices have ten minutes of picture time in them. On the back is a little screen that shows what has been shot. The things are just junk and the quality is awful. Two-dimensional.

Below the level of the table, Krak turned it on, feeling very sad.

Heller had apparently put it on a table and started it running when he and Teenie had first entered the room. The place was evidently a seneschal's office. Krak saw Teenie sit down at the desk. Heller remained standing.

He was selling her on the idea of a treaty. That was what he wanted her to do for him. Amend the existing treaty of the Hostage Queen of Flisten.

After a bit, Heller said, "It would be best if you gave up your palace in Palace City. The staff seems to want to go with you and you could take your things."

"Well, that's no hardship," said Teenie. "The wives of Lords around here snoot the hell out of me—just a bunch of cats. Could I dig my marijuana up in the palace gardens? A lot of it is ready to harvest and some of it is very valuable: Panama Red."

"I'll put Snelz in charge of the move. So that will be okay, but we won't mention it in writing. You have my word."

"And I really, truly get Madison?"

"Absolutely. You'll have to take his whole crew. If he signs over the General Loop townhouse to the government, he can take his baggage and so can they. Actually the whole lot should be returned to prison and Madison should be shot, so you be very, very careful, Teenie. He's dangerous as blazes. You've got dungeons over there: did you know I surveyed Relax Island once to update the charts? There'd been an earthquake. The whole place is just a hollow volcanic bubble. One of the cliffs had slipped. It's quite a lovely place. But don't get soft in the head with Madison: put him in one of those dungeons."

"Oh, I will, I will," said Teenie, smiling brightly.

"And now we come to Gris," said Heller.

"Oh, yes, we do, don't we?" Teenie said, smiling very broadly.

"I got him his trial but the coward fainted before he heard the whole sentence. Here it is."

She took it. She read aloud, "Said Soltan Gris is found guilty of high treason. His final execution will be done by hanging and exposure from a gibbet in the Royal prison until his body rots away; but before he is executed, he is to complete a life sentence in a prison designated by the Hostage Queen of Flisten."

Teenie began to smile with a peculiar, ferocious intensity. She read it again, savoring it. Then she said, "You hinted you would give me Gris but, brother, this is the real goods! You're a screaming genius, Whiz Kid. Oh, boy!"

"Now, there's one caution," said Heller. "His records at the Royal prison will remain on file until that sentence is completed. So you've got to return or order returned his body when he dies. Then they can string it up."

"Oh, I will, I will!" said Teenie.

"Now, I'm only doing this because you intimated you simply wanted to keep him in a dungeon. I wouldn't have suggested he be turned over to you if I thought you were going to torture him. I don't hold with torture."

"Oh, I won't," said Teenie. "I just want the comfort of knowing he's nice and safe in a quiet dungeon. I give you my word I won't even touch him."

"Good," said Heller. "Now, we're leaving a lot of this treaty, such as Gris, verbal. But there's one thing that will have to go in it. Communication will have to remain cut off with Relax Island. Planetary Defense will enforce it."

"Oh, to hell with that," said Teenie. "Who wants to talk to the outside world when you got Gris to inspect and five hundred noblemen to (bleep). Whiz Kid, you really are the most. I love you!"

And she signed the treaty and hit it with her Royal seal.

As they started to leave the room, Heller grabbed the treaty, put it in his tunic and snatched up the child's camera.

Krak looked at her watch. Ten minutes! All they'd done was talk!

She whispered to Heller crossly, "You shouldn't have made me think you were doing something else! You and your jokes!"

"It wasn't a joke," said Heller. "Maybe those catamites will get the idea they should be men. I couldn't arrange any treaty in a room with all that yowling, but maybe, too, it helped her pride to make them think it was her feminine charm that had worked."

Krak snorted. "You and other people's feelings!"

"Keep that camera and strip with my files," said Heller. "I might need it to safeguard my own reputation or defend myself from your accusations in some fight."

"Oh, Jettero, I was just fooling. I've learned my lesson. I'm not jealous anymore."

"Oh, yeah?" he said in English.

That made her laugh. "Jettero, it's not my jealousy that's liable to come between us: it's your awful sense of humor!"

"You just laughed," he called to her attention.

That broke her up. The world looked much better.

But that was that world, the world of Voltar. The fate of another world, Earth, would be settled forever this very night!

PART EIGHTY-EIGHT

Chapter 1

In the Grand Council hall, the treaty was taking its time getting back to Heller: this was due mainly to arguments occurring at every seat around the hundred-foot-diameter table, arguments which were not concerned with the treaty but with the seniority of members of each division now that there was no Lord for it. Two or three were represented only by a chief clerk and, unlike the military and police, had never had a precise chain of command below the level of nobility.

But Heller, sitting on the dais, was not impatient as he watched the paper slowly coming back. It only had two signatures left to be signed.

"Well, this will be one down and five to go," he said to the Countess Krak in a low voice without turning to look down at her. "I still can't understand why Mortiiy picked me for Viceregal Chairman. He's got lots of friends and far more experienced men for the job."

"He was smart," whispered the Countess Krak. "The military didn't jump in until the last moment and so their loyalty to him is not proven. All his friends are rebels and that wouldn't go down well with the whole population. You were never other than loyal to Cling. Furthermore, you're very popular with the population. Mortiiy thinks of you as a brother officer he can trust and, if you look at it head on, he really owes his throne to you.

He's a very clever man, really. And, of course, my Jettero is brilliant, handsome, charming..."

"And has a bad sense of humor," laughed Heller. "Well, anyway, I didn't start his reign with the slaughter of a bunch of little boys. Reigns that begin by ordering blood baths are pretty unlucky. Maybe," he added, looking suddenly bright, "maybe there *is* some hope for government. Maybe it *can* be run right!"

"Then you'd better start thinking pretty fast," said the Countess Krak. "You just said one down and five to go and, according to the notes you've got scribbled there, disposing of Earth is the last item on your agenda. Are you really going to be able to face up to ordering and arranging the deaths of five billion people?"

Heller frowned and looked down at the table before him.

"I know you, Jettero. You're thinking of Izzy and Bang-Bang and all your friends there. You've got a heart as soft as mush, for all of your tough exterior. You're probably even feeling sorry for Miss Simmons! Some of those five billion were your personal friends."

"Maybe, in spite of all those flattering reasons you just gave," said Heller, "Mortiiy was dead wrong to put me in this job." He brightened. "I know. I was just handy. He only intended it as a temporary appointment. It's very simple. All I have to do is stall this meeting on the subject of Earth and as soon as he gets a real Crown appointed, I'll simply hand it over to him as unfinished business and happily go back to the Fleet." He sighed. "That's a relief."

"I've got news for you," said the Countess Krak, and pushed into his hand a sheet of Royal proclamation paper. "When he left this conference tonight, he was so pleased with the way you had gotten things going, he wrote this. He asked me if I'd bring it back for the clerk to record."

Heller was staring at a signed and sealed sheet that appointed him first Lord of the land and Viceregal Chairman of the Grand Council. It was permanent.

He groaned. "This puts me in a bad dilemma, really. I spend a year putting a planet back together and now I have orders to blow it up."

"And you can't *weasel* out of it," said the Countess Krak. "The reason I am handing you this is so you don't do something silly and defy orders and get yourself in trouble."

"You had something to do with this," said Heller.

"No. Factually now, I didn't. He thought of it all on his own. But I will admit that it gives me great satisfaction. You are a factor of three beyond the expected life of a combat engineer. You now have a nice, safe post."

"In which all I have to do is say 'Blow up this planet,' 'Slaughter that one.' I'm going to put this conference on delay and go see Mortiiy and resign!"

"No, you won't," said the Countess Krak. "Because if you do, I'll tear up this." And she showed him another signed, sealed Royal order. It gave her back her title and citizenship and restored to her the vast Krak estates on Manco.

He hastily put his hand on hers to stop the tearing gesture. "But this is wonderful!" he said. "I am so happy for you!"

"I meant to tell you after this conference," she said, "to celebrate, I have even commandeered a palace for us." Tears were in her eyes. "Don't ruin it, Jettero."

He couldn't stand to see her cry.

He was conscious of the Homeview cameras that were suddenly on them.

The treaty was now being handed up by a violet-uniformed usher who laid it before him on the raised split-level of the vast table.

Heller thought fast. He had to hide her tears from the camera. He bent down and kissed her.

The backfeed monitors across the room brought him the sudden cheer from crowds watching him.

But he whispered, "Go get Hightee and the Master of Palace City and tell them I want to see them right away. And get out of here. You win. I will do my job."

A trifle uncertain, feeling a little bit like Nepogat the Damnable who had betrayed Prince Caucalsia in the legend, the Countess Krak hastily vanished down the back steps of the dais.

She was telling herself that nobody could prevent the destruction of Earth anyway and there was no reason to let it commit another crime and shatter her coming marriage. Besides, even though Jettero liked the place, she had always been horrified at the primitive decadence of that culture, never able to understand how a planet so potentially beautiful could be so rottenly mauled by an uncaring power elite.

As she walked away on her errand, she said to herself, "It is totally beyond salvation: all Voltar is thirsting for its blood, no thanks to Madison. To blazes with Earth. I have saved Jettero."

Chapter 2

Heller picked up the signed treaty and made a small gesture to the man on the balcony. Four trumpets and a crash of cymbals blasted through the vast hall.

Heller ranged his gaze across the throng. "Gentlemen," he said, "I wish to thank you for these concurring signatures on this treaty. I take it as a vote of confidence in the Emperor Mortiiy and regard it as an auspicious beginning to what even the most pessimistic must now begin to regard as a happy, prosperous and powerful reign auguring peace, tranquility and triumph for all the Voltar Confederation. All hail Mortiiy the Brilliant!"

The trumpets blared and the cymbals clashed in a Royal salute. Everyone in the room stood and shouted, "Long Live His Majesty!" The crowds in the streets, despite the hour, went mad with cheering.

Heller wished Vantagio, the political science major from the Gracious Palms, were there to give him some tips. This was all new to him. Poor Vantagio.

He handed the treaty to the clerk to record. He signalled for another cymbal clash.

"And now, as I am charged by His Majesty to do so faithfully, I here take up the second of the six actions to end past turmoils of this realm. To truly begin a new era, one must truly end the old."

He had thought to cheer the hall and crowds a bit and get them out of their thirst for blood. He had no liking for Lombar Hisst but neither did he want to see a man ripped to pieces physically by the two thousand or more people in this room. There had, in his opinion, been quite enough blood.

"We will now take up the case of one of the principal instigators of Royal murder and governmental decay."

The crowds on the monitors were suddenly silent. The room was still. Heller was about to bring in the product of his *horse trade*. "CAPTAIN! PRODUCE THE PRISONER LOMBAR HISST!"

Heller had ordered that Hisst be cleaned up and that he be ushered in without too much degradation. But common caution had modified his orders a bit.

A side door opened. Lombar Hisst was yanked forward. He was in a red general's uniform of the Apparatus. The only one they had evidently been able to find, since his own was scorched, had been taken off a corpse. The red was blackened by the darker, unmistakable stains of blood.

They had gotten somewhere, probably from Teenie's palace, an electric collar. It was around his neck. At the end of the chain was a burly Fleet marine. He gave a yank and Hisst stumbled forward into the glaring lights of Homeview. He looked for all the world like some ape being led on a leash.

Heller's hopes of calming the crowd down were all vanished in a puff.

The room screamed with sudden, savage hate!

The backfeed on the monitors sizzled with ferocity.

Then Heller saw that something was definitely wrong. Hisst was being tugged forward to be made to stand by the conference table, but there was something wrong with his eyes. They were always an animal yellow and a bit spooky but now they were flaring and strange.

Hisst came to a stop. He did not seem to be the least bit aware of the din that was damning him. He seemed to be speaking.

Heller called for silence and the cymbals had to sound five times before the shouts in the room ceased.

"Lombar Hisst," said Heller, "you have been brought before this Officers' Conference that you may be charged and may plead any justification for your acts. I have here a Royal proclamation on which we may write your fate which, I must advise you, is being left in the hands of this conference. I can, however, relegate you to a full trial if you have any statement which might persuade us to do so. Some mitigating circumstance..."

Heller paused, for during the whole time he had been speaking, Hisst had been mouthing words. He was not talking very loudly. Heller made a gesture to the captain of marines and the man produced a small electronic speaker and held it close to Hisst's mouth.

Hisst's voice was very strange. He was saying, "The angels are calling. Please give me a fix. Oh, hear what the angels say. Give me a fix. The angels are calling. Please give me a fix. Oh, hear what the angels say. Give me a fix...."

LOMBAR HISST WAS INSANE!

Chapter 3

The Grand Council hall was quiet with a strange hush.

Here and in the streets, over Homeview, people heard that eerie, babbling voice.

But there was no definable response. Heller breathed a sigh of relief, thinking this would come off all right after all. The people seemed distracted from the subject of Earth. Maybe, as they did not seem to be displaying ferocity toward Hisst, they had exhausted much of their frenzy. Now, if he could just keep them calm...

"Gentlemen," he said to the vast table, "I do not

think the prisoner is in any condition to answer charges and, as we all know the record, there is no point in another public trial. We know he sought to ascend the throne illegally and donned the robes of a monarch, so let us dispense with further formalities and find him guilty of that. Are you agreed?"

Heads nodded at the table. No voice was lifted in dissent. Heller took heart.

"I propose," and he turned to a clerk who was now on duty, signalling him to be very careful to inscribe what he was going to say, "that the proclamation cancels all his posts—assigned, assumed or otherwise. We shall cancel, as well, all orders, appointments, assumptions, manifestoes, proclamations, ordinances, instructions or regulations of whatever kind issued by him in writing, verbally or by others for him in their own names. We hereby cancel as well any and all pay, pay arrangements made by, for or on behalf of said subject, including all pledges and debts and any claim that could be made by him or on him. Agreed so far?"

The heads at the table nodded. Heller was simply amplifying a form common in courts-martial where an officer, found guilty of a felony of magnitude, was being dismissed from service.

Then, to this, Heller added the civil declaration used when a person was reprieved from execution without being found innocent. It was a nice touch, for Hisst had used this countless times on people for his own ends and, in fact, had used it on the Countess Krak. "He is hereby declared a nonperson. Anything he does may be declared or deemed illegal. Anything done to him is not actionable under law."

The clerk was writing busily. Heller thought with some elation that he was going to get away with this without another riot: the wrath against Earth seemed to have cooled off.

He said, "He would seem to be incapable of responding to routine communication. It seems obvious that he is not sane. Do you gentlemen agree?"

The officials at the board looked at Hisst. The marine captain had stepped away with the small voice amplifier: Hisst was just mouthing the same words as before. His eyes were weird, a sort of overbright yellow. The officials looked back at Heller and nodded.

"Therefore," said Heller, "the prisoner is relegated to the Confederacy Insane Asylum and is to remain there in custody for the remainder of his li——"

Suddenly Hisst whipped around. He roared in a deafening voice, "DOWN ON YOUR KNEES! DOWN ON YOUR KNEES, YOU RIFFRAFF! I AM THE GOD OF ALL THE HEAVENS!"

He had yanked the chain out of the hands of the marine! He held it in the air before him. "I WILL STRIKE YOU ALL DOWN! WORSHIP ME! WORSHIP ME!"

Any hope Heller might have had that the population would be less emotional about Earth suddenly went up in smoke.

The first whisper ran through the hall, "The man is mad!"

Then a louder voice: "Use of Earth material has driven him insane!"

Then, "Look what Earth can do!"

Then a screaming shout, "We've been in the hands of a man driven crazy by Earth!"

It all came in a building rush of sound. And it was capped by the howling shout from a thousand throats, "KILL HIM!"

The captain thought he had been ready. He was not.
He had had five marines surrounding Hisst.

The crowd hit them!

Daggers out, they stumbled back, trying to bar the
surge.

Twenty more marines charged in a phalanx, plowing
people away. They got to the crumbling circle.

Screaming people fought to get at Hisst to tear him
to bits.

The marines, blades held horizontally, fought to establish a ring.

People were going down, people were being tram-
pled, people howling with ferocity and rage still tried to
fight inward.

The trumpets and cymbals were blaring and clash-
ing for order.

A whistle in the mouth of the marine captain was
shrieking for reinforcements.

Fifty Domestic Police who had been stationed outside blasted through the door, stingers flashing.

Sparklewater bottles were being thrown.

Three hundred Fleet spacers armed with coils of
safety line rushed through the door swinging!

SHAMBLES!

Heller stood up. He got out his hand blastgun and
set it to maximum noise. He fired repeatedly into the air!
No result!

Then he saw through the hedge of tan uniforms that
still sought to defend the prisoner that Hisst was crawling toward this end of the room.

Heller went over the raised table in a headlong vault.

He used his arms as though he was parting waves.

The backs of the defending marines were to him.

He grabbed down and got Hisst by the collar.

He towed him free.

He crawled under the table, dragging his burden behind him.

Heller emerged back up on the dais.

Hisst swung at him.

Heller grabbed the man again in a paralyzing grip. He held him by the back of the collar.

"I GOT HIM!" shouted Heller in that piercing Fleet voice. "HE DIDN'T GET AWAY!"

A Homeview lighting man in a balcony hit him with a spot. The red uniform of Hisst was glaring bright.

Eyes in the room turned from battle and swung to the dais.

The twenty marines suddenly strung out in front of the split-level of the table, preventing further rush.

"THANK YOU ALL FOR YOUR ASSISTANCE!" shouted Heller. "BUT HE CAN'T ESCAPE AGAIN! I'VE GOT HIM!"

A sigh of relief came from the embattled throats.

The riot was over.

Chapter 4

A marine major wound Hisst round and round with chains and then, at Heller's whispered direction, wound them around some more. He carted Hisst off to an upper balcony and put him there with electric daggers pointed at his throat, on display and out of the reach of the crowd.

Army casualty teams were going through the hall, handling the injured and picking people up.

Heller sat back down in his chair. A voice sounded just behind him. "You just got a sample of what will happen if you try to give Earth an easy ride." It was the Countess Krak.

He turned. She had brought Hightee and the Master of Palace City. Heller went down the rear steps to them. He pulled their heads close to his and whispered some urgent instructions.

The Master said, "That's awfully short notice!"

"You better learn to open up your throttles, Master," said Hightee. "You're dealing with Jettero Heller. My brother wants it, he'll get it!"

"I did NOT say I would not do it!" said the wizened old man. "Crown and I have already got a good working arrangement going. I love it."

"That's better!" said Hightee. "We haven't got much time. COME ON!"

They rushed off, the Countess with them.

Heller sat back down in his chair and spent the next five minutes cursing Madison. These people were at overheat on the subject of planet Earth: "Mob hysteria" did not even begin to describe it.

He had six proclamations to issue: he had not even completed two of them.

The mop-up was still going on. It was all right. He needed the time. He became aware of somebody standing down below the raised end of the table.

It was Bis. He was laughing. "That's the first time I knew athletics went with that post," he said. "Giving a reason for the riot and then solving it to stop it is the funniest gag I think I've ever seen. You're a wonder, Jet!"

"You want this job, Bis?"

"Good Heavens! What could possibly be wrong with it?"

"Being expected to kill five billion people including friends is what's wrong with it. Here, I'll give you my tunic."

"Oh, no! But I suddenly see what you mean. Can I help?"

"Yes. Go up to that balcony and help that marine major prevent Hisst from doing anything else foolish. We're not through with him yet."

A medical Army general approached Heller and gave him the casualty figures as though this were a battle, not a conference. Because electric daggers had been set to paralyze, only knockouts and minor injuries had resulted. The general went back to the table. Heller glanced up to where they had Hisst in chains on the balcony, then he surveyed the room. He trusted passions were spent enough for him to finish this second proclamation.

He signalled for the cymbals and, when they clashed, he said in a rush, "If you will vote now on the Hisst proclamation as outlined so far, we can conclude this second——"

A violent waving of hands from the rear of the hall was accompanied by a protesting blast of shouts from there. Heller peered, then he sighed.

"Yes, Noble Stuffy," he called. "What now?"

Noble Arthrite Stuffy, a white bandage across his forehead now, surged once again up to a blank space at the conference table. "Crown, Your Lordship, sir," he said, "just half an hour ago, during the treatment of casualties, we received wonderful news. It greatly influences the sentence of Lombar Hisst."

Oh, no, thought Heller. But he said, "Tell me so we can get on with this."

"By use of our reporters and our newssheet-building

security guards, we have had the great good luck to run down and apprehend the so-called Doctor Crobe! We have him right outside. With your permission we will bring him in."

"What," said Heller, "does this have to do with Hisst?"

Noble Stuffy took that for assent and, at his signal, six watchmen brought in Crobe. He was no less a funny-looking creature than he had always been: his too-long arms, his too-long legs, his too-long nose as always made him look like a weird bird. But there was something even stranger now: instead of a crumpled captive, he was striding around like he owned the place. Before he could be stopped, he seized a chair at the table, sat down, crossed his arms and announced, "I am in charge! Take off your clothes!"

The audience gasped.

Heller looked more closely. Those weird eyes! Crobe was either high on some drug or insane—probably both!

"We have traced this man," said Noble Stuffy. "He was once employed by the government as a cellologist and was arrested for criminal misuse of cellology. He was condemned to death. He is a nonperson. Hisst used him to manufacture abominable freaks as was earlier revealed. But this was not the end of his career. He was shipped to the planet Blito-P3 and there studied *psychology* and *psychiatry*. He became an expert practitioner of these subjects and then was used by Madison for his unspeakable projects in the field of *PR*. It is our understanding that on the planet Earth, *psychology, psychiatry* and *PR* are inseparable."

"That is all very interesting," said Heller. "But please, Noble Stuffy, I wish to complete this second proclamation."

"And so do I," said Stuffy. "With the indulgence of this conference, as an influential member of the publishing world, I wish to propose that Crobe also be assigned to the Confederacy Asylum. And as he is a *psychiatrist,* supposedly expert in the treatment of the insane, I propose that Lombar Hisst be given to Crobe as a patient."

The audience gasped. Then it began to please them.

Heller unexpectedly blew up. Always an opponent of inhuman measures, he stood up and pointed a finger straight at Stuffy. "You have no idea of what you are proposing! Psychiatrists use tortures you have never even heard of! They drug their patients and send huge jolts of electricity through their brains to destroy nerve responses! And that isn't all! At a whim, they take a steel probe, push it under the eyelids and scramble the prefrontal lobes! They have no intention of curing anyone: they are simply making it impossible for the victim to get well. Ever! AND THEY KNOW IT!

"Psychiatrists say they do not believe in the soul but they work to destroy any soul a man may have. AND THEY KNOW THEY ARE DOING IT!

"I will not tolerate such an inhuman practice on anyone! Not even Hisst!"

Then he realized suddenly that he was worsening the cause of Earth. Abruptly he stopped speaking.

At the lower level of the table near him, he heard a Domestic Police general whisper to his aide, "See, Earth is so horrible even a seasoned officer cannot abide it!"

Heller stared at the backfeed monitors. He had also horrified the crowds.

Silently, he cursed. He had, without intending to, injured his chances of creating a better atmosphere for Earth.

But he was stubborn and he had his own principles. He sat down. "I will only tolerate this proposal if you modify it. Lombar Hisst will be sent to the asylum and so will Crobe. But they are to be placed in adjacent cells. They are to be held incommunicado: no one may speak to either of them, ever. I will NOT let *psychiatry* loose in the Confederacy Asylum!"

"But Crobe can talk to Hisst?" Stuffy persisted.

"Yes, but not touch him," said Heller.

"I get Your Lordship's point about not loosing *psychiatry* in the Confederacy Asylum," said Stuffy. "It would be a disaster. But so long as Crobe is permitted to 'treat' Hisst verbally, I am satisfied. I cannot possibly imagine a worse fate. Thank you."

Heller asked the table for assent and received it. He turned to the clerk and helped him complete the second proclamation. Then he sent it on its voyage for the additional signatures above the Emperor's.

At his signal, a group of Domestic Police took charge of Crobe. The man stood. He shouted, "You are all suffering from penis envy!" He was still shouting it as he was led away.

Another group of "bluebottles" approached the balcony.

Lombar Hisst was on his knees there. He was vomiting. The bluebottles gave the marine major a receipt. They slid Hisst into a black sack, put him on a stretcher and bore him away.

The proclamation, this time, since who should sign had been sorted out, made the round of the table quite quickly.

Heller got it back. He looked at it.

Two down, four to go.

Chapter 5

Heller said, "The conference has already passed a measure to abolish the Apparatus and the intelligence practices of Earth. However, the matter was not placed in proclamation form and finalized.

"His Majesty has stated that he does not wish to hear of the planet Earth again, ever. Therefore I propose, in concurrence with his wishes and requirements, that we word the proclamation as follows: 'The Coordinated Information Apparatus is abolished. Never in the future may there be a state organization, independent, devoted to the subject of intelligence.' But at this point, gentlemen, we could very easily get involved in the endless details of what Earth intelligence organizations are comprised of so that we could forbid them. And we would find ourselves mentioning the planet Earth in connection with them.

"As you know, the Army and the Fleet both have intelligence services, vital to the prosecution of a war. We do not know and have no time to untangle the various technologies of intelligence. I, for one, want to get these proclamations completed."

He got nods from the table.

"The abuses of the Apparatus were twofold. The first was recruiting criminals from the prisons to act as their personnel, and the second was to turn those vicious people loose on the population."

The instant he got it out, he knew he had made a

mistake. He had been trying to smooth out the wrath of the conference and the crowds. This analysis, while quite correct and succinct, pleasing enough to an engineer, was like throwing burning brands. It brought to vivid view all the horrors the population had been made to suffer.

Snarls in the hall and screams of rage in the streets seemed to indicate that the favored course of action right this minute would be to go find and kill any remaining Apparatus personnel. It looked like the riots were going to surge up all over again!

Vantagio, he mourned, I wish you were here instead of a target. He felt he was too green to cope with this sort of thing.

In mathematics, if you got an unexpected result, you sometimes had to use it. Maybe math would work. He would use the wrath.

He pulled out his gun and pantomimed shooting. He shouted, "WE WANT THE APPARATUS DEAD AND THIS IS HOW WE ARE GOING TO DO IT!"

It got attention.

They were listening eagerly.

"We word the proclamation that it is forbidden to use FOREIGN intelligence techniques upon the citizens of the Voltar Confederacy! And that the penalty for doing so shall be DEATH!"

It caught their fancy.

"And so that there won't be any question as to what is meant, I propose that in the proclamation we form a committee with a member from Army Intelligence, a member from Fleet Intelligence and a member from the Domestic Police, that we call it the Anti–Foreign Intelligence Committee with the duty of preventing such techniques from being used against the citizens of Voltar, that the committee have the duty of defining these, that it be placed at Grand Council level and that it be chaired by one who knows this scene and investigated it, namely Royal Officer Bis, suitably promoted. He HATES the Apparatus!"

There was a storm of applause in the hall and on the streets.

Heller bowed and sat down. He got his assent and he got the proclamation written and sent on its rounds.

He mopped at his forehead with his redstar engineer's rag.

There was a lot to this statecraft stuff. Intelligence services, no matter where, had a lot of things in common. If he had let the original proposal stand, forbidding anything known on Earth to be used by Voltar, it could have crippled Army and Fleet intelligence services, for they did many things similar to those of Earth. An intelligence service was an intelligence service. The thing wrong with the Apparatus—and the way they used the subject on Earth—was that it employed intelligence to repress their own domestic scene instead of enemies in war. And the result was that the government began to wage war on the citizens!

Three down and three to go. The next one would be tougher and the last one the worst of all!

Chapter 6

Heller called for a cymbal clash for silence.

"I know," he said, "that His Majesty wishes to begin his reign in an atmosphere of peace. It is his

dearest wish that his subjects be happy and content and
no longer disrupted by oppression and turmoil.

"Therefore, I propose, for this fourth proclamation,
an amnesty. First, I think we should include all the peoples of Calabar and anyone connected with the recent
revolt. This rescinds all rebel proclamations en masse
and also amnesties all persons on Calabar or connected
to the revolt for any crime of whatever kind as of Universal Star Time, two hours ago."

This seemed agreeable. Nobody was mad at Calabar
now. It also got General Whip off the hook without mentioning it.

Heller thought for a bit. This was going to get tricky
now. He was going to have to try to amnesty the Apparatus troops: otherwise, in bands here and there and,
within the population, incidents would continue to take
toll. He knew even proposing it could start another wave
of ferocity, maybe even killing.

He looked at a Domestic Police general at the conference table. "How long do you think it would take to
round up and try any and all persons who might have
damaged property or persons in these recent riots? I am
speaking now of the rioting citizens."

He could see the instant reaction on the monitors of
the crowds. It had not occurred to anyone that their
actions might be charged as crimes.

The Domestic Police general scrubbed at his face
with a beefy hand. "Well, Crown, Your Lordship, sir, I
am ashamed to say that it will take years. You see, we
have to reorganize the Domestic Police. Many units
joined the rioters. That will require a vast number of
arrests and trials in itself. We were hoping to discuss getting some help from the Army."

"But at the same time," said Heller with a frown, "didn't you plan on a general roundup, using what units you had intact? You know, herding citizens into stockades and holding them for weeks, maybe trying them en masse? But I was worried about how you were going to manage a house-to-house search through all the cities to round up everyone who had been actively rioting."

The crowds on the monitors were ominously silent.

"Well," said the Domestic Police general, scrubbing his face some more, "if we had help from the Army we could begin that right away."

The crowds were starting to growl. This conference was talking about THEM!

"General," said Heller, "I am assured by His Majesty that his love for his subjects is boundless. I think, to celebrate his ascension, a Confederacy-wide amnesty should be extended to all persons, regardless of crime, as of two hours ago, Universal Star Time."

The yell began very slowly and then in the streets it swelled, "Long Live Mortiiy!"

Heller felt he had it made. He was just turning to dictate the fourth proclamation when this (bleeped) bluebottle general spoiled it. He said, aghast, "You mean all the persons in jails and prisons, too?"

"Except persons already handled, such as Gris, Madison and his crew, Crobe and Hisst. It must also include a clause so that His Majesty is not constricted in removing any Lords, officials or officers he might have to, to form a new government. We should also forbid further punishment of these people, as the last thing we want is a civil war on our hands."

The bluebottle was stuck with his prisons. "But good Heavens, that would empty everything we've got!"

"They're too full anyway," said Heller.

"But some of those people committed terrible crimes!"

"I'll tell you what," said Heller. "For any already condemned criminal, we could make the condition that he must accept the amnesty with a promise to commit no more crimes, and he must be told and it must be part of the amnesty that if he or she does commit one more felony, the immediate sentence is death. I assure you that many will reform. The amnesty does not include insane asylums, as they wouldn't even understand."

The bluebottle was still goggle-eyed about it and Heller would have pushed on further except that another police general at the table spoke up.

"That amnesties all the Apparatus personnel!"

That did it. The table began to snarl. The crowds, all pleased a moment ago, starting shrieking "Death to the Apparatus."

Heller felt like telling him, you fool, there are still two or three million Apparatus people on the loose: you're going to tie up your whole police force running them down for years! We're going to have more riots, more burning buildings. . . .

He gave a signal and the trumpets and cymbals went. It took a while before he could speak again.

"Then I propose," he said, "that any ex-Apparatus personnel found engaged in any criminal act after the amnesty may be shot down *in situ*."

"I never heard of that. It sounds bad!"

"Oh, it is bad!" said Heller. "It's an ancient custom of Flisten. We'll put it right in the proclamation. Worse, we'll also add *in flagrante delicto!* That's terrible."

"But I don't know what those words mean!" cried the general.

"You can look it up later," said Heller. "There are

ladies in the crowds to which Homeview is bringing this conference. Take my word for it, it's terrible. I know this is very harsh, gentlemen."

The Domestic Police people were frowning. One of them said, "But——"

"And I was going to add, 'And to protect people's homes, the Army is to assist the police until they are reorganized and public calm prevails,'" Heller said quickly.

The Army looked surprised, then purposeful. The Domestic Police, all too aware of their shattered condition, looked suddenly pleased.

Heller knew he had the table now: that left the people in the streets and homes that were watching.

He lifted his head. The cameras were upon him. "His Majesty was very unwilling to begin his reign with any of his subjects in trouble. There will be plenty of work for everyone rebuilding buildings and parks that have been damaged. Why, I should think Calabar alone could absorb any person unemployed or newly released into the world: every city there needs to be rebuilt, quite in addition to all the construction that will be needed on every other planet in the Confederacy. His Majesty, I know, wishes to lift his whole domain of 110 planets to a grandeur never before known.

"Every person who accepts this amnesty must be told that he owes this chance to Mortiiy and that all he requires from them in return is their loyalty and their help to make this a better nation."

The crowds in the streets began to cheer.

The cameras were not now on him. He wiped his face with his redstar engineer's rag.

It had been close. He'd tell the police and Army later that *in situ* simply meant "on the spot" and *in flagrante delicto* only meant "caught in the act," if he remembered rightly.

At least he had now prevented further riots. Beneficial in its own right and necessary, it happened to be vital, if his luck held, that the name of Earth did not crop up again because of continued battling with the Apparatus: they would be utterly desperate if they thought they would be going back to prison.

Four down. Two to go. The next one would have to be quite clever. The last one, if things went wrong, would be awful.

Chapter 7

Heller heard someone back of his chair. It was the Countess Krak. She whispered, "Hightee says to tell you to stall all you can. They are in short time."

He nodded. The fourth proclamation wasn't back to him yet. He wondered how he could stall further.

Krak said, "I heard that measure. Why did you let all the criminals loose?"

"Gris wasn't the only person with a blackmail hoard. It prevents Apparatus officers from starting up in the crime business."

She didn't make too much sense out of his reply; she also detected an evasion. "You must have had another reason than that."

"Be quiet."

"But you released several million criminals on the society. Why?"

"The state has been corrupt and justice slipshod." He turned and looked at her steadily. "All right. Remember, you asked for it. You might not be the only Lissus Moam."

She caught her breath. He was alluding to herself having been a falsely condemned nonperson until just today. Tears started into her eyes. "You did it for me. To celebrate my regaining citizenship."

"Go away. You don't like softhearted people."

"I am ashamed. I love you, Jettero!"

"Well, don't hang around here being *mushy*. Go help Hightee and maybe we can save our friends. A forlorn hope, but maybe."

She suddenly kissed him. "May the Gods bless you, Jettero."

The crowds cheered. The kiss had been camera'd on Homeview. The Countess Krak was gone.

Heller muttered, to the monitors across the room, "You wouldn't be cheering if you knew I was trying to save your favorite enemy, Earth. Well, it's all up to mathematics now."

The fourth proclamation had been handed to the clerk for recording. He had stalled all he could. He stood up and signalled for a cymbal clash.

"Gentlemen, we earlier passed an informal resolution to outlaw *psychology* and *psychiatry*. I wish to incorporate that in the fifth formal proclamation which we are now about to take up. His Majesty has stated that he does not wish to hear of Earth again. If we put these subjects in a public proclamation, we will have to mention Earth and it could come to his attention. Furthermore, the names have already appeared in newssheets.

"It would seem to me that this is best covered by acceding to a demand made by the publishers who wish

to be protected against things such as lying stories and
that other Earth development, *PR*."

There was a snarl from the conference table. They
were avid to suppress anything connected with that
planet.

"I therefore propose," said Heller, "that we create
the post of Censor. Such a post, appended to the staff
here at Palace City, could prevent *psychiatry* and *psychology* texts from being published. It could also prevent
abuses under the heading of *PR*.

"Actually, I should think that the post really com-
bines with that of Royal Historian." He got table nods
in assent. "Could someone please advise me, since the
Palace City staff has been so displaced, who occupies
that post now?"

He already knew the answer. He was laying a trap.
The clique of publishers over there was nodding, all
agreeable.

A clerk stood. "Crown, Your Lordship, sir. The post
of Royal Historian was held by one who, unfortunately,
resisted the demands of Lombar Hisst. He is dead. The
post is vacant."

"Oh, woe!" said Heller. "A martyr! Well, that leaves
us with no other choice!"

They stared at him.

"One man is a public spirited citizen. He knows all
the angles of this. He has already proven his zeal by
bringing the matter to our attention. For the post of
Royal Historian and Censor and Chairman of any Board
of Censors, I propose Noble Arthrite Stuffy!"

Noble Stuffy, far across the room in the group of publishers, recoiled. "But . . . but . . . my publishing empire!"

"Oh, well," said Heller, "we all have to make our little sacrifices for the good of the people. I am sure you

can find somebody to run your paper for you." He drew himself up. "The state needs your services, Noble Arthrite Stuffy! And think how you can set an example with your paper! Think how you can uplift and uphold the purity of ethics in journalism!" He lowered his voice, "And think how thoroughly you can suppress all efforts to corrupt the population with *psychiatry* and *psychology.*"

Several other publishers grinned. The *Daily Speaker* had run the most columns lauding those subjects. They were pushing Stuffy toward the table.

Noble Stuffy finally stood in a vacant place. "Crown, Your Lordship, sir, even at great financial sacrifice, I cannot let the people down. I accept the appointment."

"There is one proviso," said Heller, severely, "I do not much hold with censorship to hide state errors or oppress dissident voices just because the state has been stupid. Where censorship is really needed is to protect the individual person against a river of manufactured lies and to protect the public from being stampeded by unprincipled villains such as Madison and Hisst. Your duty must never include the suppression of the truth. So DO NOT ABUSE THIS POST!"

There were cheers.

"I take it, then, the appointment is ratified?" said Heller.

The officers at the table gave their assent.

"Now, if you gentlemen will make room at the table for our new Royal Historian and Censor, I can have this proclamation drawn up and we can complete the signatures."

Number five. He had gotten number five! It was the key in his equation.

He offered up a prayer. Now to set the stage for
number six, the fatal one, the one which would deter-
mine whether five billion people, including his friends,
would live or die. Number six would deal with the fate
of Earth!

PART
EIGHTY-NINE

Chapter 1

A whisper behind his chair began the last fateful action of that fatal night. "Hightee and the Master say that they are ready now." It was the Countess Krak, and she promptly slipped away.

Aware that five billion lives, some of them his friends, and the future of a planet, Earth, would be determined in these coming minutes, Jettero Heller, combat engineer, not yet used to his new identity as the first Lord of the land, rose out of his chair on the dais and surveyed the turbulent room.

The crowd in the Grand Council hall had swollen to nearly three thousand people. The crowds in the streets, visible on the backfeed monitors against the far wall, had not decreased but had increased.

The new Emperor, Mortiiy, as was the custom, was leaving the conduct of the affairs of state to his Viceregal Chairman of the Grand Council, normally called Crown.

Heller drew a long breath. It was up to him now. This would be the final stroke. He must not let down Mortiiy. He must not let down Voltar. Thin as it was, he still hoped there was some chance for Earth: if he failed now, the planet would be utterly destroyed forever.

He gave his gold tunic a tug and called for a cymbal clash. Into the expectant silence he said, "Gentlemen, it is my pleasure to announce that in the nearby park, my charming sister, Hightee Heller, and the Master of Palace City have arranged an entertainment for you. I suggest, and indeed request, that you avail yourselves of this invitation and repair now to that place, leaving here only the heads of the military and our new Censor."

Nobody moved. It was a bad sign.

A voice from the back of the room called, "Crown, Your Lordship, sir! Could I call to your attention that you have not taken up the last proclamation, the destruction of the hideous Blito-P3, Earth."

He had been afraid of that. Everything depended on having no witnesses, and even then he might not pull it off.

"It is true," said Heller, "that that is what we are going to take up now. But this Officers' Conference is now scaled down to a war council. Clear the room!"

"No, no!" the people were shouting throughout the hall. "We want to hear!"

Heller scowled at them and at the flickering cameras. "We have no guarantee that Earth has no spies on Voltar. If the enemy were permitted access to every war council, we would lose every war. CLEAR THE ROOM!"

Cries sprang up. "What are you going to do?"

"We are going to plan and order executed the disposition of Blito-P3, Earth. These are matters of strategy, tactics, military orders and logistics. Such discussions are not and never will be open to the public. BUT we have provided entertainment for you while we discuss and issue our orders. There are only fifteen hundred seats set up in the park; there are close to three thousand people here: I suggest you rush unless you want to stand."

There was an instant exodus from the hall.

Heller carefully made sure that he only had the

heads of the Army and Fleet general staffs left at the
table. He indicated Bis should stay. He beckoned to a
door and Captain Tars Roke, arrived only an hour before
from Calabar, slid in and took a place. Heller sternly told
Arthrite Stuffy to sit back down when he showed a disposition to leave.

The Homeview director rushed up to the dais.
"Please, Crown, Your Lordship, sir, can't I just leave one
camera here? What you're taking up is historical!"

"No!" said Heller.

"Yes!" said the director.

"I have just begun to feel my privacy itch," said Heller. "In exactly ten seconds I will begin to think it has
been invaded. GET OUT OF HERE!"

The director fled in fright.

Heller sent the guards, attendants and clerks away.
He walked across the hall and barred the door himself—
from within.

Chapter 2

The only sound in the vast place now came from the
bank of Homeview monitors which remained, feeding
back shots taken by camera crews through the Confederacy. Two new monitors lit up, showing the scene in the
nearby park. A stage had been erected. There was a ring
of tanks and cannon. The people were filing into the
tiers of seats.

Heller went back to the immense conference table:

the five men there seemed small after the multitude which had just been crowding the room.

He gave Captain Roke a warm handshake.

"I am so glad to see you back alive, Jet, and out of the hands of 'drunks.' I was surprised to get your summons: I was dismissed, you know."

"Captain," said Heller, "welcome back to post as the King's Own Astrographer. Aside from my joy at seeing you again, you are the greatest authority in the Confederacy on the Invasion Timetable. Now gentlemen, if you will scrunch up a bit toward the dais, I don't think we'll feel so lost."

The five moved their seats and Heller took his place back on the dais. The men were close to him now.

"Gentlemen," said Heller, "we are met as a war council, senior to the Officers' Conference, to take up the disposal of the planet Blito-P3. We will write the Royal proclamation concerning its fate. His Majesty has stated that he never wants to hear of it again, ever."

"He can't help but hear of it," said Captain Roke. "It's on the Invasion Timetables. Does this thing work?" He pressed some buttons under the board edge. The console before his seat flared up. He pushed another button and a huge display, sixty by ninety feet, glowed in the face of the horizontal expanse.

"There," said Captain Roke, "you see the scheduled Voltar invasions plotted for the next hundred thousand years. They take us as near to the habitable center of this galaxy as you can get. I am sorry, Jet my dear boy, and I am truly touched at your thinking of your old teacher and giving me my post back. I would like to show my appreciation. But neither I nor anyone else can fiddle about with the Invasion Timetables. Our forefathers charted them ages ago, even before the first colonists departed from the old galaxy. These tables are balanced against expected consolidation time of new acquisitions: there is no possibility, then, of overextension.

"There, right close to the top, you see Blito-P3. I'll admit that it is not the most important target on the table: it's an oddity in that there is only one inhabitable planet in the system. Militarily, it would be of minor use in jump-offs to other targets later on, and even though it isn't vital, still, there it is. The invasion ... let's see ... yes ... 115 years from today."

"And the tables have never been changed?" said Heller.

"No, my boy. Your ancestors and mine were pretty competent people. The only changes which have occurred have been to delay a bit or advance the times. And that's what you're doing right now: advancing the time."

"We're supposed to dispose of it. Has there ever been an occasion when a planet was simply blown up?"

"Ah, yes," said Captain Roke. "Chippo. But we didn't blow it up. About thirty thousand years ago. I'll retard the screen here. See the blank? Before conquest, it developed thermonuclear devices in the absence of political stability and suffered a nuclear war that resulted in a core-boil. That was the end of it. It's on the charts now just as a mass of debris with 'spacer avoid' buoys in its orbit."

The Fleet admiral said, "Well, good. There's a precedent, then, for a planet being blown off the invasion table. We're safe in that. It doesn't much matter whether it did it to itself or we did it, a target can be removed."

"But I have a problem here," said Heller. "The main object His Majesty must have had in mind was a prevention of further contamination from this planet.

I don't know of any way to blow it up without landing on it."

"You are correct," the senior admiral said. "We don't have any missiles of a power to simply stand off and shoot. You have to insert charges at the inner face of the crust."

"That will require an army landing," said the general. "All due respect to you, Crown, Your Lordship, sir, as a very capable combat engineer, you yourself couldn't get in there with enough explosives and drills to do it. It would require a landing in force by army troops to safeguard units of engineers. Such a landing, even with Fleet sky cover, would be opposed. Battle would be inevitable and we would, as you have pointed out, be liable to contamination. The only solution I could offer is suicide battalions."

Heller was not pleased. "I don't like suicide battalions."

"Well, if we are going to avoid contamination, we can't land troops and bring them back. So it has to be suicide battalions."

"Let's review," said Heller, "His Majesty's instructions." And he turned on a playback button under the table edge and raced a strip back to Mortiiy. The voice of Mortiiy came forth. The six now present heard once more his exact commands.

"I never want to hear of Blito-P3 again! NEVER!" and then, "Use one of those blank orders to dispose of Blito-P3, Earth, any way you see fit."

Heller turned it off. "He gave me six, obviously intending the whole current situation to be calmed down. And this," he picked it up, "is the fatal number six. And it's an awful problem. You say suicide battalions, General. But the opposition might be very fierce.

I think the Apparatus had a force of two and a half million men being staged for that invasion. You wouldn't venture that many as suicides. Further, the Fleet might have to land to back the Army and engineers up. That's real contamination! This is a dilemma!"

"Well," said the general, "if we don't do something, we'll be in deliberate violation of orders."

Noble Arthrite Stuffy spoke up. "I can assure you that if no action is taken against Earth, the population will boil right over! Look at the hour of the night! The sunlit side and the dark side of this planet both have streets packed with people. Just examine those monitors there. I'm no military man, but your problem right this minute is not with suicide battalions. It's with a possible renewal of riots! That's a very nasty mood those crowds are in."

"We do thank you for your learned opinion," said Heller. He forbore to mention the role Stuffy had played in helping bring those crowds to boil. "I see on those end monitors that they're just about ready to start their entertainment. Let's watch it. Maybe we'll get an inspiration."

Chapter 3

An open end and backstage had been erected in the park, actually just a platform. Fifteen hundred seats had been erected in tiers at one side, but open space near them permitted thousands more to stand.

Three huge military bands—Army, Fleet and Palace

City—assembled on short notice, stood before and to either side of the platform. Just now, the center one—Fleet—of more than a hundred pieces, was playing "Spaceward Ho!" The floodlights sparkled on their instruments: the flash of the conductor's electric gloves pulsed in cadence as he directed them.

Then there was a long note and to its strident call, Hightee Heller marched upon the stage and the piece continued. A spotlight hit her as she marched. She wore a very daring version of an Army uniform but on her head, cocked to the side, was the dress cap of a Fleet officer. She was carrying the electric dagger of a Fleet marine.

She marched once across the stage and then made an imperious gesture. She turned and, as she marched back, up the left side steps behind her came a chorus in Army uniforms. At that moment the music changed to an Army battle song—the Army band was playing.

They paraded all the way across the stage and Hightee stopped again. She turned and up the right side steps behind her marched a chorus dressed as Fleet marines. The Palace City band joined in playing the marine battle charge.

Hightee marched to center stage and faced audience front. The Fleet band began to play "Spaceward Ho!" again. Hightee walked forward and up the steps behind her came a chorus dressed as spacers of the Fleet.

The only backdrop was the stars. The lights on Hightee and the three choruses were flashing in a marching beat. Homeview cameras flickered. The show was being carried to the packed streets and meeting places and the homes of the Confederacy. Aside from the interest of the moment, who would not watch and listen to Hightee Heller?

The routines being done by the choruses so hastily flown in from Homeview studios in Joy City were very standard routines they all knew well. But Heller was amazed she had been able to assemble it so fast. A swell of pride in his sister rose up in him: so very, very much depended on her success with this. He wondered if she had managed the near impossible and gotten the song written and fitted to music and practiced. He found he was holding his own breath.

Then suddenly all three choruses fanned into a solid line behind her, facing front, and began to mark time in place. Hightee threw a switch on her electric dagger, putting it to full intensity, and lunged.

Abruptly all three bands played a long and ominous note.

The dagger swept down, spitting sparks. And then three bands began to play, conducted by swirls of fire from the dagger, a savage piece of music.

They played through the whole tune once, Hightee conducting. Then a scarlet, pulsing spotlight hit her, and she began to sing with that searing, surging music:

We'll end off our invasion
From the culture of contagion
And blow the offending planet from the sky!
You'll find our guns quite warm,
But you've no time to reform,
Or even to request the reason why!
Your psychology *bends wills,*
Your psychiatry *just kills,*
Your drugs *that cause convulsions*
All must die!
You should have taken warning
In your very day of borning,

When you saw yourself begin to putrefy!
We'll now use all our exterminant
To blast you from the firmament
And all your tricks of spying won't apply!
We won't meet you later on,
For you'll have no other dawn.
Earth, you won't be missed!
GOOOOOOD–BYE!

There was a huge cymbal BANG from the band that went along with the last "Bye!"

But that didn't finish the song by a long way. In fact, the program was just starting.

Suddenly the first line of the song appeared against the stars by electronic projection so all the audience could see them and they could appear on the Homeview screens.

With a swirl of the dagger Hightee began to direct the three choruses. They sang and the words, blood-red, appeared in lines against the stars. They sang the whole song through again.

They came to the last cymbal bang. Hightee swept the flaming dagger to indicate the Palace City audience. She called out her command, "SING IT, EVERY-BODY!"

She and the choruses began, the words appeared against the sky, line by line. But this time she was direct-ing the audience, cupping her ear, beckoning them to sing, forcing them to sing, demanding that they sing!

The song came through to the cymbal clash again. Hightee cried, "Now everybody on Homeview! SING! SING! SING IT!"

She and the choruses, the Palace City park audience

and now everywhere in the Confederacy, even on delay—
she had them singing that song.

And they were singing it with a wave of hate!

Noble Arthrite Stuffy looked at Heller. "Did you
know she was going to do this? She'll drive those crowds
insane, straight back into riots!"

He didn't get any answer from Heller and turned to
look with horror once more at the screens. In here you
also got the backfeed from the crowds and mobs and,
truly, they were singing the song with a screaming ferocity that made Stuffy's blood run chilled. Even the
faces were contorted. Fists were shaking. The mobs were
going crazy!

The cymbal clash again. And Hightee cried,
"Louder, louder! You're singing about an enemy, not a
friend! SING IT!" And she started the song again,
words appearing across the sky:

We'll end off our invasion . . .

The roar of the voices, increased in volume, from
the nearby park swelled into the Grand Council hall.
The sound from the monitors themselves began to reach
toward hysteria.

The final bang of the song.

"Oh!" cried Hightee, "you can do better than that!
I am here in a park in Palace City, Voltar. I want to hear
your voices all the way from Flisten! SING, SING,
SING IT!"

"Good Gods," said Stuffy, "here come more riots! I
can feel it! Can't you stop her?"

"Stop my sister Hightee?" said Heller. "Never been
able to. Can't start now."

We'll end off our invasion
From the culture of contagion
And blow the offending planet from the sky!
You'll find our guns quite warm...

And on it went through again.

And then again.

And then again!

Anyone in the whole Confederacy who was anywhere near a Homeview screen was singing that song!

It was swelling from the planets in a hymn of hate!

Hightee, an expert in judging audience reactions from the stage, was putting the whole Confederacy through it and through it and through it again to obtain the exact effect which she was watching for. She took them up to frothing with that savage music and then took them beyond it.

Then, signalling with an electronic clicker held in her other hand, the words ceased to appear in the sky. But everyone knew them by this time and the music and singing continued.

Against the stars, a small dot appeared. The choruses put their backs to the audience and began to march in place, but looked like they were marching forward.

The whole audience felt they were approaching that small dot for it was getting larger.

Bigger and bigger the dot enlarged, until it was a sphere. Then bigger and bigger the sphere became until it was a planet.

And there the planet was, right before them, swirling against the night.

Heller blinked. Krak must have given them an approach shot from his files. It WAS the planet Earth! The filmy liquidness of it, like a huge blue, white and red bubble, was hanging there spinning, but too slowly to be detected. The shot had been taken from the sun side: Europe and North America were both reddishly visible on either side of the cloud-strewn ocean. The yellowish moon was even there, peeping from behind the equator. Although the picture strip had been taken from thousands of miles up, the three-dimensional illusion now appeared to hang just beyond and above the stage.

Seeing it made him feel a bit bitter. It was such a nice planet: too bad they had made so little use of the heritage Prince Caucalsia had given them—that made so many things similar culturally between Voltar and Earth. Too bad they valued it so little. It was a shame they had been so corrupted by their own primitives they had permitted themselves to go so far astray. The clutter of *isms* and hates could all be solved if they just realized that only a handful of men were using them for personal exploitation: their political creeds were just nonsense and lies manufactured for the benefit of the few, while pretending that they answered the demands of the many. And the way that culture was fixated on material possessions as a single concentration excluded it from attainment of the real and valuable things in life. A can of soup was equated on their communication lines—measured by volume of minutes—far, far more important than a man's soul.

Well, there it was, huge against the stars.

Hightee gave a signal. The music changed to the martial clamor of attack.

She cried, "Each one of you at your seat will find a pistol. GET THEM IN YOUR HANDS!"

There was an instant scramble in the tiers of seats. Yes, pistols were hanging there. They were of the type that makes only flash and noise.

Hightee drew one from her own belt. The choruses also drew. She pointed at the electronic illusion of the planet. The choruses also pointed. She yelled, "START SHOOTING!"

In a blaze of fire the choruses and audience began the barrage!

The music rose in volume. The shots began to hammer in cadence! The target was the Earth against the stars!

The music again rose in volume.

Unseen before but suddenly illuminated, a circular row of tanks appeared. They began to fire with their main turret guns, pounding at the planet with smoke and flame.

Then at a sweeping signal, an outer ring of cannon suddenly sprang into view, manned by actual gunners. They began to belch huge salvos at the target.

The music rose in fury.

Hightee gave another signal.

By optical illusion, a vast Voltar Fleet appeared all around the planet in the sky. They added a new thunder of guns to the deafening din.

Under the impact of this pounding, ABRUPTLY, WITH A DREADFUL BANG, THE PLANET BLEW TO BITS!

There was a sound like a dying scream.

There was a guttering rumble.

Something small and charred seemed to fall upon the stage.

It lay there sizzling: a small, dead, shrivelled, smoking thing.

The music suddenly shifted to a dirge.

The dirge was slow and it was awful.

A blue spotlight hit the sizzling thing. All other lights were gone.

Then, bathed in blue and with a solemn pace, thirty priests came forward from the dark.

With motions of timeworn solemnity, assisted by black burial servants who tonged the object into an open grave, the priests went through, with dirge choir music, the whole long litany of burial.

A scarlet devil suddenly appeared and scooped up what would appear to be a shrivelled, blackened soul. He turned and dumped it into a flaming pit of a Hell.

The lights were gone. Hightee was gone. The stage was empty and there was only the moan of the cold desert wind.

Chapter 4

"Gods," said Noble Arthrite Stuffy in more of a groan than a word. He daubed at his forehead, found it was still bandaged. He clenched his hand. "Oh, I really think that ruined it," said Noble Arthrite Stuffy. "I have never seen a population rise to such a fever pitch!"

"Look at the backfeed monitors," said Heller.

They all did.

The crowds in the streets were thinning.

THE PEOPLE WERE GOING HOME!

"I don't understand," said Stuffy.

"I think what you don't understand," said Bis, "is the business of a combat engineer. As a favor, Jet, tell us."

"You really want to know?"

The general and admiral and Captain Roke nodded

eagerly. They did not understand why the crowds were dispersing.

Heller sighed. Then he said, "I set it up with Hightee. And she certainly carried through. The credit is hers. All I did was take advantage of a cautionary theorem in Advanced Symbolic Logic: *The apparency of an answer can be mistaken for the answer.* A parallel is that *the apparency of a result can be mistaken for the result.* This once, it seems to have worked. The bulk of the people of the Confederacy will now think of Earth as dead. Those who don't won't be able to find anybody else all that interested.

"If you noticed, Hightee even let them sing too long. They got tired of it. They have also worked their spleen out quite thoroughly. I trust we have replaced mass hysteria with mass agreement, and *mass agreement is the true substance of reality.* Frankly, it's only combat engineer elementary mathematics."

"Wait," said Stuffy. "Completely aside from the fact that we have not handled Earth at all and now must, what you did seems like molding mass opinion. This seems very close to 'public relations.' Are you sure this isn't like Madison's *PR?*"

Bis let out a snort. "Noble Stuffy," he said, "Fleet combat engineers have been defeating and stampeding mobs of enemy people since before Madison's race learned to wear fur pants. Just yesterday, Jet defeated fifty thousand Apparatus troops in this very city, using a population-control weapon, all by himself. How'd you think we retook the place with no real casualties or destruction?"

Stuffy gawped. "I didn't know that."

"NOT for publication," said Heller. He looked again at the backfeed monitors. The people were indeed going home. And even as he looked, a couple monitors went blank as Homeview camera crews in far cities began to pack up. "We've chilled the mobs. Now let's get to work on the sixth proclamation and decide just how we are going to dispose of the *real* Earth. Unfortunately, it is NOT an electronic illusion and His Majesty has given us our orders."

Chapter 5

It was very quiet in the hall now. The backfeed monitors were going off, one by one. The main channel program now concerned weather for the coming day. At the table it threatened to be stormy.

The six sat there, a small group in this vast expanse. Heller was no longer sitting on the dais. He had taken a place at the table to be closer to them.

The Fleet admiral scrubbed his jowls. He was surveying his own console as he fed displays to it, displays which concerned the military potentials of the planet Blito-P3. "Looking at these factors, the satellites they have and so on, I think we're left no option but to blow it up: they could develop space travel."

"Technically, they might," said Heller, "though they would have to overcome gross faults in their sciences. Socially, they won't. Only two things motivate their thinking: one is commerce, the other is war. Their power elite could not see any commercial advantage in space travel, and the moment such research does not lead to internal superiority in war they curtail it.

"But actually, there is another factor which defeats them at every turn and that is an oddity in leadership. Even a casual study of their history shows that they only worship and obey leaders who kill: *Caesar, Napoleon, Bismarck, Hitler, Eisenhower* are just a few names. They revere scientists the same way: the biggest known names basically made it possible to build the biggest weapons. *Einstein,* for instance. It's a pretty primitive attitude.

"They actually revile and degrade and kill decent men who try to help them. It's as much as your life is worth to try to do anything for them that will benefit all.

"I doubt they could attain space travel before such ills as bad leadership, *socialism,* inflation and other things ate them up internally. They are actually totally incapable of doing something nationally just because it is the sensible thing to do or because it's fun. It always has to have a twist, such as who can make a million from it or who will it do in. They're pretty mixed up. As for achieving real space travel, I don't think you have a thing to worry about."

But he had not made his point. The admiral said, "Blast! No wonder the Emperor wants them disposed of!"

"When Jet was down there," said Captain Roke, "I got interested in the place and looked it up more thoroughly—though I will admit that Hisst was sitting on the key surveys. I worked out the routes to other systems that are targeted and I couldn't find one that had to go through Blito: it's a yellow-dwarf but it is off the direct traffic tracks. I was appalled by its social structure, really, and although I laughed at Jet at first when he said Prince Caucalsia might have taken some of the Voltar civilization to it, I think Jet must be right. It's a clutter of primitive and modern, but the think they use in utilizing the modern is primitive. They'll blow up culturally before they ever get to a stage of real space travel. So if it *were* disposed of, it really would have no key effect on anything else we were doing."

"Well, then," said the general, "I don't see why the Fleet can't just transport several Army biological warfare units to the upper atmosphere and we lay in a barrage of germs and defoliants and just bullet-ball the place: no landing."

"There are always survivors," said Heller. "And it would leave it on the Invasion Timetable."

"Jet is right," said the admiral. "I'd hate to put marines in there 115 years from now if bacterial warfare were used. Bugs mutate. No telling what diseases we'd be bringing back to Voltar: we'd have *real* contamination. But what I don't like about any of this is the disturbance to our operating schedules: we're committed to another invasion—Colipin—next month. And if you start deranging schedules, you wind up falling behind. We, frankly, would have to use several home-based fleets for any attack on Blito-P3, and they're needed for normal defense, especially with the recent unsettled conditions. I imagine quite a few Apparatus units escaped and will be into piracy without having heard of the amnesty. You can't double patrols with less ships."

"We're short, too," said the general. "Having to assist the Domestic Police will absorb available Army reserves."

"Well, let's see where we stand," said Heller. "The Emperor does not want to hear of Blito-P3 again and we've got to dispose of it to get it off the Invasion Timetable. If we land on it to attack, we risk further contamination of Voltar."

"My Gods, this is a dilemma," said the admiral.

"It certainly is," said the general.

Heller's heart was beating very fast but he kept his face quite calm. Would he get away with it? He picked up the sixth proclamation.

"Well, gentlemen," he said with a sad shake of his head, "the only way I can see out of this is simply to proclaim that Blito-P3, Earth, doesn't exist."

There was a stunned shock.

They thought it over.

Heller waited with bated breath.

The general looked at him. The admiral looked at him. Captain Roke looked at him. Bis looked at him. Noble Arthrite Stuffy looked at him. Their eyes were round.

Hastily Heller wrote the possible text:

ROYAL PROCLAMATION
VOLTAR CONFEDERATION
SECRET

In that the planet Blito-P3, Earth, has been found to possess elements of criminality inimical to the best interests and culture of Voltar,

In that the landing of troops upon it would risk further contamination of the Confederacy,

In that it is our Royal command that we never hear of the planet, Blito-P3, Earth, again,

The planet is officially declared to be a nonplanet.

> *It is therefore proclaimed that said planet*
> *DOES NOT EXIST AND IT WILL NOT*
> *EXIST FROM THIS DAY FORWARD FOR*
> *VOLTAR, FOREVER!*

They read it. It was the only way out. They began to nod.

A surge of elation went through Heller.

He had won! He had won for Izzy and Bang-Bang and Babe and five billion people.

He lowered his head so they would not see his grin and hastily transferred it all to the proclamation in neat script.

They signed above the Royal signature.

Now came his *coup de grâce*. THIS was the reason he had raked in Noble Stuffy and appointed a Censor.

Solemnly he looked at the ex-publisher. "Now we come to your vital part in this. Noble Arthrite Stuffy, His Majesty never wants to hear of Earth again. You therefore must eradicate every mention of these recent riots and upsets in every newssheet morgue."

Noble Stuffy gawped.

"This proclamation is YOURS to put in force! You must eradicate every reference to Blito-P3 in every book and text, on every map—a clean sweep."

"Everywhere?" said round-eyed Stuffy.

"Everywhere," said Heller. "And it is your sworn duty to prevent all future mention of that planet any-where. AND THAT INCLUDES EVEN THIS PROC-LAMATION!"

"Oh, dear!" said Noble Stuffy.

"And when," Heller continued in a hard voice, "anybody asks you what happened to Blito-P3, you are going to flinch and look sad and say it was so unspeakable it had to be censored and forbid them to even breathe its name again. Understood?"

Noble Arthrite Stuffy nodded numbly. From the look in Heller's eye he also understood Heller would probably personally break his neck if he did not comply.

So he did!

And to this day, that Royal proclamation lies in a lead case in the office of the Royal Historian and Censor.

AND THAT IS THE *COVER-UP!*

A WHOLE PLANET!

Don't doubt me. *I have seen it!* The Royal Historian and Censor, my great-uncle Lord Invay, was out to lunch! Now, how's that, dear reader? Does it make me the investigative reporter of all time or doesn't it? The answer is yes, yes, yes! I knew you would agree!

BLITO-P3—EARTH—EXISTS!

AND THE PLACE WHERE IT SHOULD BE IN THE INVASION TIMETABLE IS BLANK!

Isn't that monstrous?

And if it hadn't been removed, it would be scheduled for invasion just a few years from now.

THE PEOPLE OF VOLTAR MUST *KNOW* ABOUT THIS!

THEY'RE BEING DEPRIVED OF A PERFECTLY GOOD PLANET TO INVADE!

Despite what Soltan Gris said at the very beginning of his confession about Heller being the hero of it, I must solemnly advise you that this isn't true!

The actual villain of this whole disgraceful affair is NO OTHER THAN JETTERO HELLER!

He has been lurking behind the scenes, POSING as

a hero, when in actual, sober, solemn fact, JETTERO HELLER WAS THE VILLAIN, DOUBLE-DYED, ALL THE TIME!

JETTERO HELLER was the one who instigated the greatest cover-up in ALL VOLTAR HISTORY!

That makes him the villain. Right?

Well, enough said. You better make your voice heard to remedy this scandal. There is still time to get at it right on schedule!

PEOPLE OF VOLTAR, INSIST ON ADHERENCE TO TRADITION!

OUR ANCESTORS DETERMINED THAT EARTH SHOULD BE INVADED ON SCHEDULE.

My message to you: SWEEP ASIDE THIS COVER-UP AND INVADE!

NOT THE END

I finished the book up to here and before I wrapped it up to send it to the publisher, I read it all to Shafter (Hound wouldn't listen because he saw it had some poetry in it).

When I got all done, expecting to see Shafter absolutely stunned, he didn't stun. He laid down his wrench—I had had to follow him around while he did routine inspections which were behind—and he looked at me and said, "Young Monte, for the love of comets, you've left so many strings untied it looks like the wiring when you get to fooling with an engine and I don't stop you. You completely left out what you found on your visit to Manco and you haven't said a blasted thing about all the trouble we had over Relax Island. The book is fine so far, but you've left it at ten thousand feet. Land it, boy, land it. Finish it up in style!"

So, as Shafter is my best critic—the only one I have so far—I sweated and slaved and added an "Envoi." All for you, dear reader, so you won't be left ten thousand feet up with no landing in sight. Read on. Be careful not to crash! Readers are valuable!

PART NINETY
ENVOI I

i

Hightee Heller, after two weeks assisting me dig up old papers and logs—but spending most of her time rambling around old haunts on Manco—had to return to the planet Voltar to keep a long-arranged engagement to appear at a benefit on Hightee Heller Day, an annual event.

At the shuttleport where she was catching the deluxe spaceliner for Voltar, she gave me a pat on the shoulder and a motherly kiss on the cheek and said, "Now, don't forget to lay the real stress of your book on my brother's later life. As a writer you must see that he gets good press: he's FAR too reticent about himself. So ta-ta now. I'm leaving you in good hands. It's been fun. Good-bye."

As the shuttle took off upward and I waved, I was thinking that it might have been just fun for her—it had been deadly serious hard work for me and it would continue! I had almost worn my thumb off clicking copies of logs and documents, my ears ached with the high whine of copying recording strips. And while I had the story down to the end of the last fatal war council about Earth (and had yet to spend many hard weeks writing what you have just so quickly read), I as yet did not have the final tag ends all tied neatly. How hard, how very hard I have worked for you, dear reader!

The chauffeur was waiting as arranged by Hightee, and I was flown back to the vast estates of the Duke and Duchess of Manco where we had been staying. The estates embrace a whole range of wild mountains and a thousand square miles of fertile plain adjacent to a city— provincial, but three times the size of New York—named Atalanta.

We landed in the Rose Park and I was in luck. The Duchess, just that minute, was entering a salon.

She was tall and blonde and, despite being in her late middle age and despite children, quite beautiful. The years had been very kind to the one-time Countess Krak.

"Hello, Monte," she said. "You look quite worn. Did Hightee get off all right?"

I nodded. The Duchess of Manco usually made me feel a little bit tongue-tied and awkward: she moved with an easy grace and her gray-blue eyes looked at you with an impact. She was dressed in leather today and had probably been out supervising things around the estate.

"Your Grace," I managed, "if you will give me a little time, there are some loose ends I haven't tied up."

She smiled. "Well, come in and sit down and fire away. I need to catch my breath, myself. My latest grandchild has been running everyone's legs off all day. He's been into everything on the place! He's only seven but he takes a dozen people to keep him from an early demise. Exactly like his grandfather." And she went on to tell me, very proudly, how they'd just now fished him out of an irrigation lake when his self-built boat had capsized. His mother had evidently taken him home to the city where his father, Heller's younger son, was governor.

The park day salon was nice and cool, very rustic, all of native stone with an actual fireplace. You could have drilled a company in it. The walls were lined with paintings. There were Jettero's three sons, all middle-aged now but in the paintings still boys: two were shown in the uniforms of the Royal Academy and the third in the helmet of a speed flier. Their own daughter was shown, painted as costumed in some school play: she looked startlingly like Hightee, but she had something in the way she stood that was definitely Krak.

The Duchess called for some cool drinks and rambled on about her grandchildren, of whom she now had six. The eldest of these, at forty, had just ambitiously taken on the stewardship of the Krak estates in northern Atalanta, since he would inherit the title, and was apparently wrestling at the moment with a flood. I was not very attentive. I was trying to get a word in edgewise and get my story tied up.

I had a little list. I peeked at it and in a lull, I said, "Could you tell me whatever happened to Mister Calico?"

She laughed and gave a small, sharp whistle. In about thirty seconds a calico cat came tearing into the room and leaped up on her lap. I was stunned. "Is this Mister Calico?"

She laughed again, for the cat had looked up searchingly at me and then, deciding I hadn't meant it, went back to lapping at the sparklewater canister she was holding for him.

Then she looked a little sad. "About ten years after we returned from Earth, Jettero and Mister Calico were taking a walk up in the mountains. You realize I never did get Jettero to lead a nice, safe life, but in this case he was simply limbering up after a long session in Palace City. They weren't even hunting. And Mister Calico spotted a lepertige! He tackled it head on! Imagine jumping on a ton of lepertige! But that was Mister Calico. Before Jettero could stop him, he'd come off second best."

She sighed. Then she pointed. "That's the lepertige pelt right over there by the fireplace. It's pretty ratty for this room, I know, but Jettero would never let me throw it away. And that's what happened to Mister Calico."

The cat in her lap looked up at the name again. She said, "However, once every generation since that time, after the old one is dead, another cat gets born in the litters that answers to the name of Mister Calico without ever being told. This is the tenth one!

"You know," she continued proudly, "since we brought these cats to Manco, there isn't a single vermin left in the province. I just hope these felines don't take it into their heads to wipe out the lepertiges!"

I had my next item. "There were five ships sent from Earth to Calabar. Did they ever arrive?"

"Oh, Faht Bey's crew. Oh, yes. They operated the Fleet repair base on Calabar for some years and then retired and went home. That reminds me, I have a postcard here someplace I haven't answered. He retired as postmaster in some little town in Flisten and his daughter got the post. She's half Turkish, you know. I must get a new social secretary. When you finish your book, you wouldn't care for the job, would you, Monte?"

I cringed. These elderly people were all alike. They didn't think investigative reporting was serious business! Well, I'd show them!

"Now," I said, ignoring the offer sternly, "when all those criminals were amnestied, was there any social upheaval? I mean, a new crime wave?"

"Oh, what would make you think that? Factually,

they all seemed to think they owed Mortiiy something and most of them reformed. Let me see, it was so long ago. Oh, yes. Only one percent were ever apprehended again and executed. It was a period that was almost crimeless. I remember a party now at the end of the first year. It was sort of my amnesty, you know. But since that time the state actually hasn't had any crime waves, as you call them. Even Slum City got cleaned up."

"Well, that's fine," I said. "Now could you tell me if you ever, in any way, heard any more about a man called Izzy Epstein?"

She looked at me a little strangely. Then she shrugged and sent a footman off. He came back presently with a metal box. She opened it, took out some sheets and set the box down on the floor. I would have loved to see what was in the rest of that box but she only offered me the sheets she held. Then just as quickly she took them back. "I forgot," she said, "that you wouldn't be able to read *English*."

The sheets were very, very old and yellowed and she handled them very gently. She put them back in the box and brought out a piece of translating paper in not much better shape. She gave me that.

ii

I took an immediate photograph of the cover note and translation, and I give them to you in full:

CONFIDENTIAL
From: Censorship Clerk
To: The Duchess of Manco, Palace City

Your Grace:
Crown, His Lordship, when this was called to his attention, directed that this be forwarded to you, under seal, as a matter of personal interest.

It was brought in by a routine military survey sent by the Chairman of Intelligence.

It was found on a post in a mountain cone. The envelope, as you will note, is simply addressed, "Mister Jet." The date is concurrent with the tenth year of reign of the Emperor Mortiiy.

The translation follows:

Dear Mr. Jet:
This is just to let you know that your penthouse is all ready and waiting when you come back.

The clothes in the closets are in good shape but a little out of date. Styles have changed in ten years. Your tailor calls from time to time to see if you need anything new.

Mr. Stampi of the Spreeport Speedway called and asked if you would like to race in the new American Grand Prix. He said he reinstated all your memberships and you were right out front with him.

"Queen" Babe Corleone speaks of you often. Just the other day, at the world board meeting, she said she missed "Prince Charming" and cried a little bit. She said maybe Jerome had never forgiven her after all, because he didn't come back. She is doing fine, though. The American Rifle Association elected her Woman of the Year. There are no other mobs now, only Corleone.

She is very popular and her name is up in lights over the UN since she ordered them to pass the Women's Thermonuclear Rights Bill.

Vantagio has your portrait in the lobby of the Gracious Palms but I don't think you'd like it with all the ribbons across the chest: it makes you look like some famous politician and that's dangerous. The girls there seem to like it, though, and keep votive candles going in front of it.

I think Bang-Bang misses you. He keeps talking about the "good old days with Jet." We made him a five-star general of the army so he could show them how to drill.

Bury, I'm sorry to say, showed his true colors. After he disposed of Miss Peace and Miss Agnes, his wife disappeared. She was last seen being introduced to an anaconda at the Bronx Zoo.

You may not have heard that the mayor's wife was exiled by Babe to the island of Elba. Well, she escaped. Evidence exists that she had

*a rendezvous with Bury, also at the zoo. She
has not been seen since.*

*Twoey is not around very much. We can
barely get him in long enough to sign papers
that apply to Rockecenter interests. He's bought
all the pig farms in New Jersey and spends
most of his time there. He named a new
prize-winning sow "The Beautiful Krackle,"
but please don't tell Miss Joy, as I don't
think she'd like it. But he thought she'd be
pleased and he plagued us for weeks trying to
find out where she was so he could show her
all the blue ribbons it won.*

*I doubt you'd bother your important head
twice wondering about me. I almost died last
month when they gave me an honorary degree
at Barvard to signalize the conversion of the
last government on Earth to a corporation. I
needed you to keep me from running away
which, I am ashamed to say, I did.*

*I keep your office dusted. Your old base-
ball cap has about fallen apart where you left
it on your desk. I am afraid to touch it.*

*So anyway, Mr. Jet, when you're finished
surveying the Moon in depth or whatever is
keeping you away, your condo penthouse is
still waiting. The gardeners keep the garden up
and there isn't even any dust around. I go
there now and then and pretend you'll soon
come home. It sort of calms me. I hope you
don't mind.*

Yours very truly,

Izzy

PS: I would ask you to give Miss Joy my best but she probably doesn't remember me.

PPS: I do hope she is enjoying her life as Mrs. Jettero Heller and the wife of an officer of the Fleet.

iii

I was STUNNED!

I looked at the Duchess and said, "He knew his 'Mr. Jet' was an extraterrestrial all the time! And, just like Izzy, he simply kept his mouth shut! But HOW did he find out?" Oh, I had Heller now! caught red-handed in a flagrant Code break!

"Jettero's name was on a receipt from the Fleet pasted inside the time-sight he was given. And in the Empire State Building office, Jettero had a full library of Voltarian including a Voltarian-English dictionary. Izzy must have recognized the characters and translated the receipt.

"But there's something else: Utanc—Colonel Gaylov—reported to Rockecenter that Afyon was an extraterrestrial base. Those files all fell into the hands of Izzy. He must have put six and six together and even when he found the base was destroyed, he guessed somebody would come again or had contacts and he just left the letter."

"Amazing!" I said. I gave her back the translation after making sure I had shot a copy of it. I checked my recorder secretly to make sure it was still running. "Now, I have another on my list: Snelz. What happened to him?"

She was looking at me very oddly now. But she said, "Snelz retired as a brigadier general of Fleet marines half a century ago. He's been dead for twenty years. But listen, young Monte, I've just noticed something very odd: the questions you've been asking relate to Earth."

She pointed her finger at me. I thought that I was caught. But she said, "Now listen, young Monte, we've shown you all his papers and his logs and you MUST cover Jettero's whole career. It's brilliant! Hightee and I have to nag and nag to even get him to let the papers quote him. He won't even answer questionnaires from the encyclopedia people: he just tells them, 'See last year!' and they take it as an order and publish him as a space racer when he was young! He's quite impossible! He never gets the slightest credit for all he's done. It's VAST! Earth was just a tiny, tiny part of it. In fact, if I were you, I'd sort of shy away from it. It's too unimportant. Good Heavens, even the Colipin invasion is more interesting than that. He gave the Emperor Mortiiy an absolute fit! We lost five squadrons and Jettero got so upset he grabbed the creaky old *Retribution* and went right over there and won the war and had peace in a week. And Mortiiy, who'd gone touring to inspect Calabar, belatedly heard about it and came rushing home thinking he'd have to take over the government and he came storming into the Grand Council hall and Jettero was sitting right there and Mortiiy roared, 'What the blazes do you mean going out risking your life in that confounded war?' and Jettero just smiled and said, 'What war, Your Majesty?' and handed him the treaty of peace. And even Mortiiy had to break out laughing, he looked so innocent. But the papers never even MENTIONED it! We gave you access to the logs and files so you could really tell people about him."

I smiled. I was going to. Though not what she expected. I knew that an investigative reporter had to be very cunning, so I said, "I certainly will take your advice, Your Grace."

But whether she would have pursued it or not, I would never know.

At that moment the cat said "Yowl" and punched her with its paw and then, of all things, pointed out an upper window of the salon.

The Duchess turned and stared. She spotted something in the sky. She leaped up and she said, "Oh, no! Jettero is coming in! He's a day early!" She looked down at her stained leather jumper. "Good Heavens! I'm a wreck! No one's even been told what's for dinner!"

She rushed from the salon into the rest of the house.

The cat scampered out the door toward the landing target in the Rose Park.

I followed the cat.

iv

The spaceship came in so fast I was certain that it was going to crash.

Then it made a sudden swoop at the last moment and settled on its tail so gently, it hardly bent the grass.

Now that it was standing still, I gawped.

IT WAS A TUG!

The airlock door opened and a safety line was thrown out and a man slid down it gracefully. He was dressed in a pale blue civilian suit, without ornament but of very expensive cut. He hit the bottom with a light-footed bounce and turned. Somebody still in the ship tossed a briefcase, a box and a wrapped bouquet of flowers down to him, each of which he caught.

Belatedly, a crew from the nearby hangar was rolling out some steps. But far from being abashed as they should have been, they gave him a wave.

I was standing in a rose archway to the house. He was walking straight toward me with an easy step.

IT WAS JETTERO HELLER!

He was quite tall, very slender, the sort of man who even in late middle age keeps himself in condition. Although his features had thickened, he was still a very handsome fellow. He fixed his gray-blue eyes upon me. He said, "Where's Hightee?"

I said, "Oh, she went back this noon to Voltar."

"Oh, blast," he said, "I hoped to catch her. You must be the young man I heard she had in tow."

"The Honorable Monte Pennwell, Crown, Your Lordship, sir," and I would have knelt but he stopped me.

"Let's dispense with all the protocol. I get enough of that at Palace City." He smiled and it was a very engaging smile. "I'm home. Just call me Jet."

"Sir," I said, because I couldn't restrain my curiosity another moment, "isn't that *Tug One?*"

"Of course not," he said with a slight frown.

"But it IS a tug," I persisted. "It's got a blunt butting nose with arms. It's the same size and shape. It has a fin down the back to get rid of excess charge from Willbe Was main drives. When you opened the airlock, I distinctly saw silver handrails. It even has *Prince Caucalsia* on its nose!"

"Young Pennwell, that ship is NOT *Tug One.* But your use of the term makes me suspect you have been talking to the women of the family. Gossiping."

I drew myself up. I came to just above his shoulder. "Not gossiping. I am an investigative reporter!"

He laughed good-naturedly. "'Investigative reporter'? I haven't heard that term for nearly a century."

"I want to write the story of your life," I said.

He handed me the box he was carrying and the flowers. "Well, come on into the park salon and I will tell you all about it. No reason to keep you out here standing in the sun."

I tagged after him. He entered the room. A footman was standing there with cool drinks, smiling a welcome. Heller draped himself into a chair. A man in blue livery, evidently a major-domo, rushed in, still getting into his coat.

"Blin," said Heller to the newcomer, "take that box

and send it to Hightee. I'm sorry I missed her: I was looking forward to some do-you-remembers as we rambled
around Atalanta. Pack it carefully, as it's antique glass:
now it will have to be shipped all the way back to Pausch
Hills. The flowers are for Her Grace."

Blin relieved me of my load. The footman presented
me with a drink. Heller motioned for me to sit down.

"So what I heard was right," he said. "Dear Hightee
was helping you write a book. Do you have a publisher?"

"Oh, yes, Your . . . Jet. Biographics Publishing Company was fascinated with the idea of publishing a book
about you. They even signed a contract, without even
demanding an outline. They were avid, really." I didn't
advise him that they had assumed I must know him very
well, when actually it was not until I started this project
that I found out that Jettero Heller had been the common name of the enormously popular and fabulously
powerful Duke of Manco. They had been stunned when
they realized that there was not a single book about him
and had said, "Young Pennwell, if you've got an inside
track and can actually write the biography of Crown,
your fortune will be made!" I was going to go them one
better. What a book I had! A sky-buster!

"Well, that's fine," said Heller. "I imagine the girls
must have been assisting you."

"Oh, yes," I said. "They have been splendid—made
all your logs and things available, opened up the whole
Memorial Library to me as well."

"I imagine you've been very busy. Did you have any
other material?"

"Oh, yes sir," I said. "The most amazing thing. An
earthquake must have opened up some passages at
Spiteos out in the Great Desert. The place you pulled
down, you know. And it was my luck to find the whole

Apparatus master files." I was trying to trick him into some new disclosures, some comments I could use.

But he only said, "Imagine that," and sipped at his cool drink. "But I should imagine it gets pretty rough for a young writer. Are you not having any trouble at all?"

That reached a tender spot. "Well," I said, "there's my family. Ever since I graduated from the Royal Academy of Arts, they haven't taken my writing seriously. I've written ever so many odes and they don't even listen to them. No encouragement at all."

He shook his head and looked very sympathetic. "Well, youth has its penalties. But I don't imagine they actively put any blocks in your way."

"Oh, but they do!" I countered. "Every relative I've got has been nudging and pushing at me to take a post doing this or that."

"Oh, my," said Heller, "that must be pretty grim."

"It is!" I said, emphatically. "But they've eased up on that. Now it's something else absolutely horrible. My mother is leading a conspiracy to marry me off to the Lady Corsa."

"Lady Corsa?" he said, wide-eyed. "Why, she's the heiress to half of the planet Modon!"

"She's awfully athletic, half again my size. And she has no soul at all! She thinks writing is a waste of time."

"But, good Heavens," said Heller, "you'd wind up one of the richest men on Modon in another half-century. The lands of that planet are legendary for their productivity and the uplands are beautiful and full of game. A paradise!"

I shook my head. "Provincial," I said. "Bucolic beyond belief. All they do is dig irrigation ditches or stand around with their caps in their hands muttering about the woolly crop. Even the gentry is illiterate and they go to bed the moment the sun, there, sets. I wouldn't be able to get to the bright lights of Voltar even as often as once a year. Oh, I assure you, Your Grace, it would be DEATH!"

"You poor fellow," Heller said. "This writing must mean a lot to you."

"Oh, it does, it does. So please, Jet, tell me the story of your life."

He looked very solemn. He finished off his cool drink and put it down. "Very well, then. Where shall I begin?"

I was a bit taken aback. I hadn't realized it would be so easy. "Well, usually one begins with where he was born," I said.

He nodded. He settled himself comfortably. I got my recorder running, aching to hear his every word. Now I would get to the bottom of this. With the adroit and tricky questioning I had worked out that an investigative reporter must pursue, I would get him to reveal in his own words the substance of the most gigantic cover-up of all time.

"I was born," said Heller, "in Tapour, Atalanta Province, planet Manco, 127 years ago."

I was tense. His eyes took on the hue of nostalgia and reminiscence. Now I would get down to it.

"Then," said Heller, "I lived until now. And here I am."

I felt the very room spin. I opened my mouth. I closed it.

A bland and innocent smile remained on Heller's face.

Some footfalls were sounding in the hall. The Duchess of Manco swept in. Despite her age, she was beautiful. She was wearing a dinner gown that shimmered blue and yellow and seemed to reflect the color of her hair and eyes. Had I not known how old she was, her skill at makeup would have had me fooled.

He stood to welcome her and she kissed him. "You're a bad boy to come blasting in here a day early, catching everything in a mess. But I am delighted," and she kissed him again very warmly. Then she became aware of me. She said, "Jettero, I couldn't help but overhear what you told this nice young man. Spare him your jokes. He's really trying awfully hard and it's time you got some recognition."

"That's right!" said Heller. "Recognition! Just what I want. Recognition that I am starved. What's for dinner?"

And that was ALL I ever got out of Jettero Heller, Viceregal Chairman of the Grand Council, Duke of Manco.

So you see?

HE IS STILL ENFORCING THE HUGEST COVER-UP THE CONFEDERACY EVER SUFFERED!

But there is still time, dear reader, there is still time. The sacred Invasion Timetable can yet be restored and executed.

However, as Shafter is reminding me, I have not told you all.

V

When I got back to Voltar I was, of course, busy for a very long time writing the story you have read. Honestly, I have never worked so hard in all my life. I blackmailed Hound—he drinks—into telling people I was studying to take examination for a position, without saying which relative had won and, as Lady Corsa and her brother had gone back to Modon, I was not bothered. Oh, how I sweated.

And then the fabulous day came when I thought that I had finished, only to be told by Shafter I had my wires loose.

"All right," I said impatiently, "all right. But Shafter, I don't have any more material here. It's all written up!"

He sighed. He said, "Young Monte, have you ever realized how boring it has been for me puttering around here while you inked your fingers up? Every car you have is tuned. And you know what?"

I said, "What?"

"I think you're writing fairy tales."

"Oh, Shafter, have you turned against me, too?"

"I wouldn't do that, young Monte. But I could keep you from making an awful mistake." He went to the door of the old air-tourer he had picked up for a song (I should be more accurate: it wasn't one of my odes, for nobody will take them; it was with my unspent allowance built up while I was writing) and he opened the creaky door and pushed a panel button. He said, "Look."

I looked.

He had turned on a map. It was the Western Ocean.

"I don't see anything," I said, mystified.

"That's what I'm showing you," Shafter said. "You could be making an awful mistake. Look carefully. NOTHING!"

Believe me, it was an awful shock when I understood and verified what he was saying. Not only was there no Relax Island, THERE WAS NO ISLAND AT ALL!

"Good Heavens!" I cried. "The cover-up even extends to corrupting a Voltar planetary chart!"

"I knew you'd see it my way," said Shafter. "I'll ask Hound to pack us a lunch and we're on our way!"

We flew over there at once. Two thousand miles. The old air-tourer wasn't fast—it could only make three hundred—but it had lots of instruments and screens.

The overcast was very high and gray, the ocean was very ominous and green. At four in the afternoon we were on the exact coordinates.

"Be careful not to run into the mountaintop," I said. "I've forgotten how high it is."

"Well, you won't find out from the pilot book. There's no such island listed. But I've got a system. I've drawn a grid and we will just fly back and forth, going lower and lower, and scout this whole area of ocean."

"Don't run into the mountainside!" I said.

"I won't," replied Shafter. "For I'm quite certain there's nothing there. Besides, I'm flying with all screens live. Sit back and have another sweetbun. This is going to take time."

We combed and combed, lower and lower, splitting

through the tendrils of mist and patches of sun. Now and then we glimpsed the ocean below.

The waves began to look more and more prominent. We were finally so low, I even saw a batfish being chased by a whole school of toothers. It made me nervous, particularly since Shafter had chosen that moment to lift an interior cowl and shove in another fuel bar: I hoped we had enough of them.

The sun abruptly blinded me. It was shining under the mist, horizontally. SUNSET!

And then a weird thought hit me. "Say, Shafter, have you had a flash from Planetary Defense?"

"No," he said, skimming the waves.

"Well, for Heavens' sakes, make sure your traffic channel is operating. We don't want a warhead being slammed into us. This island is very out-of-bounds. Check your channel!"

He shrugged and put a call in. "Just testing," he said into the microphone.

"Oh, is that what you're doing?" came a Planetary Defense Base voice. "We thought you were probably looking for a place to fish."

Shafter turned and winked at me. "That's right," he said into the microphone. "But we're being careful not to run into the mountain."

"What mountain?" said Planetary Defense.

"Teon," said Shafter. "The mountain on Relax Island."

There was a silence, then, "Air-tourer 4536729-MY7. We have just issued cautionary citation on you for cruising without charts or pilot books. Please report at your convenience to Traffic Safety and get your screens and publications checked."

"Oh, here now," said Shafter, "we don't need that."

"Then probably you'd rather have a real citation for flying under the influence of tup."

"No, no," said Shafter hastily, "I'll take the cautionary one, thank you. It's not my fault your publications are hard to read. I could have sworn I saw a Mount Teon listed out here."

"You're seeing things. We're issuing the real citation. There's no such island and no such mountain. We'll monitor your progress home. Check in to court tomorrow morning. And bring ten credits for the fine. End."

Shafter turned to me. "Please don't have any other suggestions, young Monte. Give me the ten credits now so I can go to court and pay it before you get up. There's no land here, we're going home."

I was boggled. This was more than just a cover-up.

What had been the fate of Queen Teenie and Madison, the catamites, the Palace City staff and five thousand people?

Oh, Shafter had been right. I had my wires loose and waving in the air!

WHAT HAD HAPPENED?

The island was just a volcanic bubble.

Had Heller, that archvillain, sent a warship in to blow it out of the water and cover up his cover-up for keeps?

vi

I spent a very restless night. I paced. Only by dawn did I get to sleep. Hound let the sunlight in like a clap of thunder by slamming back the blinds.

"You're getting worse and worse," he said. "Now you've got poor Shafter standing in court like a common felon. Your father should have taken my advice and sent you for military duty. Charging to the thunder of guns would have made a man out of you."

"Hound," I said, "do I have a relative in the geological office?"

He raised his eyes to the ceiling. "No, you don't have a relative in the geological office. And if you don't straighten out soon, you won't have any relatives at all. They'll disown you! Plying poor Shafter with strong drink! You should be ashamed of yourself."

"He didn't tell you that."

"He didn't have to! The citation was in the morning mail slot! And here you are at two o'clock in the afternoon, sleeping it off!"

"*You* drink."

"Not in public, you little blackmailer! Get into that washroom and I'll steam it out of you!"

Actually, it did me good. It soothed the jangled nerves, even though they got all jangled again by my trying to phone while Hound shaved me. He kept brushing the mouthpiece away.

But I got hold of the editor of *The Planet,* a weekly pictorial which, I remembered, had a flavor of Voltar historical events: they liked to cover mountain slides and volcanic eruptions and such.

"About a hundred years ago or less," I said, "did you record an earthquake or anything."

"That's great," said the editor. "Who is this? Your viewer is off."

"I'm being shaved and my hair isn't combed."

"This must be my most vital call of the day," said

the editor. "Listen, whoever you are, there are approximately six earthquakes a week throughout 110 planets. And I am overwhelmed by your time and location specificity."

"Western Ocean," I said, "Voltar. Try ninety or ninety-five or eighty-five years ago."

"Listen, whoever you are, my advice is to go get chummy with a reporter who has access to newssheet files. And when you call me next time, comb your hair and turn on your viewer. Cranks," he muttered and clicked off.

It came to me in a flash. I knew where reporters hung out.

"Hound," I said excitedly, "lay out a lounge suit that's sort of wrinkled and a sloppy hat."

"You don't have any wrinkled suits!" he snapped. "Don't go accusing the footmen of not doing their jobs. Not after what you did to poor Shafter! You're trouble!"

"Listen," I pleaded. "Wrinkle one up, then. I'm going to the Ink Club in Joy City!"

He raised his eyeballs so high they clicked! When he recovered, he said, "Now you are going to go carousing with newssheet trash! You mark my words, young Monte, you'll become a hopeless drunk! If it weren't for my obligation to your father, I would go home to Flisten and abandon you to your fate!"

He wouldn't let me wrinkle my suit. He wouldn't let me wear a sloppy hat. He jawed and jawed. Oh, what I have been through, dear reader, getting you this book!

Shafter wasn't much better. Incautiously, he had given the traffic court a bit of lip and they'd doubled his fine. I gave him the additional ten credits but he kept glooming about his perfect driving record gone.

He got me to Joy City and landed near the Ink Club.

It has a huge electronic sign that simulates a river of ink that changes colors and splashes. You'd think inside they'd have fires and disasters posted up, but not so: the place is all soft gray and soothing music, somewhat like an undertaker's.

It was late afternoon. Editions were all out. It was reporter slack time. The place was jammed.

I felt extremely conspicuous with my beautifully pressed, conservative mauve shimmercloth lounge suit and perfectly brushed hat. It made me stand out like a statue in a park full of weeds.

A young boy usher saw me staring around at the tables. He must have thought I had wandered into the wrong place. He said, "Is there someone you especially wish to see, sir?"

"A reporter," I said.

He looked at me and his eyes went round. And then he broke out laughing. "Hey, you birds," he shouted, "this toff here wants to see a reporter. Do any of you splashers qualify?"

Somebody threw a canister at him. A tough-looking fellow at a crowded table yelled at me, "Don't mind the help. Come over and sit down, if you're buying."

Well, of course I was buying. I was an investigative reporter myself, wasn't I? I squeezed in at a place they made for me at a table of twenty and very shortly two waiters ran up with trays loaded with drinks.

"Well, what can I do for you?" said the tough-looking fellow, when he'd downed his. "It's two days before payday and you're a Godsend." I was paying the waiter from a roll. "Bring the table another round!" my new friend yelled, "I think the guy just robbed a bank!"

"Hey, that's a good story," said another one. "Can I have it exclusive? I'll dub you Natty the Nifty Teller

Tapper. And for another round I'll say you kiss the tellers before you will take their tills."

"No, no," I said with dignity. "I am a reporter myself. An investigative reporter, in fact."

"What's that?" several wanted to know.

"It investigates cover-ups," I said. "I'm writing a book."

"We're all writing books," my tough-looking friend said. "I got a trunk full of books. So has everybody else at this table. You got to do better than that. Waiter, bring us another round!"

"I am on the trail of a cover-up so staggering," I said, "that it will boggle everybody."

"What's a cover-up?" somebody wanted to know. "You don't cover them up. You take the covers OFF. Only then can you see what the girl looks like! You've got to be careful what you're getting into!"

"It isn't a girl I'm uncovering," I said. "It's one of the highest figures in the state. And oh, will my name be all across the sky."

"My friend," said the tough-looking one, "I think, in kindness, you have had enough to drink. But that doesn't stop the rest of us. Waiter, another round, but omit my friend here. He's drunk as a Lord!"

Five rounds later, my tough-looking friend was pretty mellow and I got him to listen.

"I've got to get access to newssheet files stretching back maybe ninety-five years. I'm searching for a specific disaster."

"My friend," he said, "what you need is a reporter. No editor is going to let you near his files. Now, as you've been buying so handsomely, any of us here would be glad to help, except for one fatal thing: nobody lasts ninety-five years in this business."

"Old Shif did," said somebody, pointing.

My tough-looking friend turned.

A gray-haired old wreck was sitting at the end of a bar across the room, all by himself, staring at an empty canister.

"Hey, he might know. Buy us one more round, Natty the Nifty Teller Tapper, and I'll introduce you for free."

Five minutes later, my tough-looking friend, with me beside him, was telling Shif, "Here's somebody that's insisting on buying you a drink. Bye-bye, Natty, drop around when you've tapped another till." And he left.

"Drinks," said old Shif, "always cost something. What is it this time?"

"I am trying to discover any strange occurrence in the Western Ocean, sometime between a century ago and now, probably maybe ninety-five years ago, maybe not." And I signalled the barman to bring a canister of tup. The barman hesitated until I flashed a bill to show him I was paying.

Old Shif watched the canister arrive. "Maybe you better be more specific."

I decided to confide, he looked so old and wise. I leaned over and whispered in his ear, "I'm trying to find out what happened to Relax Island."

His head whipped around toward me. Something flashed in his eyes. Was it fear?

Then he did the incredible. He pushed the canister of tup right back at the barman!

Without looking at me, Shif said, "I'm sorry. I can't help you."

Oh, was I certain now! Yes, indeed, there was a cover-up! I grabbed the canister and put it back in front of him. He did not touch it.

This was an emergency. I signalled to the barman for a keg. The barman saw my money, picked one up and put it on the bar in front of Shif.

"That won't help," said the aged reporter. "Young man, as a friendly gesture, all I can tell you is to forget it. You are in Censor territory."

My certainty surged!

I know how these clubs operate. The attitude of that barman clearly showed that old Shif was in debt to the place. I grabbed the young boy usher and gave him a whispered message.

Two minutes later, the manager was standing there, holding an account sheet in his hand. "I don't know what you want with this," he said to Shif. "It was about to be written off as a bad debt."

Shif pointed at me. "He called for it, I didn't," said Shif.

I grabbed the bill. It was a year overdue. It was for more than I had on me. I grabbed out my identoplate and stamped it.

"No, no!" said Shif. "You're tempting me beyond endurance!"

"Good," I said.

"Bad," said Shif. "This is DANGEROUS!"

I was absolutely positive then that not only the Censor but Heller himself must be behind this Relax Island cover-up!

"Give me an account sheet with his name on it," I told the manager. "Mark it for the next year and leave the amount blank."

The manager stared. Old Shif sat there kind of crumpled. The blank sheet came. I stamped it. But I held onto it.

Seconds ticked by. Then slowly, slowly, old Shif

reached out for the sheet. He gripped the corner of it and used it to pull me close to him.

He whispered in my ear. "Don't ever tell anyone it came from me. Go and see Pratia Tayl, Minx Estates, Pausch Hills."

vii

Because it was late in the Voltar year, Minx Estates was not in bloom. But from the air, as we landed, one could tell it was very prosperous. It had garden walks amongst the shrubs, and statues of naked nymphs peeped forth. The vast house was a mansion of three stories and higher gables. A small hospital nestled in the trees at the back. A pool, in the shape of a heart, steamed in the late afternoon sun.

We landed on the target and I got out. What seemed to be a bundle of furs in a reclining chair at the pool side suddenly stirred and said, "Oooooooo! What a beautiful young man!"

I advanced cautiously. An old face of at least 150 peered out of the furs. Excessive makeup did not hide her years. "Sit down, sit down!" she cried, indicating a lawn chair beside her. "Tell me all about yourself!"

"I am Monte Pennwell," I said. "Do I have the honor of addressing Pratia Tayl?"

"Oh, my goodness. Not only handsome but also polite. Yes, indeed, I am Pratia Tayl, or at least that name will do. Now you just make yourself at home."

Things apparently happened very fast at Minx Estates for all its surface serenity. Pratia began to chatter at three hundred miles an hour, asking all about my family, of which she had heard, and all about my friends and interests. And while she was doing so a young man with bright green eyes and straw-colored hair came up with a tray of canisters and a jug of pink sparklewater and Pratia said, "Thank you, son," without even taking her eyes off me, and then a woman came out of the house with some sweetbuns. She had bright green eyes and straw-colored hair and Pratia said, "Thank you, daughter," and went right on chattering at me.

An elderly dowager, escorted by an elderly man with bright green eyes and straw-colored hair, entered the front gate and passed us en route to the small hospital at the back, and Pratia, barely halting her chatter at me, said, "Good afternoon, Lady Tig. Good afternoon, son." When they opened the hospital door, I saw the sign on it, *Cellology Beauty Clinic.*

I had no more than read that when a very sporty air-speedster landed and two men got out. They both had bright green eyes and straw-colored hair. When they came over to give her a peck on the cheek, she interrupted her barrage at me long enough to say, "Boys, meet Monte Pennwell, the writer. You know of his family. Monte, my grandsons Jettero and Bis." They shook hands and went off to the house and I cut into Pratia's chatter.

"Good Heavens," I said, "are all these children YOURS?"

"Oh, these are just some of them," said Pratia with a proud simper. "Most of them have married and are in practice. You should see my grandchildren!"

"Do they all have bright green eyes and straw-colored hair?"

"Oh, yes," said Pratia. "Aren't they beautiful? I even have three great-grandchildren already and they have them, too! Adorable. But I was wondering, don't you have an Aunt Bit? I think I went to school..."

A really ancient hag came out of the house and stalked over to us. She cut right across Pratia's chatter. She said, "Will this guest be staying for supper?"

Pratia said, "Oh, I'm sure he will, Meeley. Be certain that you serve something stimulating. And he will be staying the night...."

"No, no," I said quickly. "I have to be home for a family dinner. But...but," I said to the old hag, "she called you Meeley. Are you...well...are you the former landlady of..."

"That (bleep)?" said Meeley. "Hah!" And she stalked off.

"I'm sorry you can't stay the night," said Pratia. "My bed is awfully soft."

It just shows you the menaces which surround the profession of an investigative reporter! You should be impressed with the dangers I ran getting this material for you, dear reader.

Swiftly, I said, "I only came to find out about Relax Island."

Her bright blue eyes went round. She was suddenly silent. She stared at me.

Hastily, I explained, "I heard a rumor you could tell me. You see, it's no longer there."

She nibbled at a sweetbun. Then she said, "Prahd wouldn't like it if I told you."

"Prahd?" I said. "Prahd Bittlestiffender?"

"Are there any other Prahds? He is still the King's

Own Physician, but he runs this little beauty clinic here when he isn't busy at Palace City." Suddenly she looked brighter. She raised her voice and called, "Ske!"

A man in a butler's uniform came out of the house shortly. "One of the girls said you called, Mistress. I didn't quite hear. I'm getting pretty deaf."

"Ske?" I said. "By any chance, you aren't the one-time driver of . . . of . . . ?"

"That (bleep)?" said Ske. "I'll have you know I've been butler here ever since old Bawtch died. I'm respectable."

"Bawtch?" I said. "The chief clerk of . . ."

Pratia cut me off. She said, "Ske, Prahd won't be here tonight, will he?"

Ske shook his head and went off to do whatever butlers do.

"Oh, goodie!" said Pratia. "He won't be here at the clinic so he wouldn't know you'd been here listening. I can tell you after all!"

I sat forward on the edge of my seat.

"So that's settled," said Pratia. She didn't say anything else.

"Well?" I said. "Well?"

"Oh, Monte," she said, "you amaze me. Don't you know that a girl can't possibly impart secrets unless it's in bed?"

I gawped.

"Don't look so prim," she said. "It's a long story. I couldn't possibly tell you unless you spent the night."

Then I smiled. I nodded. I knew I had nothing to fear from a woman who was 150 or 160 years old. After all, I DID have to get the story.

I sent Shafter and the air-speedster home.

Little did I know what I was letting myself in for!

Oh, Gods, what I have been through and how I have suffered, dear reader, getting you this vital tale!

I did not have the least inkling of the shocking experience that awaited me!

I should have read it from the smile on the face of Pratia Tayl when I helped her to rise and go in to dinner, a smile which stayed there all through the meal.

PART NINETY-ONE ENVOI II

viii

Feeling pleasantly full of a delicious dinner, I was led by Pratia into an imposing bedroom. It had floating chairs. It had an enormous floating bed. The place was all white and gold and was decorated with natural-color cupids on the walls and in the cloudy ceiling. I suddenly looked again. The cupids, in singles, doubles and clusters all were leering!

Pratia sat down in a soft and ample chair. She picked up a bag which had been lying there. Out of it she took a needle and some long strings, then she shook out a pile of tiny, colored hoops. I knew what all that was: ladies of quality often make circular mats of different designs and thread small hoops of various colors on strings by the thousands. I was reassured. I started to sit down on a couch.

"No, not there," said Pratia. "On the bed!"

I sat down on the huge bed: it was wondrously soft and fleecy but strangely it did not sink, keeping one supported.

Pratia put a needle through a hoop. "You are really a nice young fellow," she said. "So, take off your clothes."

I flinched.

"No take-off-the-clothes, no story," said Pratia.

Well, she wasn't attacking me. With considerable reluctance, I kicked off my shoes and socks, removed my jacket and my shirt.

Pratia had stopped threading. "All of them," she said.

Unwillingly, with my back to her, I removed the rest.

"Now lie down on your back," she said. "If you're so modest, you can cover yourself with the sheet."

Although she was watching, she was still in the chair. It made me brave. I lay down on my back. I pulled the sheet over me.

Pratia let out a sigh. And then she said, "All right, girls, you can come in."

Through the door, giggling, came two girls!

I instantly pulled the sheet up to my throat!

"These are my great-granddaughters Asa and Lik," said Pratia.

Asa was about twenty-one. She was quite thin. She was quite pretty. She had green eyes and straw-colored hair.

Lik was about nineteen. She was plumper. She was very pretty. She, too, had green eyes and straw-colored hair.

"Girls," said Pratia, "this is a real, live author named Monte Pennwell. Isn't he nice?"

The girls promptly began to get out of their clothes, shedding them with an alarming speed.

I hysterically pulled the sheet up over my head!

"Now, don't get alarmed," Pratia said to me. "They are both virgins. I wouldn't dream of letting them indulge in actual sex. I am just making sure I am bringing them up right. We're very proper people: I wouldn't condone letting them touch their brothers and it's almost never that we get a nice young man to practice on."

"No," I said in a panic, surging up. "I'd better go!"

Pratia smiled that strange, intense smile. "No practice, no story," she said. "And it's some story, I assure you."

I steeled myself. I was an investigative reporter, I told myself. If I were going to be true to my craft, I must not flinch at the little bumps in the road. I lay back down.

Suddenly, Asa's face was looming over me. "Now, all I'm going to do," she said, "is just give you a nice kiss. Boys and girls kiss all the time, so there's nothing wrong with that, is there?"

I shook my head, not really knowing if I was agreeing with her or telling her not to do it.

She put her palms on my cheeks and gave me a nice, gentle kiss. At least it seemed so. But an electric thrill went through me.

Asa drew back. She was sitting on her heels beside me. "Now you see? Just a simple, innocent kiss."

Pratia had stopped knitting. Her blue eyes were very intense. Her tongue was playing along her upper lip.

Asa leaned over me again. I could not see much through the screen of her straw-colored hair. She was kissing me on the cheek.

I felt my toes clench. My heels straightened out with a jerk.

Asa was sitting back, looking down at me, grinning.

I raised my head and looked around, startled. Where was Lik?

The girl's bare feet were visible on the floor, heels up, on the other side of the bed.

I felt my eyes roll right up into the top of my skull as a shuddering groan filled the room.

Asa giggled.

Pratia smiled happily.

Lik, kneeling on the other side of the bed, pulled her head out from under the sheet. "Oh, boy!" she panted. "That was goooooooood!"

Pratia began threading hoops again. "You've been a nicely behaved boy, Monte Pennwell. So you just lie still and I will tell you the story of Relax Island."

ix

"It all begins," said Pratia, threading small rings with her needle, "about five years after the ascension of Emperor Mortiiy to the throne.

"Things were very calm in the whole Confederacy. There was prosperity. A great deal of building was in progress. Practically everyone had forgotten all about Hisst and certainly, since it had had no publicity in the first place, Relax Island was the furthest thing from anybody's mind.

"Then one day, right here at the gate, a fisherman showed up from the Western Ocean shore. He was an old man and very brown, very ragged and poor. He had walked all the way from the village of Wayl, a distance of nearly five hundred miles.

"He wouldn't talk to anybody but me, so they brought him out to the summerhouse where I was and he stood there twisting his shade hat around and around and he said he had a message for me. And would I pay?

"I told him that depended. He fished into a straw bag he had and brought out a sealed glass canister. He held it near me but wouldn't let go of it.

"I looked through the glass and read, 'If whoever finds this message will take it to Pratia Tayl, Minx Estates, Pausch Hills, she will give him two hundred credits.'

"That's a lot of money. He said that he had found the bottle floating off the breakwater at Wayl. My curiosity got the better of me. I paid him and he gave me the canister and went away.

"I cut the seal and spilled the whole roll of paper into my hand. I spread it out. It said:

Tell Papers Headline

HUGE PLAGUE WIPING OUT RELAX ISLAND
POPULATION DYING LIKE FLIES

The exile colony of Queen Teenie, Hostage Monarch of Flisten, not only imperilled but doomed!

Unburied dead littering the roads are making an unbearable stench.

The piteous moan of infants rends the air.

Death stalks from the crown of Mount Teon down to the southernmost cliff, planting its crushing hooves into the guts and brains of this defenseless and shuddering population.

No medical supplies exist.

Unless immediate help is received, there is no hope.

PS: For God's sakes, get this to the papers, Pratia!

"Well, you can imagine the shock I went into! I instantly got on the viewer-phone. I showed the message. I called editor after editor, publisher after publisher.

"Some reporters came out and I showed it to them along with the canister.

"And then you know what happened?

"NOTHING!

"The next day, there wasn't a single mention of it in the papers, not ONE line! Oh, I was upset.

"Now, you know that by this time Prahd, although he was the King's Own Physician, didn't have too much to do. Mortiiy was very healthy and Prahd had finished cleaning up the removed Lords long since. Cling was still alive but he had special nurses. So Prahd, to while away the time, opened the little hospital here as a cellology beauty clinic for the dowagers and women of Pausch Hills. He was here three days a week and when he next came, I showed him the message.

"He scratched his head. He looked at the date on the message and saw it was only two weeks old and he said there might yet be time. He viewer-phoned Palace City to try to get hold of that BEAUTIFUL man, Jettero Heller—Duke of Manco is his right name now, but I always think of him as dear Jettero, such a LOVELY man. Such grace . . . Where was I? Oh, yes.

"But dear Jettero—I certainly would love to talk to him someday. I have to worship him from afar. You have connections, Monte. Someday could you introduce me?"

"It's possible," I said, lying there naked between the two girls. "But please, please, tell me!"

"Oh, goodie. Anyway, dear Jettero was on some kind of a tour to way off at the other end of the Confederacy and nobody knew when he'd be back. The Grand

Council was meeting only once a month and that was three weeks off.

"Prahd didn't dare approach Mortiiy about it, of course, but he has lots of influence. And he contacted the Lord of Health who, in view of the emergency, cleared it with Planetary Defense.

"Prahd didn't want to go right in with a big medical team and cause a stir, so he got a Royal ambulance and, when I volunteered, he disguised me as his nurse and . . . What's the matter, Asa?"

X

Asa had been sobbing quietly for some time but I had not given it much attention. Now she said, brokenly, "Lik had some and I didn't. I'm all hot and frustrated and I think I'm going to have a nervous breakdown. I'm lying here next to him and I ACHE!"

"Oh, dear," said Pratia in quick sympathy. "By all means, go ahead: I couldn't live with myself if I tortured children."

Asa moaned her thanks.

Lik popped up and looked down into my face. "I also feel deprived. I didn't get a chance to give him a nice kiss."

I turned my head away from her.

"Oh, come now, Monte Pennwell," said Lik. "Certainly a kiss never hurt anyone, especially from a girl who prides herself on being chaste."

Pratia grinned expectantly and sat forward in her chair.

I turned my head back, offering my cheek.

Pratia was beginning to pant.

My eyes went round! Asa's groan filled the room.

Pratia's needle and hoops were crushed between her quivering hands.

Lik gave me a gentle pat upon the cheek. "Now, you see?" she said, "It didn't hurt a bit. You are a good boy, Monte."

"Oh, he is that," said Asa, panting.

"Gran-gran, can't we hear this story another time?" said Lik.

"No, no!" I said. "Please, please. What happened on the island?"

Pratia blinked her eyes a few times and then got back to putting her needle through hoops once more.

She sighed. "So we got passed by Planetary Defense and we landed on the island.

"You never saw such a peaceful scene. The flowers were blooming and beautiful, the air was very soft. The palace steps were burnished, the paths were swept. And here and there in the little nooks, catamites were making love to each other.

"They hadn't even noticed that we landed! Thinking it was because we were at the palace back door and that no one had spotted the ambulance—since Prahd had driven quietly—we rushed in through the palace.

"We rushed up a stairs and down a hall.

"Five officers were sitting there outside Queen Teenie's bedchamber. Their senior saw us and held up his hand. He frowned.

"'No, no' he said, 'you can't go in. We're just now changing the guard.'

"There was a shuffling sound on the other side of the door. It opened and five officers marched out adjusting their clothes.

"The senior in the corridor saluted the senior coming out. He said, 'We are here to relieve you, sir. Is there anything we should know?'

"The officer who had been in charge of the watch finished buttoning his tunic. 'It's warmer than usual. My advice is to advance to the attack at once.'

"Before the relieving officer could answer, Prahd swept him aside and we rushed into the room.

"Teenie was lying on her bed. Five years hadn't changed her much and she still wore her ponytail. A beautiful smile was on her mouth and she was stretching lazily. Then she saw us!

"She leaped up and rushed over. She was in total alarm!

"'You're from the mainland!' she cried. 'What's wrong? You're in doctor's clothes. Is somebody sick?'

"We showed her the message and she blew up. She swore for a full two minutes without stopping. Then she went into action.

"She got on some clothes—something they call a *bikini top*—and she grabbed a piece of chain and she assembled five real guards. We got into the ambulance and at her direction went roaring down to the south end of the island.

"Apparently Madison and a gang he'd had lived in a village there, miles and miles from the palace and on the edge of a cliff. It was very picturesque; the houses had thatched roofs and tile floors. We stopped in front of the biggest one: it had a sign on it that said *Press Office*, but it was where Madison lived.

"A woman came out whose name, I gathered, was

Flip. She tried to kneel but Teenie went right by her.

"Madison was lying on the bed. Teenie threw the message at him. He looked at it and then at her. He tried to get up!

"WHAM! She hit him with the chain and knocked him right back in bed!

"'You *son of a (bleepch)*,' she screamed at him. 'Are you trying to get us evacuated out of here?' And she hit him again. Then she started hitting the furniture and she nearly wrecked the place!

"The woman Flip was wailing at Prahd and it was an awful row.

"And you know what the plague was? Madison had a cold!

"When the scene calmed down a little, Prahd, as long as he was there, examined him. 'The cold,' he said, 'is just an allergy. You're allergic to something here.'

"And Madison said, talking in a whisper to Prahd, 'I'm allergic to no headlines.'

"Teenie heard him and sailed in again. 'That's all you ever talk about, you (bleepard)! I'll give you a headline!' and she hit him across the skull with the chain, slashing it open.

"That seemed to satisfy Teenie and she went outside and started lambasting some of Madison's crew for letting Madison make trouble.

"Madison broke down and wept. 'All my genius is gone,' he said. 'Ever since I began to sleep with Flip, I am deserted by real ideas. I started to PR the governor and almost got him executed and then Teenie found out and put me in a dungeon for three awful weeks. I'm a failure. I can't even get a minor revolt going! She won't even let me start up a paper!'

"Well, Prahd sewed up his head and consoled him

and he even gave him some gas he could sniff so he wouldn't be so impotent with Flip and that was the end of the plague.

"But you know Prahd. Or maybe you don't. But he can always find something wrong with people's cells. Here we were with an ambulance chock-full of medical supplies and an estimated week to handle a plague and no plague to handle. But there were five thousand people or maybe six with warts and such and their staff doctor was nowhere near as good as Prahd, so they started going through the villages shaping people up.

"They didn't need my help so I moved in with Teenie and we had a great old time gossiping. I was younger then, you know, and I really enjoyed myself.

"I'd lie on one bed and Teenie would lie on the other and we talked and talked about everything under the sun, moon and stars."

Pratia let out a deep sigh of fond nostalgia. "Ooooh! Those officers!"

"Wait a minute," I said, propping myself up between the two girls, "Didn't Prahd get jealous?"

"Prahd? Oh, Monte, you are so naive. Prahd has never touched me. He's a cellologist and it's against his professional ethics to (bleep) his patients. And I've been a patient of his for ages!"

"But all your children have green eyes and straw hair," I protested. "I know from the record that your first child by Gris had green eyes and straw hair. . . ."

"And so did the second," said Pratia. "Oh, I see. You didn't know that I conceived on my nuptial night at the Royal prison." She smiled in fond memory. "What a night! And two months later, there I was, pregnant. Wonderful."

Asa murmured, "Go on and finish telling him the story, Gran-gran. I always love to hear it."

Lik was playing with the hair on my chest. "Yes, go ahead, Gran-gran. You're just getting to the good part."

"Oh, yes," said Pratia. "Well, anyway, I suddenly noticed I was using up my quota of officers much, much faster than Teenie. I have always been a believer in conservation, so one night when we took a break for dinner, I asked her what that was all about.

"And she said, 'It's spots.'

"And I said, 'What spots?'

"And she said, 'The spots you touch.'

"And I said, 'Well, I never! Tell me more!'

"Now, it seems she'd been trained by somebody called *Hong Kong whore*, some professor at some high institute of learning, and she could make her body do the wildest things internally and she knew all the nerves in somebody else's body and all the spots to touch. She showed me and it was absolutely marvelous! I'd never heard of such a thing.

"So I got to thinking and I asked around and I found out they were short of fuel bars and would run out in a few months. They were cut off from all communication with the outside, but Teenie wasn't too worried until I pointed out that the little rods she used to train the women with wouldn't work anymore.

"So I made a deal with her. I would get her twenty tons of fuel bars, enough for fifty years at least, if she would teach me all these tricks.

"Prahd was straightening teeth and ingrown toenails and he'd found that some of the inhabitants were descendants from the Teon sea people of ages back, so it wasn't too hard to get him to report that the plague was under control but would take another couple weeks.

"Well, those two weeks were just about the greatest in my life. Some electronics crook in Madison's outfit had made her all the necessary screens and probes and she'd taught all her maids with them, so she went to work on me."

She went on talking. But, staring at her, I couldn't make the things she was saying reach my startled wits.

Her mouth was moving.

Asa was listening in pleasure.

Lik was gleaming in fond delight.

Pratia's mouth was forming words.

No sound at all was reaching me!

And then I realized that I hadn't really gone insane. The two girls had simply lifted up the edges of the pillow my head was on and it was covering my ears!

I batted the obstruction off my hearing with an impatient hand. "... and having performed so elegantly before the whole island population, I was graduated *Magna Cum Loud.*" Pratia sat back with a sigh.

The girls were panting.

Pratia smiled at last. She shook her head. "How fleeting are the yesteryears. Alas, the two weeks were over."

"Now comes the sad part," said Asa with a sigh.

xi

Pratia sat in nostalgia. The girls lay on either side of me, inert. At last Pratia began to insert the needle into hoops once more.

"So we went back to the mainland," Pratia said, "the throng on the palace terrace waving us good-bye with . . ."

"Wait. Hold it!" I said. "I know for a fact that Soltan Gris was in a dungeon there. You haven't mentioned him."

Pratia looked at me with her blue eyes. "Gris?" she said.

"Yes. Did Teenie torture him to death or what?"

Pratia let out a gentle laugh. "Oh, Teenie might get angry but she was never cruel: you'll note she didn't even keep Madison in a dungeon. But as to Gris, she probably got tired of his screams after pulling a couple fingernails. Maybe he just wasn't any fun to torture. Possibly he just fainted any time he saw pincers or tongs.

"You see, the dungeons were very deep there: way under the mountain. Not the place you'd go for a pleasant walk. Oh, I asked her about him but she just shrugged. Probably it was a case of vengeance satisfied.

"Well, anyway, when we got back to the mainland, Prahd reported that without fuel the place could become unhealthy. Dear Jettero wasn't back yet so they authorized the shipment."

"Now comes the very, very sad part," said Lik.

"Prahd," continued Pratia, "went over with it to see that it arrived all safe, and just as he was leaving, Madison whispered to him, 'You wait! I'll put this island on the map yet!'

"Well, Prahd didn't think anything of it. But he hadn't been home here three days when . . .

"BANG!

"A tremendous earthquake! Tidal waves!

"RELAX ISLAND HAD BEEN BLOWN TO BITS!

"Dear Jettero came back and he questioned Prahd but Prahd told him, 'It couldn't have been the fuel! Every bar was in its own insulated container!'

"And dear Jettero said, 'The only way it could have blown up was by taking every bar out of its carton and stacking them all together!'

"And Prahd said, 'But I told them all specifically not to DO that!'

"And Jettero said, 'I know what happened. Madison said he'd put it on the map: he didn't. He took it off forever. It was only a volcanic bubble. I warned Teenie. *Madison blew up Relax Island just to get a headline!*'

"And the sad part of it was," said Pratia, "he didn't even get a single mention of it in the papers. Not even his own obituary. And that was the end of all of them, and Relax Island, too."

xii

Both girls began to sob. They clutched at me for comfort.

Pratia let out a shuddering sigh and then she said, "Well, cheer up. The evening is still early. Asa, wipe your tears away and turn on the music."

The girl let go of me and sprang up from the bed. She opened a big white console and fed the slot a strip.

There was a thunder and then a beat. The volume bashed my ears. The whang and wow of electronic instruments began to rip the tortured air. I had never in my

life before heard such sounds. They hammered you and
somehow worked at you and made your hips twitch.

> *Psychedelic sunset!*
> *Woo-oo! Woo-oo!*
> *Psychedelic sunset!*
> *Woo-oo! Woo-oo!*
> *Psychedelic sunset!*
> *Woo-oo! Woo-oo!*
> *Psychedelic sunset!*
> *Woo-oo! Woo-oo!*

Lik's open lips were close beside my ear. "Isn't
it divine?" she whispered. "Gran-gran copied Teenie's
whole library onto strips. Oh, listen to that *Punk Rock!*"

"Lik!" yelled Pratia above the pulsing din. "Don't
just lie there. Do your duty!"

The girl leaped, her body jerking, and rushed to a
bureau. She got a drawer open, hips bucking to the
rhythm as she worked. She got out some greenish leaves
and papers and began to roll thick, fat cylinders about
three inches long.

Still bucking to the music pulse, she handed one to
Pratia. With slamming heels and heaving thighs she
pushed one into the clutching grasp of Asa. Then she
leaped across me and as her hair jerked near my face,
crammed the end of a cylinder in my mouth. Fire sprang
up from her hand. "Drag deep!" she yelled at me as she
applied the flame. "Suck it down into your lungs and
hold it."

The smoke almost strangled me. "What is it?" I
coughed.

"Panama Red! The very best! I see I got to teach you how to use a joint! DRAG! DRAG! Oh, listen to that *rock!*"

I expelled the sweetish smoke.

Head jerking in the music din, Lik took a drag. She sucked it down into her lungs and held it. Then she let it out. "Oh, Heavenly!" she crooned.

Asa had gotten back on the bed, white fog wreathing from her mouth. She jammed her joint between my lips and cried, "DRAG! DRAG! Then you'll hear the music!"

I dragged and got through coughing. I stole a look at Pratia. She was sitting there, head wreathed in smoke. Through it her eyes peered avidly.

"All right, girls!" cried Pratia. "You can practice your lessons now! HAVE AT HIM!"

A wondrous soft feeling was suddenly enwrapping me. I felt like I was floating, detached.

The music was suddenly wonderful beyond all imaginings as "Psychedelic Sunset" pounded on.

But something else was happening.

With searching fingers, the two girls were seeking out my spots. Before my eyes there was a blur of hands. I fixated on a finger that was probing at my throat.

A joyous feeling began to spread through me.

Two angels on the ceiling were leering down.

More joints.

More music.

Hours later, I slept.

xiii

A horizontal shaft of sunlight came in the low window and pried at my eyelid.

I moved my head. A pain went through it.

I looked toward the chair where Pratia had sat. It was empty.

I looked to my right: there lay Asa, mouth partly open, sound asleep.

I looked to my left: there was Lik. She had a dreamy smile upon her face as she slumbered. Her arm was flung across my chest.

It seemed to me to be a very good idea to get out of there. My throat felt parched. I was hungry. I ached.

Using careful strategy, I disengaged Lik's hand and laid it gently on her thigh. Inching slowly, slowly, I worked my way from out between them down toward the foot of the bed. I was certain I could make it.

My head reached the level of their thighs. Now, with just a final jerk of my legs, I would be upright and free.

I surged up.

YOW!

One of them had grabbed my hair!

"Come back here!" said Lik.

"What's the matter? Don't you like us?" Asa said, looking around into my face.

"Gran-gran is gone," said Lik. "We can skip the fancy stuff."

"*Yeah, man,*" said Asa. "We can get down to the real business!"

"No, no!" I said. "I've got to go home! My head is killing me!"

Lik stuck her eyes very close to mine. "Aha!" she said. "His eyes are all red."

"Only one remedy for that," said Asa.

Lik leaped out and got a joint and, before I could stop her, crammed it in my mouth. She lit it. "Drag deep and you'll feel better."

Amazingly, I shortly did. A woolly cloud seemed to fill me.

Each of them took some drags.

They sat there watchfully to be sure I did not walk off, but then, looking carefully at my expression, they were finally assured I wasn't going to.

Asa got up, found a strip and put it in the console. Music was shortly booming through the room, that weird electronic music with the heavy beat. A man was singing against a chorus:

> *My mama never told me*
> *About the birds and bees.*
> *My papa always told me*
> *To stay off all boys' knees.*
> *So I have had no training,*
> *My appetite to vex.*
> *I have to find out on my own*
> *What there is to sex.*
> *So please excuse ferocity*
> *In ripping off your clothes.*
> *If you decline, please be assured,*
> *I'll punch you in the nose.*

> *Oh, now let's do it all again.*
> *I think I've got the hang.*
> *But I can't believe the birds and bees*
> *Get such a huge end bang!*
> *STICK IT TO ME, BABY!*

"My sentiments exactly!" said Asa and she made a grab for me.

I would have escaped but I collided with Lik.

She slammed me hard on the chest and knocked me back on the bed.

The speakers slammed into my ears with their heavy beat.

Asa's scream made the bottom end of the curtains fly out the window.

"Now, just have a quiet puff," said Lik.

I was surely puffing.

Marijuana smoke soared into the air.

A cupid grinned when Lik's voice said, "Me, now me!"

Lik screamed and the marijuana smoke and the curtains flew away.

The marijuana butt was burning on the floor.

Trying to wrap the sheet around me, I scrambled back from the bed. "Oh, my Gods," I said, "I may have made both of you pregnant!"

Asa was wrapping a robe around her. She laughed. "No worries about that, Monte Pennwell. Prahd hands us out birth control pills."

My clothes were on the floor and I was edging toward them. Suddenly I stopped and stared at them. I shook my head. "Pratia told me that you both were virgins!"

"Hah!" said Lik. "And there won't be any virgins left in the whole Confederacy when we get through spreading Teenie's stuff around! We're only learning now, but you just wait."

I picked up my pants, still clutching the sheet about me. But I was hit with a new thought. "Does Prahd . . . ?"

"Oh, Heavens, no," said Lik. "What a thing to infer. Prahd never touches anyone around here. Why should he, when he's got nurses by the score? Come on, Asa, let's clean this boy up. He has a dirty mind."

They hit me like two lepertiges about to tear their prey limb from limb.

They threw me into the shower.

The water poured down in a steaming cascade.

They jumped in with me.

Their heads were just a blur.

Asa's hand reached out and unclipped a rod vibrator from its hook on the bathroom wall. She held it there a moment while it shook.

Lik's hand reached out and grabbed a block of soap.

The shower jets were pushing steam. "Stand still!" cried Lik.

I screamed.

The slippery block of soap flew out and hit the bathroom wall. Asa was laughing as her hand scrabbled on the floor for it. "Now me! Now let me do it to him!"

The shower jets went stronger.

I screamed again!

Water was pouring out of the drain and vanishing. "Now wasn't that lovely, Monte?" said Lik.

They were wrapping a huge towel around me. I was shaking like a leaf in a storm.

"I know what we should do," said Asa. "We'll fix him up as a present for Har."

"Who's Har?" I trembled.

They were both in loose robes now and they sat me down at a makeup table. It had lots of mirrors.

I said, "I look AWFUL!"

"Nothing like putting a new face on it to meet the day," said Lik.

She powdered my face with a spray can.

Asa took some blue paint from a pot. She put it on my eyelids. Then she took a black pen and drew in eyebrows and huge lashes.

Lik put spots of red on my cheeks.

Asa painted my mouth scarlet so it was very big-lipped.

They stood back and admired their handiwork. Then Asa grabbed a filmy negligee and slipped me into it. I stared down at the frilly collar.

"Oh, you look so pretty now," said Lik.

"I feel terrible," I said. "I've got to go."

"Pish, pish," said Asa. "The sun is hardly up." She grabbed three joints.

I made a feeble effort to leave but they towed me over to the bed. Asa put a joint in my mouth and lit it.

Lik, dragging at her own, went over to the player and put a new strip in. Shortly, the whining beat of the music was pounding the walls.

Two on one is lots of fun,
When you can't have three.
It's now begun for everyone,
So let's all have a spree!
When we're all done, another one
Will start with you on me!
HUMP IT, HONEY!

A new voice came into the room!

"And how is everybody this fine morning?"

I stared. A youth with green eyes and straw-colored hair had entered. He was about twenty. I cringed. I realized this must be one of their brothers! He would undoubtedly shoot me!

He had some bags that seemed to be full of grass or hay. He went over to the bureau and opened a lower drawer. "Just harvested some gold Colombian out on the farm," he said.

He threw the bags in the drawer and took a bundle of rolled joints from his pocket and tossed them at the girls. "A present for you," he said. "It's marvelous."

"Oh Har, dear brother," said Asa, "how sweet you are to us. But we have a present for you, too."

"Its name is Monte Pennwell," said Lik.

"And I think you'll find it marvelous, also," said Asa.

"It's more or less a virgin," said Lik.

"Oho!" cried Har, walking over.

I stared at him round-eyed.

He had a painted face!

"If he seems a little used up," said Asa, "remember that it's just from girls."

"Ho, ho!" said Har. "You mean he's never had it real Earth-style?"

Lik giggled and shook her head.

A group of three cupids, with arms around one another, were leering down at me from the ceiling.

Asa's hand seized my wrist when I would have bolted.

The negligee they had put on me went slithering down on the floor. I yelped. "Hold him still!" cried Har.

The speakers bulged with the music beat:

Will start with you on me!

I yelped again but Har groaned.

One of the cupids seemed to be diving through space, hands held together, knees bent, ecstasy on his face. He was going down and down and down past clouds while moans and music filled the room.

Then the diving cupid mysteriously became me in its place.

I was diving and the clouds were rushing by.

I screamed suddenly while I dived and exploded.

I was standing in the bathroom rubbing a wet towel against my face.

My clothes were lying in a tangle on the floor. I reached down and picked them up.

Sloppily dressed, I stood at the door. I looked back into the room. I frowned as Asa's voice sounded, "Oh, Har. Me now, oh, Har, please!"

Lik's voice came with a strangled sound, "Not yet. Not yet. Not yet!"

I shook my head even though it made it hurt.

I closed the door behind me and the music dimmed to a whisper.

XIV

Nobody was about. I found a viewer-phone in the hall. I did not turn the viewer on. I called Shafter to come and get me.

Outside, the morning air was chill. I went over to the landing pad and sat down on a bench.

Somewhere behind me, I heard a noise. I turned. A man was clearing up debris outside the door of the hospital, throwing things into a trash box. He had on an old doctor's smock, very stained. After a bit he picked up the box and headed for the kitchen disintegrator: his course lay across the landing pad.

When he got close, I suddenly recognized him. It was Prahd! The once straw-colored hair was heavy now with gray, but his eyes were as green as green emeralds. He was long of limb and had a jerky walk as though hung together with hinges.

He dumped his trash and turned around. He saw me sitting there.

"Who are you?" he said. "One of the children's shiftless friends?" There was an edge of contempt in his voice, possibly brought on by my very rumpled appearance. It stung me.

I opened my mouth to give him an acid reply when suddenly, despite my fog, inspiration hit me. And then and there I proved my worth as an investigative reporter. Despite being banged half to pieces, despite marijuana aftereffects, I could still function. I don't mind telling you that what I pulled off was absolutely brilliant! A coup in its own right.

"My name is Pry," I said. "I am a medical student."

He stopped. I could see the interest kindle. "Well, what are you doing here?"

"It's private research," I said. "Just for my own interest. Lately I've been studying genetics. I ran into the strange case of a brown-eyed man and a blue-eyed woman who had only green-eyed children."

He sat down suddenly on the other end of the bench and looked at me closely. "Where did you get this?" he said.

In true investigative-reporter style, I lied. "One of my professors said he had heard from a colleague long ago that it could happen. And he cited the children of Pratia Tayl."

"Are you hinting at something?" said Prahd.

"No, no," I said, my brilliance overriding my splitting headache, "I would never dream of questioning the ethics of the leading cellologist in the land. I just slipped in here this morning in the hope of getting a glimpse of some of the green-eyed progeny. Then I will know that it is indeed true that a brown-eyed man and a blue-eyed woman can have green-eyed children, and I won't have to believe the genetic axioms anymore. I find them tiresome anyway."

"Oh, come now," said Prahd, the sanctity of the medical and cellological axioms at risk. "You can't make a decision on a single case."

"You're going to say," I said, "that it is an atavism, but that won't hold, for it seems to be consistent and breeding true. The percentage of atavistic reoccurrences are ... I forget the percentage. ..."

"Nineteen," said Prahd. "But you are simply floundering around. It is NOT an atavism. You students are all too willing to go diving off into the brush instead of holding the line. I assume now that I can talk within the bounds of professional discretion?"

"Absolutely!" I said.

"The old colleague of your professor was alluding to the case of an officer of a defunct organization who was married in the Royal prison and whose bride conceived on her wedding night. When the child was born it had to be registered and it excited some professional interest; but the paper I filed on it might now be lost, for it was long ago."

"No one cited a paper," I said, ignoring my headache and continuing to surpass myself with investigative reporter brilliance.

"Then that's the trouble," said Prahd. "They don't teach students as thoroughly as they used to in my day: they leave it up to people like myself to straighten them out.

"The case traces back to another, far-off planet that doesn't exist anymore. I was on duty there and this same officer came to me, injured. One of his testes had atrophied in youth, the other had been crushed. In effect, he had been emasculated.

"Now, on this far-off planet there were very few available Voltarians and it would have been a scurvy trick to give him testicles from the race there, as it is very short-lived. Further, there was the matter of operational emergency.

"The only possible solution was to take cells of my own testes and cause them to manufacture full organs in his scrotum."

"Amazing!" I said. "Does one run into these emergencies often?"

"Fortunately, seldom. It is a very unique case. I was rather proud of the result, actually. But on the other hand, it had strange consequences. This officer was quite unprincipled.

"In a valley there, near the hospital, with his new equipment, he impregnated some thirty women. The offspring all had green eyes and straw-colored hair, even though black eyes and hair were the racial dominance.

"Not only that, but this officer actually married two women in a very distant city on that planet and he impregnated them and at least a dozen other women there."

"And the offspring all had green eyes and straw-colored hair?"

"Every one of them!" said Prahd.

"Well, how did you know that, if they were born after you left?"

He looked at me strangely. I had to get a quick grip on the situation, for the marijuana and headache had made me incautious. I was floundering, the sunlight hurt my eyes. I said, "But Pratia calls more than two people 'son' and 'daughter' and this officer was sent to an island before the second child . . ." I broke down, trying to think.

Just then Ske the butler passed, evidently bound for the markets, and he said, "Good morning, Master Pennwell. Did you have a nice night with Lady Pratia?"

Prahd's hand was gripping my front collar. He yanked me close. "Who the blazes are you, anyway?"

Unfortunately for Prahd, it yanked my face upward. My eyes lighted on an attic window!

A face was there, peering through the curtains.

The hair was gray and matted.

The eyes were wild, quite insane.

But even age did not fully change him from his pictures.

IT WAS SOLTAN GRIS!

Despite the throttlehold on my throat, despite my hangover, elation coursed through me! Not even the jar when Prahd threw me down could wipe out my triumph.

Pratia must have gotten him as part of her trade for fuel!

But how monstrous! Here he was, surrounded by his worst enemies—Ske, Meeley and even Bawtch—before he died! How they must torment him and gloat! What glee they must feel with him locked up there in the attic!

I was staring at those insane eyes and then I further understood. He was carrying another man's sperm: every time he had impregnated a woman it had been not for himself but for Prahd! How devilish Prahd had been, siring babies all over the place without a single blot on his professional ethics!

And there Gris was, still under the sentence of death: Teenie had simply delegated it to Pratia! No wonder his prison records still existed! The sentence had never been completed!

And Pratia had had him (bleeping) himself crazy all these years siring another man's children!

A TERRIFIC, MONSTROUS ADDITIONAL COVER-UP!

The insane eyes withdrew from the attic window.

I giggled in Prahd's face.

Hangover or no hangover, I knew right then that I was one of the greatest investigative reporters that ever lived!

I had found Soltan Gris!

XV

For three days after I got home I was not much good for anything.

My heart was pumping overtime, though I realized this must be because I simply was not used to marijuana. My eyes continued to be bloodshot, caused, of course, by my rubbing them too often. My throat was dry, but only when I wasn't drinking water. It was also bruised deep inside, a condition occasioned, naturally, by Prahd's grip. The body contusions and chafed (bleep) just showed that I was not used to sex.

The doctor that Hound called asked if I'd been mauled and chewed by a snug and wanted to give me numerous shots for snug-bite. I said no, but Hound said yes and the reaction from the shots was far worse than any illness I might have had.

These people were far too nosy and it was with great relief, on the fourth day, when they finally let me out.

The bruises had turned yellow. I ignored the ruptured veins. I grabbed Shafter and made him pack the old air-tourer. I had things to do!

In my pocket nestled a note I had blackmailed out of Prahd. It was on the stationery of the King's Own Physician and it said I was a medical inspector. He had quickly seen the light when I had told him that my great-uncle, Lord Dohm, at the Royal prison, would be fascinated to know where his prisoner, Soltan Gris, had gotten to and, further, that the neighbors in that elegant neighborhood might object to mobs burning down Minx Estates if they found the hated Gris was not only alive but in the attic there. Prahd had seen the light, all right! I marvelled at the way I was rapidly picking up the skills of an investigative reporter: I could do them so well now that even the after-haze of marijuana could not dull them.

And neither could these broken veins and bruises! I was heading for the Confederacy Insane Asylum on the chance that Doctor Crobe and Lombar Hisst were still alive!

If there had been a cover-up on so many other things, might it not be true that their TRUE condition might also be masked? Perhaps they had just been the victims of political opportunism and chicanery! It might be that they were illegally held!

What a coup if I established THAT!

The Confederacy Asylum is far, far to the north. There is a wasteland there that borders a vast ocean near the northern pole of Voltar, a dismal place, covered most of the year with ice.

It was the autumn season and the quarter of the year which covered the north with perpetual night had not quite arrived, though Voltar's sun was awfully low on the horizon on these brief, remaining days.

After an overnight stop at a midway air hostel, we arrived in the twilight of a 10:00 A.M. dawn.

As far as one could see, there were small huts and buildings. They ended at a cliff edge far above the sullen northern ocean.

Shafter landed on the target marked Reception Center. Wrapped in an electric-heated jacket and covered by a snow mask, I stepped out into the shrieking, icy wind.

A guard flinched at the letter and hastily directed me into the building and down a long hall to the office of the Resident Keeper.

Strangely enough, the official was a cheerful, bright young man with black eyes and charm. The sign said his name was Neht.

He came right out of his chair when I handed him the note. His hair rose faster than he did but the speed of his recovery told me all I needed to know: his appointment was political rather than technical and was held by INFLUENCE.

I didn't remove my snow mask. I said severely, "There have been rumors of mistreatment of inmates, denial of medical care."

To my astonishment, his alarm did not just switch to charm. It went right on to laughter. "I can't imagine where that came from," he said at length. "We have a staff of physiological doctors unrivalled in skills. You will forgive my seeming mirth. Actually, it is relief. There has been criticism of a different kind: that our employment of gerontological technology on inmates adversely affected our budgetary burden. No, no, inspector, you will not find *mis*treatment here. The bodily illnesses of the insane—and they are many—are extraordinarily well cared for. And I can assure you that this task is performed, despite its difficulties: you see, the insane do tend to bash themselves around. But we patch them up, regardless. You see, we are forbidden by law to tamper with their nerves or damage them, but I assure you that, when they get ill or even scratched, they are cared for at once."

"You spoke of gerontological technology," I said. "Are there abuses there?"

"Some say so," replied Neht. "But personally, I am proud of it. By extending age in inmates, it can be argued that the cost of running this place is heightened. But you must realize that, despite the short northern growing season, we actually EXPORT food to northern government installations: the inmates, many of them, seem to find relief in working outdoors despite the weather, as it gets them out of their cells. So, what does it matter if we extend age? Sometimes, though rarely, aging is attended by calming reflections, if senility does not set in. Just the other day we discharged a man who had reached 195. He said his wife would be dead by now, so there was no one left to keep him insane and he went away as happy as could be."

"Nevertheless," I said, still severe, "this does not get you out of an inspection."

Of course he complied. With the specter of a cancelled appointment being issued by the Emperor, he was all obligingness.

There ensued an hour of walking from barracks to barracks and hut to hut. I went through the charade of trying to talk to this patient or that. They stared at me blankly or thought I was a cloud and one even gave me a carefully stamped drawing receipt for two billion credits—except, despite his motions, he was holding neither an identoplate nor a paper. One was pushing a single-wheel cart through a yard. It was upside down; I asked him why he did not turn it right side up and he whispered to me that if he did, somebody would put something in it.

Although walls were scarred up, the huts and barracks were well kept. Although the inmates were strange, none of them were physically injured or ill. The dispensary and hospital were clean and busy and no fault existed there.

Finally I turned to Neht. My investigative-reporter skills would be needed to the full. I said, "I see no extremely agèd people here. I doubt very much that you are using gerontological techniques to keep them alive. Frankly, I am beginning to suspect that you are killing the older ones off!"

That got through his bland, black-eyed charm. "Oh, not so!" he cried. He studied the situation for a moment and then he said, "Come with me!"

His way led to the record office. There sat huge arrays of consoles. He cleared away a covey of fluttering clerks and sat down at one, fanning his fingers over the keyboard. He was causing case records to flash by age.

He kept up a running fire of comment, "You see? One-ninety-one. Two hundred and three. One-eighty-nine. One-ninety-two..." This one and that one, he went on and on. It dawned on me that there must be at least a half a million inmates in this place. This was going to take all day!

My wits were sharp. I said, in an acid voice, "I see you are avoiding the political prisoners."

That stopped him. He forgot his charm and gawped. "We don't have any political prisoners here!"

"Oh, yes, you do!" I said in as deadly a voice as I could manage. "Or, that is to say, you DID until you killed them off."

"Oh, here now," he said. "That is very brutal talk. They would fire the whole staff if anything like that happened!"

"Precisely," I said. "I happen to know there is truth in my allegation. You HAVE had political prisoners. I know the names of two."

He shook his head, confused. Then he said, "There never have been any such here. You have been misinformed, Inspector."

"Punch in," I said, "the names of Dr. Crobe and Lombar Hisst!"

Instantly he relaxed. He even chuckled. "Oh, those!" he said. "They're not political prisoners. They're as insane as anybody ever got."

"Punch them in," I said sternly.

He did.

AND THERE THEY WERE!

Neht tried to explain that the reason they had not come up on his gerontological console was that Hisst was only 170 and Crobe was only 180. I would have none of it.

"Political prisoners," I said. "I must inspect them!"

He shook his head. He pointed to the notation on Hisst's card: *INCOMMUNICADO. May only speak to Crobe.* And then on Crobe's card: *INCOMMUNICADO. May only speak to Hisst.* "They are not permitted to talk to anyone! Nobody ever goes to see them!" Neht said. "Those are Royal orders!"

"Aha!" I said. "From another reign! And what am I carrying but Royal orders? The charge is proven. You DO have political prisoners here, prisoners no more insane than you or I. Well, thank you, Neht. I shall now go back and make my report that the Confederacy Asylum——"

His charm was gone completely. "Please!" he wailed. "Those two are as mad as mad!"

"That can only be proven by an interview in depth with both of them. And WITHOUT you or your staff coaching or jabbing pins in them! Because I like you, Neht, and do NOT want to cause trouble for you, I will accord you this favor!"

"Oh, thank you," he said in a faint voice and rather huntedly beckoned for a guard.

I swelled with elation. Investigative reporter skills were absolutely fantastic!

Here came my next coup!

PART NINETY-TWO ENVOI III

xvi

The hut was isolated. It stood upon a point which jutted like a finger from the cliffs above the sea. Two thousand feet, straight down, the Northern Ocean roared, battering its heavy green fury against the basalt barricade, using for battering rams great floating islands of white ice.

We had to go through a locked gate before we could enter upon the point. The guard used a plate to unfasten the bars. "It's past noon," he said. "The cleaning crew have probably just come and gone, so you will find them reasonably sanitary. It's a good thing: usually you can smell that hut clear from here."

We walked along a path between the two vertical cliffs. The wind from out of the northern pole moaned dismally. A flurry of snow beat at my mask. This was a gruesome place—think of being incarcerated here for nearly a century!

After a walk of a hundred yards, we arrived at the hut. It was rectangular, built of heavy insulating block like all these huts, a kind of a fortress standing lonely by itself in the teeth of icy winds. It had two doors on the shore side.

The guard approached the left-hand door. "I'll let you see Number 69,000,000,201 first." He consulted his list. "Yes, that's somebody once named Crobe. Now you must be very careful, for both of these are quite mad. I've been here sometimes guarding the cleaning detail while they work and to ensure that nobody speaks to them."

"Have they ever attacked anybody?" I said.

"Not that I recall."

I became even more certain that this was what I said it was—political expediency. This guard had been coached by Neht, that was obvious. "You're not going in with me," I said. "My interview is technical but it may contain state secrets. So let me in there and stand well clear of the door."

He looked a little uncomfortable. Then he hitched his greatcoat around him, dropped his stungun off his shoulder into his hand, put his plate against the door and gave it a shove. He glanced in and then, with another look at me and a shrug, walked off thirty feet.

I repressed a thrill of excitement. I was about to see the notorious Doctor Crobe!

I walked in.

My eyes adjusted to the sudden gloom.

The whole hut was really just one oblong room; dividing it in the center was a string of vertical bars.

I scanned the area I had entered. It was a very capacious room. It was even furnished. It had shelves of books.

Somebody was bent over a tub of some sort. He turned around.

IT WAS CROBE!

His nose was too long; so was his chin. His arms looked more like the legs of birds. He had no hair left at all. He was wearing a coat, but if the cleaning crew had given him a fresh one, it was already dirty.

"You're just in time," he said, as though my visit was a daily occurrence. "The fermentation is completed and I've just hooked up this tube. Let it drip a little longer into the canister and you can test it. I think it is the best I have ever made."

"What is it?" I said.

"*Home brew.* I save half of my dinner every day and dump it in this tub. It ferments quite nicely." I saw he had a lid over the tub and a tube came out of its center, going through several coils before it dripped a clear fluid out the end.

He removed the canister which had been receiving it, quickly putting another in its place. "Now," he said, "sit down on that comfortable couch and try this."

I was amazed. This was no madman. He was even smiling pleasantly. I sat down on the indicated couch and he handed me the canister, making a sign then that I should sip.

I was cautious. I removed my snow mask but I only pretended to drink.

"Oh, goodness, go ahead," said Crobe. "You're not depriving me! I have gallons and gallons of it." And he indicated a rack of jugs on the far wall.

Well, it couldn't kill me. I tossed it down.

PURE FIRE!

It scorched my throat like acid! I couldn't talk!

He watched me carefully. Then he said, "Ah, no convulsions. Which means the *fusel oil* has distilled off. Can you still see?"

I coughed. "Of course I can see. Good Gods! What is this?"

"The very finest *Kentucky bourbon* or possibly *white*

mule. One of the many gifts to Heavens from the planet Earth. I learned how to make it from a professor there in a higher institute of learning called *Bellevue.*"

A glow was springing out of my stomach. My alarm faded. Actually, I suddenly felt very good. I looked around. I said, "I see you also have a lot of books."

He smiled at the shelf. "They're a bit dog-eared now, but Noble Stuffy insisted they be brought for me from the townhouse long ago. He seemed to think I might need them."

I stared at their titles. The letters? didn't make any sense.

"Psychology, psychiatry," said Crobe, "and all the works of Sigmund Freud. All the basic texts of *psychotherapy* on Earth. But they won't let me use it here. They are very unenlightened and retarded. I could clean out this whole asylum for them but every day they gag me before they let the cleaning crew in. However, I have lots of friends, such as yourself, dropping around all the time. Have another *shot?*"

He poured me one from a jug and then took one himself. He shuddered as it went down. He said, "Gods!" and after a second, "but that's good." Then he sighed. "I wish they'd let me have some retorts, for without them I can't make *LSD.* So you'll just have to be content. Drink up."

I threw down the second drink. It sizzled like the first. But shortly, the room looked quite rosy.

"Well, we've wasted enough time," said Crobe, glancing at his wrist where he had no watch. "I have other patients coming in, so you'll just have to rush it a bit. Now lie down on the couch and start talking."

I lay back. I said, "What about?"

"Does it matter?" he said. "We will simply begin by

free association. You leave it to me. Just say anything that jumps into your head."

Well, of course, the first thing that jumped into my head was the continual plotting of my family to manage my life for me. I said, "If my book is not a success, I am finished utterly. My uncles will crush me into some awful job or I'll have to marry that ghastly Lady Corsa and spend my life, much like you, in a cultural desert, Modon, an exile."

"Ah," he said, "trouble with your mother!"

"How did you know?" I said.

"Obvious," he said. "Sigmund Freud covered it like a blanket. An *Oedipus complex!* I can get to the bottom of your case at once. It is a classic example of *psycho-pathology.* You see, there is the *anal passive,* followed by the *anal erotic.* Then there is the *oral passive,* followed by the *oral erotic.* There is also the *genital* stage but no one ever really reaches that. These are ALL the mental stages there are. Everything is based on sex. Sex is the single and only motivation for all behavior. So there you are."

I thought maybe it was the *white mule.* "I don't quite understand."

"That's because you have yet to achieve insight into your condition," said Crobe. "But it is VERY plain to me. Your mother did not let you play with her nipples when you were a baby. Correct?"

"I don't think so," I said.

"You see? And that inhibited your natural sexual out-lets! ALL your trouble with your family comes from that. This will inhibit you from freedom of expression and movement. The cure is simple. Just face up to the fact—and you MUST face up to it—that you are arrested in the *oral erotic* stage. You will NEVER find any remission of symptoms unless you ride roughshod over your repression and find yourself a nice young man and practice, unremittingly, *fellatio.*"

I stared at him.

"I see I am being too technical for a layman. I am giving you pure Freud. Your insanity can be cured only by a life of dedication to making love only to young boys and men—orally, of course. Now, I am sorry," and he glanced at his watchless wrist, "but your appointment is over for the day. However, you are now cured so you need not come back. My calendar is overfull."

xvii

I rose up from the couch. "Well, I certainly thank you for your therapy," I said. "And I can understand how busy you must be, but do you mind if I ask you for your professional opinion?"

"About what?" said Crobe.

I got out some puffsticks—I had taken to smoking them since I had seen that all the reporters did at the Ink Club. I offered one to Crobe and was about to light it for him when he ate it. I didn't know they were comestible. I lit my own.

"Doctor Crobe," I said, "you may very well have been illegally incarcerated here."

"I've said so all the time," he replied. "These barbarians do not appreciate *professional* technology."

"Do you know the man who put you here?"

"I certainly do. I saw him issue the order. I would have run away at once the way I am supposed to, but they restrained me."

"So you know that it was Jettero Heller."

He flinched a little, looked around. We were still alone. He nodded.

"What is your professional opinion of that man?"

Crobe sat back. He rubbed his overlong nose. He stroked his overlong chin. Finally, he said, "You can appreciate that I have made a considerable study of Jettero Heller. Our doctor-patient relationship goes back many years. He disregarded my earliest advices to him and so, you understand, I cannot be held responsible for his mental state. Had I been permitted to give him true professional help—his physiomental composition was entirely wrong for Mission Earth—none of this ever would have happened."

He sighed and then he tapped the top of his radio. "I have, of course, followed his subsequent career, but anything I have heard of him only confirms my first spontaneous analysis." He shook his head sadly. Then he got busy fortifying himself with a long gurgle of *white mule*, after which he sat and stared out into space.

"What was that analysis?" I prompted.

Crobe recalled himself. "Of what?" he said.

"Jettero Heller," I prompted, eagerly.

"Oh, him. Well, I can tell you but you must remind me to explain if I go in too deep for a layman to follow. It is a very difficult case, not well covered in some points by the textbooks.

"To begin with, he likes height. This is very grave, for it is a deviation from normal *alto-phobia*. I know, therefore, that he suffers from *alto-libido*."

I stared.

"Yes, very grave," said Crobe. "But that is far from all. He likes to go very fast. This is a condition of *velocitus-libido*.

"The next symptom is no less strange. Everyone knows that people are just riffraff, yet—and I witnessed this myself in the early days when he was my patient—he is pleasant to people. This shows that he has *urbanus-populi-libido*. Very bad.

"He also erects a façade of pretending to be fair to others—an utter sham, but it takes many people in, since it is, in fact, a fixation. An utterly craven insistence on justice for others. This detects that he has *justitious-libido*.

"Now his record—although it is very confidential, he is no longer my patient and I can disclose it to you—shows that he is very athletic. He runs and jumps and exercises and engages in sports. This reveals deep-seated *lascivus-libido*—roughly translated from professional language, a love of sports. Damning.

"*Libido* means a desire, craving or love of something. But in Heller's case, it is a deviation since it is NOT confined to sex. As the word *libido* is used constantly by Freud to describe the gravest mental conditions, you can begin to see where this is leading us with Heller.

"Now, were it to stop there, possibly we could classify the man only as extremely neurotic. But unfortunately, it doesn't. A résumé of his career discloses that he persists until he gets a job done. This puts us in very dangerous waters. According to the best texts, it means," and he paused and frowned, "that he is *achiever-oriented!*

"Nor is this all: unlike the normal person, he does not get confused or dispersed easily. According to the most exacting *psychology* authorities, this is equally bad. He is *GOAL—ORIENTED!*"

Crobe sat back and sadly looked at the floor. "Actually, I hate to tell you the last and worst thing, it is so very awful."

"Oh, you must," I said.

"Well, it is pretty technical," said Crobe. "While it is just standard Earth *psychology*, it may exceed your grasp. Now let me define the word *schizo* for you: it means split or divided like two of something. Do you follow that?"

I said that I did.

"Very well," continued Crobe, "then you must realize that *schizophrenia* is a very dreadful psychosis. A *schizophrenic* is an insane person, as any *psychologist* or *psychiatrist* on Earth will tell you.

"And so, to return to the case we are examining, you are aware that he once called himself Jettero Heller."

"That's right," I said.

"But NOW," said Crobe, with a meaningful look, "he calls himself the Duke of Manco! TWO NAMES! TWO IDENTITIES! SCHIZOPHRENIA!"

He sat back and shook his head. "So we are forced, then, to conclude that the man in question is totally, utterly and completely insane!

"HE should be the one in here. Not I!"

He sat for some time, lost in thought. Then he said, "But I should not be spending my valuable time discussing this with a layman. It is a matter only understood, in its awful enormity, by fully trained Earth professionals. You must excuse me now. I have to get busy making more *white mule*."

He started to get out of his chair.

xviii

I stopped him from rising. "Wait!" I said. "My business is not done." I pointed at the bars which divided the room.

It was very dark in the other half and I had not been able to see clearly.

There was a swivel glowplate at the top of the couch. I tipped it up so it would shine through the bars into the gloom.

A shadowy shape was sitting there, a sort of small mountain on the floor. The chin lifted and the light struck into yellow eyes.

LOMBAR HISST!

His hair was totally gray. His skin was so deeply wrinkled it seemed to have chasms. The face looked blank.

"Oh, him," said Crobe. "I gave him ninety-some years of *psychoanalysis*, but for the last five or so, he refuses to talk. Actually, it is a *psychiatric* case and requires the expertise of a *neurosurgeon*. You see, the *frontal lobe* has become too involved with the *parietal lobe* of the brain, causing the inevitable *biofeedback* predicted by the magnificent Earth scientist Snorbert Weener in his work, *Stybernetics*, based on his constant association with *pigs* at the *Massachusetts Institute of Wrectology.* Believe me, it would cause Weener to absolutely *squeal* with rage and wiggle his tail if he knew his vital work was not being applied. Ah well, the mighty are often forgotten.

"Now, it so happens that I am certified by no less august a body than the *American Meddle Association*—the group that is dedicated to making all the money for medical doctors possible, no matter how—to perform this simple operation. It is textbook, done constantly on Earth. In fact, it is mandatory! But these unenlightened barbarians here are denying me my tools.

"Factually, I only need one tool. It is the standard one employed by all *psychiatrists* everywhere for this elementary and vital operation. It is called an *ice pick* and it isn't even expensive to buy: one can be purchased in any *hardware* store.

"All the *psychiatrist* has to do—he must be qualified of course, but that's easy, one just hangs a piece of paper on the wall—is insert the *ice pick* up under the left eyelid, shove it all the way up and sweep it from left to right. Then one slides it up under the right eyelid and does the same. It severs the nerves of the prefrontal lobe quite effectively. And so simple. Why, one day, at *Bellevue*, I asked for a demonstration and the leading *neurosurgeon* there simply rushed out into the waiting room, said 'Watch!' and in a trice he had operated on over fifty people: they were impoverished black people, charity cases. Only a small percentage, no more than seventy, died on the spot. The remaining fifteen never gave anyone any trouble after that. Economical, too, they only lived a couple of years. Saves the state money! Earth *psychiatry* is nothing if not practical. They trained me well!"

He got himself another shot of *white mule* and as he sipped it, deeply sighed, "Ah, well, there he sits, deprived utterly of real professional help."

"Well, didn't the *psychoanalysis* make him sane?" I said.

"Oh, that it did," said Crobe. "He just won't talk.
He doesn't even say anything when they come in each
day and lift him up to clean away the excrement and
urine. Sane as can be. Just obstinate."

I looked through the spaced vertical bars, but Hisst
was just sitting there on the floor, yellow eyes glinting in
the glowlight. He did look obstinate.

I found I was drinking another *shot* of *white mule.* I
felt a sudden surge of confidence. I was willing to wager
anything that Lombar Hisst would talk. I was sure he
was simply waiting for an investigative reporter to come
in so that he could tell the real truth about his role in
Mission Earth.

I put down the canister, missing the table. I put out
my hand to say good-bye but unfortunately knocked a
jug of *white mule* over. It lay there gurgling but Crobe was
examining my palm, muttering that it was significant
there was no hair on it.

"Thank you for your time, Doctor Crobe," I said. "I
must be going now."

"Pay the receptionist," said Crobe, "but if you
(bleep) her, that will be extra. However, I do not advise
it. It is not that most of these receptionists at *Bellevue*
have syphilis, since they associate with *psychologists,* it is
that you would be departing from my professional Earth
psychiatric advice. You realize that Heller came to grief
solely by not following my prescription and refusing to
have his limbs shortened. So don't descend down his disastrous trail. You are clearly *oral erotic,* a textbook case of
Freud, and your only chance of mental recovery lies in
finding, as any Earth *psychiatrist* would verify, some good-
looking boy and doing it constantly. Good day. Next
patient, please!"

XIX

The guard seemed a little surprised to see me. He came forward and locked Crobe's door. "Well, you got out of that alive," he said.

I gestured at the other door. "Open it!" I said.

"You mean you're going into the same room with Inmate 69,000,000,202? It says here on the record that he used to be prone to violence. See, right here on the back of the card it says, 'Warning: he almost killed a cleaning steward once.'"

I looked at the date. It was almost seventy years ago. "Since that time," I said grandly, "he has had decades of standard *psychoanalysis.*"

"What's that weird smell?" said the guard. "Oh, it's your breath. You didn't drink anything he gave you, did you? Maybe I should rush you over to the hospital and have your stomach pumped!"

"Don't infer a Crown inspector doesn't know his business," I said haughtily. "Open the other door!"

He shrugged, applied his opening plate and I walked in. I looked back and glared at the guard, for he was standing there with stungun ready. He shook his head, but leaving the door ajar, he walked off about thirty paces.

I looked back into the room. It was quite dark. The fumes of the spilled jug were seeping through the slotted bars making the whole place reek. Crobe was just lolling over there, drinking from a canister, more *white mule.*

Lombar Hisst was sitting very still. I had not realized what a very big man he was: even with his haunches on the floor, I saw the yellow eyes were level with my shoulder as I walked up to him. I stood in the path of his gaze.

Suddenly he looked straight at me.

In a perfectly normal voice, he said, "Could I have one of those puffsticks?"

Accommodatingly, glad of the time it gave me to phrase my first questions, I reached into my pocket and got out a box. I extended it.

He took one, still sitting there in quite a mannerly way. He put it in his mouth.

"Could I have a light?" he said.

I reached in my pocket again and found a firestick. I squeezed its shaft.

It flamed.

I extended it close to the end of Hisst's puffstick.

SUDDENLY HE SEIZED MY WRIST!

The power was bone-crunching!

With his other hand he grabbed the shaft of the falling firestick.

With a roar quite like a lepertige he surged to his feet!

He threw me with a twist, as though I were a doll, straight against the far wall!

I had not hit before he grabbed a cover from the bed.

He touched the flaming shaft to it and it burst into flame!

He swished the blanket as though it were a whip and rushed up to the bars!

He screamed as he flogged fire through the bars, "I'm sending you to HELL, you hear? I'm sending you straight down to HELL NINE, DIRECT!"

He was hitting the bars with the flaming blanket!

Gouts of fire were flying off and spraying into Crobe's room.

"You and your *psychoanalysis!*" shrieked Hisst. "I've waited decades just for this!"

Crobe had sprung up, clutching a jug of *white mule* to his bony breast. He added his screeches to the din. "Keep those blasted angels on your own side of the bars!"

A gout of fire was racing now across Crobe's floor, eating puddles of spilled *white mule*, spouting tongues of blue.

"No, no!" screamed Crobe. "You're getting angels all over me!"

Lombar still lashed the bars with fire.

I found my legs and sprinted for the door.

The guard was racing up. As I exited, I hit him.

The stungun flew into a snowbank.

In a tangle of arms and legs, the guard and I went pinwheeling down the path away from the hut.

Lombar raced out.

He was wrapping the flaming blanket around him.

Spurts of blue fire were following him out of the door.

Suddenly there was an awful roar!

The jugs of *white mule* had blown up!

The whole roof of the hut blew wide in a geyser of red and blue.

And there went Crobe sailing skyward!

Just as the roar of the explosion died, I heard Crobe's voice. In tones of exultation the doctor cried, "Look, I'm flying! I'm flying! I WAS AN ANGEL AFTER ALL!"

Abruptly, high in the air, carrying his *white mule* bomb, Crobe exploded with a tremendous BANG!

Lombar Hisst, wrapped in the burning blanket, was racing toward the far point of the cliff.

He reached the edge. He was still running. He tried to spring up in the air.

He was bellowing, "*I'M* GOD! *I'M* THE REAL GOD! MOVE OVER, YOU (BLEEPARD), SO I CAN RULE THE UNIVERSE!"

He went plunging, a blazing fireball, two thousand feet down toward the water, a spectacular arc.

He struck a piece of floating ice in a final gout of bursting flame!

He slid off to be crushed in the thundering surf against the cliff, a charred and roasted nothing, ground to pieces in the cold, green sea.

Crobe and Lombar Hisst were very, very dead.

XX

I promised Neht I'd hush the matter up.

I did not tell him I would not put it in this book. I am an investigative reporter. I have learned fast at my trade. Lying to get access is a key technique of that profession—with cheating here and there and a dash of misrepresentation. For what are lies to the riffraff when I can bring the truth to you, dear reader? You should be grateful to me for becoming so adept at my chosen profession. Bob Hoodward, I assure you, could not have practiced better.

And so I sailed off southward with Shafter at the controls. I was going to make one last visit to Hightee Heller: I had to check something very vital to these revelations.

With a stopover at a northern hostel so I could recover from a mysterious headache and spots before my eyes, and where I could also dress the next morning in something more suitable than singed snow clothes, we came at last to the landing target of Hightee Heller's home in Pausch Hills.

I did not wait for any attendant to appear. I knew the place now and so just walked in.

I saw a butler shortly, a very big man, sitting in a hall polishing silver. I said, "Inform Hightee that Monte Pennwell is here to talk with her."

He went off and so I wandered. I was looking for, perhaps, a correspondence room where she would have her letters: just a few moments alone with her personal files might be very rewarding.

The door to the art salon was open. I saw another door to a room beyond it: that might be the correspondence room. An investigative reporter must not even heed the meaning of privacy. I glanced over my shoulder. No one was watching me. I began to cross the art salon.

Here was where Hightee Heller kept many of her gifts. People sent them to her from all over, even today. It was a sort of museum but I wasn't interested in that.

I was just passing a table in the middle of the vast room when my eye chanced to catch the writing on a card. I stopped right there!

Somebody had taken the interplanetary shipping wrappers off. The card said:

HAPPY HIGHTEE HELLER DAY
With Love

Jettero

IT WAS THE SAME BOX I HAD SEEN HIM
CARRYING ON MANCO!

Apparently it had been delayed in shipment from
that planet.

I hastily glanced around. Any clue was worth inves-
tigating. No one was in sight. I stepped to the table.

Evidently a footman had prepared it so that all Hightee had to do was remove the ribbon and top cover, making it easy for her to receive and examine whatever it was.

The box itself was quite large: it was covered in a
crinkly gold paper the like of which I had never seen
before. The ribbon was two inches wide and ended in a
huge rosette. Very foreign looking.

It took me only an instant to remove the ribbon and
the cover.

I took some packing paper out and then didn't know
what I was looking at. There was a horizontal round ring
suspended five inches above a wider base. From the ring,
each separately wrapped in paper, hung a dozen figurines, apparently made of glass.

In the center of the base was set a green rectangular
box but the rest of the base was blue and totally transparent. Taped to the bottom of that base and partially
seen through it was a slip of paper, printed, with writing
on it, like an invoice from a store.

THE LETTERING!

Had I seen it before?

Oh, any clue was welcome.

I MUST HAVE THAT PIECE OF PAPER!

To get it, I had to remove the strange device from the box.

I started to lift it. I had underestimated its weight from the ease with which Heller had carried it.

I struggled to get it removed. It kept catching on the wrappings. Finally, I wrestled it over to the center of the table top, knocking the wrappings and box to the floor as I did so. But at least I had it sitting there.

I ignored the strangeness of the gadget. My task now was to lift its edge up and get at that taped paper.

There were some levers around the edge. In lifting it, I must have touched one. The thing went *CLICK!*

I clawed at the tape under it—what strange stuff, transparent and sticky. I had to use my fingernail.

AHA! I HAD THE PAPER!

The edge of the platform, when I released it, hit the table with a thump.

The ring began to turn!

THE THING BEGAN TO PLAY A TUNE!

I went into a panic that the noise might be overheard.

I stared at it. Then I grabbed one of the levers on the edge and yanked it.

IT PLAYED LOUDER!

The ring went faster!

The paper sleeves flew off the figurines. They were glass dancers!

They were turning in a circle now and dancing to the music.

YE GODS, BUT THAT WAS LOUD!

Frenziedly, I yanked up and down on the levers!

ANYTHING TO STOP IT!

IT WENT FASTER!

The dancers were now whirling madly.

Their glass toes, which had sounded like small bells, were now more like high-pitched gongs!

I gave one more yank at the levers.

It was too much.

The figurines suddenly flew away, sundered from the ring.

They sailed through the air.

They shattered with small tinkles on the floor!

The whole device let out a vibrating *WHAM!*

A yellow spring flew out of it and hit me in the face!

A voice!

The butler!

"WHAT IN BLAZES ARE YOU UP TO?"

He grabbed me by the collar!

He lugged me to the door.

He pitched me, seat first, onto the landing target!

I lit on my butt with a skid and a puff of dust.

The butler's voice again. He was standing in the door, dusting off his hands.

"Monte Pennwell, do not land here anymore!" he said.

Actually, I had been misled: I had believed they did not have any security here. But who needed it, with that butler around!

I did not know if this was Hightee's message. Never mind, relentless investigative reporter that I was, I had what I had come for!

I could even ignore Shafter's amazed look.

xxi

We flew at once to the Royal Institute of Ethnology. I raced to the Department of Unconquered Planets.

I was in luck: a junior assistant professor there was familiar with my family name. I promised him advancement I knew very well I could never effect, if he would translate the paper. He was naive enough to accept.

They have machines and dictionaries there and all sorts of contrivances for decipherment of alphabets and meanings, anything short of an outright military code.

It took him only two days and I sit now in my tower study with the translation before me. It says:

TIFFANY'S
FIFTH AVENUE
New York, New York
Customer: General Jerome Terrance Wister
(Retired), U.S. Army Reserve
Address: 5606 Central Park West
Charge to: Grabbe-Manhattan Bank
c/o Israel Epstein III
President

1 Antique Glass Animated Dancer Music Box
18th Century, Venetian
$21,000.00

Note: No Credit Card Necessary

And the date is ONLY THREE WEEKS AGO!
ANOTHER MONSTROUS COVER-UP!

With a viewer-phone call I just made ten minutes
ago to the Reliable Spacetug Building Company, I
learned that ten years after his return from Earth and
one week after he had received Izzy Epstein's letter, Heller commissioned the construction of an exact duplicate
of Tug One, even down to the phantom duellist in its
gym. He paid for it himself—and how easy that was,
since, as Duke of Manco, he received one percent of its
huge annual revenues, the usual remuneration for a duke
but quite enough to buy ten such tugs a month. According to the old chief engineer at Reliable, now retired and
garrulous with age (and who had been very proud of the
job they did on it—"all gold, silver and jewels, ran like
a watch"), they built it in three months (a record), loaded
it with digging disintegrator tools (note that), test-flew it
and then Heller "took it on a shakedown cruise that
lasted three weeks." The tug has long been the pride of
the company, for it is nearly indestructible and is in service right up to today. "He uses it to jink around the Confederacy planets: a powerful man in his position has to
be in a lot of places fast, and even though many think
it eccentric to use those monster Will-be Was main
drives just to get home for a weekend from Voltar to
Manco, it makes good sense."

Little does he know!

Probably feeling sorry for "poor Izzy" and his
friends, it is vivid now that Heller went and dug him out
a new Earth base, probably in one of the hills near the
roadhouse in Connecticut, less than an hour's easy drive
from the Empire State Building or the condo. He's probably got the descendants of Connecticut deputy sheriffs

Ralph and George still thinking they are part of the Maysabongo Marines and drawing the corrupted payoff of their fathers as they watch the old bootlegging roadhouse for him.

By now he has probably attended the funerals of all his one-time friends, has given their progeny a leg-up into high positions and is very likely known as "Uncle Jet," the fellow they have to keep cooking the Social Security and army records for so nobody will notice he is 127 years old, a totally giveaway age for that planet's short-lived people. They probably keep backing him up ten years at a clip so he never gets above sixty-five. But he must look to them like he is fifty. Maybe he puts white powder in his sideburns to further the deceit.

Oh, you can excuse it by imagining a conversation between him and Lord Bis, the head of the Combined Service Intelligence Committee. He and Bis would be agreeing it was a very good thing for Heller-Wister to maintain his exalted five-star-general U.S. Army status, even though it is just reserve and never active. By being in the background there, they would agree, any space military adventure on the part of Earth would be known to Voltar long before it happened. But as Earth firmly believes that nothing can go faster than light, a supply line for any Earth attack on Voltar more than twenty-two light-years long would make any attack extremely unlikely. So you would have to regard such a conversation as an utter sham and see it just for what it is:

AN EXCUSE FOR THIS MONSTROUS, FINAL COVER–UP!

xxii

And what is this last, biggest cover-up?

Well, dear reader, I will tell you.

We already know he is hiding the existence of a whole planet.

But now the matter becomes MUCH more serious!

Jettero Heller, Duke of Manco, is DEPRIVING VOLTAR OF SOME OF THE MOST MAGNIFICENT DEVELOPMENTS EVER HIT UPON IN THIS WHOLE UNIVERSE!

Now, let me take these things up one by one and I will soon convince you.

PR: The skills of PR, even to the tiny degree I have been able to utilize them, have literally saved my life. They are jerking me from total, hounded and depressed anonymity to a position where my name will blaze across the sky. People will no longer be able to push me around and make nothing of my writing. Utilizing only a tiny fragment of PR, I have rooted out the TRUTH. And after this it will be "Yes, Noble Pennwell" and "No, Noble Pennwell" and "I'm shivering in my boots lest you frown at me, Mr. Pennwell!" One assuredly cannot discount the vast value of this technology, now known only to Earth and available nowhere else!

INTELLIGENCE SERVICES: Unless you can spy upon your own population, you cannot keep them in

line. The riffraff will get out of hand and impudent—
even revolt—unless spies and armed spy forces are
planted on them at every street corner. How else can a
government get even with those they do not like? How
else but by provoking them into crime and then arrest-
ing them? Unless you can make continual trouble for citizens individually and keep them at each others' throats,
then they may unite and in a screaming wave overwhelm
the government! On Earth they have developed those
skills to a very fine point and practice them in every
country. Only there can our power elite learn how to do it!

. BEVERAGES: When you think of what we call
strong drink, it becomes a laughing matter. Tup and
varieties of sparklewater are absolutely nothing. They
merely make one relaxed and cheerful. NOT ONE OF
OUR DRINKS IS REALLY EFFECTIVE! It takes
white mule to really throw one into the land of I-Don't-
Care. None of our drinks cause one to cast away his
inhibitions—they don't even make anyone see double.
What a powerful surge is available from Earth beverages.
I know. I have felt it. Yet how to make them is ONLY
available in full from Earth!

MUSIC: You have to experience the scorching beat
of Punk Rock to really appreciate what Earth could do
for the whole artistic universe. I swear, there is nothing
like it ever heard before, anywhere else. The wild abandon of it doesn't even have to be in tune! And the sentiments are not hidden at all! Only Earth could develop
such music. Only Earth can teach us how to properly
play it and thus sweep aside our too-smooth and com-
plicated melodies and chords. Punk Rock gets right down
to it! It beats your eardrums in!

DRUGS: This is just cabal and propaganda. I have
experienced marijuana, the most powerful of these drugs,

and I frankly did not care a snap what happened! I
simply let them do anything they liked to me and
enjoyed it. DRUGS YOU NEVER HEARD OF ARE
AVAILABLE FROM EARTH! IT IS THE SOLE
SOURCE OF THE THRILLS YOU CAN EXPERI-
ENCE!

PSYCHOLOGY and *PSYCHIATRY:* These are obviously the most advanced population-control techniques
ever heard of anywhere. Imagine a government having a
corps of doctors it can use to kill anyone it doesn't like
and no questions asked! That's POWER! Imagine the
boon of a state monopoly in bending the minds of children, making them into anything it wishes, even animals
just grazing in the fields!

Now, it must have been quite obvious to you, dear
reader, for I rely on your intelligence, that the only reason Lombar Hisst remained insane was because the
skilled and qualified Doctor Crobe was FORBIDDEN
the use of his normal tools. Had he been able to properly
treat Lombar Hisst as he proposed, all would have been
well! And only Earth has that technology.

SEX: Oh, sex and sex and sex. Before Earth shed its
divine light on this subject, who knew anything at all
about sex? We are all so unenlightened, we are so dread-
fully inhibited on the subject that it is a matter of weeping. Teenie was a master of it, a divine Goddess, sent to
us from Earth to lead us out of darkness. Today we could
have innumerable varieties of sex if we only knew the
whole story from Earth. We could have oral sex and anal
sex rampant in every salon. We could have mass orgies.
And we could have incest as a common way of life. They
know how to do these things on Earth. Pratia is not
imparting her divine wisdom: she is hoarding it because
she is just a *voyeur* now. She is not even letting this

enlightenment escape outside her own family, and I doubt very much, since she has a wandering wit, that she is teaching accurately. The place to get the REAL information is EARTH! It is a paradise of wallowing, rampant sex perversion! Wonderful!

CATAMITES: All this stupid fuss that was made about catamites is a cover-up in itself.

I will have you know that when Doctor Crobe *psychoanalyzed* me, I was IMPRESSED! It was a stunning revelation to know why my life had been so tortured and so grim.

Never had I suspected before that I was merely *oral erotic.* Failure to know that has almost wrecked my life!

Just as soon as I get this book into print, I am going to hunt up Har and importune him or blackmail him or anything and force him to let me do it to him every day.

And, oh, I am certain there will be many changes in my life.

So I will owe my very sanity to Earth, the only place where such wisdom comes from!

So now that I have explained it, you can see the vast dimensions of this last cover-up.

JETTERO HELLER is denying the whole Voltar Confederacy, the rest of the universe, if you please, of these colossal benefits!

But WHY he is doing it is the best of all.

Now you will recall what the learned Doctor Crobe said about two identities? Good!

Look at Heller!

He has TWO identities on Voltar alone.

On Earth he is known as Wister and maybe others!

So, hold your hat, we come to the most awful cover-up of all:

JETTERO HELLER has MORE than TWO identities. That makes him a *schizo-schizophrenic!*

He is not only just the real villain of this piece.

HE IS INSANE!

THE WHOLE OF THE VOLTAR CONFEDERACY HAS BEEN GUIDED FOR NEARLY A CENTURY BY A MAN WHO IS COMPLETELY AND UTTERLY CRAZY!

Oh, let's forget for the moment the imagined successes of the Confederacy during that period, since they are hardly to his credit. That Voltar, since he took over as Crown, has never lost a war is simply a tribute to the Army and Fleet, and wars have been few, remember that! And let's not harp upon the fact that Voltar has never in her history been so prosperous internally: when everybody is employed and working cheerfully, you can't help but have prosperity. His popularity doesn't count, for it is based on the fact that he is never in the news and there are no investigative reporters around to tell people the TRUTH!

The multiple identities would prove it by itself that Jettero Heller is insane. But there is a REAL BIG PIECE OF EVIDENCE YOU MUST NOT OVERLOOK!

By submerging Earth, JETTERO HELLER HAS COST VOLTAR THE STAGGERING BENEFITS THAT WE COULD GET FROM EARTH!

I have listed them above. It should be plain to you, dear reader, that only a madman would underprivilege Voltar that way! A vicious, dirty trick to play on all of us!

SO!

That spot is blank on the invasion tables.

The planet Earth belongs there.

Those tables are SACRED!

The time for the invasion is still a few years in the future!

There is AMPLE time to mend this hideous, psychotic cover-up engineered by a madman!

So I give you the vital battle cry:

RESTORE EARTH TO THE INVASION TABLES AND INVADE!

I will drive it home in the very best way I know. Read this and it will lift your heart, Voltarian, with a THRILL!

ODE TO EARTH

O Earth, O Earth, you luscious globe,
You beckoning, wine-fat treasure-trove,
You whet our hunger as you spin
And lure us with your wealth to win.
You saved my life with your PR.
I triumph now without a scar!
Your spy techniques are quite sublime
And can be used to undermine.
And who could think but to extol
Your psych and psych for mind control.
Who would refuse to cut their fug
If offered some divine Earth drug?
Who can deny that men will drool
For just one shot of good white mule?
And no musician would heed sneers
If he had Punk Rock to drown their ears.
And who, pray tell, would show aversion
To lovely butt and mouth perversion?
And Earth, you number in your riches
Sex that converts girls to (bleepches).

Did I say sex? Oh, you excel!
Sex is the thing you do so well!
Never has such concentration
Been levelled at self-gratification!
Nowhere else in the universe
Did anyone dream that sex came first!
We thank the Gods that you are weak
And believe so well when your leaders speak.
We praise to the Lords your internal squabbles.
We'll just step in and grab your baubles!
It is so nice you can't unite,
For you won't offer any fight.
We are so thankful for your schisms
Brought on by all your social ISMS.
For all your wealth, you stand around
And eat suppression, finely ground.
Your leaders lead you to the slaughter.
You're as easy to rape as a poor man's daughter!
So we'll throw you on your back
And insert us in your crack
And rape and gut until you squirm
And fill you full with our bullet sperm!
And when your dead carpet the streets,
We'll roll right in with Rocking Beats
And loot you of your luscious hoard
Of the wisdom and lust that I've adored.
We'll suck you dry!
Our thirst you'll quench
With the dripping blood of every wench!
And when you are then but a husk,
To me, you'll smell like lovely musk.
And to Voltar as slaves we'll bring
Every virgin for a fling

And have here in our native land
All the things that made you grand!
Until this happens, I will rave
And beg and plead until you, slave,
Are captured there and put in chains
To let us pick your luscious brains.
And then at length establish here
Your culture as a proud veneer
Upon our peoples far and wide
So that their semen runs like tide
Up into your legs spread wide!
For with your culture, we will nurse
A whole enticing universe,
And from your womb, tomorrow springs
As you lie weeping with slashed-off wings.
So cower there, O Earth, we come!
And we will beat the funeral drum
For bodies slaughtered on your plain
That died in agony and pain.
Don't plead, O Earth, for mercy now!
Your time has come and this I vow:
Each thing you know we will suck up
And toast your death with blood in cup!
Surrender? No, it is too late.
Just weep while soldiers fornicate
Upon your grave up there so high,
So soon to be our Voltar sky.
But, cheer up, Earth! When soul has flown
It will in Voltar find its home.
Your wisdom wise like graveyard flowers
Will come to us and will be ours!
So, Earth, just bare to us your breast
And let us suckle you in death!

*VOLTAR! SEEK NOT MORE OF MY PERSUASION!
LAUNCH ON TIME THE EARTH INVASION!*

THE (TRIUMPHANT) END!

(To be published immediately after The Triumphant End)

LETTER FROM MONTE PENNWELL
TO HIS PUBLISHERS

TO: BIOGRAPHICS PUBLISHING
            COMPANY
         COMMERCIAL CITY
         PLANET VOLTAR

GENTLEMEN (though I am certain there
is not one in the shop!):

I have just received back for author's
approval the edited copy of my book.
I AM OUTRAGED!
I am so angry, I have never been so
angry!
I hardly know how to start screaming
at you!
You have changed the name of every
single Lord in the book! I demand you use
the real ones I used!
You ink-spattering dabblers and med-
dlers!

You have changed the U.S. Army name that Jettero Heller used on Earth. It wasn't *Wister!* I gave the REAL name!

And if this were not effrontery enough, YOU HAVE CHANGED MY NAME AS AUTHOR! "Monte Pennwell," indeed! THAT IS NOT MY NAME! My family name is one of the most honorable and respected names in the whole Confederacy and I INSIST THAT YOU USE IT!

It is a wonder to me you didn't change the names of New York and Turkey!

THIS IS VILLAINOUS!

I WILL HAVE YOUR HEADS!

YOU SIGNED A CONTRACT!

I know my rights!

If you DARE to dicker around with me, I will take you RIGHT TO COURT and sue you for a BILLION CREDITS!

This book deals with corruption in government. I don't care if it attacks the leaders of the state! YOU IDIOTS! That's why I'm writing it!

There has been a MONSTROUS COVER–UP! This book is intended to EXPLODE it into view!

The people of Voltar are being VIC-TIMIZED! They are being denied posses-sion of a planet RICH IN WISDOM!

They are being misled and manipulated by an archvillain WHO IS INSANE!

I must get the word to them so they

can RISE AS ONE MAN and SCREAM THEIR FURY at this DECEPTION!

Earth is right there aching to be TORN TO PIECES!

We could FEAST upon it!

You LACKEYS!

You MINIONS of a VILE and CORRUPT MADMAN!

HOW DARE YOU LABEL THIS AS A WORK OF *FICTION!*

How dare you insert an introduction that REFUTES EVERYTHING!

How dare you infer that I am simply an IMAGINATIVE WRITER?

Oh, let me tell you, you're in *REAL* TROUBLE!

I have PROOFS!

I have hundreds of pounds of COURT RECORDS! I have a WHOLE FORTRESS FULL OF DOCUMENTS! I have all my notes and copies of the logs and records on Manco. I have my recordings of all interviews! I even have the Gris strips of every move Heller ever made!

I am armed like an Army with *FACTS!*

They won't dare touch me!

I am shouting out the spirit of a great crusade! Invade Earth at ALL COSTS! We cannot afford NOT TO!

For an instant, I will throttle my rage and demean myself by trying to appeal to

your reason even though it is quite obvious
you have none!

You must not let yourselves be brow-
beaten by the VILE Duke of Manco into
foregoing the HUGE benefits of invading
Earth.

Look what that planet has done for me
already! It has made me into a MAN! As
soon as this book is published, I will haunt
the house of Har and do my Earth thing
with him until I get completely well! I
have been assured by a great Earth authority and *psychiatrist* that it will handle all
my family problems. AND I MUST HAN-
DLE THEM! THEY ARE UNBEAR-
ABLE!

They are plaguing me about jobs and
even proposing the UNTHINKABLE: that
I marry that AWFUL Lady Corsa in that
AWFUL rustic Modon. I am going completely MAD!

This book must be a roaring success!
DO NOT MEDDLE WITH IT! My very
soul, nay, even my SANITY depends upon
it utterly!

You are going to ABIDE by your contract.

You are going to PUBLISH THIS
BOOK!

OR YOU WILL BE COMPLETELY
RUINED!

IF YOU DON'T PUBLISH IT, I
WILL *SUE!*

And VOLTAR HAS GOT TO
INVADE EARTH OR I'LL TEAR THIS
GOVERNMENT APART WITH WHAT
I KNOW!

That's what you are up against!

BEWARE!

I suppose you are going to threaten me
by saying you will publish this letter. YOU
ARE TOO SNIVELLING A PACK OF
COWARDS TO STAND UP. I DARE
YOU TO PUBLISH IT!

DOWN WITH TYRANNY!

DOWN WITH DENYING US THE
GOODIES OF EARTH!

And DOWN WITH YOU AND
YOUR DEVIL MASTER, HELLER!

I've got to stop writing because this
paper will CHAR from the intensity of my
RAGE!

I am sending the manuscript back to
you. I am NOT going to work for DAYS
and DAYS reverting these names to the
real ones. I am already worn out sweating
for FREEDOM FROM DENYING US
EARTH!

(Bleep) you!

                              THE AUTHOR!

**Biographics Publishing Company
Commercial City
Planet Voltar**

My dear Monte Pennwell:

We have, as of this date, received back the manuscript of the book.

We regret to inform you that due to pressure of work in our editing department, the changes we made will have to remain changed, just the way we changed them.

It was puzzling to us why you wished to defame your own immediate ancestors and relations, some of whom were on the Grand Council at that time, so we have also omitted the list of those Lords from the text without changing them.

You will be pleased to know that our company is very prosperous and influential now and that some changes have been made in our management. Several members of your family took a sudden interest in publishing and pooled their petty cash and bought the company. The editors you were dealing with originally, and to whom you are objecting so strongly, are no longer with us. So we can look forward to highly amiable relations, I am sure.

We do regret the necessity to give you the pen name *Monte Pennwell* as author, but if you will read the small print of the contract you signed, it not only reserves to the publisher the right to make any editorial changes, it also states he can change the names of the characters and that he alone determines what cognomen is used for the author. You should have read the contract more carefully.

However, we will publish, at the end of the book, your letter, so the reader will know that changes were made. This should reassure you.

Also, you should be pleased to know that the book WILL be published, but more of that later.

Now, you have raised the question concerning whether this book should be published as fact or fiction. And we are very pleased to be able to handle this point.

There is, however, a difficulty. You speak of proofs. Before embarking upon a fact book, one normally retains a verifier and so we did, a MOST reliable firm. We made every effort to support your allegations. And we wish to condense his report for you:

DRUGS ON TAYL FARM: Recent accidental brush fire swept over area and no crops exist. Marijuana farming there unverifiable.

MAN IN TAYL ESTATE ATTIC: King's
Own Physician gave verifier immediate
access there to inspect. The place was
being repainted. No evidence of any prisoner there.

WITNESSES: Pratia Tayl, grandchildren
and great-grandchildren recently left, with
staff, for some property Tayl seems to have
owned on the Southern Continent. The
place is deep in the jungle and inaccessible
to process or subpoena servers or court
officers. The King's Own Physician stated
it was just a usual annual vacation. But
these and other witnesses that might come
up in litigation do not seem to be available. Both the Duchess of Manco and
Hightee Heller slammed off their viewer-
phones quite angrily when the verifier
mentioned your name and I do not think
they would be willing to furnish any
proofs.

GRIS RECORDS: The verifier called at
the Royal prison and found they have a
witnessed statement there to the effect that
every scrap of material related to the confession of Soltan Gris and any trial have
been properly destroyed. The person wit-
nessing it was a man named "Hound," but
we have no reason to think this is your
valet as the name is common amongst
yellow-men. The only confession copy existing is the one you dictated. No proof.

SOLTAN GRIS: He is not alive, as you
state. There is a body hanging to rot at
the Royal prison. It had recently been
freshly retarred: they do this to slow decay.
However, from the tar, the verifier was able
to get fingerprints and the body is indeed
that of Soltan Gris. The warder said these
bodies last for a long time so there is no
telling exactly when he was executed and
the justiciary seems to have misplaced the
record of that.

CROBE AND HISST: Superintendent
Neht at the Confederacy Asylum was
extremely helpful to the verifier. He said
there were no political prisoners there.
There is no trace of a Hisst or a Crobe in
their prison records. The verifier was
shown a place on a point such as you
describe, but he said the charred place
there was just where they burned trash.

YOUR OWN NOTES: You allege to have
made copies of logs, etc., on Manco and
stated that you had voice recordings of
interviews. Your driver, Shafter, the one
who is on probation for drunk driving, was
interviewed. He remembers having a packet
as part of the original manuscript but he
said that when he was bringing it to us
there was a sudden squall and it fell out of
the air-truck into the Western Ocean. He
could not swear to what was in it.

RELAX ISLAND: Sons of some local

publishers were interrogated concerning
this: they became very angry with the verifier and would not substantiate that the
island ever existed.

SPITEOS AND THE APPARATUS: The
Lady Corsa was quite helpful. The old pile
of black rocks out in the Great Desert is
indeed still there. You apparently gave it to
her and she showed the verifier all around:
they have been handling soil erosion. She
even defended you, saying it was not really
your fault you got strange ideas and that
all you needed was more fresh air, exercise
and a firm hand. She laughed quite amus-
edly at the idea of the place being full of
documents. She explained the recent heavy
truck tracks as having been made by a
shipment of fertilizer, which, I think you
will agree, was very quick-witted of her in
that you could easily have been arrested for
failing to report such a discovery of government documents.

In short, there is no cover-up. There
couldn't have been, you see, because there
is no evidence of anything remaining to
have been covered up.

So, of course, your book only qualifies
as a work of fiction and I am sure that
you will be happy now on that point.

Frankly, I am certain the former management of this company expected an
entirely different kind of manuscript from

you. We won't nuance with words and say that you deliberately misrepresented the book beforehand so that you could get a binding contract, but when they were dismissed they certainly seemed to be of that opinion. Vociferously so.

You see, as some experts on publishing advised them, very little is publicly known about the Duke of Manco, aside from the fact that everything goes smoothly when he is around. The public only knows that when Mortiiy the Brilliant retired to Calabar sixty years ago and his son, Prince Wully, ascended the throne, Wully was promptly dubbed "Wully the Wise" because he never did a thing without consulting the Duke of Manco first.

This great man won't even give out data to encyclopedias and they have to rely on what they know of his youth as Jettero Heller.

So such a work as the "Life and Times of the Duke of Manco" (which, I may remind you, is what you told everyone you were writing) would have sold like sparklewater in the desert. It quite probably would have brought you the fame and fortune for which you seem to thirst.

This absolute rot about being an investigative reporter is clogging your wits, if we might loosen our own pen for a moment. It is not that you have not achieved something: the death of three men is not nothing. It is a very good thing for you that two were insane and the third a notorious traitor: Otherwise you would, as a reward for your "PR study," be doing time in prison for willfully and knowingly hounding them to their deaths, contrary to the Anti-Harassment and Inviolability of Personal Privacy statutes introduced in the last century. We could forget driving an eccentric old lady and her offspring into exile and you may, of course, be fatuous enough to believe that the betrayal of the Duchess of Manco and the almost deified Hightee Heller is something you can live down, but we believe this sudden assimilation of "PR technology" and your inexplicable use of such debased maliciousness could lead to self-harm and you should be warned to abandon it for your own good.

Do not, whatever you may be thinking or supposing, blame the Duke of Manco for anything you might think is going on. Surprisingly, he feels sorry for you.

We showed him this manuscript and he read it in his rapid fashion and then simply sighed and said, "The poor fellow. It got to him."

It was a very cryptic statement and we asked him his advice concerning the publishing plan. But he merely chuckled and

said, "Go ahead. It might wake them up."
An amazing man!

Now let us take up this matter of the
contract: It is true that one existed, duly
signed, and it is valid. But talking of a
billion-credit suit is nonsense. In the first
place, the sum is preposterous and never
has been heard of in court annals. In the
second place, there has not been, on the
part of the publisher, any violation of it.

And here is the good news you have
been waiting for. The company is going to
publish the book, and every clause of this
contract—which you should have read—will
be honored. So you can cheer up at this
point.

Now, the contract undertakes to publish this book by you but it does NOT say
where or *when*.

We consulted various legal experts but
they could come up with no solution. It
was left to Lord Bis, a distant cousin of
yours, by the way, and who heard of it
while chatting with the Royal Historian,
another member of your family.

Lord Bis looked the project over—read
the manuscript in fact—and came up with
a most *admirable* solution, as I know you
will agree. From his position as Chairman
of the Intelligence Committee, he noted
that the invasion of Earth, a blank slot on

the invasion tables, would have been due to
come up just a few years hence.

This brilliant man told us that all we
had to do was hold the publication until
that unutilized invasion date had fully and
irrevocably passed and could not possibly
be returned to: it would then be too distant in the past.

When that occurred, Lord Bis advised,
we could send the book with one of the
usual survey parties to the planet Earth
and, through the auspices of publishing
connections there, publish the book solely
and only on the planet Earth. And there
was no need, in meeting the terms of the
contract, to publish it on Voltar at all!

He commented that the population
there would regard it just as a work of fiction and that it would not cause them to
strengthen their defenses as, he says, the
planet is "quite muddly," as he put it.

The brilliance of the solution becomes
quite manifest when you realize, as he
pointed out, that there is no Code break
involved: The planet Earth does not exist,
so it is outside the Space Code regulations!

So your book is going to be published
after all. I know you will think that is
wonderful. And there is no slightest tinge
of contract breakage. Your publishers are
taking care of you straight down the line.

We are sorry that we have no slightest

idea of how you can be paid royalties. And
this is too bad. For we understand that
your mother went absolutely livid when she
read what Crobe said about her and that
you intended to become a *fairy* or a *cata-
mite* and she cut off your allowance, dismissed your valet and driver for being so
lax and sold all your vehicles.

So it is a very good thing that you
have such tender and endearing friends as
old Doctor Prahd Bittlestiffender. It was he
who informed us, when we asked, that His
Majesty had issued a Royal order about
you. It is not often that a young, aspiring
bridegroom is the subject of a wedding
order.

I do wish to congratulate you on your
forthcoming marriage to the Lady Corsa.
You are very lucky that it will be by Royal
command since it saves the tedium of
waiting.

I understand that the Lady Corsa's
brother and two of his hunting companions
have come over from Modon in their family space yacht with some lepertige nets to
make sure you get safely to the wedding
and safely back to Modon, which I thought
was very courteous of them and a true
brother-in-lawly gesture. As a matter of
fact, as you receive this letter, you are
probably already in their custody.

Your bride is a fine, strong woman,

very patriotic and willing to do anything for her country and to suffer certain deficiencies for the sake of raising the social status and connections of her family by allying it to ours. A true powerhouse of a woman! So I am certain she will treat you very well, such as giving you money to buy shoes for walking in the mountains, an exercise of which she is extremely fond. It will give you lots of time to think.

And, who knows, in fifty years, you might even get back to Voltar from Modon for a visit, although I would advise, even then, a disguise.

So we are all agreed, then? Fine. I will see you at your wedding tomorrow.

Your Great Uncle
Cuht
New Managing Director
Biographics Publishing Company

THE TRUE AND FINAL END
OF MISSION EARTH

About the Author
L. Ron Hubbard

Born in 1911, the son of a U.S. naval officer, the legendary L. Ron Hubbard grew up in the great American West and was acquainted early with a rugged outdoor life before he took to the sea. The cowboys, Indians and mountains of Montana were balanced with an open sea, temples and the throngs of the Orient as Hubbard journeyed through the Far East as a teen-ager. By the time he was nineteen, he had travelled over a quarter of a million sea miles and thousands on land, recording his experiences in a series of diaries, mixed with story ideas.

When Hubbard returned to the U.S., his insatiable curiosity and demand for excitement sent him into the sky as a barnstormer where he quickly earned a reputation for his skill and daring. Then he turned his attention to the sea again. This time it was four-masted schooners and voyages into the Caribbean, where he found the adventure and experience that were to serve him later at the typewriter.

Drawing from his travels, he produced an amazing wealth of stories, from adventure and westerns to mystery and detective.

By 1938, Hubbard was already established and recognized as one of the top-selling authors, when a major new magazine, Street and Smith's *Astounding Science Fiction*, called for new blood. Hubbard was urged to try his hand at science fiction. The red-headed author protested that he did not write about "machines and machinery" but that he wrote about people. "That's just what we want," he was told.

The result was a barrage of stories from Hubbard that expanded the scope and changed the face of the genre, gaining Hubbard a repute, along with Robert Heinlein, as one of the "founding fathers" of the great Golden Age of Science Fiction.

Then as now he excited intense critical comparison with the best of H. G. Wells and Edgar Allan Poe. His prodigious creative output of more than a hundred novels and novelettes and more than two hundred short stories, with over twenty-two million copies of fiction in a dozen languages sold throughout the world, is a true publishing phenomenon.

But perhaps most important is that as time went on, Hubbard's work and style developed to masterful proportions. The 1982 blockbuster *Battlefield Earth*, celebrating Hubbard's 50th year as a professional writer, remained for 32 weeks on the nation's bestseller lists and received the highest critical acclaim.

"A superlative storyteller with total mastery of plot and pacing."—*Publishers Weekly*

"A huge (800+ pages) slugfest. Mr. Hubbard celebrates fifty years as a pro writer with tight plotting, furious action, and have-at-'em entertainment."—*Kirkus Review*

But the final *magnum opus* was yet to come. L. Ron Hubbard, after completing *Battlefield Earth*, sat down and did what few writers have dared contemplate—let alone achieve. He wrote the ten-volume space adventure satire *Mission Earth*.

Filled with a dazzling array of other-world weaponry and systems, *Mission Earth* is a spectacular cavalcade of battles, of stunning plot reversals, with heroes and heroines, villains and villainesses, caught up in a superbly imaginative, intricately plotted invasion of Earth—as seen entirely and uniquely through the eyes of the aliens that already walk among us.

With the distinctive pace, artistry and humor that is the inimitable hallmark of L. Ron Hubbard, *Mission Earth* weaves a hilarious, fast-paced adventure tale of ingenious alien intrigue, told with biting social commentary in the great classic tradition of Swift, Wells and Orwell.

So unprecedented is this work that a new term—dekalogy (meaning ten books)—had to be coined just to describe its breadth and scope.

With the manuscript completed and in the hands of the publisher and all of his other work done, L. Ron Hubbard departed his body on January 24, 1986. He left behind a timeless legacy of unparallelled story-telling richness for you the reader to enjoy, as other readers have, time and again, over the past half century.

We the publishers are proud to present L. Ron Hubbard's dazzling tour de force: the *Mission Earth* dekalogy.

"I am always happy to hear from my readers."

L. Ron Hubbard

These were the words of L. Ron Hubbard, who was always very interested in hearing from his friends and readers. He made a point of staying in communication with everyone he came in contact with over his fifty-year career as a professional writer, and he had thousands of fans and friends that he corresponded with all over the world.

The publishers of L. Ron Hubbard's literary works wish to continue this tradition and would very much welcome letters and comments from you, his readers, both old and new.

Any message addressed to the Author's Affairs Director at Bridge Publications will be given prompt and full attention.

BRIDGE PUBLICATIONS, INC.
4751 Fountain Avenue
Los Angeles, California 90029